pawn

BOOKS BY TIMOTHY ZAHN

DRAGONBACK SERIES

*Dragon and Thief**
*Dragon and Soldier**
*Dragon and Slave**
*Dragon and Herdsman**
*Dragon and Judge**
*Dragon and Liberator**

QUADRAIL SERIES

*Night Train to Rigel**
*The Third Lynx**
*Odd Girl Out**
*The Domino Pattern**
*Judgment at Proteus**

STAR WARS® NOVELS

Heir to the Empire
Dark Force Rising
The Last Command
Specter of the Past
Vision of the Future
Survivor's Quest
Outbound Flight
Allegiance
Choices of One
Scoundrels
Thrawn

The Blackcollar
*Blackcollar:
The Judas Solution*
A Coming of Age
Cobra
Spinneret
Cobra Strike
*Cascade Point and
Other Stories*
The Backlash Mission
Triplet
Cobra Bargain
*Time Bomb and Zahndry
Others*
Deadman Switch
Warhorse
Cobras Two (omnibus)
Conquerors' Pride
Conquerors' Heritage
Conquerors' Legacy
The Icarus Hunt
*Angelmass**
*Manta's Gift**
*The Green and the Gray**

*A Tor Book

pawn

A CHRONICLE OF THE SIBYL'S WAR

timothy zahn

TOR

A TOM DOHERTY ASSOCIATES BOOK

NEW YORK

PAWN

Copyright © 2017 by Timothy Zahn

A Tor Book
Published by Tom Doherty Associates
175 Fifth Avenue
New York, NY 10010

www.tor-forge.com

Tor® is a registered trademark of Macmillan Publishing Group, LLC.

The Library of Congress Cataloging-in-Publication Data is available upon request.

ISBN 978-0-7653-2966-0 (hardcover)
ISBN 978-1-4299-4707-7 (e-book)

Our books may be purchased in bulk for promotional, educational, or business use. Please contact your local bookseller or the Macmillan Corporate and Premium Sales Department at 1-800-221-7945, extension 5442, or by e-mail at MacmillanSpecialMarkets@macmillan.com.

First Edition: May 2017

Printed in the United States of America

0 9 8 7 6 5 4 3 2 1

pawn

one

On her last day on Earth, Nicole Hammond woke from her hung-over stupor to the sound of vague and distant voices, the reek of booze and blood, and the rough slap of someone's hand against her cheek.

"Wake *up*, bitch."

She rolled off the mattress onto the hard wooden floor, her cheek stinging as she tried to drag herself back to consciousness. She pried open her eyes, wincing as the early-morning sunlight blazing through the window burned into them.

It was Bungie.

Damn.

She reversed her movement, rolling back toward the mattress and groping beneath her pillow for her knife.

Bungie was faster. "Uh-uh," he said, snatching up the pillow and tossing it aside.

Nicole swore under her breath as her bleary eyes took in the empty spot where the pillow had been. Her knife was gone.

So was the tattered wallet where she'd stashed her share of last night's take.

Damn, damn, *damn.*

"Where's your knife?" Bungie demanded, taking a step toward her and planting one foot squarely in the middle of her mattress.

"I don't know," Nicole said, the words coming out slurred from a painfully dry mouth. She glanced over at the bedroom door, hoping Jasp might have heard the commotion. Surely Bungie wouldn't want to take on Jasp in his own place.

"If you're counting on Jasp, don't," Bungie said, a dark sort of smirk in his voice. "Last I saw he was still at the party. Looking for someone to take you off his hands."

Nicole felt her heart sink. Jasp had the nicest place of anyone she knew, and she'd hoped she could sweet-talk him into letting her crash here at least another couple of weeks. But like everyone else before him, he'd apparently had enough of her sleeping off hangovers on his floor.

A second later, her heart leaped again as a horrible thought suddenly struck her. Had he given her to Bungie? Was that why the big ugly ape was here? To collect her and take her to his place?

God, no. Please, no.

"Get dressed," Bungie went on, his dark smirk going just plain dark. "I need a doctor."

Nicole blinked away more of the mental haze. She'd assumed the smell of blood had been coming from her, that she'd bitten her lip or maybe vomited before collapsing on her mattress last night.

But it wasn't. It was coming from the bloody rag Bungie was holding pressed against his left side.

So Bungie had gotten into another fight. Big surprise. "What did you—?"

"Just get your damn clothes on," he snarled.

"Yeah, keep your shirt on," she muttered, getting unsteadily to her feet. She staggered a moment as her head suddenly went all dizzy, but the chair where she'd dropped her jeans and sweatshirt was right there beside her, and she was able to grab on to it before she fell over. The clothes reeked of booze and sweat, but she didn't want to take the time to go hunting for something clean. Especially not if Bungie was going to bleed on her.

"Come on, come *on*."

Nicole didn't answer, concentrating instead on getting dressed. Her head was throbbing twice as hard as it had been when she first awoke, and she desperately wanted a drink. But Jasp wouldn't appreciate it if she helped herself to his supply without asking first.

Luckily, she wouldn't have to. Once she was dressed, she'd drive Bungie over to Packer to get fixed up, and Packer always had some booze lying around. She could easily talk him out of a drink or two for her headache while he sewed Bungie up.

As she pulled on her clothes, and as Bungie cursed under his breath behind her, she listened to the voices whispering through her pounding head.

They were louder than usual today.

In fact, she couldn't remember them ever being as loud as they were right now. Certainly not since the first time she'd heard them, four years ago on the day after her fifteenth birthday. Trake had introduced her to whiskey at that party, and for a long time afterward she'd just assumed the voices were a normal part of a hangover, like the buzzing in her ears and the sweats and the dry mouth and the headache.

But over the years she'd slowly come to realize that the voices weren't something that anyone else experienced. The voices were totally and uniquely her.

She'd been scared when she first figured that out. She'd heard about people with strange voices whispering at them, usually as part of a creepy story about a serial killer or someone who'd walked off a ten-story building.

Nicole's voices never told her to do anything like that. They never told her to do anything. They never even called her by name, like they did in most of those stories. Usually she couldn't even make out any words, like she was listening to a radio that was playing too softly.

Over time, she'd gotten more or less used to it. Even when the voices stopped being just a part of every hangover and started coming at odd times of the day or night it didn't bother her too much.

Though she sometimes wondered if she was going insane when she woke up in the darkness and heard the whispers.

"What the *hell* is taking you so long?"

"Almost ready," Nicole said, making a face into her sweatshirt as she pulled it over her head. This was not exactly the way she'd hoped to sleep this one off.

But she didn't have much choice. Bungie was part of Trake's group, and he was hurt, and if she didn't help him, she could find herself out on the street with no one to take her in. It wasn't like Trake couldn't get someone else to play lookout and distraction for him—the Philadelphia streets were full of people who would jump at an easy job like that. "Let me get my boots," she added, hurrying toward the window.

"You got shoes right there."

"Those are wet," Nicole said over her shoulder.

"You throw up on 'em?"

"I stepped in a puddle."

"Oh, for . . ." His voice trailed off into a rumble of muttered curses.

She actually *had* stepped in a puddle, though not exactly a soaky one, if Bungie bothered to check to see if the shoes were wet. Not that she cared.

But her boots were near the window, and getting to the window got her to her window box.

And that was what she really cared about. She needed to see if, sometime during her weekend binge, her whiskey-soaked brain had remembered to water her flowers.

It had. Even just a glance showed her that the dirt was still moist, and the plants themselves seemed to be doing fine.

"I swear, if you're mooning over those damn plants—"

"I'm getting my damn boots," Nicole shot back, grabbing one and leaning against the wall for balance as she pulled it on.

She ran her eyes over her small collection of plants, then lowered her gaze to the window box itself. That small wooden box was the single constant in her life, the one thing that had been with her since she left her grandmother's house four years ago. In that time some of the plants had died and been replaced, and some of the planter's wood trim had chipped or broken off. But she didn't care. She'd carried that box everywhere, and when Jasp threw her out she would make sure that her plants went with her.

She just hoped that whoever Jasp pawned her off on wouldn't have a basement place like Packer's. The flowers needed their sunlight.

"Ready," she said, zipping up the last boot and turning back to face Bungie. "Do we need to score a car, or—?"

She broke off, feeling her eyes widen. In the short time it had taken her to dress, the rag Bungie was holding to his side had gone from merely red with blood to dripping with it.

This wasn't his usual deep scratch. This was something a hell of a lot more serious.

"Already got a car," he grated. He was still standing upright, but he was starting to sway a little. "Give me a hand, huh?"

Nicole moved to his uninjured side, steadying him and helping him across the room to the door. The stairs down to the street were the trickiest part, and there were a couple of times when she thought she was going to lose it and send both of them tumbling to the next landing. But with one arm around Bungie and the other hand on the rickety railing they finally made it.

Trake had better appreciate her going through all this. Bungie damn well better appreciate it, too. "Which one?" she asked, shivering as the cool early-morning air hit her sweaty skin.

"There," Bungie said, pointing to a BMW crookedly parked beside a fire hydrant. "You drive." He pressed a set of bloody keys into her hand.

"Where are we going?" she asked as she steered them toward the car.

"I already *told* you—the hospital," he rumbled. "Put me in the backseat—this side, right here."

Balancing Bungie on her arm and shoulder, she got the car unlocked and opened the back door. "Easy now—watch the ribs," he warned. "Watch the *ribs,* damn it!"

A minute and some more cursing later, she had him settled. She closed the door, then hurried around the hood and got in behind the wheel. "VA hospital's closest," he told her between clenched teeth as she closed her door. "We'll try there."

"Do they take non-vets at the VA?" she asked, wincing as she touched wetness on the seat beside her. Definitely a good thing she hadn't bothered with clean clothes.

"They'll take me," Bungie told her, his voice dark. "Come on, come on—I'm *bleeding* back here."

"I just meant it might be better to try somewhere else," she said, turning her head to look over the seat at him.

And caught her breath. From somewhere under his shirt he'd pulled out a gun.

Not the little .22 she'd seen him wave around when he was playing tough. This gun was a lot bigger, and a lot nastier.

And she'd seen it before somewhere. "Where did you get—?"

"Drive," he said. The quietness of the order was somehow scarier even than his usual yelling.

Hastily, she turned back and fumbled the key into the ignition, an unpleasant tingle between her shoulder blades. The car started, and she pulled out into the street.

What the *hell* had the big idiot gotten himself into this time?

She'd walked past the VA hospital only once, a couple of months ago, but she remembered the way. Luckily, early-morning traffic in this part of Philadelphia was always light.

And as she drove, she tried to think.

This was bad. Dangerously bad. Bungie was as addicted to fights as he was to alcohol, but the worst she'd usually seen him with was bruises and maybe a few cuts. Packer was pretty good with those, though Nicole had never figured out where Bungie got the money to pay the old medic's ridiculous fees. She probably didn't want to know, either.

But minor cuts didn't bleed like this. Bungie didn't have the skill to boost a late-model car like the BMW, either.

And in all the years he'd been hanging around Trake and his group he'd never had a gun like that.

So: felonies. Probably up to his neck in them. Even if the VA hospital was willing to treat him, the minute they cut off his shirt and saw that big bleeder they'd probably call the cops. If it was a gunshot wound, she was pretty sure they *had* to call them.

But that wasn't Nicole's problem. She'd take him in, because buying points with Trake was a good idea and arguing with a bleeding man holding a gun wasn't. But the minute he was out of sight, she would get as far away from him, his gun, and his stolen car as she could.

In fact, it might not be a bad idea to get out of the neighborhood completely for a few days. She had a little money saved—

She made a face. No, she didn't. Everything she had was in her missing wallet.

Had Jasp taken it? He could have noticed that she put it under her pillow every night. But Jasp didn't seem like the type for something that petty. More likely, she'd lost it somewhere at last night's party. Maybe she'd lost her knife there, too.

Or maybe one of Trake's guys had lifted it while she was too drunk to notice. There were enough jerks hanging around who would do something like that just for the fun of it.

Which still left her with no money and a burning need to lie low for a while.

Where could she go? She didn't know many people outside of Trake's group, and most of those also knew Bungie. Someplace farther out, maybe out of the city completely?

That might not be a bad idea. She'd been trying for months to get Trake to move her up from lookout to pickpocket, but he always said she needed more practice. Living and scoring on her own for a few days might be the chance to prove that she could do that.

The one thing she would absolutely *not* do was call her grandmother and ask for help. She'd face Bungie and his new gun before she'd do that.

"There!"

Nicole jerked her attention back from unpleasant thoughts of her future to unpleasant thoughts of her present. The hospital was straight ahead, its VETERANS ADMINISTRATION sign prominent beside the drive entrance. "Is there an emergency room?" she asked, looking around. "I don't see a sign."

"Who said anything about an emergency room?" Bungie growled. "That lot over there—that'll be where the doctors park. Go."

Nicole frowned. She'd seen enough TV to know that doctors

had special stickers on their cars for hospital parking lots. How did Bungie expect her to park in there without drawing attention they didn't want?

But she didn't dare argue the point. Not with Bungie in pain. Especially not with Bungie in pain and holding a gun.

"There," he said, leaning over the backseat beside her, his breath unpleasantly hot in her ear, the gun twitching at the edge of her vision. "Getting out of his car—see him?"

"Yes," Nicole said. The man was in his late twenties, about Bungie's age, with short hair and a professional-looking suit. The car he was getting out of was bright red, with the kind of spindly-spoked wheels she'd always liked. There was no way to tell if he was a doctor, but he certainly looked like one.

"Get beside him," Bungie ordered. "Come on, *move* it."

Nicole pressed down on the pedal, sending the car leaping forward.

The doctor closed his door and did something with his key ring, making the lights flash and the horn give a short toot. Turning toward the hospital building, he headed briskly past the other parked cars. Nicole watched him out of the corner of her eye as she reached his row and turned into the narrow lane.

"Get beside him and stop," Bungie said, and there was a sudden surge of cool air at the back of Nicole's neck as he lowered the rear window.

"Wait a second," Nicole said as she suddenly saw where he was going. Bad enough to be riding in a stolen car with him. But to help him with a *kidnapping*? That was a whole new level of bad. "How about I park here and go bring him to you? Okay? You know I can do it—just like how I got that guard out of the way a couple of weeks ago? You can rest here, and I'll bring him back—"

"You ever try to outrun a bullet?" Bungie interrupted.

Nicole swallowed hard. "No."

"Tell you right now, this isn't the day to try," he said quietly. "Now get beside him and stop."

The doctor, his mind apparently on other things, didn't seem to notice them until Nicole stopped the car. He looked up, a sort of mildly curious expression on his face—

"You a doctor?" Bungie demanded.

The man took a second look, and Nicole saw his expression stiffen. "The hospital's right there," he said, pointing at the big building behind them. "They can take care of you."

"How about *you* take care of me?" Bungie said, lifting the gun into view over the windowsill. "Get in the car."

A wave of fresh nausea swept through Nicole's already queasy stomach. He was doing it. He was really, truly, doing it. "Easy, Bungie," she said carefully. "This isn't worth it. We can find another—"

"Shut up, or I'll kill you both," Bungie snarled. "I've already killed one man today. I'm in the mood. Get in the car, Doc. *Now*."

It took the doctor a second to find his voice. "Look. I can see you're upset—"

"How about seeing that I've got a gun?" Bungie cut him off. "Get in the damn *car*."

"I don't have anything to treat you with," the doctor protested, his voice starting to crack. "Let me take you into the hospital—"

"You got a medical bag?"

The doctor swallowed. "In my car. But it's not much more than a first-aid kit."

"Good enough," Bungie said. "Let's go get it. Nice and slow."

The doctor's eyes flicked to Nicole. "Better do as he says," she said. "He's not in the greatest mood."

"Yeah, I can see that," the doctor said grimly. "Fine."

He turned and headed back toward his car. Bungie tapped the

back of Nicole's head with his gun in silent order, and she let up on the brake, letting the car roll alongside the doctor.

Across the lot, a couple of other doctor types were chatting together as they walked toward the hospital, and Nicole found herself gripping the steering wheel tighter. If the doctor decided to risk shouting a warning to them . . .

Apparently, Bungie was thinking the same thing. "What's your name, Doc?" he asked out the window.

"McNair," the man said. "Sam McNair."

"Got a family, Sam?"

"No."

"So no one would miss you if I blew you away?"

A muscle in McNair's cheek tightened. "Take it easy," he said. "I'm not going to make trouble."

They traveled the rest of the way in silence. Nicole kept the car beside the doctor, her brain and head throbbing. Had Bungie *really* killed someone?

Maybe he had. It would explain the car and the gun. Probably his wound, too, if whoever he'd killed hadn't gone quietly.

And now he'd said it out loud, and in front of a witness. So where did that leave her?

She didn't know. All she could do was hope the doctor fixed Bungie well enough to travel, and that she could ditch him before the cops caught up with him.

They reached McNair's car. "My bag's in the trunk," he told Bungie. "Wait here and I'll go get it."

"Better idea," Bungie said with a grunt. "Stand right there—right *there*—where I can see you. Put it in park, Nicole, and give me a hand."

He seemed weaker than he'd been when they'd left Jasp's place, staggering as Nicole helped him out of the backseat. But his eyes were wide-open and alert, and she could see by the strain in his jaw and neck that he had his teeth clenched. Running on pure willpower now.

"Okay, Doc," he said, keeping his gun pressed against his side where it wouldn't be so visible to anyone passing by. "Nice and slow."

Not that there *was* anyone passing by. In fact, as Nicole glanced around, she realized that for the moment the three of them were completely alone in the parking lot, probably as isolated as it was possible to get in a big city.

She hoped all that seclusion wouldn't make Bungie feel secure enough to do something stupid.

The voices were getting stronger.

McNair led the way to the rear of his car and pulled out his key ring. For a second he seemed to hesitate, maybe wondering whether he dared risk hitting the panic button instead of the trunk release. Bungie didn't say anything, but just took a step closer to him. The doctor's cheek tightened, and with a quiet thunk the trunk popped and swung smoothly open. "Good choice," Bungie rumbled. "Get it."

For a second the two men locked eyes. Then, McNair's cheek twitched again and he reached into the trunk and pulled out a black doctor-style bag. With his free hand, he reached up to close the trunk.

There was a puff of air on the back of Nicole's neck, and a pair of arms slithered like snakes around her shoulders and locked together solidly across her chest.

A startled scream tried to explode from her throat. But all her muscles were suddenly frozen in place. Bungie spun around to face her, snarled something disbelieving as his gaze jerked upward to something above her head. He grabbed at Nicole's arm, his fingers tightening around her rigid flesh as he swung his gun to point over her shoulder.

McNair gasped something and grabbed Bungie's gun arm, either trying to wrestle the weapon away from him or else drag it off-target from wherever it was aimed. Bungie snarled and swung the arm back at him, slamming the side of the gun against the other's forehead. McNair staggered, but managed to keep his grip. Bungie tried to bring the gun back around, but he was pulling against all of McNair's weight, and it wasn't working. The voices in Nicole's head gave a sudden, shrieking gasp.

And out of nowhere two more figures appeared, one behind Bungie and one behind McNair. The newcomers' arms darted around the men's shoulders and their hands locked together, just like the arms that were holding Nicole.

But the attackers weren't muggers or random strangers or security guards from the hospital.

They weren't even people.

They were taller even than Bungie, at least six and a half feet tall, with thin bodies and arms and pure black eyes. They had no noses, their mouths seemed to be little more than wide slits, and their heads were completely bald. Their skin was a pale, silvery white that glistened in the early-morning sunlight. As Nicole stared in disbelief, the creatures unfolded large, shimmering butterfly-type wings from their backs. The wings stretched up and out into the morning breeze.

An instant later, the world vanished.

Not the way it disappeared when Nicole drifted off into a drunken sleep, going gradually blurry as consciousness faded away. This disappearance was sudden, complete, painless, and terrifying.

Maybe not quite complete. She couldn't see the car or the

parking lot or the Philadelphia skyline or even Bungie and Mc-Nair. The whole world seemed to have turned a black so total that she felt like she could stretch out her hand and run her fingers through it. But she *could* still see the arms wrapped around her chest.

With nothing else for her to look at, and with another scream trying desperately to escape her frozen throat, she forced herself to concentrate on the arms.

Her attacker's skin wasn't silvery white, like she'd first thought. Instead, the skin itself was pure white, with an overlay of criss-crossing silver threads that gave it its metallic sheen. The fingers were interlocked together, but as she looked closely she could see that there were six fingers on each hand instead of five, and that the two on the ends both seemed to be thumbs.

That would have freaked her out, she thought dully, if her mind hadn't already been completely freaked out by all the rest of it.

Don't worry, Nicole. I won't let you go.

Nicole felt her breath catch in her still-frozen throat. Suddenly, for a single moment, the normally wordless voices in her head had spoken words.

And they'd spoken the words to *her.* Not to somebody else, but to *her,* Nicole Hammond. Personally.

The horrifying stories of voices telling people to kill themselves were running through her mind when the blackness in front of her was ripped away like that street magician she'd seen once pull the black cloth off his hat.

But it wasn't a pigeon that appeared in front of her, like it had from the magician's hat. It was Bungie and Dr. McNair, standing exactly where they'd been when Nicole's world disappeared. The silvery-white butterfly people were also there, one of them still standing behind each of them.

But they were no longer standing in the hospital parking lot. They were in a tall-ceilinged round room with dim overhead lighting and hundreds of glowing or flashing colored lights dotting the room's curved walls. Between the lights, the walls seemed to be covered in a crosshatch of the same kind of silvery threads that were on the butterfly people's skin.

From somewhere in front of her came a sudden whooshing sound, and a section of the wall that didn't have any lights swung open, letting in a dazzling blaze of light. Through the ringing in her ears she heard the sound of footsteps, and as she squinted against the light she saw the black silhouette of a figure walking toward them. She couldn't see a face in the glare, but from the way it walked she had the impression that it was a shortish, broad-shouldered human instead of another butterfly person.

Abruptly, it stopped. For a moment it stood still, and Nicole found herself tensing. Then, with a snort, it stepped to the side of the opening and bit out a couple of words in some crazy foreign language.

A moment later another shadow from outside the round room appeared and walked toward them, this one much taller and broader than the first shadow. As it came close, some of the reflected light bounced back from the walls onto its face and body and Nicole was finally able to make out some details.

It wasn't just a big person, like she'd thought. Nor was it another of the butterfly people. Its face was utterly unlike anything she'd ever seen, reminding her somehow of a squashed shark face, complete with sets of gills on its neck. Its body was even worse, looking like it had been made by pouring a thousand glass marbles into a mold. The shoulder and hip and knee joints didn't seem quite right, and the creature's hands were thick and broad, like the paws of some horrible movie monster.

Nicole tried to shrink back, another scream boiling up inside her. But she still couldn't move, and this scream was just as unable to escape her paralyzed throat as all the others had been. The marble monster stopped two feet away from her and reached out his hands.

And for the second time that horrible, terrifying morning, the world went black.

two

There had been many times over the years when Nicole had looked forward to sleep. When the world was crashing down around her head, sleep had often been her only escape.

But this sleep wasn't an escape. It was restless, full of frightening dreams of glass monsters and giant butterflies and men and women staring down at her and babbling in strange languages.

The worst part was that she wasn't sure that all of those hazy images were, in fact, dreams.

And whether she was dreaming or lying half-awake, through all of it she could sometimes hear the faraway voices, once again wordless.

When she finally came fully awake, she found herself alone in a small room, squarish like a normal room instead of the round one she'd first seen after the parking lot disappeared. She was lying on a mostly comfortable bed, with a soft light coming from small gaps in each of the corners. The walls and ceiling were a pale gray, with a sheen that seemed to imply they were made of metal. A pair of tall white racks stood beside the bed, one on each side of her, with three boxes loaded into each of them. The boxes were connected with wires and clear plastic tubing, and from the upper box on each side another tube came out and into a taped-over spot on the inside bends of both her elbows. It was sort of like the IV setups she'd seen, only with boxes instead of plastic bags like they used in hospitals. Across the room were a chair and a small desk with a built-in computer screen.

Nicole looked around, listening to her heart thudding in her chest. It was a hospital room, obviously. Probably in the VA hospital where Bungie had tried his insane kidnapping stunt.

But why was she in a hospital at all? Had she been shot? She couldn't remember anything like that happening.

Unless the butterfly people, the round room, and the marble monster had been dreams. Hallucinations, maybe, after hospital security jumped her and Bungie. Maybe during the struggle someone had shot her.

But then shouldn't she hurt somewhere? Packer had told her about a guy he'd patched up once who'd been shot ten years earlier and still wasn't able to move his arm without it hurting.

Maybe one of the machines was pumping in drugs. That could explain why she wasn't hurting. But shouldn't there at least be a whole bunch of bandages somewhere on her?

She lifted her head and looked down at her body. To her surprise, she was no longer dressed in her jeans and sweatshirt, but was instead wearing a blue jumpsuit sort of thing with a black belt and low black boots. There were no bandages anywhere that she could see, or any indication that there'd ever been any.

On the plus side, she didn't smell like booze and vomit anymore.

She was still gazing down at her new clothing, wondering when hospitals started using jumpsuits instead of those flimsy robe things, when there was a softer version of the whooshing she'd heard in the round room and a door half-hidden behind one of the racks slid open.

Nicole tensed, her mind flashing back to her nightmares about butterfly people and marble monsters. To her relief, it was a normal woman who stepped into the room. Her face was cheerful and heavily freckled, her reddish hair tied back in a tight ponytail. She was wearing a jumpsuit like Nicole's, except that hers was red instead of blue.

"Good morning, Nicole," the woman said. Her voice was melodious, with the kind of pleasant English accent that Nicole had always liked. "It *is* Nicole, correct?"

It took Nicole two tries to get her voice working through an unexpectedly dry throat and mouth. "Yes, I'm Nicole," she confirmed cautiously.

"My name's Allyce," the woman said. She crossed to one of the racks beside Nicole and peered at something on one of the sides that Nicole couldn't see. "I'm your doctor. How are you feeling?"

Nicole's first instinct was to say she was fine. People who complained about feeling bad got left behind on jobs and didn't get a share of the take.

But there was something in Allyce's voice that made Nicole think that maybe she really did want an honest answer. "My throat's kind of dry," she said, taking a quick mental inventory of her various body parts. Surprisingly, especially so soon after a binge, her head wasn't hurting. Had they found a new cure for hangovers? "My stomach hurts a little, too."

"Probably hunger." Allyce pointed to the tubes running into Nicole's arms. "We've been feeding you and filtering out your wastes intravenously, so your stomach hasn't had a lot to do lately." She smiled. "I know what you're thinking, that dialysis usually means a lot of discomfort. Fortunately, this system is completely painless."

Nicole looked at the tubes again, her stomach tightening around the empty hole inside it. That hadn't been what she'd been thinking at all. "Was I sick?" she asked anxiously. "Was I hurt? What happened?"

"No, no, you're fine," Allyce assured her. She did something to the box, then stepped around the rack and started unfastening the tube connected to Nicole's right arm. "We just needed you to be under for a few days while we fitted you with your neural-link translator."

Nicole stared at her. "A few *days*?"

"No worries—the implantation went fine," Allyce continued. "How's your head, by the way?"

With an effort, Nicole dragged her mind away from the idea that she'd been lying here for days instead of just a few hours. No wonder her hangover was gone. Only—"My *head*?"

"Yes." Allyce finished with the tube and drew a circle in the air with her forefinger above Nicole's right temple. "Specifically, this area right there."

Nicole frowned, focusing her attention on that part of her head. It *did* feel a little strange, now that Allyce mentioned it. And the breezes from Allyce's movement were strangely cold right there. Carefully, she reached up and touched the spot.

And jerked her hand away. All the hair from her temple to her right ear was gone. In its place was a slightly lumpy grid that seemed to be made up of slender, stiff lines, circles, and spirals.

"It's all right," Allyce said quickly. "The procedure's finished, and it went fine. And there are never any side effects." She turned her head and pointed to the same place on herself. "See?"

Nicole stared, her stomach tightening even harder. Partially hidden beneath Allyce's hair was the same grid thing Nicole could feel on her own head. Allyce's threads were bright silver, and there were small globules at most of the intersections. It was like a strange tattoo, only made of metal instead of ink. "What is it?"

"As I said, it's your neural-link translator," Allyce said. She leaned over and started removing the tube from Nicole's other arm. "It's so that you can understand all the different languages that are spoken here."

"You mean foreign languages? Like Spanish and French?"

"Spanish, yes," Allyce said. "I don't think there are any French speakers here at the moment. But there are others. Plato speaks Greek, for instance, and there are one or two even stranger ones." She finished with the tube and stood up. "Come. It's time for proper introductions."

Slowly, Nicole eased herself off the bed. For having spent several days not moving, her muscles seemed in reasonably good shape. Unless Allyce was lying about how long she'd been there. "Where's Bungie?" she asked. "Is this the veterans hospital?"

"Your two friends will be joining you shortly," Allyce promised. "As to where we are, I'll let Plato explain that."

She reached for Nicole's arm. Automatically, Nicole twitched away. Allyce took the hint and let her hand fall back to her side. "Come—I'll take you to them," she said instead. She walked to the door and touched a small plate beside it. The door opened with another whoosh, and she stepped out into a gray-walled hallway.

Not sure she wanted to do this, but with no better ideas, Nicole followed.

The hallway was like a longer version of the room they'd just left. Its walls and ceiling were made of the same gray metal, with the same kind of indirect lighting glowing from the corners and from a few spots along the edges where the walls and ceiling met. The floor, fortunately, wasn't just more bare metal, but was instead covered with a slightly bouncy wall-to-wall mat that reminded her of dark red pizza crust. There were other doors along both walls, and ahead she could see a couple of gaps that probably led into other corridors.

Oddly enough, there were no windows or skylights or any other natural lighting. The handful of hospitals she'd visited over the years had all had lots of windows. Even their hallways had had some light coming into alcoves or waiting areas.

Were they in one of the hospital's inside work areas? Or maybe down in a basement?

"Unfortunately, the translator is audio based and can't help with these," Allyce commented as they walked past the first closed door. "But you'll catch on quickly enough."

"Catch on to what?" Nicole asked.

"These," Allyce said, pointing to the next door.

Nicole frowned, slowing to a stop. There was a small white plate beside the door, right about eye level and a foot or so above the same sort of touch switch that Allyce had used to open that first door. She'd seen plates like that before in hospitals, with the room's name or identifying number on it.

Only the black characters etched into the plate weren't any sort of letters or numbers she'd ever seen. Some of them were curvy and complicated, like the letters on Chinese take-out menus. Others were sharp-angled with maybe something curly added on. "What are they?" she asked.

"That's the room number," Allyce said. "This one is *postinda*-three-three-six-one-five. Don't worry—as I said, you'll catch on. Plato will give you a copy of the manual later—that will help." She reached for Nicole's arm, remembered in time, and pointed ahead. "Come—breakfast is waiting."

They passed three more doors before Allyce reached the one she wanted. Beside each of the doors, Nicole noted, were number plates with the same strange squiggles.

The room Allyce ushered her into was several times larger than the room Nicole had woken up in. At first glance, it looked like a small cafeteria, with half a dozen people in blue jumpsuits seated around one of the tables and a few others in green and/or red outfits at some of the others. A serving counter was set up against the far wall.

Only there wasn't anyone at the counter, like there was in a normal restaurant, but just some trays with cups and plates of food on them. The tables were also oddly shaped, with eight sides like stop signs instead of normal round or square ones. The chairs were high-backed and looked a lot more comfortable than the cheap plastic ones at the fast-food places she got to eat at sometimes.

She took another look at the people . . . and only then did she notice that not all of them were actually *people*.

She stopped abruptly just inside the doorway, bouncing another half step forward as Allyce, caught by surprise, bumped into her. "What is it?" Allyce asked. "What's the matter?"

"That," Nicole murmured tensely, bumping into Allyce a second time as she took a quick step backward. The shark-faced marble monster who'd come at her when she'd first arrived at this place was sitting at the table with the blue-jumpsuited men—

"Oh, for goodness' sake," Allyce said, a note of exasperation briefly coloring her calm voice as she tried without success to push Nicole the rest of the way into the room. "That's just Kahkitah. Go on, he won't hurt you. Go *on*, Nicole—I can't get in until you do."

Nicole swallowed hard. The whole room had gone silent, with all faces turned to her and Allyce, including the nightmare face of the marble monster.

Still, it wasn't making any move toward her this time. Maybe it was just some new kind of robot, something the hospital cleaning staff used to clean up dangerous spills or collect bedpans or something.

Whatever it was, she decided, standing in the doorway wouldn't gain her anything. With an effort, she forced her feet to resume moving.

"That's better," Allyce said as she slipped around from behind Nicole and again tried to take Nicole's arm. This time, Nicole let her. "Come on, we'll start out slow. Let's take that table over there and I'll get you something to eat while we wait for Plato and your friends."

Watching the marble monster out of the corner of her eye, Nicole let Allyce lead her to an empty table. The men in the blue jumpsuits watched her the whole way, but the marble monster himself simply returned to his meal. Nicole chose a chair where she could see both the monster and the door, and gingerly sat down while Allyce went to the serving counter and brought back one of the trays.

Like the room and hallway, the meal wasn't what Nicole had expected. The main bowl contained a thick yellow paste with oddly shaped bits of other colors mixed in, like someone had taken butterscotch pudding and poured in several different children's breakfast cereals. The two smaller plates beside it held what looked like burnt toast and perforated red marshmallows. The mug contained water with what looked like frozen pieces of lemon floating in it. "What's this?"

"Breakfast," Allyce said. "Go ahead, try it. Trust me, it tastes better than it looks."

Nicole had heard that one before, usually from her grand-mother, and it had never, ever, been true. But her stomach was feeling emptier than ever, and the aromas rising from the food didn't smell all that bad. Picking up the oddly shaped spoon lying beside the bowl, she steeled herself and dug in.

For once, the meal was a pleasant surprise. The pudding dish was hot, and tasted more like Italian food than pudding mixed with cereal. The burnt toast was also good, reminding her of a type of breaded chicken she'd had once. The red marshmallows were only fair and unlike anything else she'd ever eaten, though the taste did remind her of the way a Japanese restaurant smelled.

But the long days of eating through a tube in her arm had left her ravenous. She ate everything, including the marshmallows, down to the last crumbs of burnt toast.

"I would say your appetite has definitely returned," Allyce said as Nicole scraped the final bits of pudding from the bowl. "That's a good sign. Would you like some more?"

Nicole looked over at the trays on the counter. Her grandmother had told her that eating too much made you look greedy. Trake had said that a full stomach slowed you down.

But she was still hungry, and neither of them was here to complain at her. "Would that be okay?"

"Absolutely." Allyce's smile turned brittle. "If there's one thing this place has plenty of, it's food. I'll get you another tray."

She picked up Nicole's tray and headed back toward the serving counter. Nicole watched as she moved between the tables, running their brief conversations over again in her mind, trying to figure out what exactly the other woman wanted from her.

She *did* want something, of course. Everyone did. And the nicer or friendlier a person was, the bigger the hook hidden behind the smile and kind words. Allyce wanted something, and sooner or later she was bound to let a glimpse of that hook slip out.

Nicole was still thinking over the possibilities when the door whooshed open and Bungie strode in.

He looked surprisingly good, especially considering the shape he'd been in the last time she'd seen him. His head, like Nicole's, had been half shaved, his newly acquired pattern of silvery thread glistening in the light. But otherwise he looked awake, alert, and steady on his feet.

He stopped a pace inside the door, just as Nicole had, probably to assess the situation, just as Nicole had. His gaze swept the room, his face expressionless as he looked at the people and marble monster. He glanced into the hallway behind him, then strode toward Nicole's table. As he did, another young man stepped into the cafeteria, a thoughtful look on his face. He watched Bungie cross the room, then headed over toward the serving counter.

Bungie reached Nicole's table and dropped into the chair beside her. "What the hell's going on?" he demanded quietly.

"Don't ask me," Nicole murmured back. "All I know—"

"Yeah, well, I *am* asking you, aren't I?" he snarled back. "What the hell is this place? Who the hell—*what* the hell—are these people?" He jerked his head toward the marble monster.

"I already said I didn't know," Nicole said, feeling her throat tighten. She'd hoped the lack of emotion in his face meant he'd decided to play it cool. Instead, it had been a mask he'd put on to hide the anger and fear bubbling under the surface.

She hadn't personally seen all the crazy stuff Bungie had gotten himself into. But she'd heard enough stories, and anger or fear was usually a big part of the mix. And if there was one thing they didn't need right now, it was Bungie doing crazy stuff. "It's okay," she said in as soothing a voice as she could manage with her heart pounding in her throat. "If they were going to hurt us, I think they'd have done it already."

"Yeah?" He jabbed a finger at the silver threads on his head. "What do you call *this*?"

"It's a translator," Allyce said, appearing at Nicole's side and setting a fresh food tray in front of her. "How are you feeling, Howard?"

"The name's *Bungie*, bitch," Bungie bit out, glaring up at her. "Yeah, that's the same stupid story Pretty Boy here said. You think I'm stupid?"

"She's telling the truth," another voice put in.

Nicole turned to look. It was the young man who'd come in with Bungie, another of the food trays in his hands. "Here's your breakfast," he continued, setting the tray in front of Bungie.

"What the hell is this?" Bungie demanded, glaring distastefully down at the tray. "It looks like kitchen scraps."

"It's actually pretty good," Nicole said. "That stuff that looks like—"

"Did I ask?" Bungie cut her off, his voice gone ominously quiet. "Huh? Did I ask?"

Nicole clenched her teeth. "No."

"So here's what's gonna happen," Bungie said, his voice still quiet. "You, Pretty Boy, are going to get me some *real* food. Then you're going to get me a drink, and *then* you're going to show me the way out of here."

"You finished?" the young man asked calmly.

Nicole winced. Angry, afraid, and quiet. Bungie was on the road to crazy, all right.

This was *not* going to end well.

Bungie looked the young man up and down. "Yeah, I'm finished. For now."

"Good," the young man said. His voice was still calm, but there was a new edge to it that sent a shiver up Nicole's back. "Let's go in order. First: The name's *Jeff,* not Pretty Boy. Second: This is the food we have this morning. Eat it or go hungry—your choice. Third: If by *drink* you mean alcohol, forget it. There isn't any aboard."

Nicole frowned. *Aboard?* What kind of word was that to use with a hospital?

Either Bungie didn't notice the odd term or didn't care. "Like hell there isn't," he snarled. Abruptly, he shoved back his chair and stood up. "If you got people, you got booze. *I want a damn drink.* So you go get the whiskey, or I'm gonna—"

"Or you're going to *what?*" a deep voice challenged from the doorway.

Nicole turned. The man standing just inside the room was short and broad-shouldered, with black hair framing a dark, craggy face. His eyes were on Bungie, his expression holding the same hard animosity that Nicole had seen on way too many cops throughout the years. Standing uncertainly behind him was McNair, the doctor from the parking lot, his new translator glinting from his half-shaved head.

And even though the figure in the round room had been only a silhouette against the bright light, Nicole had a strong sense that this dark-haired man was that same person. The man who'd said incomprehensible words to her and the others just before the marble monster had come at her.

Someone across the room ground out more foreign words—"I said you're going to do *what?*" the broad-shouldered man repeated, taking another couple of steps toward their table.

A fresh chill ran up Nicole's back. This time, she'd been looking at the newcomer's face when he spoke . . . and his lips and mouth hadn't matched the words he was saying.

In fact, she was pretty sure he'd actually stopped talking before he'd finished asking the question.

But that was impossible. How could he keep talking after he'd stopped talking? Was he one of those ventriloquist people?

"I'm gonna crack some heads, that's what," Bungie growled back, taking a step away from the table and looking the newcomer up and down. If he was bothered by the other's strange mouth and lip pattern, he didn't show it. Probably hadn't even noticed it.

Again, the broad-shouldered man said something incomprehensible. This time, he was still talking gibberish when he also started speaking English. "You need to take a minute and think about what you're proposing," he said, his voice even colder than Bungie's. "Even if you were to win such a fight—and I guarantee you wouldn't—what then? Do you propose to find a door and simply walk home?"

Bungie snorted. "Give me one good reason why I can't."

There was another quick series of nonsense words—"Because we're currently a thousand light-years from Earth," the man said calmly. "Everything you've ever known is far, far behind us.

"And you'll never see any of it again."

Once again, silence filled the room. Even Bungie seemed unable to find anything to say.

But he recovered quickly. "Yeah, right," he said. "You must think we're stupid or—"

The other man snapped something—"Do you understand Greek, my friend?"

"Because if you think—" Bungie stopped. "What?"

More jabbering—"Because that's what I'm speaking right now," the other man said. "The reason you're hearing English is because of the translator grafted to your head and brain." He gestured to the marble monster and said something else—"Kahkitah, speak some of your language to him."

Nicole jerked violently as what sounded like a rapid-fire series of birdcalls suddenly filled the room. She had just enough time to see that the marble monster's shark gills were vibrating in time to the sounds—"Plato speaks the truth," the words came over the chirping. "You're hearing the language of the Ghorf people as yours. I *think* you're hearing it that way," he added, suddenly sounding a little confused. "Of course I can't hear what *you're* hearing. But I hear your language as mine, and I'm told it also works the other way."

The broad-shouldered man—Plato?—spoke again. "Kahkitah's easily confused, but I'm sure you get his point," he said. "And even you, Bungie, must have figured out by now that this technology isn't even close to possible on Earth."

"Then where *are* we?" Nicole asked, trying hard to keep her voice calm. "You said we were in *space*?"

Plato said something—"You're aboard the *Fyrantha,* a large spaceship traveling between the stars."

Bungie threw a hooded look at Nicole. But he had a reputation for never backing down. Looking back at Plato, he folded his arms across his chest. "Yeah? Prove it. Open a window or TV screen or something and let's see outside."

Plato snorted and spoke, his tone sounding sarcastic. "If you can find either of those, you're welcome to take a look," he said. "Better still, find a door and leave. I won't try to stop you."

He turned around and continued speaking as he gestured to McNair. "Don't just stand there, Sam. Come in and have breakfast."

"What?" McNair asked distantly, his eyes on Kahkitah.

Plato spoke again—"I said come in, sit with your friends, and have something to eat," he said, gesturing to Nicole's table. "The day's work will soon begin."

With an effort, McNair tore his eyes away from the creature. "They're not my friends," he said, his voice hardening as he looked at Nicole and then Bungie. "And whatever you think I'm going to do for you, you can forget it. You kidnapped me for nothing."

Plato eyed him for a moment after he'd finished—waiting for his own translator to finish its work, Nicole realized. Then he gave a sort of barking laugh and started speaking. "You misunderstand, Sam," he said. "You weren't the target. Nicole is the only one we needed."

McNair had started walking stiffly toward the table. Now, abruptly, he stopped short. "What?" he demanded. *"Her?"*

Plato nodded as he spoke again. "Indeed. She's one of the rare ones—a Sibyl—and we need her—"

"Wait a second," Bungie interrupted, glaring at Nicole. "You want her—*what*? What do you want *her* for? She's a nobody. A useless drunk."

Nicole dropped her gaze to the tabletop, feeling her face flush with embarrassment and shame. *Nobody. Useless. Drunk.* With all the strange things she'd experienced since waking up, she'd almost forgotten.

But he was right. She was useless. All she'd ever had was Trake and his group, and that was gone now. Gone forever.

And suddenly, she really, *really* wanted a drink.

Plato spoke—"Of course she's an alcoholic," he said. "Most Sibyls are. They have a unique brain chemistry, and the most common Earth-side manifestation of that is addiction to alcohol. Of course, we need her to be completely sober before she can be of any use, which is why there's no liquor aboard."

"What the *hell* are you babbling about?" Bungie demanded. "What brain stuff—what are you talking about?"

"I'm talking about the unique brain chemistry," Plato said, "that allows her to listen to the ship."

Nicole frowned, her growing craving for a drink suddenly forgotten. "Listen to the ship do what?"

Plato spoke—"The *Fyrantha* will tell you what needs fixing, and sometimes tell you how exactly the repairs are to be made," he said. "Your job will be to relay those instructions to your work crew."

Nicole looked at Plato, then at Jeff and Allyce. If this was a joke, no one was laughing. "That's crazy," she said.

"No argument here," Allyce agreed. "But it's still true. Tell me, did you ever hear voices in your head? Things you couldn't really explain or make out?"

"Yes, but—" Nicole threw a furtive look at Bungie, wincing at the expression on his face. She'd never told Trake or any of his people about the voices. "They were coming from *here*?"

"Actually, they were coming from the Wisps who were on Earth at those times," Allyce said. "It was their communications with the *Fyrantha* while they were picking up other people that you overheard."

"You mean those UFO crazies were *right*?" Bungie demanded. "Those damn butterfly things have been flying around the world all these years?"

Plato spoke—"They don't fly anywhere," he explained with strained patience. "They locate their target, port in and grab him or her, then port out again."

"That's how we all got here," Jeff said. "The *Fyrantha* needed workers and sent the Wisps to get us."

"This makes no sense," McNair insisted. "You said Earth was, what, a thousand light-years away? You can't snatch people from that kind of distance."

Plato rattled off some words—"Two hundred years ago you couldn't have a conversation with someone on the other side of the planet, either. Is it so strange to think that someone more advanced than us could come up with an equally miraculous invention?"

"It's nonsense," McNair said flatly. "For one thing, nothing can travel faster than the speed of light. For another, it's flat-out ridiculous. Why would anyone with technology like that invite a bunch of cavemen like us to come in and fix up their ship for them?"

"It wasn't exactly an invitation," Jeff said grimly. "I was snatched straight out of my computer repair shop. Plato was pulled off a construction site."

"Everyone has their own story of how they got here," Allyce said. "But don't worry. We're well treated, and there's plenty to keep us busy. You'll get used to it."

"No, I don't think so," McNair said stiffly. "I don't know why I'm even here when all you wanted was her. Fine. Send me back and we'll call it even."

Plato spoke, shaking his head. "I'm afraid we can't."

McNair's eyes narrowed. "What do you mean, you can't?" he demanded. "Of course you can. Just turn this thing around, or crank up whatever machine you used to bring us here. Whatever it takes."

Plato spoke. "The *Fyrantha* will not allow it. But don't worry. As Allyce said, there'll be plenty of useful work for another doctor—"

"The *ship* won't allow it?" McNair drowned out the rest of Plato's words. "The *ship*? Who the hell's in charge here, you or it? You get on that machine and you *send me the hell home*."

Plato shook his head and said a single, flat word. "No."

McNair's face darkened. "Listen. I don't know who you are, or who made you king of this little—"

Plato bit out something in a tone that all by itself made McNair stop in midsentence. *"Enough,"* the translation came.

Once again, the room went quiet. Plato continued in the same ominous tone—"We don't raise our voices here, Sam," he continued. "We don't threaten each other, and we *absolutely* don't fight. We settle any and all differences in a polite, civilized manner. Is that clear?"

"And if I don't feel like being a sheep today?"

Plato spoke—"Then try harder. The ship doesn't like it when we fight."

McNair threw Nicole a disbelieving look. "The *ship* doesn't *like* it?"

Plato was talking again—"And you don't want to make the ship unhappy. You don't want the food dispenser to suddenly dry up. You don't want the lights to go out. You don't want your room's temperature to drop to forty below zero."

"You'd really do that to us?" McNair demanded.

Plato spoke—"We don't run the *Fyrantha*, Sam. It's not up to us. So. No fighting or arguing. Is that clear?"

"Perfectly," McNair said between stiff lips.

Plato shifted his gaze to Bungie and spoke again. "Clear?"

Bungie snorted. "Buncha cowards," he bit out. "None of you ever been hungry or cold before?"

Plato spoke—"You've never been hungry or cold like this. Clear?"

Bungie looked at McNair. The doctor looked back at him.

And with a sudden tightening of her stomach, Nicole saw the flash of understanding between them. Bungie was a street thug and kidnapper. McNair was a high-class doctor and kidnapping victim.

But neither wanted to be here. And both were prepared to do whatever was necessary to get home.

Even if it meant working together.

"Fine," Bungie said. "Clear."

Plato nodded and spoke again. "Now, eat your breakfasts, both of you, and we'll sort out your duties." He looked back at Nicole as he continued. "You, of course, already have your assigned task. When you're finished, you'll be taken to your work area and Allyce will instruct you."

Nicole looked down at her tray. If Plato was telling the truth, she'd been kidnapped because of the voices she'd been hearing all these years. Voices that were supposed to tell her how to do things.

Only they weren't doing that. They never had. Aside from that one moment of clarity when the butterfly person had been holding her in the darkness, she'd never even heard a complete sentence out of them.

Should she tell Plato that? If it really was the only reason she was here, maybe that would persuade him to send them all home.

Only Plato had already said that wasn't going to happen.

Which meant Nicole had to stall somehow until she could figure out what else to do. She had to stall like crazy. "All right," she said, picking up the spoon again. The first part of that stalling, she decided, would be to eat very, very slowly.

And hope that whatever Bungie and Sam came up with, they would come up with it fast.

three

Nicole had perfected the art of slow eating back in third grade when she'd decided she hated school. She'd gotten pretty good at it, too, sometimes pushing her breakfast long enough to miss the entire first half hour of the class day.

Eventually, her grandmother had figured it out and called her bluff. After that, Nicole was given a rock-solid specific time to be finished eating, after which the cold leftovers would be taken away to form the basis of that night's dinner.

Now, that self-training was once again coming in handy. But there were only so many times even Nicole could chew a given bite, or pretend to get something caught between her teeth, or fake a sip of water going down the wrong way. Especially when Jeff and Allyce were sitting there, patiently watching her every move. Even more especially when Bungie and Sam finished their meals long before she did and left with Plato.

She could only hope that whatever plan they were cooking up could be set into motion quickly. Finishing the last of her own meal, she reluctantly announced herself ready to go.

From the way Plato had talked she'd assumed it would just be her and Allyce who would be heading off to the job site he'd mentioned. To her surprise, it turned out that the whole group of blue-jumpsuited men at the other table was also going with her.

Including the big marble monster, whose name was lost in all the rest of the weird stuff that had been thrown at her in the past hour. Not that she would probably be talking much to him anyway.

That resolve apparently also worked the other way. Not only did the marble monster not talk to her as they all walked down the gray corridors, but neither did the rest of the group. A couple of the men at the front kept up a quiet conversation between them along the way, but most of the rest didn't talk at all. Not to each other, and certainly not to Nicole. Even Allyce, who'd been chatty enough an hour ago, seemed to have run out of things to talk about.

The sole exception was Jeff.

"Plato considers all of us to be a single repair crew, but we often end up breaking into two separate groups," he told Nicole as they walked along. "Most of the time it's hard to get more than two or three of us working on the same project—just isn't enough room. Though we'll probably all work together today—the area we were working before you came along is plenty big. But don't worry, the *Fyrantha* probably won't overload you with details until you're ready for that."

"Sure, that makes sense," Nicole said, not understanding even half of what he'd just said. "Are you the one in charge?"

Jeff snorted. "Hardly," he said. "No, Carp's the crew foreman—he's the balding guy up front. The thin guy he's talking to is Levi, the assistant foreman. He runs the second crew when we break into two squads."

"Oh," Nicole said, memorizing the limited views she could see of the two men's faces when they turned briefly toward each other as they talked. The first rule of survival in an unfamiliar group, she knew, was to find out who the boss was, figure out his hook, and play to it. That was the best way to keep the rest of the gang at a safe distance.

The problem was that none of the usual rules worked here. If Jeff and Plato were right about the ship giving them free food, then working against hunger was out. If there wasn't anything to buy, money was out. If there weren't any jobs to do, and no cops to watch for or distract, everything she'd done for Trake was gone.

So what was left?

Given that Carp was a man, and Allyce seemed to be the only other woman around, there was one other obvious hook. But Nicole had no intention of going that direction unless she absolutely had to. She'd been down that road before, and it was nothing but pain and trouble and more pain.

And usually fights. If Plato wasn't lying about the ship not liking it when people fought, all the more reason to steer clear of that one.

"I don't know how much Allyce told you," Jeff continued, "but we're currently working in the *sevko*-four part of the ship. *Sevko* is one of the letters. I guess you'd call them letters. Susan—she's a Sibyl in one of the other work areas—thinks they're more like full syllables that the Shipmasters use to label the macro areas of the ship. Everything inside a given macro is then divided into corridors and rooms and labeled with sets of numbers."

"Sounds complicated," Nicole murmured, feeling more lost than ever. She was definitely going to have to find a protector here, if only to make sure that if Bungie snapped he didn't snap in her direction.

Jeff might be good for that. He seemed like the helpful type, and guys like that sometimes also saw themselves as white-knight protectors of young women.

But right now, her main problem was still how to hide the fact that she couldn't hear the voices the ship was supposed to have. But there might be a simple way to slide that one past them. Plato surely wasn't going to trust a newcomer like Nicole with giving anyone orders, which meant he would have another Sibyl on the job to make sure Nicole was telling the truth and not just scamming everyone. If she could find a way to trick that other Sibyl into giving the crew the instructions without saying anything about them herself, she might be in the clear, at least for now. "Where's your other Sibyl?" she asked Jeff.

An instant later she knew that had somehow been the wrong thing to say. To her left she heard a quiet catch in Allyce's breath, and to her right Jeff stiffened and threw a wary look at her. "What do you mean?" he asked cautiously.

"I just thought someone could explain how this is supposed to work," she said, the words falling over each other. Was she not supposed to ask about other Sibyls? Jeff had just mentioned one— were the rules different for her? "In case I get something wrong."

Jeff's tension disappeared. "Oh," he said, sounding as lame as she just had. "No, the other Sibyls are off with their own work crews. It'll just be you." He pointed ahead down the hallway. "Here we are."

Nicole looked. Carp and Levi had stopped at a section of corridor that was set back a few inches from the rest of the wall. They did something at the far end, and the panel slid along the floor like a long closet door, disappearing into the section of wall beside it. Behind the door was a shallow room with a few dozen black, multipocket vests hanging from hooks along the back and toolboxes and strange-looking machines arranged neatly on the floor beneath them. "This is the work site?" she asked, staring into the long closet in confusion.

"No, this is where we gear up," Jeff said. "We keep these closets locked, but the code's pretty simple—someone will give it to you later. Come on, I'll get you your vest."

Nicole had already noted that the vests were equipped with lots of small and medium-sized pockets. What she hadn't realized was that most of the pockets were already full.

"What *is* all this?" she asked as she squirmed around, trying to get the garment to rest comfortably on her shoulders. It was a lot heavier than she'd guessed, with some of the bulkier items pushing her arms awkwardly away from her sides.

"Yours is mostly food and water," Jeff said. "Plus a screwdriver, wrench, and a couple of other general-purpose tools. We'll be away from the hive most of the day and need to bring our lunch with us."

"How much are you expecting me to *eat*?" Nicole asked, peering down at the bulging pockets. Maybe she shouldn't have taken that second tray at breakfast.

"Oh, you're carrying our food, too," Jeff said, as if it were obvious. "Our vests are already loaded with tools and replacement parts. You don't have any of that, so you carry all the food."

"Oh." Nicole hefted the weight on her shoulders. It still seemed like an awful lot of food and water for nine people. Even if one of those people was a big marble-covered monster.

"You'll also need this," Allyce said, holding out her hand.

Nicole frowned. Lying across the other woman's palm was something that looked like a half-melted version of the small plastic squirt gun she'd had as a child, with a metal cylinder wedged into one end. "What's that?"

"Your inhaler," Allyce said. "It has the drug you'll need to hear the ship."

Nicole's first reaction was a flood of quiet relief. So she wasn't *supposed* to be hearing the voices yet? That was a huge weight off her shoulders.

Her second thought was more like a slap across the face. They were expecting her to put unknown *drugs* into her body?

That scared her. She'd done everything she could through her nineteen years to avoid drugs. She'd tried weed only once, and it had made her sick to her stomach and determined never to try it again. Cocaine, heroin, and meth were straight out—she'd seen what those did to kids in her neighborhood, not to mention some of Trake's group, and there was no way she was going to let that stuff anywhere near her. Designer drugs were a total crapshoot, and could kill you faster than an angry dealer with a new gun to play with. And every single one of the hallucinogens terrified the hell out of her. Alcohol, especially a good whiskey, was the only thing she'd never been able to turn down or control, and that was more than enough of a load across her neck.

"Go ahead," Allyce urged. "Take it."

Gingerly, Nicole picked up the inhaler. It wasn't much heavier than her old squirt gun, either. "What's in it?" she asked.

"As I said, the drug that allows you to listen to the *Fyrantha*," Allyce said. "It's in powder form, rather like asthma medicine. I gather you never had asthma?"

"One of the kids at school had it," Nicole said, turning the inhaler over in her hand. "What kind of drug is it?"

"It's magic pixie dust," Carp growled as he worked the fasteners on his vest. "Who cares what it is?"

"*I* care," Nicole said firmly. It was risky to stand up to the boss, she knew, especially a boss who might be the key to her survival until she could get out of here. But this was something she needed to get straight right from the beginning. "I want to know if it's going to make me dizzy or throw up or something. Or get hooked."

"Oh, no, it's nothing like that," Allyce assured her. "It lets you hear the *Fyrantha* for about three minutes, that's all. None of the other Sibyls has ever complained of any side effects."

At the edge of Nicole's vision, she saw Jeff shift from one foot to the other. Was he uncomfortable about something?

But uncomfortable about what? Was this some kind of con game? A practical joke?

Or was it something worse? Was Allyce pulling something nasty?

But Allyce's face held nothing but pure sincerity. And Nicole really couldn't see what a con game would gain anyone. Maybe Jeff was just impatient to get going. "Okay," Nicole said, still not happy with any of this but knowing there was nothing she could do about it. They could hold her down and stuff the dust down her throat if they really wanted to. "How do I work it?"

"We'll tell you when we're at the job site," Carp said impatiently. "Come on—we're already running late."

A sudden bird trilling filled the corridor. Nicole jumped, then remembered that was how the marble monster talked. "But how can we know where the job site is until she tells us?" the confused-sounding translation came.

"Gee, let me think," Carp said sarcastically. "Our last job was in *sevko*-four-nineteen-five. Before that we were in *sevko*-four-nineteen-four, and before *that* we were in *sevko*-four-nineteen-three. You want to take a wild guess where we're probably working today?"

For a long moment the marble monster just stared at him. Longer, Nicole suspected, than it took for the question to translate.

At least one other person in the group apparently thought so, too. "It's okay, Kahkitah," Jeff said soothingly. "Come on, Carp, lay off him, will you?"

"No, I want to hear his answer," Carp said, his eyes still on the marble monster. "Come on, Fishface, shake those brain cells into action—"

He broke off as Kahkitah suddenly warbled. "We're going to work in *sevko*-four-nineteen-six!" the big Ghorf said excitedly.

Carp shook his head in mock amazement. "Whatever would we do without you?" he said. "Grab your kits and let's go. Kahkitah, you get the sealer."

Reaching into the closet, he grabbed the handle of one of the boxes and strode away. Levi and the other men each took another of the boxes and marched off behind him. Kahkitah stood still another moment, probably waiting for the translation to finish, then went to the closet and dragged one of the larger machines into the hallway. He worked a lever, and the machine extended wheels from its underside and a loop from its top. Wrapping one hand around the loop, he headed off after the others, rolling the machine behind him.

"Come on," Jeff said to Nicole, picking up a kit of his own and sliding the closet door closed. "As you may have noticed, Carp hates waiting."

Two minutes later, they caught up to Carp and the rest of the crew standing beside a wall in another of the hallways, this one longer and wider than the others Nicole had seen.

A plain hallway, with no sign of open cabinets or warning signs or even holes in the wall or floors. "This is the work site?" she asked Jeff, looking around in confusion.

"It will be in a second," Carp said, beckoning as Kahkitah came up to him. "Come on, get it open."

Kahkitah apparently didn't need this one translated. Parking his machine beside Carp, he crossed to the wall on the far side of the hallway. Crouching down, he took hold of a handgrip Nicole hadn't noticed before, and with a convulsive surge that seemed to start at his ankles and ripple up all the way to his head, he reared up and backward.

And to Nicole's amazement, the entire section of the wall came with him, a good twenty feet of it, swinging up like the side of a sandwich-vendor truck. Kahkitah swung the panel nearly all the way to the ceiling, then shifted his grip and pushed it the rest of the way up. He held it there while two of the men in the crew scurried to the ends of the panel and did something that seemed to fasten it in place.

Kahkitah eased his hands away and stepped back again. Nicole watched the open panel another moment, just to make sure it wasn't going to come crashing down, then focused on the open space behind it.

It was a complicated-looking mess. There was a massive spider-web of wires and tubes fastened to the back wall, along with dozens of oddly shaped boxes that ranged from cigarette-pack size all the way up to something bigger than the dish Nicole's grandmother had used for their yearly Christmas turkey. The wires seemed to start at one of the boxes, most of them then traveling outward like spokes of a wheel and disappearing into the back wall. Over all the wires and tubes was a shiny coating, like the whole thing had been covered with plastic or varnish.

"Okay, Sibyl, you're up," Carp said briskly, pulling out a pen and something that looked like a big cell phone from one of his pockets. He tapped the corner of the phone, then positioned the tip of the pen at the top. "Any time."

"Hold the inhaler vertically," Allyce instructed, positioning the device in Nicole's hand so that the squirt gun end was pointed toward her and the half-melted grip was going straight up. "Put the tip in your mouth, and as you squeeze the top take a quick, deep breath. It'll shoot pretty hard into the back of your throat, so try not to gag on it."

Steeling herself, Nicole gave it a try.

The first attempt didn't work very well. She apparently didn't squeeze the thing hard enough and all she got was a mouthful of a shockingly sweet powder. Carp snorted something under his breath, but the rest of the group merely stood and waited. Nicole tried again, and this time felt a strange coolness as the powder flew down her throat into her lungs. For a second she had to fight against the urge to cough, wondering if and when she would know if it had worked—

The five-three-three circuit is broken.

Nicole twitched violently. Without warning, the murmur in the background had suddenly become a single, utterly clear voice in her head. *The six-seven-three circuit is broken—*

"Well?" Carp demanded.

"The five-three-three circuit is broken," Nicole said, trying to unfreeze her brain. With the silvery thing they'd glued to the side of her head, Plato's and Kahkitah's translated voices at least *sounded* like they were coming through her ears. The *Fyrantha's* voice sounded like it was coming from three inches behind her eyes. "Also the six-seven-three circuit—"

The three-one controller has incomplete output—

"The three-one controller has incomplete output," Nicole said, hoping desperately that she could keep up with the voice.

"Hold on, hold on," Carp said, writing furiously on the phone with his pen.

"I've got it," Levi said calmly, writing on his own phone. "Keep it coming, Nicole."

The five-five junction box is damaged—

"The five-five junction box is damaged—"

The six-eight-three-three ready fire symbol axe is damaged.

Nicole frowned. The *what?* "The six-eight-three-three ready fire symbol axe is damaged," she stammered. The words sounded as bizarre coming out of her mouth as they had coming into her brain.

Apparently they did to everyone else, too. "The *what*?" Carp demanded.

Nicole braced herself. "The six-eight—"

"I got the numbers," he interrupted. "What the hell was the rest of it? Ready fire symbol?"

"She probably meant a rectifier simplex," Levi said. "There's one between those two dipple modulators on the left."

Carp snorted. "Oh, for the love of—"

"Hey, take it easy," Jeff spoke up. "These probably aren't words she's ever run into before."

"Even Kahkitah has trouble with them," someone else added, "and he's been hearing them for two years."

"Yeah, well, Kahkitah could hear them for *twenty* years without them sinking in," Carp said acidly. "So is that it? Hey—Sibyl—look alive. Is that it?"

"That's all I heard." Nicole looked at Allyce. "Unless the powder's worn off. Should I try it again?"

"No, it should still be active," Allyce said, peering briefly into Nicole's eyes. "If the voice has gone silent, it means that's all the *Fyrantha*'s going to give you. For now."

Nicole felt her throat tighten. Up to now she'd managed to shove that particular bit of creepiness into the back of her mind. But with Allyce's words, it had suddenly rushed back to the forefront.

The ship was talking to her. A big, alien ship was *talking* to her. To *her*.

"Okay, let's get on it," Carp said, digging into one of his vest pockets and pulling out a tool that looked like a combination socket wrench and screwdriver. "Tomas, figure out which of those junction boxes is the five-five. Levi, Jeff, tag the rest of the modules and start getting them off. The rest of you, find the circuits she listed and start peeling off the sealant."

"What do I do?" Nicole asked.

"You stay out of the way and don't touch anything," Carp said as he headed to the wall.

Kahkitah whistled another birdsong. "You may stay here by me," he offered, sounding almost shy. "I won't have other work until they need more heavy lifting to be done. I'd appreciate the company."

Nicole eyed him. Big, strong, but clearly not very bright. She'd known people like that, and they usually got nothing but abuse and contempt from everyone else around them. If Carp's attitude was any indication, Kahkitah probably got a lot of the same here, too.

Hanging out with someone like that would be excruciatingly boring, and it could damage her reputation with everyone else. Still, if her attempts to work Carp or Jeff went south, it might not hurt to have a little friendly muscle in reserve.

"Thank you," she said, stepping to Kahkitah's side. She stood as close to him as she dared, trying not to wince at the odd look and texture of his hands and marble-studded arms. Figuring out this one's hook, she thought distantly, would be a hell of a challenge.

Nicole had seldom had the chance—or the inclination—to watch people while they worked at regular jobs. Now, as she and Kahkitah gazed at Carp's team, she discovered that it was every bit as boring as she'd always suspected.

They spent the first few minutes figuring out exactly which of the wires and boxes were the ones the voice had identified. Then Carp, Levi, and Tomas used various tools from their vest pockets to unfasten the boxes from the wall. While they did that, the rest of the crew set to work with flat-bladed knives, prying up parts of the plastic coating that sealed all the wires to the wall.

It took almost an hour to get the boxes free and disconnected from the wires and tubes that came into and out of them. The plastic coating was pretty hard to remove, or maybe it was just hard to remove without damaging the stuff underneath. The men were still working on that part as Jeff and Levi settled themselves cross-legged on different sections of the floor and began taking apart the boxes, laying the pieces in neat rows or half circles around them.

They were all still working at their various tasks when Carp called lunch.

Nicole's general boredom was interrupted for a couple of minutes as she passed out her collection of food bars and water. She rather expected the men to sit down together, or at least clump in twos or threes to chat while they ate, but to her surprise they all headed off in different directions, either going somewhere down their current hallway or else finding other hallways or open rooms. Apparently, they had enough togetherness during their work time.

Which left Nicole and Kahkitah alone. Kahkitah had his own set of food bars, but he accepted a bottle of water from her supply and settled down on the floor in a sort of half-kneeling, half-sitting position. Nicole sat down beside him, nibbling at her vaguely Tex-Mex-flavored food bar and wondering what Carp would say and do if she rearranged the positions of the pieces Jeff and Levi had so painstakingly laid out. Probably not a good idea.

There was some more birdcall whistling. "Tell me about yourself, Nicole," the translation came.

"What?" she asked, frowning.

More whistling. "Tell me about yourself," Kahkitah repeated. "We've been told only your name. I want to know more."

Nicole snorted. "Why?"

Still more whistling. Nicole tried to hear something recognizable in the sounds—familiar birdcalls from the city parks, or bits of music, or *something*—but it was never anything but meaningless trilling noise. "Because you are now part of our crew," Kahkitah said. "As you have seen, you and I will usually have little to do. It would help pass the time if we could talk together while the others work. Unless your goal is to watch them and learn how to do the repairs yourself?" he added, as if it were an afterthought.

A pretty stupid afterthought. But then, he wasn't exactly the brains of the group. "Yeah, well, the first thing you need to know about me is that I couldn't learn how to do the stuff they're doing," she said. "Not in a million years."

Kahkitah waited for the translation to end, then made some more birdcalls. "I didn't know humans could live that long."

Nicole rolled her eyes. "It's an expression," she said. "It's a way of saying I'm stupid."

Birdcalls—"That's not true. Why do you speak untruths?"

"Who says it's not true?"

More birdcalls—"I do. You're a Sibyl. That means you're smart."

"No, it means I've got a broken brain," Nicole growled. "I already knew that."

Kahkitah was silent so long Nicole started to think he'd given up on the conversation. Then, he began trilling again.

But this time, the sound was softer, as if he were trying to whisper. "I watched you, Nicole," the translation came. "I watched you in the dining room, and as the others worked. You're alert to things around you. That speaks of intelligence and foresight."

Nicole shook her head. "Just speaks of me trying to stay alive. Nothing more. It's survival, not intelligence."

Birdcall—"I disagree. But even if you're right, the *Fyrantha* is a new opportunity for you. Here, no one will be able to hurt you."

"No one was hurting me back home, either," Nicole said. The words came out reflexively, as they had so many times before.

They were mostly true. "That's what all the watching and getting out of the way was for."

Birdcalls—"You speak of Bungie? Did he hurt you?"

"I told you no one was hurting me," Nicole insisted. "Bungie isn't exactly the nicest guy on the block. But he never hurt me."

Birdcalls—"Do you wish protection against him?"

"I *told* you, he never hurt me."

More birdcalls—"Do you wish protection against him?" Kahkitah repeated.

For a long moment Nicole thought about getting up and walking away. Kahkitah was stupid, she was stupid, and this was a stupid conversation.

But then she looked up into his eyes. Disturbing, alien eyes . . . and yet, somehow, his eyes and posture reminded her of an earnest, friendly dog.

Nicole had always wanted a dog. Her grandmother had always said they couldn't afford one. "Look," she said, trying one last time. "Bungie's an idiot—I'll give you that. He's also trouble. Been that way the whole time I've known him. But it's not like I can walk away and never see him again. Not if Plato's telling the truth about where we are."

Another pause, then more trilling. "But here you have choices," Kahkitah said. "You may not be able to walk away. But you don't have to remain close."

"We were never close," Nicole said, grimacing at the very thought of hanging around Bungie on any kind of permanent basis. "And I'm not planning to start now. But I've got to get along with him, just like I have to get along with all the rest of you."

Kahkitah seemed to think about that. Then, he gave a three-toned whistle that sounded almost like a sigh. "There is an evil spirit within him," he said. "He concerns me. You will let me know if he becomes a danger to you?"

"You'll be the first," Nicole assured him. Well, it would be either him or Jeff, depending on whether she needed muscle or brains. "Now if you'll excuse me, I have to eat."

Birdcall. "Of course."

The food bars were filling but small, and Nicole's meal didn't take very long. Even so, by the time she was finished Kahkitah had leaned his body backward at a painful-looking angle against the wall, closed his eyes, and gone to sleep.

For a few minutes Nicole considered taking a walk and seeing what else might be around here. But everything looked alike, and she didn't want to risk getting lost. Alternatively, she could hunt down Carp and get started finding his hook. But it might look suspicious if she moved on him this quickly.

So with nothing better to do, she got up and went over for a closer look at the mess of wires and boxes on the wall.

It was a tangle, all right. She'd seen that while the others worked. Kahkitah's idea that she could ever learn how to fix stuff like this was completely ridiculous.

Still, seen up close, it wasn't as bad as she'd thought. It was still a tangle, but the wires were different colors, as were the connector things on most of the boxes. The colors didn't always match up, but they did so enough times to form a kind of pattern.

She would still never figure out how to do this kind of work. But still, it wasn't as bad as she'd thought.

She was still studying the equipment, tracing the wires and tubes with her eyes just for the fun of it, when the rest of the crew began to drift back.

The afternoon went about the same as the morning had. Levi and Jeff found whatever was wrong with the various boxes and replaced the parts from their kits. The others finally got the rest of the plastic peeled off, at which point replacing the wires was a quick and relatively easy task.

They were midway through the replacement, and Nicole was listening to her stomach rumble and wondering what dinner would be like, when they had a pair of unexpected visitors. Unexpected and, for Nicole, at least, very much unwanted.

Plato and Bungie.

Plato made some comment in Greek as the two of them arrived. "How's it going?" the translation came

"Almost done," Carp said, eyeing Bungie. "Maybe half an hour to replace the wires, then another half hour to reseal."

Plato spoke again. "So not much to see. Too bad. But that's all right. Bungie can watch that part and at least see how you close down a job. He can learn the rest of your routine tomorrow."

"What do you mean?" Carp asked suspiciously.

Plato spoke—"I mean he's on your team now."

"Lucky us," Carp said, eyeing Bungie some more. "What exactly does he do?"

Plato said something that sounded sarcastic. "What he does is work with your team. The specifics you'll have to figure out on your own."

"No," Carp said flatly. "Sorry, Plato, but no. I already got all the unskilled dead weight I can use."

Plato snorted and rattled off more Greek. "Well, then, you'd better train him quick," the translation came. "Because he's yours."

"Why?" Carp demanded, jabbing a finger at Nicole. "Because of *her*?"

Plato shrugged and spoke. "Partly because of her. Mostly because I don't have anywhere else to put him. Allyce and Sam say he's healthy enough for light work and I can't have him sitting around doing nothing."

"And you don't care if my fix rate goes to hell?" Carp shot back.

Plato replied—"Your fix rate's going to be fine. You've already got the best of the bunch, which is another reason to give him to you. Sam tells me the streets of Philadelphia are violent. Bungie survived them, so he must be able to learn *something*."

Carp snorted. "You'll forgive me if I'm not optimistic."

"Hey, bring it on, smart mouth." Bungie jumped into the discussion. "Anything you can do, *I* can do."

"Yeah, that'll be the day," Carp said with a sniff.

Plato waved a hand and said something cheerful-sounding. "Then it's settled. Good. See you all back for dinner." With a nod at Nicole, he turned and strode away.

Carp watched him go. Then, abruptly, he spun back to face the others. "What are you looking at?" he snarled. "Back to work. Fishface, get the sealer over here."

Hastily, the other men resumed their work. Kahkitah twittered and headed to the big machine he'd brought from the supply closet and got a grip on the dragging loop. "Let me know when you're ready," the translation of his birdsong came.

Bungie's hand closed around Nicole's arm. "You okay?" he asked quietly into her ear.

Nicole winced at his touch. But Kahkitah was watching, and she didn't want him thinking Bungie was hurting her. "I'm fine," she said. "Where did Plato take you?"

"Nowhere special," he said. "Back to the hospital rooms. We went by a place he called the rec center, too. Kind of like the game room at Paco's, but no pool table or pinball. You been here all day?"

"Mostly," Nicole said. "You and Sam looked like you were planning something. Are you?"

"Who, me?" Bungie asked innocently. "I'm not planning anything." He snorted softly. "At least, not till I figure out where Plato stashed my gun."

"Yeah." Nicole braced herself. She really didn't want to ask this. "Back before we came here, you said that you'd killed some-one. Were you—I mean—?"

"Remember Jerry?" Bungie asked, his voice eerily casual. "Said I cheated him on that liquor store thing?"

A shiver ran up Nicole's back. She'd heard about that deal. Bungie *had* cheated him. "Yes."

Bungie shrugged. "He's not saying it anymore. Not saying any-thing else, either."

Nicole felt her throat tighten. Now she remembered where she'd seen that gun before. "That was Jerry's gun, wasn't it?"

"Hey, I *had* to take it away from him." Bungie patted his injured side gently. "His next shot might have hit something important."

"Oh."

Bungie chuckled, a dark, unpleasant sound. "Oh, don't sound so worried. I'm not gonna do anything till I'm good and ready. And like I said, I need my gun back."

There was a sudden grinding sound. With an effort, Nicole tore her attention away from Bungie and looked back at the work site. One of the men—a Canadian named Bennett—was using Kahkitah's machine to spray a thin, shiny mist over the new wires the team had installed. As she watched, the liquid dried into more of the tough plastic coating. Bennett played the nozzle back and forth until he'd covered the whole area, then shut off the machine. "Done, and done," he announced.

Carp stepped over to the wall and gave the work a quick but careful look. "Okay," he said, gesturing. "Everyone back. Fish-face? You're on."

Kahkitah stepped to the edge of the raised wall and braced his big hands against it as Bennett and one of the other men pulled the sealant machine back out of the way. Two of the other men went to the ends of the panel and released the locks, and Kahkitah lowered the section of wall carefully back into place.

"And that's dinner," Carp announced with tired-sounding satisfaction. "Good work, everyone. Let's stow the gear and go eat."

Four

Over the next month, in fits and starts, Nicole settled into her new life.

At first she missed alcohol. Missed it terribly. She ached for the taste and for the familiar and welcome fog it brought. The days seemed to stretch out, with evening and nighttime hours she'd almost forgotten even existed suddenly returning to full awareness. Her moods swung wildly, from relief to anger to excitement to long and bitter crying in the privacy of her room.

But gradually, the aches faded and the cravings subsided. There were still times when she missed what had once been her most loyal companion. But slowly those regrets became less and less frequent.

The rest of the adjustment wasn't nearly so hard. By the end of the first week she'd memorized all her co-workers' names, faces, and quirks, plus the faces and quirks of people like Allyce, whom she saw only occasionally in the living or work areas. Most of them were people she could probably get along with, or at least could fake getting along with, with only a couple on her list of people to avoid as much as possible.

One of the latter group was Dr. McNair, or *Sam,* as Plato insisted everyone call him. His anger at being snatched from his hospital's parking lot cooled a bit after the first few days, but it never went any cooler than a dark, brooding resentment. Much of his anger was focused on Plato, which Nicole thought was unfair since Plato had already said he wasn't the one actually running the *Fyrantha*.

Even more unfair was the fact that a lot of Sam's remaining animosity seemed to be directed toward her, which was completely ridiculous. Nicole hadn't asked for this any more than he had. But straight thinking didn't seem to be Sam's strong point, at least not in this particular matter.

Fortunately, Plato assigned him to the medical center with Allyce and another doctor named Lena, and unless someone got hurt out on a job all three doctors seemed to stick close to that one area. As long as Nicole stayed healthy, she should be able to avoid Sam until he finally calmed down. If he ever did.

By the end of the second week she'd become fully accustomed to her translator. In fact, she became so used to it that her brain stopped noticing those first couple of seconds of foreign speech and only picked up conscious focus again when the English translation kicked in.

Adjusting to the physical device itself proved somewhat trickier. For several of those first days her scalp itched furiously as the hair started growing back, and incautious scratching of the area was a good way to catch her fingernails on the translator's metal lines and circles. Several times an itch turned into a jolt of pain as her nails dug into the still-tender skin around the translator, and more than once she managed to hit one of the handful of slightly jagged edges hard enough to draw a few drops of blood.

By the end of the third week she finally had the *Fyrantha's* layout and room-numbering scheme figured out. There were still times when she got turned around, especially when their repair work took them to a more distant part of the ship. But even then, she could usually figure out from the nearby room markings how to find her way back to the group of rooms, facilities, and connecting hallways that everyone simply called the hive.

Her own room in that complex was a strange mixture of the simple and the luxurious. The furniture was simple and compact, with the same basic layout as the cheap motel rooms her family had stayed in on the rare occasions when her grandmother had the money to take them someplace out of town overnight. But it was her own space—her own, private space, with a lock on the door and everything—which was something she'd never had before. She had a bed, a comfortable padded chair, a couple of lights, her own private bathroom, and even a nice-sized TV built into one of the walls.

Granted, there was nothing to watch but what seemed to be nature documentaries set on exotic alien worlds, with commentaries that her translator annoyingly wouldn't translate. But it was still something to do in her free time when she didn't feel like socializing.

And by the end of the fourth week, she'd finally mastered her job as Sibyl.

That was the hardest part of all, and it was as hard on the rest of the team as it was on her. There was a huge amount of technical language she had to learn, as well as methods and equipment descriptions that she had to correctly relay to Carp and the other workers. Not always successfully, either, and there were several times when the whole bunch of them wasted hours on something that turned out to be a misunderstanding on Nicole's part.

The fact that Carp wasn't a patient man didn't make it any easier. Nor was he reticent about expressing his thoughts and frustrations, usually in a loud, angry voice, and always right in front of everyone else. More than once during those first weeks Nicole had to fight to keep back tears as he told her in a clipped, barely civil tone exactly what he thought of her as a Sibyl, as a woman, and as a human being. Usually in that order.

Jeff sometimes tried to intervene, and Kahkitah was invariably distressed at her humiliation. But Carp didn't seem to care. Still, for all his loud temper, his outbursts and anger never lasted very long, and within a few minutes he would be back to normal. Occasionally, he even went so far as to compliment Nicole when she had some insight or timidly made a suggestion that proved worthwhile.

And then there was the *Fyrantha* itself, which seemed determined to keep her under ever-increasing pressure. Before Nicole was fully comfortable with one level of her new job the damn ship invariably upped the ante. First it was new technical terms for her to memorize, then it was increasingly complicated repair instructions that she was supposed to repeat word for word to her crew, and *then* it was not one but *two* sets of entirely different instructions for the two different squads of the crew.

And when Nicole finally struggled her way to some kind of proficiency at that, the instructions started coming in two different chunks, which then required her to move between the two squads, trying to keep the messages clear in her mind and hoping she didn't get them mixed up. That happened once, and Carp made like he would never let her hear the end of it.

There were times—lots of them—when Nicole seriously considered giving up and telling Plato she was done. But each time she kept going. Part of it was because she was afraid to find out what Plato would do if she refused to work, the other part because there was no way in hell that she was going to let Carp's opinion of her turn out to be right.

Back home, Trake had always told her she would never be more than the group's lookout or distraction. Even when she'd tried to make something better of herself, like her attempts to learn how to pick pockets, he and the others had treated her efforts with contempt or amusement.

True, all she was doing here on the *Fyrantha* was inhaling some dust and repeating what the voices in her head said. But she was at least doing that accurately, which was still apparently more than Carp had expected. Maybe it was more than Nicole had expected, too.

And slowly, so slowly that she didn't even notice it happening, she began to realize that her kidnapping had possibly been the best thing that ever happened to her.

True, in many ways the *Fyrantha* was a prison. But so was her life before that Wisp swooped in and grabbed her. Here, at least, she had her own room, plenty to eat, and no muggers, killers, cops, or crazy street people lurking around every corner. None of Trake's friends or enemies were here, which meant she never had to keep one eye over her shoulder making sure no one robbed her, groped her, or put a knife in her back.

There was no whiskey, of course, and there were times when she lay awake in her darkened room, sweating profusely and unable to sleep, desperately wanting a drink. But by the end of the first month even that was starting to fade.

In fact, there was really only one thing that kept her from persuading herself that the *Fyrantha* was the idyllic home she'd never had.

That one thing was Bungie.

He was always there—at her work, during her meals, even at the times when she was trying to socialize and figure out her co-workers' hooks. He was seldom helpful at any of those times, either. During working hours he mostly loafed, or else pleaded helplessness due to his mostly healed injury, or simply disappeared to wander the area around the work site.

Sometimes he even carried out small bits of sabotage when

no one was looking. Nicole caught on to those events only when the next whiff from her inhaler suddenly showed a completely new problem that hadn't existed before.

Twice it earned her a scolding rant from Carp about making sure she'd given the team the complete list of repair information before they started work. Both times Nicole had to just stand there and take it.

Bungie had stood silently off to the side and smirked.

She'd thought about turning him in. She'd thought about it a lot. But something always held her back, always made her take the blame for whatever he'd done this time.

Part of it was fear. She'd never actually seen him hurt a woman, but there were a lot of stories about his behavior, and she didn't doubt a single one of them. And there were way too many places aboard where Bungie could catch her away from the others.

Part of it was distrust. It would be her word against his, and no one had *ever* taken her word over someone else's. Once she blamed him for something and was brushed aside, no one would bother listening to anything she might call him on in the future.

But part of it—maybe even the biggest part—was that she really didn't want Plato to lock him up or send him away. Bungie was the one connection to her past life that she still had, and even in her new safety and comfort she sometimes felt a perverse longing for the Philadelphia streets.

Bungie seemed to realize that, too. Even while he was going out of his way to antagonize everyone on the ship, from Plato to Sam to the members of the other work teams when they ran into them in the corridors or dining room, he was careful not to push Nicole herself too far. He was also careful to back off his other interactions before they got to the point of blows or even loud arguments, which Plato had warned him against that first day.

Nicole's first theory was that this was part of some plan he and

Sam had come up with, that Bungie was maybe acting as a distraction while Sam worked behind the scenes on a scheme to get them home. But Bungie was just as unpleasant to Sam as he was to everyone else. Her second theory was that he was hoping to make such a nuisance of himself that Plato would eventually get exasperated enough to send him home. True, he'd already said he couldn't do that, but Bungie probably figured he'd been lying.

It wasn't until that first month was past that Nicole finally figured it out.

Bungie simply hated life here.

In fact, the more Nicole thought about it, the more she realized that the things she found most pleasant about the *Fyrantha* were probably the very things Bungie most despised. There were no street toughs he could intimidate, threaten, or scam. There was nothing to steal, and even if there had been there would have been nowhere to fence it. There were no drugs, no alcohol, no mood-altering substances, no excuses to kick up trouble. There were no games except the ones the workers had made for themselves, no movies except the nature shows on the room TVs, and no food except the rotating menu delivered to them in the dining room.

Worst of all, there was no money. Money was how people like Bungie kept score on how their lives were going. When he had it, he was big and powerful and king of the world. When he didn't, he was small and angry, ready to cheat and lie and stab people in the back to get that feeling of power again.

She hoped he would eventually come around. This was his new life, and if Plato was right it was his new life forever. The sooner he accepted that things would never change, the better it would be for everyone.

It was at the end of the fifth week that everything suddenly changed.

". . . and then rewire the secondary core coil," Nicole repeated, listening hard to the voices echoing through her mind. Sometimes there was a last-minute addition, like the *Fyrantha* had just remembered something. Or, the way Jeff had once explained it to her, like the ship had just run a fresh diagnostic and found a minor problem the first sweep had missed.

But this time, there was nothing. "That's it," she confirmed.

"Okay," Carp said, tapping the end of his stylus absently against his cheek as he looked through the notes he'd made on his notepad. "Looks like a pretty even breakdown between mech and tech. Levi?"

"Agreed," Levi said, nodding. "I'll take Jeff, Duncan, and Bennett and get started on the transfer node."

"Fine," Carp said. "The rest of us will tackle the coolant pump assembly." He glanced around, paused for a longer look. "Well, well—imagine my surprise."

Nicole looked around, wincing already at what she assumed was the problem.

She was right. While she'd been focusing on the *Fyrantha's* instructions, and Carp and the others had been busy taking notes, Bungie had once again slipped away.

She looked back at Carp, bracing herself. Lately, he'd gotten into the habit of blaming her when this happened.

To her relief, this time he didn't bother. "Whatever," he said. "Let's see. More of us will be here at the pump than the transfer node, so this is where we'll meet for lunch."

"Sounds good," Levi said. "Let's get to it."

The workers sorted out their equipment boxes, and Levi led his crew off down the corridor toward the broken module Nicole had identified. "Kahkitah?" Carp called, beckoning to the big Ghorf. "Get this open, will you?"

Kahkitah lumbered obediently over to the wall panel, and Nicole braced herself. The question, she knew, had to be asked. "Do you want me to go look for Bungie?" she asked Carp.

"Some reason why you want him back?" Carp countered.

Nicole hesitated. There was actually a very good reason to make sure Bungie stayed where they could see him: the fact that he was likely to get into trouble anywhere else. Only a few days ago he'd figured out how to get into one of the atmosphere-filtering rooms, and she'd caught him throwing switches and changing settings apparently just for the hell of it.

A quick whiff from her inhaler had enabled her to reset everything and relock the door after getting him outside. As far as she knew, neither Carp nor any of the others had any clue as to what had happened. But it had been a close call.

She should definitely have called Carp in on that one, she knew. But again, the combination of fear and nostalgia had kept her quiet. Her threat to turn Bungie in had gotten him out of the filter room and kept him mostly docile for a while after that. Maybe she could keep him under control, especially if he was getting resigned to his new life, and that would be the end of it.

Besides, as long as she had her inhaler she should be able to fix anything he messed up. "I was just worried that he might get lost," she said instead.

Carp's gaze flicked past her down the hallway, his lips tightening. Nicole's tentative efforts to get close to him over the past couple of weeks had gone nowhere, stifled by a combination of Carp's impatient and grating personality, Bungie's continual hovering presence, and Nicole's own diminished urgency for finding a way off the ship. Still, she'd learned enough about his expressions and body language to see that he was currently torn between not wanting Bungie around any more than absolutely necessary while also knowing that he was accountable for the man's actions and safety.

Responsibility won. "Sure, go ahead," he said reluctantly. He eyed the pump machinery behind the wall—"And take Kahkitah with you," he added. "Doesn't look like we'll need him for a while."

He snorted. "If he has to bend Bungie's head a little to get him back here, don't sweat it."

"I understand," Nicole said. "Come on, Kahkitah."

"Where are we going?" the Ghorf asked as they set off down the hallway.

"We're looking for Bungie," she told him, peering down a cross-corridor as they passed. The *Fyrantha* was a big ship, and unless he'd left a trail of bread crumbs there was no practical way to know which direction he might have gone.

Unless he'd already started messing around and broken something. If he had, another jolt from her inhaler might give her a clue to his location. She pulled her inhaler from her vest pocket—

She stopped as Kahkitah put a large hand on her arm. "There's no need," he said. "The effects of the first should still be present. If the *Fyrantha* is speaking, you'll hear it."

"It can't hurt to be sure," Nicole said, trying to disengage her arm from his hand.

To her annoyed surprise, he merely tightened his grip. "The effects will still be present," he insisted.

"Yes, thank you," Nicole said, her annoyance moving rapidly toward anger. She was the Sibyl here, not him. If she wanted an extra puff of magic powder, that was her call. "I think I can tell when—"

The lefnizo-*four Door Three has a short circuit,* the voice came in her head. *The conducting metal must be removed from the contacts and the system reset with the keylock control.*

"Fine," she said, finally shaking off Kahkitah's hand and dropping the inhaler back into her pocket. "It's *lefnizo*-four. Come on."

Nicole hadn't been to the *lefnizo* section of the ship yet, but the numbering pattern she'd memorized should put it just past the *marsarvi* section, where the team was currently working. The *lefnizo*-four room should be close in toward the ship's portside hull, which was a flat, featureless wall running at the left-hand side of all the rest of the *Fyrantha's* rooms and other hallways. She took a moment to orient herself, then picked one of the hallways that should take her in the right direction and started walking.

The door she was looking for turned out to be closer than she'd expected, though somewhat trickier to find. That first hallway dead-ended in a group of rooms similar to those where Nicole and the others lived back in the *postinda* section, and she and Kahkitah had to find another hallway that circled around them. Eventually, they ended up in the extra-long hallway that ran right along the portside hull.

They found Bungie crouched beside an unusually large door set into a tall, curved wall, digging at the lock mechanism with a screwdriver. "What are you doing?" Nicole demanded as she and Kahkitah came up.

"What's it *look* like I'm doing?" he growled back. "Give me a hand here—I want to get this open."

"Come on, Bungie, you need to stop all this," Nicole said, fighting to keep her voice steady. Trake could get results by yelling at Bungie; Nicole couldn't. "Sooner or later you're going to wreck something we can't fix, and Plato will have to do something to punish you."

"Plato can stuff it," Bungie said, peering past the screwdriver tip into the mechanism. "You think I'm quitting now, you're crazy. Don't you see what we've got here?"

Nicole took another look at the door. It was much bigger than most of the others she'd seen aboard the *Fyrantha*, a good five feet wide and reaching nearly to the top of the eight-foot-high ceiling. Its identification plate was also larger, maybe four or five times bigger than any of the other room IDs. Aside from that there wasn't anything remarkable about it. "It's a door," she said. "So?"

"So this." Bungie tapped the big number plate. "You see any other doors or rooms around here that are labeled by just *one* letter and *one* number?"

"That's indeed unusual," Kahkitah agreed, his bird whistles sounding thoughtful. "What do you think it means?"

"It means there's something in here they don't want us to see," Bungie said, turning back to his work. "Good enough reason for us to get inside. Come on, Nicole—the damn ship talks to you. Figure out how to get this open."

"What if it's something dangerous?" Nicole countered. "What if it's an outside door or a fuel tank?"

Bungie snorted. "What, a gas tank with a big door in it? Don't be stupid."

"It could still open up to the outside," Nicole said, feeling a tightness in her stomach. She'd seen Bungie in this mood before, and he wasn't going to let go until he got a look behind that door.

Unless she let him wreck it. That was what the *Fyrantha* had said, wasn't it? That poking around with his screwdriver had caused a short circuit?

Only that didn't necessarily mean the door was broken so that it wouldn't open. It could mean that he'd broken the lock so that it wouldn't stay shut.

Either way, she had to get him out of here. "Come on, we have to get back," she said. "Carp's already mad that you sneaked off again. If we head back now—"

"Whoa!" Bungie said sharply, his eyes on something behind Nicole.

She spun around, expecting to see Carp or even Plato. But it was just a Wisp, moving along the long corridor toward them.

Nicole took a deep breath, feeling herself wilt as the sudden tension flowed out of her. "It's just a Wisp," she said, eyeing the tall silvery being closely. They didn't see a lot of Wisps around the living and work areas, but she occasionally caught sight of one moving silently along the corridors on some unknown mission. For a while she'd wondered if their presence meant that someone else had just arrived, but since no one new had joined their little group she decided that wasn't right.

"Yeah, just one of the little bastards who kidnapped us," Bungie bit out, still glaring at the Wisp as it glided delicately past them, heading forward along the long hallway.

"This one isn't one of the ones who did that," Nicole said.

"How the hell do you know *that*?"

Nicole opened her mouth . . . closed it again. Now that he mentioned it, she had no idea. "I don't know," she admitted. "I just do."

For a long moment he stared at her. Then, with a grunt, he turned back to the lock. "Whatever."

"No, wait, please," Nicole said, wincing as he jabbed the screwdriver back into the lock. If she didn't stop him, he was going to break something for sure. "Let me try."

"Why?" he asked suspiciously. "So you can make sure it stays locked? 'Cause if you do, you and I are going to have problems."

Kahkitah stirred. "You mustn't threaten her," he said, sounding embarrassed at having to talk to someone else that way. "Plato says we're to be polite and civil to each other."

"Plato can stuff that, too," Bungie said. He eyed Nicole another second, then stood up and slapped the screwdriver into her palm. "Just make sure you don't wreck it." He glanced around, frowning. "Where'd it go?"

"Where'd what go?" Nicole asked.

"The damned butterfly," Bungie said. "It was here a second ago."

Nicole peered down the hallway. The Wisp had disappeared, all right. "Probably went into some room down there."

"I don't think so," Bungie said darkly. "There aren't any."

"There are rooms and compartments everywhere," Kahkitah reminded him, craning his neck to look that direction.

"Not over there," Bungie told him. "You've got the long hallway with no doors at all, and you've got this thing"—he thumped his hand on the big door in front of them—"and nothing else on this side until the hallway dead-ends about fifty yards up."

Nicole shaded her eyes, frowning harder. From what she'd seen back in the *sevko* and *postinda* sectors, she'd assumed the portside hull hallway ran the entire length of the ship. Had they really made it all the way to the *Fyrantha's* front end?

"Never mind," Bungie said, giving Nicole a not-so-gentle nudge toward the door. "Get busy."

Nicole felt her stomach tighten as she knelt down and peered into the lock mechanism where Bungie had been poking. If he'd managed to bend some piece of metal around until it had created a permanent short circuit, she would have to take the whole thing apart in order to fix it. That would require another whiff from her inhaler to get repair instructions from the ship, along with probably a bunch of tools she didn't have. And probably wouldn't know how to use even if she had them.

But she couldn't see anything obvious. With the tip of the screwdriver, she pried open the small keylock control panel and studied the pad. She'd helped Jeff and Levi do half a dozen system resets during her time aboard, and this pad looked like all the others they'd used. She'd try the standard code first, she decided, and if that didn't work she would use her inhaler and hopefully get the default lock code from the ship. She punched in the code, then touched the two enter/apply keys.

To her surprise, the door popped open. Apparently, this door's default wasn't to be locked, but to be open.

If she'd immediately thrown herself against the door, she might have been able to push it closed and maybe reset the lock. But in the first moment of surprise, that thought never occurred to her. Before she could do more than goggle at the open door, Bungie grabbed the edge and started pulling. "Out of the way," he ordered.

There was nothing for Nicole to do but scramble to her feet and hastily back up. The door was heavy, and even with Bungie pulling with his full weight it came only slowly open. Nicole circled around behind him, her heart thudding with both anticipation and fear as she peered through the opening.

She'd been right. The door did indeed open to the outside.

But it wasn't the outside Plato had warned was out there, an outside of space and stars and stuff. Instead, beyond the door was a peaceful country landscape, with trees and bushes and low hills, with a cheery greenish-blue sky and a sweet-smelling breeze rustling through the leaves and rippling through the tall grass.

Behind her, Bungie swore. "That lousy, stinking liar," he rumbled, his breath hot on the back of her neck. "Like hell we're wherever the hell he said we were. We never even left the damn ground."

Nicole frowned at the landscape. It certainly looked like Plato had lied to them.

But there was something odd about the scene, something that sent a warning shiver through her. "Bungie—"

She broke off as he shoved past her, banging her shoulder against the edge of the door as he did so. "What are you—?"

"Come on," he said, grabbing her wrist and pulling her through the doorway.

"Where are we going?" she asked, struggling to keep her balance as she rubbed her shoulder with her free hand.

"Where do you think?" he retorted, leading her around a cluster of half a dozen low bushes. "We're getting the hell out of here and going home."

Nicole focused on the bushes as they passed. The plants were about chest height, shaped like old Christmas lights, with wide bases just off the grass that swelled outward and then tapered up to their tips. They had thin branches, blue-green leaves, and dark purple berries.

They didn't look like any plants she'd ever seen in the parks in Philadelphia. Or anywhere else her grandmother had ever taken her.

"Wait!" Kahkitah called from behind them, his whistling voice on the edge of panic. "Come back! You can't go in there—it's not allowed. Please—come back!"

"Why?" Nicole called over her shoulder, struggling to free herself from Bungie's grip. "What's out here?"

"It is not *out*!" Kahkitah called. "It is not allowed!"

"So stay out!" Bungie shouted back.

"Maybe we should go back," Nicole suggested, still trying without success to break free as he dragged her along. "Or I could go back, and you could keep going?"

Bungie didn't answer. He led the way through a stand of tall, thick grass, and Nicole saw that he was steering them across the more or less level ground that lay right in front of them to the right. Seventy or eighty yards ahead was a low structure made of stone that she hadn't spotted before. The building wasn't much bigger than one of the play structures at the park she'd gone to when she was little, but it looked a lot sturdier than any of those had been. It was half-hidden by the grass and bushes, and there were some trees arching over its roof that probably gave it some welcome shade when the sun was in the sky. More trees stretched out behind it, reaching into the sky as far back as she could see. There were lots of cutout windows in the structure's sides, probably for ventilation.

She could also see several shadowy figures moving around behind those open windows. Children at play, maybe?

But this didn't look like any kind of city park she'd ever seen. Certainly not a Philadelphia park. There was no skyline, for one thing. Even with trees this tall, there should be at least a few buildings visible against the greenish-blue sky.

She stopped short, her eyes widening. The *greenish-blue* sky?

An instant later she was yanked off her feet as Bungie kept moving. Or rather, as he tried to keep moving. With his hand still clutching Nicole's wrist, her unexpected stop pulled him off balance, wrenching her arm and yanking them both down in the grass. "You *stupid*—" he snarled.

And broke off as a sudden flash of green light lit up the ground to their left. Reflexively, Nicole ducked, twisting her head around to look.

Where there had been only bushes and tall grass a minute ago, a dozen creatures had suddenly appeared.

They were definitely not children at play. They were shorter than Nicole, the tallest maybe three and a half feet tall, with light brown fur on their arms and legs. They wore dark brown leather-looking smocks draped over their chests and upper legs and sandal-like shoes tied around their ankles and feet. Their long necks and smallish heads were also furry, with short, upright ears, long noses, and black eyes. They were like nothing she'd ever seen before, but at the same time there was something about them that popped the thought of upright weasels into her mind.

And each of them was carrying a slender, four-foot-long black tube.

Her mind had barely registered all that when the whole group dashed out of their partial concealment behind trees and bushes and charged across the plain, their black tubes spitting out flashes of green fire.

Not like the laser blasts or flamethrower bursts she'd seen on TV or in movies. These were like nothing else she'd ever seen.

Like nothing on Earth.

Nicole screamed, a cry of horror and fear and hopelessness that came boiling out of her mouth without any conscious thought as the air lit up around her. She threw herself onto her face in the grass, her body tingling with the horrible anticipation of the shot that would burn away skin and muscle and bone and kill her.

She was going to die. Here, pressed into the weeds of a world whose name she didn't even know, a group of alien weasels she had no quarrel with were going to blast green fire into her back, and she was going to die. From behind her came the thudding swish of furry legs as the weasels charged toward her through the grass. She tensed and waited for the end—

A second later, with green bolts still flashing over her head, the running feet swept past without even pausing and continued on across the field.

It was another couple of seconds before it penetrated Nicole's suffocating swirl of fear that she was still alive. It took a couple more before she could gather enough nerve to open her eyes and cautiously raise her head.

Her ears hadn't lied to her. The weasels had indeed run past the two humans sprawled on the ground. They were still on the move, in fact, dodging in and out of each other's paths like they were performing some kind of crazy group dance.

She frowned. Was this some sort of game? *Were* they really just some alien children at play?

And then, as the weasels continued to weave their pattern, a new spray of green shots slashed outward from the stone building she and Bungie had seen earlier. Three of the weasels jerked as some of the bolts sliced across them, and Nicole half heard, half felt, a tingling high-pitched scream echo across the ground. The scream was cut off, and the three weasels toppled to the ground. As they did so, the rest of the weasels threw themselves forward and to the sides, some into tall clumps of grass, others seemingly trying to get behind trees or bushes.

But for that first paralyzed second, Nicole hardly noticed them. Her eyes were locked on the three crumpled weasels, her brain once again twisting in the hellish reality of this place. She'd seen dead bodies before, on the Philadelphia streets, and she knew the utter stillness that no one still alive and breathing could ever quite achieve.

All three of the fallen weasels were dead.

They weren't children. And this was no game.

Another green flash, a closer one, slashed across the ground at the right-hand edge of Nicole's vision. Steeling herself, afraid to move but even more afraid that something might be sneaking up on her unawares, she eased her head and eyes in that direction.

It was one of the weasels, lying flat on the ground behind the group of bushes she and Bungie had passed on their way in. He was peering along the barrel of his gun, and as she watched he fired another green bolt through the bush's lower branches in the direction of the stone building.

And then, to her bewilderment, he tucked his gun close in to his chest and rolled onto his back and then onto his stomach, ending up behind a different section of the bushes.

She frowned. What in the *world*?

An instant later, she got her answer. A green bolt from the direction of the stone building sizzled through the spot where the weasel had just been lying, blasting through the branches and sending burned and blackened leaves wreathed in yellow fire fluttering to the ground.

She nodded to herself, the sudden rush of excitement as she figured it out almost making her forget the danger she was in. "He was changing position so the people in the building would shoot back at the wrong place," she murmured.

There was no answer. "Bungie?" she asked, her fear suddenly flooding back in. Had he been shot? Bracing herself for the worst, wincing as the weasel behind the bushes fired again, she looked at the place where Bungie had been lying.

Bungie wasn't there anymore.

Clenching her teeth, she eased up onto her elbows and started crawling slowly forward, the way she'd seen soldiers do on TV. Directly ahead was a particularly thick clump of grass, surrounded by a circle of lower blades that shouldn't wave as much as she passed through it. If she could get to the taller grass and look around it, she would have a better view of the stone building.

With the green bolts still lancing back and forth, and with an occasional high-pitched scream from dying weasels stabbing in her ears, the crawl to the tall grass seemed to take forever. But finally she was there. Gathering her courage, hoping desperately that she hadn't come all this way just to get her head blown off, she eased her eyes around the side of the grass.

There, to her relief, was Bungie. He was still alive, seemingly still even uninjured, crawling stealthily toward the blazing battle.

A second later the utter irrationality of that struck her. He was crawling *toward* the battle?

He'd gone insane. That was the only explanation. Sometime in the past minute, the strain of being attacked by alien weasels had pushed him over the edge.

Maybe he even thought he was one of them. There was some sort of thing like that, she remembered hearing once, where people who had been kidnapped changed sides and joined them or something. "Bungie!" she hissed toward him, trying to pitch her voice so that only he would hear her. "Bungie, come back. *Bungie!*"

"Quiet," he snarled back, pausing his crawl long enough to turn around and glare at her. "You want to get me killed?"

Nicole blinked in confusion as he resumed his crawling advance. This made no sense. If he didn't want to get killed . . .

And then, like a kick in the gut, she got it.

Bungie hadn't gone crazy, and he wasn't trying to join the battle. He was trying to get to the three weasels who'd been killed in that first attack.

He was going for a gun.

Nicole cursed under her breath. Bungie still groused twice a week about how he still didn't have a clue about where Plato had stashed the gun he'd brought with him. With three exotic weapons just lying there being ignored, of course he would go after them.

"You," an unfamiliar voice said quietly from behind her. "Blue-clad."

Frowning, Nicole turned her head.

The weasel she'd seen shooting and rolling around earlier had moved to the very edge of the line of bushes, to a spot where he could see Nicole but couldn't be seen by the people in the stone building. He was staring at her, his eyes unblinking.

And he seemed to be talking to her. "Wha-what do you want?" she stammered.

The weasel gave out a series of quiet squeaks, barely audible over the muffled noise of the battle. "The other," the translator built into Nicole's head murmured. "Does he hope to steal the weapons of our lost companions?"

A quick lie came reflexively to Nicole's lips. But it would be a waste of breath. A few more seconds and it would be obvious what Bungie was up to. "He isn't going to shoot at you or your friends," she assured him, wondering belatedly if he could even understand her. Had whoever was running the *Fyrantha* given these creatures translators, too?

Apparently so. "Then why does he want them?" the weasel asked.

How was she supposed to answer that one? "There are some . . . disputes . . . between us," she said, picking her words carefully. For all she knew, this could be some scheme Plato had set up to get Bungie to do something wrong. They did elaborate cons like this all the time on TV. "He just wants the gun to make sure people will listen to what he has to say."

The weasel's ears twitched and he squeaked again. "If he touches one of the weapons, I will kill him."

"You'll *kill* him?" Nicole echoed, wondering if she'd actually heard that right. "But why? I said he wasn't going to hurt your friends."

"He will not take our weapon," the weasel said. "I will not say more."

"But I can't stop him," Nicole pleaded. "He won't listen to me."

"Then he will die," the weasel said. "If you wish to preserve his life, you must find a way to keep him from the weapons."

Nicole turned back. Bungie was nearly to the crumpled bodies. Somehow, she had to crawl through the storm of green fire, get to him, and persuade, or force, him to stop.

Or she could stay where she was, protect herself as best she could from the battle, and call the weasel's bluff.

Or watch Bungie die.

Maybe if he hadn't been so rotten to her back in Philadelphia she would have been more willing to take the risk. Or if he hadn't been so nasty to everyone here. Besides, this mess was all his fault. He'd fiddled with the door, he'd dragged her into the middle of this, and he'd decided to steal a gun. Whatever happened now was his fault.

He was nearly to the bodies and weapons now. Nicole watched as he crawled those last few feet, her chest tight, wondering if the weasel behind her would have a clear shot or if her own head or shoulder might be in his way. Maybe she should move a little farther to her left, where she'd be safer. Easing up onto her elbows, she started sidling across the grass—

And dropped flat onto her face again as something huge suddenly blew past her from behind. Out of the corner of her eye she caught a glimpse of Kahkitah's back as the Ghorf disappeared from view. There was a yelp and a strangled curse from that direction, followed by a loud rustle of something plowing headlong through the grass. Even as Nicole tried to figure out the odd sound, Kahkitah reappeared, dragging a cursing Bungie behind him by one leg. As they passed, Kahkitah flicked his free hand toward Nicole. "Come now," he ordered. "Come quickly."

Nicole looked over her other shoulder at the weasel. He was watching her closely but didn't seem inclined to interfere. Swallowing hard, she got gingerly to her feet and headed off after Kahkitah, keeping hunched over and as low to the ground as she could. Once again, her back tingled with the expectation of a burning blast of green fire.

Once again, nothing happened. A dozen agonized seconds later, with Bungie still swearing, they escaped back through the door.

Five

Plato, to no one's surprise, was furious.

"I should have you whipped," he bit out as he paced back and forth across the treatment room. There wasn't much space for pacing, really, not with Nicole, Bungie, Sam, and Allyce all in there with him. But Plato didn't seem concerned about the possibility of running one of them down. "Or even thrown out an airlock. What in the name of *hell* did you think you were doing?"

"Yeah, go ahead—throw us outside," Bungie snarled back. "Just give me my gun first and watch what happens." He jabbed a hand behind him in the direction of the ship's front. "Squirrel brains splattered all over the place. That's what happens."

"Hold still," Sam ordered, grabbing for Bungie's gesturing hand.

"And *you* can just get the hell away from me," Bungie snapped, yanking the hand out of his reach. "I don't need you pawing at me like some—"

"He said *hold still!*" Plato thundered.

For a couple of heartbeats he and Bungie glared at each other. Then, reluctantly, Bungie let Sam pull his arm back down onto the treatment table. "Fine," he muttered. "Whatever."

"You're a fool, Bungie," Plato said contemptuously. "A stupid fool. Those cuts could be infected, or laced with poison. It would serve you right if I let you refuse treatment."

Nicole looked down at her own wrists and forearms, cringing a little at the crisscross of scratches she hadn't even noticed she was picking up as she crawled through the grass.

Allyce had assured her that the clear liquid she was painting over the scratches would protect her from dangerous infections. But given that Allyce also admitted she didn't have any direct experience with the plants, Nicole couldn't help but wonder if the doctor even knew what she was talking about.

Still, right now, Plato's anger seemed more dangerous than any germs she might have picked up. The big man paused at one end of his path long enough to send a glare at Nicole, then resumed his pacing. "And as for being outside, you weren't," he added to Bungie. "Outside is the emptiness of space, where vacuum and cold would have a race to see which one killed you first."

Bungie snorted. "Yeah, right—"

"Where *you* were is what the Shipmasters call the testing arena," Plato continued. "It's off-limits to those of us whose job it is to maintain the *Fyrantha*." He stopped abruptly and jabbed a finger at Bungie. "And you will *not* go in there again."

He swung the finger around to point at Nicole. "Neither will you. Is that clear?"

"Hey, whatever you say," Bungie said sarcastically. "How come you never mentioned this testing arena? While you're at it, what else about this damn place haven't you told us?"

"I've told you everything you need to know," Plato said, his tone icy. "The *Fyrantha* tells Nicole what needs fixing. You and the rest of your crew fix it. You go where she tells you to go; you stay out of places I tell you to stay out of. That's how we all get fed and stay warm and keep on living. Anything about that changes, I'll let you know."

"Right," Bungie said. "Because you're the boss. You get to make decisions like that."

"Exactly," Plato said. "And to give you some extra time to let that sink in, you're both confined here until further notice. Kahkitah?"

Bungie's eyes widened. "*What?* Why, you stinking bastard son of a—"

Kahkitah lumbered in from the hallway. "Yes, Plato?"

"Nicole and Bungie will be staying here until I say otherwise," Plato told the Ghorf. "You'll make sure they don't leave."

Kahkitah looked at Bungie, then Nicole. "They're staying *here?*"

"Right here, right in this room," Plato confirmed, pointing straight downward in emphasis. "I'll have lunch and dinner sent in for all of you. If they're lucky, I'll let them go sleep in their own beds tonight. *If* they're lucky." With a final glare at Bungie, he strode past Kahkitah and disappeared down the hallway.

The door slid shut behind him. "Don't worry, it's not a punishment," Allyce assured Nicole as she started wrapping a thin gauze around Nicole's scratched forearms. "He just wants you under observation in case other symptoms start to present."

Bungie sniffed. "Sure he does."

"No, really," Allyce insisted. "You can be diagnosed and treated quicker if you're already here. "

"It's for your own good," Sam added.

"Sure," Bungie said. "Whatever."

For another minute the two doctors worked in silence. Then Sam peered over his shoulder at Nicole. "So what was it like in there?" he asked.

"*Out* there," Bungie corrected tartly. "Plato can flap his mouth all he wants, but we were *outside*. Nicole saw it. So did Fishface." He gestured to Kahkitah. "Go ahead, Fishface. Tell him."

"I'm really not sure," Kahkitah said hesitantly. "The sky on the

far side seemed to curve toward the ground. It might indeed have
been an inside room, just as Plato said."

"*I* didn't see anything like that," Bungie countered. "All I saw
was trees against sky over there."

Kahkitah hunched his shoulders. "My eyes are different than
yours."

"*Different* doesn't mean *better*," Bungie shot back. "I know what
I saw."

"Yes, of course," Kahkitah said hastily.

"And so did Nicole," Bungie added. "Right?"

"I really wasn't looking that far," Nicole said diplomatically. Of
course, Bungie hadn't been, either. But she didn't dare mention
his attempt to steal a gun, not with Kahkitah and the doctors
here. In fact, this whole line of conversation was probably one
they should get off of as quickly as possible.

Bungie seemed to have figured that out, too. "Fine," he said.
"Maybe it *was* just a big room. Whatever."

"So what was it like?" Sam persisted. "Plato said it was a testing arena. What was it testing for?"

"For fighting," Kahkitah said, sounding confused and horrified
at the same time. "There were strange beings in there *fighting*
among themselves."

"You surprised by that?" Bungie asked. "Come on, Fishie. Fighting is the natural state of everything. People, nature—everything."

"It's not exactly *fighting* when it's in nature," Sam murmured.

"It's stuff killing other stuff," Bungie retorted. "Call it whatever you want. It's still fighting."

"But there isn't supposed to be any such fighting here," Kahkitah said, sounding even more bewildered. "The *Fyrantha* is to
be a haven of peace. Plato has said so, many times."

"Yeah, like Plato knows jack," Bungie said with a sniff.

Kahkitah cocked his head. "Jack?"

Bungie rolled his eyes. "Never mind. You two finished?"

"I am," Allyce confirmed, giving Nicole's forearms a final look and then refastening her jumpsuit sleeves over the bandages.

"Me, too," Sam said. "What kind of fighting was it? Hand-to-hand, like karate? Or were there weapons involved?"

"So then you probably have somewhere else you need to be, right?" Bungie asked, ignoring Sam's question.

"Allyce said we need to be monitored," Nicole reminded him.

"So hook up something to monitor us with," Bungie said. "You got all kinds of fancy gadgets, right?"

"Can we do that?" Sam asked Allyce. "There are certainly a lot of places I'd rather be."

"I suppose," Allyce said, looking doubtfully at Nicole. "I don't know if that's what Plato had in mind, though."

"To hell with Plato," Bungie retorted. "You don't want to be here. We don't want you here. So figure something out."

"I suppose we could wire in sensors to monitor your functions," Allyce said slowly. "Presumably any new symptoms would manifest *somewhere* in a standard profile."

"So do it," Bungie said.

Allyce looked at Sam. "Fine by me," Sam said. "Even bored is better than hanging around these two."

"All right," Allyce said. She still sounded doubtful.

But that doubt didn't get in the way of efficiency. Five minutes later, she had the sensors set up. It looked a lot like the system Nicole had been hooked into when she'd first awoken aboard the *Fyrantha*, but without the feeding and cleansing tubes.

"Great," Bungie said when she'd finished. "Now go have fun somewhere else."

"I'll be in the office if you need me," Allyce said. She tapped

Nicole's bandages. "And if something presents, I'll be right here."

"Nothing's going to happen," Bungie said. "Just make sure Plato doesn't forget about feeding us."

"I'm sure you'll never be out of his thoughts," Sam said sarcastically. "Come on, Allyce."

They returned their equipment to the storage drawers and left the room. "You, too," Bungie said to Kahkitah. "Out. We need some privacy."

"I don't think I should," Kahkitah said, making no effort to move to the door.

"*Listen,* Fishface—"

"It's all right, Kahkitah," Nicole interrupted. Bungie certainly wasn't going to try anything wired to Allyce's equipment. "I'll call if I need you."

Kahkitah hesitated another moment. Then, without a word, he turned to the door and left.

"Dumb as a rock," Bungie said with a contemptuous snort. "Okay. I figure we'll wait until tonight, when everyone's asleep. You can get the door open again, right?"

"What are you talking about?" Nicole asked carefully. Was he actually suggesting—? "You want to go back *in* there?"

"No, *out* there," Bungie corrected with a glare. "I still think Plato's blowing smoke." He waved a hand impatiently. "Never mind. Doesn't matter what the hell—or *where* the hell—the place is. What matters is that they've got guns."

"Which they're not shy about using."

"They're not going to be shooting like that *all* the time," Bungie said. "I figure we catch them at night when they're sleeping, grab one of the guns, and we're as good as home." His eyes narrowed. "Unless you don't *want* to go home."

"Of course I do," Nicole lied.

"You sure?" Bungie persisted. "'Cause I've seen how you look at Jeff."

Nicole blinked. "I haven't been looking at Jeff," she protested.

"Yeah, don't worry, I'm not going to shoot Pretty Boy," Bungie said. "Not unless I have to. All we want is for them to show us how to get home. I figure a couple of arm or leg shots to show we're serious, and they'll be lining up to beat the snot out of Plato until he's ready to cooperate."

"We'd do better to wait," Nicole said, searching desperately for an excuse to keep from having to go into that battle zone again. "Plato's going to be watching us like a hawk. We have to give him time to forget."

"Sounds great," Bungie said sourly. "Except that the first job we get tomorrow will probably be to fix the door." He frowned with sudden thought. "Only—wait a second. *You'll* be the one giving the orders. If you keep your mouth shut about the door, there's no way anyone else will ever know. Right?"

"Unless the *Fyrantha* passes the order to one of the other Sibyls," Nicole improvised. She actually had no idea what would happen if she ignored an order. But it made sense that the ship would eventually give the job to someone else.

Regardless, she had no intention of leaving the door in its current half-locked condition, where Bungie could go in and out any time he wanted. Whatever he ended up doing, and whenever he ended up doing it, she needed to keep control of the situation.

"Fine," he said impatiently. "What's *your* idea?"

Nicole chewed at her lip. After weeks of watching Carp and the others fix broken systems, she had a pretty good idea how things worked aboard the ship. If the door repair went the same way as every other job, there might be a way to do this.

In fact, if she was *really* clever, there might be a way for her to shove the majority of the responsibility straight onto Bungie's own shoulders. Then, when he failed, he couldn't blame her. "You probably damaged the keylock control when you jammed in that screwdriver," she said. "If you did, the ship will tell me to have the control replaced. All you have to do is get hold of the damaged control before they throw it out. They're usually about the size of your palm and pretty thin, so it should be easy to hide in one of your pockets. Once we have it, we should be able to go to the door any time we want, swap out the new control for the broken one, and key in the reset command to get back in."

"Or we could skip a step and just break the new one after they put it in," he suggested. "Not like I can't get a screwdriver whenever I want."

"Maybe," Nicole said, feeling her heart rate pick up. For all she knew, he might actually be able to break in that way. That would take her right back to the free-for-all situation she was trying so hard to avoid. "But you'll have to break the new one exactly the same way you broke the old one. Otherwise, there's no guarantee the door won't just lock down."

Bungie grunted. "Whatever. Fine—I'll get the broken one."

"And then we'll wait a few days before we try it?" Nicole pressed. "Long enough for Plato to stop watching us?"

"Sure." Bungie eyed her closely. "But *just* until Plato stops watching us."

"Of course."

"Good." Bungie peered at his bandaged arms and started fastening his jumpsuit sleeves up around them. "'Cause I'd hate to think you weren't going to help us get home just because of Jeff. That's how accidents happen."

Nicole swallowed hard. "I know," she said, the words sounding hollow in her ears. He would do it, too, she knew. He'd already done it at least once, back in Philadelphia when he thought one of Jerry's runners was paying too much attention to his then girlfriend. The kid had been in the hospital for a week after Bungie finished with him.

"Good," Bungie said again. He finished with his sleeves and got up onto the treatment table, stretching out on his back and folding his arms gingerly across his chest. "I'm gonna take a nap. Wake me when lunch comes."

Nicole had expected the *Fyrantha* to order the door fixed the next morning. She was right. She'd also expected the repair to consist of swapping out the damaged keylock with a new one. She was right on that one, too. Finally, she'd expected Bungie to fail in his attempt to steal the old keylock before Carp dumped the day's scrap into the recycle slot.

She was wrong.

"I don't believe it," she said later in her room, turning the damaged keylock over in her hands. "How come Carp didn't notice it was missing?"

"Because it wasn't," Bungie said, his voice practically glowing with self-satisfaction. "I'd already swiped one of the other replacements when no one was looking. I just put the new one in the scrap bucket when I took the old one out. I didn't think Carp would look that close at every piece of garbage before he tossed it."

"I guess not," Nicole agreed, trying to sound enthusiastic as she slipped the keylock into her pocket. "Okay, then. We'll wait until they've forgotten about all this, then see if it'll get us in."

"Sounds good." Bungie extended his hand. "Only *I'll* hold on to it."

Damn. "It'd be better if I kept it," she improvised. "If Plato gets suspicious, he'll probably search you before he searches me."

"Yeah, and if Jeff's hands start poking around, *he* might find it," Bungie retorted. "Come on, give."

Reluctantly, Nicole handed the keylock back to him. "Just promise you won't go without me."

"Would I do a thing like that?" Bungie asked in the closest thing he had to an innocent voice. In all the years he'd been hanging around Trake's group, Nicole had yet to see that act work. On anyone.

"Because if anything happened, I'm the only one the *Fyrantha* will talk to," Nicole reminded him.

"Yeah, fine," he said, stuffing the keylock into one of his pockets and getting leisurely to his feet. "Take real good care of yourself. I'll see you in the morning."

six

Bungie had wanted to wait no more than a week before heading back into the testing arena. Nicole had argued for at least two months, privately hoping that after such a long delay Bungie might lose interest and forget the whole thing.

Either Bungie sensed her strategy, or was just his usual impatient self. His compromise was two weeks.

Nicole, naturally, didn't get any further votes.

She thought about going privately to Plato and warning him about Bungie's plan. But whatever Plato did, it would be obvious to Bungie that Nicole had been behind it, and she'd seen what he did to people he considered traitors. She thought about sneaking off to the testing room door and seeing if she could sabotage it in such a way that even the damaged keylock wouldn't get them in. But if she got caught she would be in trouble with Bungie *and* Plato, and she couldn't afford to make two enemies at the same time.

She even thought about deliberately injuring herself, or making herself sick, so that she wouldn't be able to replace the keylock when the time came. But that wouldn't buy her more than a temporary delay, and again ran the risk of bringing Bungie's anger down on her.

And so, fourteen days exactly after their first visit, Nicole found herself hunched over beside the testing room door, swapping out the keylock for the damaged one. She finished the job and keyed in the reset code, hoping desperately that it wouldn't work.

The universe had never been much for granting desperate wishes, at least not hers. Once again, the door popped open.

Back in the hive area, the lights automatically dimmed during the "nighttime" hours, though they never went lower than a twilight gloom. The hallways she and Bungie had traveled on their way here had been likewise dimmed.

The same cycle apparently applied to the testing arena as well. The greenish-blue sky was muted, and the lights around the rim had faded to about the level where Philadelphia streetlights usually started to come on.

And now that Nicole was looking for it, she could see the way the sky at the far side did indeed curve down below and behind the hills and trees.

It was a room, all right, just as Plato and Kahkitah had said. A *big* room, certainly, at least a football field long and probably longer. But it was still just a room.

Somewhere deep within her, a part of her had been hoping Plato was wrong. That there was indeed a whole world out there beyond the battle area. It would have meant there was someplace else to go, someplace Nicole could escape to if Bungie decided to push too hard and she had to get away or risk getting killed.

But there wasn't any such escape path. They weren't on Earth, or even some alien world. They were indeed trapped together aboard a floating coffin flying between the stars.

Back on that last morning, she'd thought about getting away from the city. She'd gotten away, all right.

"There," Bungie muttered into her ear, pointing over her shoulder. "See?"

Nicole shook away the memories. "Where?"

"At the base of that tree," he said. "See? He's just sitting there."

Nicole frowned. Then she saw it: an indistinct figure, looking like a misshapen person sitting with his back to the tree. Beside him, a long pole pointed almost straight upward.

And though it was hard to tell in the relative gloom and patchwork of shadows, she was pretty sure the figure was facing the stone building that had been the focus of the weasels' attack the last time she and Bungie were here. "Careful," she warned. "He looks like he's on guard duty."

Bungie grunted. "Not for long he's not. Stay here." Lowering himself to the ground, he headed off toward the figure at a stealthy crawl.

Nicole winced. But there was nothing she could do, even if she'd wanted to. She certainly wasn't going to go over there with him.

On the other hand, if the guard spotted Bungie, there was a good chance he'd spot her, too. It wouldn't be smart to be standing out here in the open when that happened.

The line of bushes where that one weasel had been shooting was about ten feet away. Staying low, Nicole slipped over to it and settled onto her knees close to the near edge. From there she could keep an eye on Bungie's progress, while hopefully being a little harder to see.

Though if shooting started, the bushes weren't going to give her much protection. There were a dozen tears and blackened spots where all those blasts of green fire had slashed through them. The second bush in line, in fact, had had much of its central trunk or stem or whatever shot away. All the leaves on one side had withered, while those on the other half were still going strong. Idly, she poked at the burned stem where it met the ground.

She frowned, peering closer. The dirt there wasn't dry, like she'd expected for something indoors, but was actually quite damp. In addition, now that she was paying attention, she could see something shiny down there among the bush's roots. Carefully, she brushed some of the dirt away with her fingers, uncovering a long, thick copper-colored wire that was both cool and wet.

She nodded to herself. Of course. An enclosed forest like this would have to have some sort of watering system built into the ground. Maybe a feeding system, too.

Of course, the whole idea of a wire somehow transporting water was pretty weird. But she'd seen stranger things aboard the *Fyrantha*. If she ever needed to know anything about the system, the ship would surely explain it to her.

Carefully, she brushed the dirt back over the wire and tried to straighten the stem, feeling a twinge of guilt and loss. Her own window box plants were long gone by now, she knew. Unless Jasp had continued to water them . . . but he'd probably dropped the whole thing in the Dumpster two days after she disappeared.

This bush would probably die, too. But she could at least try.

She ran her fingers over the watering wire, getting them wet, then shook the drops off at the base of the still-green part of the stem. She repeated the operation until the ground around the bush had the same moisture level that her window box soil had right after she'd watered it. She had no idea whether it would be enough, but it was the best she could do.

From across the room came a soft thump. Nicole looked up, her heart leaping into her throat.

Whatever the noise had been, it wasn't the sound of Bungie getting caught. The guard was still sitting where she'd seen him earlier, his weapon still pointed into the air beside him.

Nicole frowned. She hadn't really paid attention before, but that weapon was much longer than the guns the weasels had been using earlier. Did a longer gun mean a more powerful gun? The greenfire guns hadn't seemed to work very well against the stone building, she remembered. Maybe they'd brought in this bigger gun hoping it would do a better job.

There was another quiet thump, and this time she saw a bush near the guard's tree shake a little. Bungie must be nearly there.

And then, so suddenly that it made her jump, Bungie lunged into sight from some bushes behind the guard. He grabbed the weapon and wrenched it away from the figure.

And froze.

Nicole frowned, her heart still thudding. Had something gone wrong? She stared across the gloom, trying to figure out what had happened. Bungie was just holding the weapon, staring at it as if it had somehow paralyzed him.

Even more bizarre, the guard hadn't reacted to the attack. He was still just sitting there, facing the stone building. There was a sort of slithering hiss from somewhere to Nicole's left—

And Bungie toppled face-first to the ground as an arrow suddenly erupted from his shoulder.

Nicole gasped with horror, her own shoulder pulsing with sympathetic pain. Bungie rolled half over onto his side and scrambled to his feet, staggering again as another arrow hissed its way into his left thigh. He snarled with pain and rage and struggled back to his feet, throwing himself forward just in time as a third arrow narrowly missed him. Leaping into a stumbling run, he headed back toward Nicole and the door.

He'd gotten maybe three steps when another arrow caught him in his upper right arm.

Nicole frowned. This last arrow hadn't come from her left like the other three, but had come from the direction of the stone building.

But there was no time to wonder about that. Bungie was still on his feet, loping toward her in that same awkward running limp, the long weapon clutched in his hand. Another two arrows shot past him, one from each direction this time—

"Get it open!" he shouted, his voice twisted with pain and anger. *"Now!"*

Nicole leaped to her feet and ran to the door, her back tingling with the terrible fear that the next arrow would be hers.

But she reached the door without the anticipated flash of agony. She hit it at a dead run, kicking away the screwdriver Bungie had used to prop it open and shoving against it with everything she had. A second later Bungie slammed into the heavy metal beside her, swearing over and over through clenched teeth.

Their combined momentum did the trick, opening the door far enough for them to get through. With a final curse Bungie threw himself out into the hallway, the weapon clattering loudly as he tossed it onto the floor ahead of him. Nicole was right behind him, grabbing the door as she passed and reversing direction. If their attackers made it across the open area before she got it closed, she and Bungie were dead.

But they were apparently satisfied with driving the intruders away. She got the door closed and latched, and for a moment sagged against the panel, her knees shaking with reaction. Then, steeling herself, she turned to Bungie.

There was a fair amount of blood seeping out into his jumpsuit and onto the spongy red floor. Still, there was a lot less than she'd expected, what with three arrows sticking out of him. He was certainly bleeding less than most of the gunshot victims she'd seen over the years.

"You just gonna *stand* there?"

Nicole snapped herself out of her macabre train of thought. "Sorry," she apologized. "Sorry. What do you want me to do?"

"Find a cart or something," he said, his voice shaking a little. "No way I'm walking very far like this."

"Okay," Nicole said, trying to think. She had no idea where an actual cart might be, but the supply closet they'd been working out of that morning had a couple of large welding platforms on wheels. Maybe she could put him on one of those and drag him back to the hive. "Do you want me to hide the gun first?"

Bungie snarled something under his breath. "*What* gun?"

Nicole frowned, and for the first time focused on the prize Bungie had brought out of the testing arena.

Only to discover that what he'd risked death to steal wasn't a gun. It was nothing but a slender pole, maybe eight feet long, with a pointed tip and a nasty-looking axe about a foot back from the pointed end. "But they were all using guns," she protested, staring at the weapon.

"Sure they were," Bungie snarled. "Two damn *weeks* ago."

Nicole winced. And since she was the one who'd insisted on the delay, this whole fiasco was now her fault.

She should have known that was where it would eventually end up.

"I'll go find a cart," she said, looking both ways down the long portside hull hallway. Nothing was visible in either direction, and it was a hell of a long way back to the hive. Maybe instead of trying to use a welding machine she should go back to the medical station and see if there was a wheelchair or something she could borrow.

"Never mind—forget the cart," he rasped. "That pumping room yesterday. Remember? We'll go there."

"And do what?" Nicole countered. "You need a doctor."

"No kidding," he ground out. "So get me to that room and then go get Sammy boy to come fix me up."

"But—" Resolutely, Nicole clamped her mouth shut. It wasn't

much of a plan, but it wasn't worth arguing about. At least it didn't entail her lugging him back to the hive across her shoulders. "Fine. Come on, I'll help you up." A sudden thought struck her, and she picked up the spear-axe thing he'd brought out. It was heavier than it looked, probably solid metal. "Here—use this like a walking stick."

The pump room was a lot closer than the hive. It was also a lot farther than Nicole remembered it. But with sweat, effort, and a lot of Bungie's cursing, she finally got him inside and settled as comfortably as possible in the cramped space. She left the spear-axe propped up against the side wall where he could get to it if he needed to stand up, then hurried back to the hive.

Sam wasn't happy at being dragged out of bed. He was even less happy at Nicole's evasive answers to his questions. It took the better part of ten minutes to persuade him to come with her, another five to get the medical travel bag, and another ten to get to Bungie's hiding place.

At which point, as Nicole had expected, the doctor's simmering resentment blossomed into full-blown anger.

"How the *hell* did this happen?" he demanded as he knelt beside Bungie, his fingers probing at the arrows' entry wounds. "Where in the world did you find—Oh, no," he interrupted himself, glaring up at Nicole. "The *testing arena*? After Plato told you not to go there?"

"No, we decided we wouldn't go there *before* he told us not to," Bungie shot back. "*Ow!*—watch it."

"Yeah, that's real funny," Sam growled, pulling out a pair of scissors and starting to cut away the jumpsuit material around the arrows. "Serve you right if I turned around and walked away."

"You're not gonna do that," Bungie countered. "You're also gonna keep real quiet about this."

"Oh, am I?" Sam said sardonically. "Give me one good reason."

"Because you want to get out of this damn place as much as we do." Bungie pointed at the spear-axe. "And that's how we're gonna do it."

Sam frowned at the weapon. "You think we're getting out of here with a *halberd*?"

"You asked me once if they were fighting with weapons in there," Bungie reminded him. "There you go."

Sam snorted and turned back to his work. "Yeah, I can just see us holding Plato up at halberd-point and demanding he send us back."

"Don't be stupid." Bungie hissed loudly as the doctor eased one of the arrow shafts back a little. "That's just a sample. They've got lots better stuff in there."

"They've got bows and arrows, anyway," Sam said, rubbing his chin. "Okay, here's the deal. Even with a topical, this is going to hurt. A lot. It'll be easier on both of us if we go back to the hive and I put you under a general."

"No," Bungie said flatly. "Plato sees me like this, and it's all over. He'll weld the damn door shut or something. You just douse me with that healing goo, and we'll call it a day."

"And then what?" Sam countered. "You just waltz in at breakfast tomorrow like nothing happened? That salve's good, but it's not *that* good. Especially not with serious muscle damage like this. If it had been bullets instead of arrows you'd have bled to death half an hour ago."

"Yeah, getting shot was lucky, all right," Bungie said.

"I'm serious," Sam insisted. "You're going to have trouble walking for at least a week, and if you don't take it easy you might end up with a permanent limp."

"So I'll just hang out here for a few days," Bungie assured him. "Nicole can bring me food bars." He tapped one of the pipes behind him. "I've got plenty of water."

"And how is she supposed to explain your disappearing act to Plato?"

"She doesn't have to explain anything," Bungie said. "I disappeared, and she doesn't know where I am."

"He'll never believe that."

"So what?" Bungie said. "What's he gonna do, lock one of his precious Sibyls in her room until she talks? Not a chance. All he can do is yell and stomp, and she can handle that."

Sam looked up at Nicole. "Nicole?"

Once again, the idea of turning Bungie over to Plato flicked across Nicole's mind. Once again, she pushed it firmly away. For all the trouble Bungie had put her through, he was still her only connection back to her old life.

More importantly, even if Plato locked him up for a while, he would eventually be back out with the work teams. Bungie walking free and clear and looking for payback against a betrayer wasn't something Nicole wanted to face.

And he was right about Plato probably not punishing her for his disappearance. One of the eight Sibyls had gotten sick a week ago, and Plato had had to frantically shuffle Nicole and the other six around on double duty to cover for her until she was well enough to go back to work.

He would be furious at Bungie's disappearance. But as long as Nicole stuck to her story, there wasn't much he could do. "It's worth a try," she told Sam.

The doctor shook his head. "You're both crazy," he declared.

"Hey, you want to come with us when we leave this damn place?" Bungie asked pointedly. "If you do—"

"Yeah, yeah, I got it," Sam interrupted, pulling a hypodermic injector from the bag. "Shut up, and hold still."

As he'd warned, the anesthetic was only partially effective, and Nicole found herself twitching with Bungie's every grunt and groan. But the doctor knew what he was doing. One by one, he cut each of the arrows near the exit wound, then carefully worked the shafts back out through the skin and muscle. Each of the wounds erupted in fresh blood as the arrow plugging it was removed, but Sam had healing salve and bandages ready. In the end, Bungie lost a lot less blood than Nicole had expected.

Finally, after nearly two hours, it was finished.

"Here are some painkillers," Sam said, handing Bungie a small bottle as he stowed his gear back into the bag. "You're going to hurt like hell when the topicals wear off. Don't take more than one every twelve hours. I'll come back tomorrow night and check on you."

"Don't bother," Bungie said, peering closely at the bottle's label and then slipping it into a pocket. "Last thing I want is a parade going back and forth for Plato to follow. If I need you, I'll send Nicole."

"Fine," Sam said. "Whatever. Speaking of parades, I realize a red blood trail on red flooring isn't all that obvious, but you should still do something about that."

"Yeah." Bungie looked at Nicole. "I think he means you."

Nicole suppressed a sigh. He could have said something about this while she was just standing around watching him pulling out arrows. "Fine," she said. "I'll take care of it."

"You can use these," Sam said, handing her a packet of small paper towels. "They're specially treated to absorb blood. Just be sure to get everything." He closed his bag and stood up. "And if Plato finds out about it—"

"I threatened to beat you up," Bungie said impatiently. "Now get lost."

"You're welcome." With one final look at Nicole, Sam headed off down the hall.

"You'd better get busy with the blood," Bungie told Nicole, carefully shifting around into a more or less lying position. "And then get me some food bars, huh?"

There'd been times over the years when Nicole had had to scrub bloodstains from carpets and clothing, and she knew what a long, excruciating chore it could be. To her relieved surprise, cleaning up Bungie's blood trail was nothing like that. Between the nonabsorbent characteristics of the red flooring and the highly absorbent liquid in Sam's cleaning towels, a single swipe was enough to completely remove the dribblings of blood. The whole job, all the way back to the testing arena, took barely fifteen minutes.

She'd finished with the floor, and was checking the door itself for stray bloodstains, when she heard footsteps.

She froze, her heart suddenly pounding. From the rhythm of the steps it sounded like there were at least two people coming toward her. The long portside hallway was still empty, which meant the footsteps had to be coming from one of the cross-corridors.

She hissed between her teeth, trying desperately to think. If that was Plato and someone else, probably Carp or Kahkitah, the last thing she wanted was to get caught right here outside the testing arena door. She had to find somewhere to hide, and fast.

Only there wasn't any such place. Heading down the hallway toward the rear of the ship and the hive would take her straight across every one of the cross-corridors, and even in the relative darkness Plato would have to be blind to miss her. Taking the long hallway the other direction would be even more useless. As Bungie had pointed out on their first visit, that end of the hallway dead-ended fifty yards away, and there were no rooms along it where she could take refuge.

But if she went all the way to the end, lay flat on the floor, and held perfectly still, it was just barely possible that a quick look would miss her.

The footsteps were getting closer. A slim chance, she decided, was better than none. Stuffing the bloody towels inside her jumpsuit, she slipped around the curved wall of the arena and headed as quickly and quietly as she could down the hallway.

She was maybe twenty yards in, wondering how far into the gloom would be far enough, when the footsteps abruptly stopped. "You," a voice called from behind her. "Stop."

Nicole froze, her heart suddenly thudding even harder. That wasn't Plato or Carp, or anyone else she'd met aboard the *Fyrantha*.

Slowly, carefully, she turned around.

The other was standing in the center of the hallway near the arena door: vaguely human-shaped, but taller and wider than most people. It was taller even than Kahkitah, with no more than six inches between the top of its head and the hallway ceiling. Its entire body glistened in the dim light—covered with shiny metal, or maybe even made of it. Its legs were thick and flared outward into feet that were more like big round cones than actual feet, sort of like the hairy legs and hooves of Clydesdale horses. The thing had no face that she could see, only a ribbed and perforated plate that reminded her of an old-style knight's helmet.

And that face—or that lack of face—was pointed squarely at her. "Yes?" she called back timidly.

The figure seemed to think about it. Then, it lifted an arm and beckoned to her. "Come."

Nicole's legs were trembling with fear, her whole body screaming at her to turn and run away as fast as she could.

But there was nowhere to run. The only door that was even within reach was the big one that led into the arena, and even that wasn't really an option. Not with the metal man standing almost close enough to lean over and touch it.

Unless Nicole could get him to move the wrong way, maybe with a feinted attempt to get around him, then get the reset code punched in and the door open before he could change direction and come toward her. Something that big and heavy-looking had to also be slow and ponderous, especially with those ridiculous feet. With enough of a head start, surely she could outrun or out-maneuver it.

"Come," it ordered again.

With an effort, Nicole forced her feet to start moving. On the other hand, the arena was home to people with bows and arrows and no hesitation about using them. Maybe it would be better to forget the feint and just try to duck past the figure and make a run for it. If she could get to the next cross-corridor, and if the metal man was as slow as she hoped, she might be able to lose it in the maze of hallways and rooms.

Unless it was armed.

Swallowing, she studied the figure's hands and hips as she approached, looking for signs of a gun or other weapon. There didn't seem to be anything there, but all the glinting from the metal made it hard to see details. The figure turned its head and shifted position—

Nicole caught her breath, her feet grinding to a halt so fast that she nearly fell on her face. Stretching out from the figure's back was another whole section of body, also covered with metal. This part was long and thick like a horse's, and had a second pair of thick legs with the same conical ankles and feet at the rear.

The thing facing her wasn't just a big man. It was a nightmare straight out of her grandmother's tattered Greek mythology book.

The thing was a *centaur*.

"Come," the centaur said. It cocked its head. "Don't be afraid. I won't hurt you."

Once again, Nicole's body screamed for her to do something— *anything*—that would get her away from the impossible creature standing before her. Once again, there was nothing she could do. Fighting back sudden tears of fear and helplessness, she resumed walking.

She made it to within ten feet of the centaur, decided that was close enough, and stopped. "What do you want?" she asked, fighting to keep her voice steady.

There was another pause. Nicole clenched her hands into fists at her sides, her fear briefly punctuated by a flash of anger. Some of Trake's friends liked playing this same silent-stare game, probably figuring it made them look like the boss in some overblown gangster movie. To her, it just made them look like pretentious half-wits. For a huge armored man-horse to pull that same trick was just plain stupid—

"You were inside the testing arena tonight," the centaur said.

—and with a sudden creepy flash of belated insight, Nicole suddenly understood. The centaur wasn't playing games. He was simply doing what Nicole and everyone else aboard the *Fyrantha* did every day: waiting for someone's alien speech to be translated before replying.

What had thrown off Nicole's perception was that she wasn't hearing his own form of speech first, before her translator kicked in and gave it to her in English. Either his voice wasn't audible to human ears, or else his helmet was handling both ends of the translation.

And with that, suddenly, the creature somehow seemed less scary. He might be big and alien and covered in metal armor, but he couldn't get through a simple conversation without a translator any more than she could. "Yes, I was," she acknowledged. "A friend and I both went in."

A pause—"We were informed humans don't fight," he said. "Why then did you go into a field of battle?"

Nicole felt her lip twitch. Plato's ominous warning about not fighting flashed to mind, along with his warning of what would happen if anyone strayed across that line. "May I ask who you are?" she asked, stalling for time. "Names are important to us."

There was the usual pause—"My name is Fievj," the centaur said. "I'm of the clan and the people of the Lillilli."

"I'm Nicole," Nicole said. "I'm a human. But I guess you knew that. Were you in the arena? Because the only person I saw in there didn't look anything like you." She grimaced as something that hadn't sunk in at the time suddenly struck her. The figure had been so still . . . "In fact, I'm not even sure he was alive."

"He wasn't," Fievj confirmed calmly. "He had died in battle earlier in the day. The Micawnwi propped him against a tree as a decoy. They hoped to lure the Cluufe defenders into an attack, thus betraying their archers' positions."

Nicole stared at him, a chill running up her spine. The idea itself was creepy enough, but Fievj's cold-blooded description made it even creepier. "Are you one of the—that first group you said?" she asked. "I'm sorry, I don't remember the name."

"The Micawnwi?" Fievj waved a hand. "No. Neither am I of the Cluufe. I'm an observer, watching their battle from afar." He cocked his head to the side. "You do not fight, either, or so we've been told. Yet your companion risked his life to steal a weapon from the arena. Why?"

"He didn't know he was risking his life," Nicole told him. The moment of distraction had passed, but it had bought her enough time to come up with a story. It wasn't brilliant, but it was at least plausible. Hopefully, that would be good enough. "He didn't know it was a weapon, either," she continued. "You see, there are a lot of times when we have to open whole sections of wall to get to the machinery behind them, and sometimes the locks that are supposed to hold those sections against the ceiling don't work like they're supposed to. Bungie saw the pole and thought we could use it when we needed something to prop up one of those sections."

She held her breath as her explanation worked its way through Fievj's translator. "What about your Ghorf?" the centaur asked. "He was brought to the *Fyrantha* for precisely that reason. Isn't he strong enough to hold up those wall sections?"

"Oh, definitely," Nicole assured him. She'd seen Kahkitah do it, too, once pressing a wall section against the ceiling for two straight hours. "But sometimes we're working two jobs at the same time, and if both sets of locks are broken we're kind of stuck. Anyway, like I said, Bungie saw the spear-axe thing and figured it might work." She shrugged. "He didn't count on getting shot at."

The pause this time seemed much longer than any of the previous ones. Nicole stood as still as she could, feeling fresh sweat breaking out on the back of her neck. Maybe Fievj's translator was just taking its time.

Or maybe the centaur was doing some hard thinking. That was never good.

"Why did he go into the arena the first time?" Fievj asked.

"That was mostly by accident," Nicole said. "We were working on the lock and the door popped open. We'd never seen anything like it before on the ship, and we wanted to look around."

A shorter pause—"Yet when the battle began, he moved *into* danger instead of away from it."

"I know," Nicole said, trying for a mix of rueful and exasperated. She had no idea whether Fievj could pick up on her tone of voice, but better to be safe than sorry. "He told me afterward that he panicked and got himself turned around. He was mostly crawling with his eyes closed—didn't realize he wasn't heading toward the door. If Kahkitah hadn't gone in and grabbed him, I don't know what would have happened."

"It might have been instructive."

Nicole frowned. That was an odd comment. "Or he might have been killed."

"Perhaps. Why did *you* go inside this second time?"

Nicole hesitated. This part of her story was going to sound a lot less plausible than the excuse she'd spun to him for Bungie. But it was all she could come up with on the fly. "The first time I was inside people were shooting into the bushes near the door," she explained. "When we went in tonight, I wanted to see how much they'd been hurt, and if I could do anything to fix them."

Another too-long pause. Fievj was doing way too much thinking tonight. "You wanted to fix the *bushes*?" he asked, sounding incredulous.

When a lie was teetering on the edge, sometimes the only way to get through it was to say it again louder. "What's wrong with that?" she countered. "I like plants. They're part of nature, and we humans like nature. I used to keep plants in a box at my home, and I took them with me whenever I had to move." She waved toward the arena. "I'd go in there every day if I could. And if there weren't always people shooting at each other."

"The other humans have expressed no interest in such things," Fievj said.

"Most of them probably don't even know about it," Nicole said. If repeating the lie didn't do the trick, the next best strategy was to try to change the subject. "What's all that shooting about, any-way? Is it a school? Are they training for a war or something?"

"Where's your injured companion?" Fievj asked. "He needs medical attention, does he not?"

Carefully, Nicole let out the breath she'd been holding. Apparently, Fievj knew the change-the-subject ploy, too. And he didn't want to talk about what Nicole had seen. Which was totally fine with her, as long as it got her out of here. "The doctor's already treated him," she said. "He said he'll be fine once he's had some rest."

Fievj seemed to straighten up. "Then I take my leave," he said. "Perhaps someday I shall speak to him in person."

"Maybe," Nicole said, frowning. Change the subject *and* then cut the questioning short?

Not that she wasn't just as happy to see him go. But there was something here that felt wrong. "Will I see you again?" she asked.

Fievj took a step backward, the movement of his four legs reminding Nicole more of a big dog than of a horse. "We shall meet again," he confirmed. Without waiting for a response, he walked past the arena door and headed down the cross-corridor. Nicole strained her ears, listening as his four feet thud-thudded along the dark red flooring and faded into silence.

She took a deep breath and let it out in a sigh. There was no way to know if he'd completely bought her story, but he'd apparently bought it enough to at least put an end to the questioning. She took another deep breath—

Something touched her shoulder.

She jerked violently, throwing herself a couple of foot-tangling steps forward, trying desperately to get away from whatever it was that had sneaked up behind her. She spun around, nearly falling down in the process—

She'd thought it might be another centaur like Fievj. She'd feared it might be something even more horrible.

It was only a Wisp.

Nicole staggered to her right, putting a hand against the wall to steady her rubbery knees. "Damn it," she breathed. "Don't *do* that."

The Wisp didn't answer. But then, they never did.

Nicole frowned. On the other hand, they never seemed to stand still, either. They were always on the move somewhere, with no apparent interest in the activities of the repair crews they were passing.

In fact, now that Nicole thought about it, the only time she'd ever seen any of them standing still was when they'd grabbed her, Bungie, and Sam.

Yet here this one was. Just standing there.

Staring at her.

With an effort, Nicole found her voice. "What do you want?" she asked.

For a moment the Wisp held its position. Then, still without a word or gesture, it glided past Nicole and headed down the hallway. It reached the arena door and turned down the same cross-corridor Fievj had taken.

Was it doing some sort of leisurely pursuit? Or was it on night duty, here to keep track of anyone roaming the *Fyrantha's* hallways when they were supposed to be sleeping?

Nicole took another deep breath. Her lungs, she reflected sourly, were certainly getting the full workout tonight. To say nothing of her heart.

Or all the rest of her, for that matter. This evening had definitely been one giant meat grinder.

Pushing herself away from the wall, she headed wearily toward the pump room where she'd left Bungie. She would pick up a few food bars from one of supply closets, make sure he was settled down for the night, and then head back to the hive.

It had been one hell of a day. She could hardly wait to see what tomorrow would be like.

seven

Back in Philadelphia, Trake's activities had often kept him out into the early hours of the morning. It was the schedule most of his friends also preferred, and when she was lucky Nicole had been allowed to tag along.

Still, most of those late nights had been followed by equally late mornings, so she'd usually been able to get the necessary hours of sleep.

Here on the *Fyrantha,* the standard routine was just the opposite: relatively early evenings, followed by relatively early mornings.

The two schedules, Nicole discovered to her bleary-eyed regret, did not work together at all.

She was slogging her way through breakfast, fighting to keep her eyelids open and noting how much harder it was to follow Jeff's and Kahkitah's morning chatter when she was half-asleep, when Sam arrived. He got his tray, but instead of going off to eat by himself as he usually did, he headed straight for Nicole's table. He stopped at her side and nodded toward one of the unoccupied tables. "Over there," he said curtly. "We need to talk."

"About what?" Jeff asked.

"Something that's not your business," Sam said. "Nicole? Move it."

"Stay put," Jeff told her, glowering up at Sam. "If he's got something to say, he can say it to all of us."

"No, that's okay," Nicole said, hastily getting to her feet. Her fogged mind had finally figured out that the doctor wanted to talk about Bungie, and that was definitely a conversation she wanted to have in private. She scooped up her tray, followed Sam to his new table, and sat down beside him. "You want to make it a little more obvious?" she growled.

"Make *what* obvious?" he growled back.

"That we've got a secret," she said. "Next time you want to draw attention, wave a flag or wear a sign or something."

"Yeah, I'll try to remember that," Sam said. "Your big stupid pal Bungie's gone."

Nicole stared at him, her breakfast suddenly forgotten. "What are you talking about? Gone where?"

"If I knew that, he wouldn't be gone, would he?" Sam said with strained patience. "I went to check on him this morning, and he wasn't there. Where did he go?"

"I don't know," Nicole said, thinking hard. Bungie had been all right when she'd delivered the food bars to his hiding place, right after her run-in with—

Her stomach tightened. "The centaur," she said.

"The *what*?"

"The centaur," Nicole repeated. "Fievj. One of the—I forget the name of his people. Lilly something. He found me while I was cleaning up the blood trail and wanted to know what we were doing in the arena." She frowned. "Or maybe it was the Wisp—they both headed off the same direction. Maybe they're working together."

Sam shook his head. "You've lost me. Start at the beginning."

Nicole gave him a quick summary of her back-to-back confrontations outside the testing arena. "I'd already cleaned up the blood, so I don't know how they could have found him," she said. "Maybe they've got some special gadgets that can tell where the blood was."

"Or else Bungie was swearing loud enough to be heard two corridors away," Sam said, his voice suddenly thoughtful. "You say the Wisp showed up out of nowhere?"

"Well, it must have showed up out of *somewhere*," Nicole said. "I just don't know where. I didn't see any doors down that corridor. Though now that I think about it, there was another Wisp who disappeared down that way the first time Bungie and I went into the arena. So there must be a door somewhere."

"Maybe," Sam said slowly. "Or maybe the teleport room is down that way."

Nicole frowned. "You don't know where it is?" she asked. "Weren't you watching when they took us from there to the medical center?"

"No, because I wasn't awake," Sam said bitterly. "They knocked out all three of us. I was just thinking that if the Wisps can go from here to Earth, why can't they also pop in and out of places around the ship?"

Nicole turned that one over in her brain a couple of times. "Then why do we see them walking around at all?" she asked. "And why would they have to go down that one hallway to pop into the teleport room?"

"How the hell should I know?" Sam demanded. "I'm just thinking out loud."

"Okay," Nicole said, easing back from him a little. "Take it easy."

"I *am* taking it easy," he snarled. "It's *your* boyfriend who's missing. Don't you even care?"

"Of course I care," Nicole said. "And he's not my boyfriend."

"*He* seems to think he is."

"I'm not responsible for what he thinks," Nicole ground out. "Don't worry, we'll find him. As soon as I've got my team working, I'll go look at the pump room and see if he left me a message. Was the spear-axe still there?"

"It's called a halberd," Sam said with more strained patience. "A *halberd*. And no, it wasn't. Wherever he went, he took it with him."

"Or whoever took him took it, too."

"Let's hope the hell not," Sam said darkly. "If they did—" He broke off. "Fine. Just make sure you let me know—*immediately*— if you come up with anything." He glanced over his shoulder toward the door, then abruptly stood and picked up his tray. "See you later," he added, and headed toward one of the other tables.

Nicole frowned. What in the world—?

"Nicole!" Plato's voice boomed from the door. "Where are—? Oh, *there* you are. Grab your crew and head out to *lefnizo* sector."

Nicole turned. Plato was standing just inside the doorway, glowering in her direction. "Sure," she said. "As soon as we're done eating."

"As soon as *we're* done, or as soon as *you're* done?" Plato countered. "Looks to me like everyone else is finished."

Nicole glanced around the room. The rest of her crew were indeed just sitting and waiting. "I'll be ready in a minute," she promised, scooping up a spoonful of her breakfast and shoveling it into her mouth.

"You'll be ready *now*," Plato said tartly. "Come on—everyone up. You've been falling behind schedule the last few days."

"That's not Nicole's fault," Jeff said as he and the others stood up.

"It's not ours, either," Carp seconded. "It's that idiot Bungie. I warned you up front that he was going to screw up our fix rate."

"Maybe you'd rather I just lock him in his room?" Plato shot back.

"I could live with that," Carp said.

"I'll bet you could." Plato looked around the room. "Where is he, anyway? Nicole?"

"I haven't seen him since last night," she said, more or less truthfully.

Plato snorted. "Idiot. Anyone see him, tell him the clock's ticking and that he'd better get his butt out to *lefnizo*." Turning, he strode out of the room.

Jeff walked over to Nicole and picked up her tray. "Come on," he said, starting for the door. "I'll hold the tray—you can eat as we walk. We can bring the dishes back after work."

"Are we in *that* much of a hurry?" Nicole asked, scrambling to her feet to follow him. The rest of the team, she saw, were already filing out the door.

"Probably," Jeff said over his shoulder as he picked up his pace to catch up with them. "Every so often one of the Shipmasters suddenly shows up and tells Plato we're falling behind and need to get hustling."

"But how are we supposed to go any faster?" Nicole objected. "I tell you everything the *Fyrantha* tells me. Once we finish, we're done. Right?"

"Plato obviously thinks we can do more," Jeff said. "Maybe if we started working faster you'd get more instructions. I don't know—it doesn't make sense to me, either. But when they lean on Plato, he leans on us. That's how it works."

"Sounds like back home," Nicole muttered as she fell into step beside him and scooped up another spoonful. "Who are these Shipmasters, anyway? What do they look like?"

"No idea," Jeff said. "Far as I know, Plato's the only one still here who's ever seen them."

"What do you mean, still here?"

Jeff shrugged. "The story is that the Shipmasters have been snatching people from Earth for a long time. Maybe as long as a few decades. Don't know if I buy that myself, but that's the story."

"You'd think the people would have been missed," Nicole murmured. A few *decades*? How bad a shape was the *Fyrantha* in that it needed that much maintenance?

And why her and Carp and Jeff, of all people? She'd already seen at least four types of aliens aboard the ship. Five, if you counted the Wisps. There must be hundreds of different types out there in the universe—surely someone would be better at this job than people from a primitive world like Earth.

For that matter, why didn't the Shipmasters do it themselves? They'd built the damn thing, hadn't they? How come they couldn't fix it?

"Oh, and that other thing Plato said, about the clock ticking down?" Jeff continued. "That means Bungie's running on what we call *down time*. Those are the days when you can't do any work. Kind of like sick days and R and R lumped together. Each of us gets two days of that every month, plus our usual break days."

"Plato never said anything about that."

"That's because he'd rather no one ever used down days unless they were sick," Jeff explained. "You haven't been, so I guess he didn't bother to mention it."

"Ah," Nicole said. "Plato does that a lot, doesn't he? Forget to mention things, I mean. Or is it just me he doesn't like?"

"It's not just you," Jeff said. He sighed. "Look. You see what this place is like. We're slaves here. The Shipmasters say they'll take us home when the ship is all fixed, but no one believes that. There's nothing to do except watch those nature shows or play whatever games we can cobble together. Plato has to keep us in line, because the Shipmasters keep *him* in line. There are no carrots here, just sticks."

"What?"

"Carrots and sticks," Jeff said. "Rewards and punishments. You hadn't heard that term before?"

Nicole winced. She never liked having to show her ignorance of things. "Probably. I just forgot. So all we've got is each other?"

"Yeah, for whatever that's worth," Jeff said. "There are some friendships here. Not many. You try to get along with the rest of your crew and everybody else, but you're more acquaintances than friends. That's just the way it is."

"What about us?"

He looked sideways at her. "What *about* us? I like you fine, but . . . this place really isn't conducive to . . . anything more."

Nicole stared down the corridor at the backs of her teammates, a piece of her soul crumbling inside her. The *Fyrantha* was so much easier and safer than her old life that she'd managed to completely miss the real core of what things here were like.

But now she saw. And as she thought back over the past few weeks, all her more or less fond memories of the crew's time together began to crumble to ash. Everyone made an effort, but she could see now how hollow it all was. "Yeah," she murmured. "That sucks."

"It sucks big-time," Jeff agreed. "It's a drab existence. But it *is* existence. And we were mostly used to it." He paused. "But then you came along. You, Sam, and especially Bungie."

"And *Bungie's* the one Plato doesn't like?"

"Bungie's the one who scares him spitless," Jeff said grimly. "I don't know what the Shipmasters have over him—he doesn't talk about it with any of us grunt workers—but he seems deathly afraid that Bungie's going to do something to ruin things for everyone."

Nicole snorted out a curse. "You mean for all us slaves?"

"Yeah, I get what you're saying," Jeff said. "But be careful what you wish for. Things are never so bad they can't get worse. And to be honest, you're not helping things poking around that arena."

"You telling me I shouldn't go back?"

"I think Plato's made that pretty clear."

"I suppose," Nicole said. "So what happens to Bungie if he runs down the clock?"

Jeff made a face. "If he runs out of down time before he runs out of AWOL, he stops eating."

Nicole winced. Even with Sam's magic healing cream there was no way Bungie was going to be up and working in less than a week. "I thought the *Fyrantha* had plenty of food," she murmured.

"It does," Jeff confirmed. "That's Plato's way of keeping people from loafing or taking a day off just for the hell of it."

"No exceptions?" Nicole asked.

"Sure, but they're mostly if you're injured on the job," Jeff said. "If that happens you get to stay on full rations until the docs say you're well enough to go back to work. But somehow, I doubt that's what happened to Bungie." He looked sideways at her again. "And don't tell him that part, okay? He strikes me as the type who might whack his leg with a hammer just to get a few days off. No offense."

"No offense," Nicole assured him. "Actually, that *does* sound like him."

"So if you see him you might want to tell him that he's looking at a forced diet if he doesn't come back soon," Jeff said. "You finished?"

Nicole scraped one last bite from the bowl. "Yes," she said, laying the spoon on the tray. "Thanks."

"No problem." He paused long enough to set the tray down at

the side of the hallway, then continued on after Carp and the others. "We'll pick it up on the way back."

The past two days had been spent working on pump rooms and electrical switching areas in the *lefnizo* sector, not too far from the arena door and the pump room where Nicole had left Bungie.

Her main concern earlier that morning had been that he might accidentally make enough noise that one of the team would hear him. Now, her main fear as they all gathered by the sector's equipment closet was that he'd taken it into his head to move to more spacious or comfortable living quarters even closer to the day's work area. Or worse, that he'd managed to pick the exact room they were about to work on.

"Whenever you're ready," Carp said sarcastically.

Nicole blinked, silently cursing herself. Still half-asleep, and with Bungie's vanishing act weighing on her mind, she was having serious trouble slipping into her normal routine. "Sorry," she said. She pulled out her inhaler and gave herself a good jolt.

The electrical locus in lefnizo-*two-six-six-nine has short circuits in the two-nine junction, the three-one junction, and the one-one-nine-seven rectifier simplex . . .*

Listening with half her attention, Nicole relayed the *Fyrantha's* instructions. It looked like another of what Jeff called twofers: two entirely separate jobs the team would have to split up to deal with. Still, though Carp was clearly the best mechanic of the group, Levi ran a decent enough second, and Jeff and Duncan were better than either of the other two on straight electronics repair jobs. Today's twofer looked like one mechanical and one mostly electrical job, which should let the crew split along its usual lines.

And with the two groups out of sight of each other, Nicole should have a chance to slip off to the pump room and see if she could figure out what had happened to Bungie. Idly, she wondered how Carp would handle things if the *Fyrantha* started giving them three jobs per day instead of two.

—and you are needed in Arena Four. Proceed to the lefnizo-four *Door Three immediately.*

Nicole's musings vanished in a violent twitch. What in the *world*—?

And then, suddenly, her fogged brain caught up with her.

It was Bungie. It had to be. He must have watched her punch in the reset code yesterday and then sneaked back into the arena last night after she left him. Possibly looking for a more secure hiding place; more likely still hoping to get hold of one of those greenfire guns they'd seen their first time inside. The *Fyrantha* had spotted him, realized he wasn't supposed to be there, and was calling on Nicole to get him out.

Or else he'd gone in there and gotten himself killed, and the ship wanted her to dispose of the body.

Damn. She'd meant to go back and swap out the keylocks again. Only somehow she'd never gotten around to it.

"Nicole?" Carp asked.

Belatedly, Nicole realized she was standing in the middle of the hallway, her mouth was hanging open, and Carp and the others were staring at her. "What?" she managed.

"You okay?" he asked.

"Sure," she said. "Fine. You get it all?"

"Yeah, I think so," Carp said, still staring. "You need to go to the medical center?"

Nicole frowned. Did she look *that* sick? She opened her mouth to tell him she was fine—

And then, almost too late, she caught the golden opportunity she'd just been handed. She needed to get to the arena, and she didn't want any of the group to know she was going there . . .

"Yes, maybe I should," she said. "But I can help get the gear to the work site first."

"That's okay—we can handle it," Carp said. There was something in his eyes, an odd intensity that worried her. "You just go get yourself checked out."

"You want me to go with her?" Jeff volunteered.

"No, I'm all right," Nicole said hastily. "I'll be back soon."

She backtracked a couple of hallways until she reached a cross-corridor that would take her safely out of their sight. Once there, she followed it all the way to the portside hull, then turned into the portside corridor and headed toward the front of the ship.

She took the last part of the trip carefully, peering around every corner, hoping she wouldn't run into any of her crew. But all the cross-corridors were empty, with no humans, Wisps, or wandering centaurs. She reached the arena door with a sigh of relief and punched in the reset code.

Nothing happened.

She frowned and punched in the code again. Still nothing. She tried a third time, then dropped to one knee and peered in at the mechanism.

The damaged keylock hadn't looked all that different from a good one, which was how Bungie had managed to do the scrap bucket switch in the first place. But there *had* been a couple of minor but distinct differences.

Those differences were no longer there. Sometime in the past twelve hours, someone had come here and swapped out the trick keylock with a new, undamaged one.

That job should have come through her team, which would at least have given her advance warning. Clearly, someone had beaten them to it.

And Nicole no longer had any way to open it.

She got back to her feet, thoroughly confused. Why in the

world would she have been told to go to the arena if she couldn't get in? Didn't the *Fyrantha* realize that the keylock had been changed?

Of course it knew. That was the whole point of these messages that she and the other Sibyls were sent. The ship was always running diagnostics to see what needed to be fixed.

Unless her summons hadn't been about going *into* the arena, but merely coming to the arena door. Where she was out of sight of everyone who knew her . . .

She spun around, fully expecting to see Fievj in his bright centaur armor striding toward her, maybe with a weapon in his hand this time. But again, there was no one in sight. Not even a Wisp.

Could the Wisps be waiting for her down the dead-end hallway? Had she been brought here to learn the secret of how they appeared and disappeared from there?

And if it did have something to do with the teleport apparatus, like Sam thought, did that mean the *Fyrantha* had decided it was time to send her and the others back to Earth?

She stared at the arena door, running that thought through her mind, trying to decide how it made her feel. She felt safer here than she ever had in Philadelphia, and had thought she was reasonably happy. But that was before Jeff's grim analysis of their situation. Had her earlier contentment been solely the result of some rationalization thing that her mind had created in order to keep her from being miserable?

She didn't know. But for the moment it wasn't important. Bungie and Sam certainly wanted to go home, and if the ship was ready to let her in on the secret, she needed to listen. She could always send the others back and then decide whether or not she really and truly wanted to join them.

Only how could she learn anything if there wasn't anyone here to show her?

And then, she finally got it.

"Damn," she muttered at her own stupidity. Pulling out the inhaler, she gave herself a whiff.

Enter the arena with the code six-seven-two-nine-four-three-eight.

She frowned. So it *wasn't* the hallway. The ship did indeed want her to go into the arena. Had she been right the first time about Bungie being in there?

Only one way to find out. Dropping the inhaler back into her vest pocket, she punched in the code.

The door popped open. Taking one last look around the still-deserted hallway behind her, she pulled the heavy metal panel back a couple of feet and slipped inside.

The place looked about the same as it had last night, except that the sky was much brighter, more like the daytime lighting that had been going on her first trip inside. The trees, bushes, and waving grass seemed just as inviting as always, and there were no indications that the place was even inhabited, let alone inhabited by people with bows, halberds, and greenfire guns.

But *someone* was clearly still here. The dead body was no longer propped up under the tree.

Nicole took a deep breath. At least the body hadn't been removed and replaced by a dead Bungie. "Hello?" she called tentatively. "Bungie?"

There was no answer. She hesitated, then pulled out her screwdriver and wedged it between the door and jamb. There was a keylock on the inside of the door, too, and the code the *Fyrantha* had given her would probably work just as well from this direction. But then again, it might not, and she had no interest in getting trapped in here.

Taking a deep breath, she moved warily into the chamber. "Bungie?" she called again.

Still no answer. Ahead and to her left were the low forested hills where the weasels with the greenfire guns had come from on her first visit. It was also the general area from which one of last night's bowmen had taken potshots at Bungie. Ahead and to her right, separated from the wooded hills by a tall ridge of mossy rock, was the low stone building where the other group of greenfire gunners had been. One of the archers who shot Bungie had been firing from there, as well.

Under the circumstances, neither choice of direction struck her as very appealing. But she couldn't just stand at the door all day. If Bungie was in here, she had to make at least a reasonable effort to find him.

During both of the attacks she'd seen, it had been the people from the trees who'd shot first. Maybe that meant the people in the stone building weren't as aggressive. If she'd been Bungie, she decided, that was the direction she would have gone.

It was as good a coin toss as any. Hoping that this wasn't as stupid as it felt, she started across the open ground toward the building.

She'd covered maybe fifteen steps when a bush six feet away suddenly rustled.

Nicole jumped, nearly biting her tongue. "Bungie?" she called nervously.

The bush rustled again. Then, from around the lower edge, a small face peeked out. An alien face, small and dark-eyed, with a flat snout and wide, lipless mouth. It reminded her of something halfway between a bear and a koala, with maybe a little alley cat thrown in. It didn't make a sound, but just stared across the waving grass at her, an intense look on its face.

Or maybe that was how the face always looked. "Hello," Nicole said carefully. "Have you seen someone who looks like me—?"

She broke off as, with a horrendous crashing of leaves and

branches, a six-foot-tall version of the same creature bounded into sight from behind another clump of bushes thirty feet away. It gave a single screeching howl and charged.

Nicole jerked, sheer panic freezing her feet in place. There was no chance she could make it back to the door, she knew, not with the speed the creature was making. There was no way she was going to fight it, either—she couldn't see any weapons, but at six feet tall and with its whole body as wide as Plato's shoulders, it could kill her just by knocking her over and sitting on her.

Still, Kahkitah was big, too, and even more nasty looking. This thing was wearing clothes—the same kind of smock and sandals the weasels from her first visit had been wearing, only this one was dark red instead of brown—and if it could figure how to put on clothes it was hopefully smart enough to think. If Nicole could convince it that she wasn't a threat, maybe it would leave her alone.

If not, it would at least probably be a quick death.

So she stood still, remembering to keep her empty hands in sight like the cops always ordered people to do. The creature continued its charge, its feet kicking up clouds of dead leaves as it ran. It reached the bush where the smaller version of itself was still peering out at Nicole.

And abruptly came to a jarring halt, its feet scattering more leaves as they skidded briefly across the ground. Leaning over, it snatched up the smaller koala bear, which gave a sort of gurgling yip as it was hauled upward through the branches. Holding the small one to its chest, the big koala bear began backing away.

And suddenly, Nicole got it.

"It's all right," she called, lifting her hands a little. "I wasn't going to hurt him. Or you. Really."

The words were barely out of her mouth when she belatedly realized that to the koala bear her speech was probably just so much noise. She was trying to think of some way to use gestures to get her point across when the big koala bear stopped. It cocked its head, and Nicole heard some deep grunts coming from its half-open mouth—

"Who are you?" the words came through Nicole's translator. "What do you do here?"

Nicole swallowed hard. The koala bear might not be charging at her, but its voice still had an ominous edge to it. "I'm a Sibyl," she said. "I'm one of the people who were brought here to fix the ship. I thought one of my friends might be in here—he's been hurt—and I was looking for him. That's all."

The koala bear leaned a little closer, its head and upper chest angling out over the smaller koala bear's head. "What ship is this you speak of?"

"*This* ship, the one we're in," Nicole said, waving a hand around her. "This room is part of a big ship."

The koala bear gave a little squeak and more grunts. "Impossible," the creature insisted. "There is no rocking of tides. No smell of sea air. This is not a ship." It seemed to wilt a little. "This is a nightmare."

And then, to Nicole's amazement, the huge keglike body seemed to collapse in on itself. She caught a shimmering glimpse of a thick forest of body hair that had been standing on end as it folded to lie flat against the koala bear's skin.

And when the process was over, the creature clutching its young to its chest was slightly shorter, much thinner, and far less terrifying. With a final measuring look at Nicole, it turned and started back toward the trees.

Nicole should just let them go, she knew. She'd gotten away without getting killed, and that was all she'd ever wanted from the encounter.

Anyway, she had more than enough on her plate. Bungie was still missing, she herself was standing in the middle of a huge room full of trigger-happy people, and Plato would probably skin her alive if he found out she'd been in here again. Her best move was a quick look around and an even quicker retreat.

But there was something about the way the big koala bear was walking that reminded her of too many of the people in the darker parts of Philadelphia. She could sense the creature's feelings of weakness, of fear, of despair—

"What's your name?" she called impulsively.

The koala bear stopped. Slowly, it turned around. "Repeat?"

"I asked what your name was," Nicole said, already regretting having opened her mouth. Whatever the alien's problem was, there was nothing Nicole could do about it.

Still, she'd started the conversation. It would be rude to just turn and walk away now. She continued to stand there, waiting, as the koala bear seemed to consider. Then, hesitantly, it walked back to her. Setting down the smaller alien, it bowed. "I am Mispacch, Woman-fifth of the Micawnwi," she said.

"Hi," Nicole said, wincing at the ridiculousness of the word. "I take it this is your child?" she added, gesturing toward the smaller koala bear.

"Yes," Mispacch said, touching the child gently on the back of its head. As she did so, Nicole spotted the glint of metal beneath the flattened hairs on the side of the older alien's head. "This is Son One. His sister, Daughter One, is yonder behind the trees."

Nicole frowned. All the trouble to have two kids, and she couldn't come up with something better to call them? "Don't they have names?"

"Our people don't assign names until a child's fourth birth-cycle," Mispacch said. "By then, personalities and characteristics are evident, and an appropriate name can be chosen."

"Ah." That made sense, she had to admit. Her own name, according to her grandmother, meant *victory of the people,* which was about as far from Nicole's actual life as you could possibly get. "How long until that happens?"

Mispacch dropped her hand from Son One's head. "They will never have names," she said quietly. "They will both die here in this place. As will I."

Nicole frowned down at the child. "I don't understand. Are you all sick?"

"My children are starving," Mispacch said. "As am I.

"We are all of us starving to death."

eight

Nicole felt her eyes go wide. *Starving?* "What in the world are you talking about?" she demanded. "The *Fyrantha* has tons of food."

"This *Fyrantha* you speak of may indeed have food," Mispacch said. "But the dispenser in our living space does not."

"The dispenser?"

"The machine that provides our food."

Nicole nodded, finally understanding. So that was why the *Fyrantha* had sent her here. Something was broken and needed fixing.

Except she wasn't in the fixing business. She was just the Sibyl. If Mispacch's food machine needed to be worked on, she would need to bring in one of the crew.

Only who? Carp wouldn't be interested, especially if he knew this place was off-limits. Neither would Levi or any of the senior men.

But there was Jeff. Not only was he younger than the others, but he'd already said that he liked her. He might be willing to bend the rules for a good cause. "Sounds like it's broken," she told Mispacch. "I'll get one of our repair crew and see what he can do."

"There is no use," Mispacch said. "The dispenser isn't broken.

It's deliberately reducing the amount of food it gives us, a little less each day."

"That's ridiculous," Nicole scoffed. "What makes you think it's deliberate?"

"Because the Masters told us it was."

Nicole stared at her. "Wait a second. Someone is starving you on *purpose*? What in hell's name for?"

"They don't intend for us to all die," Mispacch hastened to assure her. "They've told us about another dispenser with plenty of food. We need only take possession of it."

A creepy feeling settled in between Nicole's shoulder blades. "Let me guess," she said. "It's in that stone building over there?"

Mispacch touched her mouth. "True."

"And there are other people there who aren't letting you get any of it?"

"Also true," Mispacch said. "But that too is not unreasonable. Their food also comes from that dispenser. They have already said they'll kill anyone who tries to take it from them."

Nicole grimaced. So it boiled down to a turf war, like dozens of others she'd seen.

Only this one was being played for higher stakes than simply who could deal on which street. And apparently it was for the entertainment of some group she'd never heard of.

Or had she? Were Mispacch's Masters the same as Plato's Shipmasters? "So what are you going to do about it?" she asked. "Just sit here and starve?"

"Not all of us, no," Mispacch said. "Only the women and children."

"Because if your buddies with the bows and arrows—" Nicole broke off. Had Mispacch just said—? "The women and *children* are starving?"

"I've said already there isn't enough food for all," Mispacch said, some impatience creeping into her voice. "The men—the fighters—cannot be allowed to become too weak to fight." She spread her hands wide. "How do you not understand?"

"Oh, I understand just fine," Nicole snarled, a cold rage settling into her gut. She knew how that worked, all right. There had been plenty of times when she'd had to sit back and watch Trake and his buddies divide the take from some score and then throw a few scraps to the women who'd had to put up with them through it all.

Back then, there'd been nothing she could do about it. Here, maybe there was. "Doesn't mean I like it, but I understand," she added, digging into her vest pockets and pulling out three food bars. "Here."

Mispacch seemed taken aback. "What are these?"

"They're food," Nicole said, wiggling them a little in her hand. "One each for you and your children."

Hesitantly, Mispacch reached out a hand. Then, she drew it back. "I cannot," she said sadly. "Any extra food must go to the men. If they cannot fight, all of us will die."

"I can get more for them," Nicole said impatiently. "But these three are for you. Go on, take them."

Mispacch's body hair flared briefly, then flattened out again. This time, from her closer perspective, Nicole could see that the end of each hair split into several more hairs, umbrella-like. That was probably what had made the Micawnwi's larger size look solid. "I'm sorry," she said. "I cannot."

Nicole ground her teeth together. This was getting both ridiculous *and* stupid. "At least take a couple for your children."

Mispacch hesitated, then reached out and delicately took one of the three bars from Nicole's hand. "They may share one," she said. "The other two must go to the men."

She gave a whistle and began tearing away the food bar's

wrapper. From the bushes a dozen yards away another small Mi-cawnwi appeared and scampered through the grass. Son One had meanwhile settled himself at his mother's feet in a sort of cross-legged yoga pose that hurt Nicole just to look at it. His sister joined him, and Mispacch carefully broke the bar in half.

And then paused, staring at the food. "What now?" Nicole growled. Was she going to have to force the damn food down their throats?

"The smell is odd," Mispacch said. "I fear there is something in this that we cannot properly digest."

Nicole felt her nose wrinkle. That possibility hadn't even oc-curred to her. Certainly Kahkitah never seemed to have a prob-lem with the food in the dining room. "What do you mean by *properly*? Like it'll give you the runs or something?"

"I don't understand that word," Mispacch said. "I fear the food will make them ill."

Nicole looked down at the two children. Even with their alien faces, there was no mistaking the intensity with which they were staring at the food in their mother's hands. They were hungry, and were clearly willing to chance it. "I guess you're going to have to try one after all," she told Mispacch.

"Yes." Once again, the Micawnwi hesitated. Then, with a sud-denness that was almost startling, she brought her hand up and took a big bite from one of the halves. Nicole caught a glimpse of a double ring of bright flat teeth, and then the bite was gone. "It's done," Mispacch said. "Now we wait."

"How long?" Nicole asked, suddenly remembering her own shrinking schedule. Even if she pretended she'd walked really slowly, there was only so much time she could squeeze out of a supposed round-trip to the medical center.

Still, with the crew split in half, each group might assume she'd simply come back and was hanging out with the other one.

That should theoretically give her until lunchtime before she was missed.

Of course, if Carp talked to Sam or Allyce later and found out that Nicole had never shown up, there would be a whole different level of hell to pay. But she would cross that bridge when she got to it.

"Only a few minutes, I think," Mispacch said. "Our bodies process food quickly."

"Mmm," Nicole said, searching for something else to say. She'd never liked awkward silences, and this situation had the potential to be the king of awkward silences. "So tell me what happened to you and the rest of your people back there. How did you get here?"

"We were on a shopping trip with a group from my neighborhood and a group from a different neighborhood," Mispacch said. "It's a ritual sharing of the marketplace that goes back to the peace exchanges of many centuries ago. I was searching among items of clothing for my children when a group of strange beings with glowing wings appeared. They took hold of us, and we were soon in a large metal room filled with strange electrical instruments."

"You were all in the same room?" Nicole asked, thinking back to the round teleport room where she and Bungie had arrived. "How many of you were there?"

"We are forty." Mispacch made a grunting sound. "Or we were when we first arrived. Yes, we were all in the same room."

Nicole pursed her lips. Her teleport room had been way too small to accommodate forty Micawnwi and the Wisps who'd grabbed them. That meant there were at least two such rooms aboard the *Fyrantha*. That could be a useful bit of information somewhere down the line. "What happened next?"

"Strange creatures came," Mispacch said, her body giving a

sort of quivering twitch. "They called themselves the Masters and forced us into another group of metal rooms that they called the hive."

"The hive?" Nicole asked, frowning. She'd assumed someone in her group—Plato, probably—had given their rooms that name. But apparently it was in general use around the *Fyrantha*. That might mean it was one of the Shipmasters' terms, which might give her an idea of the kind of people they were.

That, or it was simply how her translator always translated that concept.

"Yes," Mispacch said. "Even then, I assumed we had all been drugged to unconsciousness and were somewhere within our city, and that this was the playing out of some ritual I'd never heard of."

She paused, her eyes steady on Nicole. "Then the creatures spoke, and told us we were no longer on our own world."

"No, you're not," Nicole confirmed. "We're aboard a spaceship called the *Fyrantha,* traveling somewhere between the stars."

"Between the stars," Mispacch murmured. "Some of our story-tellers speak of such travel. But those tales were always assumed to be fiction."

Nicole nodded. "Same with us."

"But why do we travel so?" Mispacch asked. "What is the purpose of this voyage?"

"I don't know," Nicole admitted. "Still trying to figure that out. What happened after that?"

"At first, very little," Mispacch said. "There are five dominant men among us, and they spent some time establishing their leadership hierarchy. Mostly, we all searched for a way out of the ten rooms of our hive prison. In one of the rooms were two machines, one of which provided food and the other water."

"In ever-diminishing amounts."

"Yes, but not at first," Mispacch confirmed. "In the beginning the supply was more than adequate for us all. All were fed to satisfaction, including the women and children."

"How many women and children are there?" Nicole asked.

"Ten women and four children," Mispacch said. "There are also three young boys, but they are nearly to the age of maturity and it's been decided that they'll be counted among the fighters."

Which therefore granted them a full share of food. Nicole was willing to bet that they were related to whoever had come out on top of the status dog pile. This thing sounded more and more like the way Trake did things. "So when did the food supply stop being adequate?"

"After the third day," Mispacch said. "The supply of water has continued unchanged, but the amount of food has decreased with each passing meal."

"Is that when the men graciously invited you and the children to take a hike?"

"Again, not at first," Mispacch said. "For two days the men continued to divide the food equally, each getting less but none being refused." She hissed something Nicole's translator apparently was unable or unwilling to translate. "On the third morning of the smaller portions a voice spoke from the food dispenser. It named itself the Oracle and told us about the additional machine inside a large chamber which we would now be permitted to enter. The Oracle promised the other dispenser would more than make up our current shortfall, but also warned that it was under the control of enemies who would first have to be defeated."

"Have you seen these enemies?" Nicole asked.

Mispacch hissed again. "All too closely," she said grimly. "Two of our men went into the chamber to search out this dispenser. Only one came back, with a description of small but fierce creatures who had killed his companion and driven him away with weapons and arrows."

"Did he give you a description?"

"Even if he hadn't, I've also now seen them." Mispacch gestured to Nicole. "They are shorter than us, shorter even than you, with thick brown body hair, long necks, and small heads. Their snouts are long and their eyes black." She ran a hand down her reddish outfit. "They wear garments similar to this, but in brown instead of red."

Nicole frowned. The description sounded awfully similar to the weasel things she and Bungie had run into on their first trip in here. Weasel creatures, moreover, that had also been trying to capture the stone building.

But who had they been trying to capture it from? Apparently not the Micawnwi—from what Mispacch had said it didn't sound like her people had ever been in control of the building. How many alien groups were in here, anyway?

More to the point, both sides in that earlier war had been using greenfire guns, not halberds and arrows. Had those other weapons been lost or destroyed?

"The Oracle told us that a storage closet in our hive would now be unlocked, and that inside we would find weapons equal to those of our new enemies, which it named the Cluufes. But it also warned that the Cluufes would not be easy to defeat. It urged the men to spend a few days first in learning how to use the weapons."

"Which of course they didn't?"

"No, they did," Mispacch said. "They worked and trained for two days before attacking." She made another untranslatable sound. "But they also realized that spending those days on less and less food might leave them too weak to fight. It was then that they decided that the food must henceforth be reserved solely for the men."

"Okay," Nicole said, thinking hard. If whoever was manipulating this—the Oracle or the Masters or whoever—if they were cutting off the food supply from outside the Micawnwi quarters, there was probably nothing Jeff or anyone else could do about it. The arena stretched well past the dead end in the portside hull corridor and a similar blockage on the starboard side of the ship, which meant her team had no access to anything on the arena's far side.

But if the food was being cut off by tweaking something inside the dispenser itself, they might be able to fix it. "Okay," she said again. "There might be a way to make the dispenser give you more food. Let me go see if I can get someone to come in and look at it."

"Can't *you* come and examine it?" Mispacch asked hopefully.

Nicole shook her head. "Sorry, but I'm not really one of the repair people."

Mispacch's hairs bristled. "You said you were."

"I'm part of the crew, yes, but I'm only the Sibyl," Nicole said. "I listen to the ship and tell the others what to do."

"A foreman, yes?" Mispacch said.

"No, I'm not—I can't do anything," Nicole insisted. "Really."

"Can't you at least look?" Mispacch pleaded. "Calling others would take time—"

Abruptly, she broke off. Turning away from Nicole and the children, she buried her face in the nearest bush and threw up.

Sometimes, especially when Nicole was really, really drunk, the vomiting seemed to go on forever. With Mispacch, to her relief, the whole thing was over much faster. "You okay?" she asked as the Micawnwi slowly straightened up again. "I mean . . . you know what I mean."

"I'm unharmed." Mispacch took a couple of deep breaths, her hand pressed hard against her stomach. "I was right. Your food is of no use to us." She cocked her head. "Won't you please come and look at the machine?"

Nicole sighed. Thirty seconds ago, she'd been ready to walk out the door and try to figure out how to broach this subject to Jeff. Now, staring into Mispacch's face, she realized with a sinking feeling that she was stuck. If she turned her back on these people now, she would worry about it all day. "Fine—I'll look at the damn thing," she said. "You well enough to travel? Good. Let's go."

Nicole had known from the start that the arena was big. On her first visit she'd estimated it could be as big as a football field.

She'd been wrong. It was a whole lot bigger.

And the sheer size wasn't the most amazing part. Past the first line of hills and trees, the ones visible from the arena door, were more hills, along with grassy hollows, more trees and bushes and plants so weird that she couldn't even mentally categorize them, and lots of grass of different colors and sizes. The arena was also peppered with craggy rocks, some of them forming ridges that seemed to cut the landscape into smaller sections, while other narrow spires stuck straight up nearly to the glowing greenish-blue sky, almost like natural signposts whose signs had been lost. At one point she and the three Micawnwi even had to cross a narrow stream that wended its way down from a set of hills and disappeared somewhere past a line of purple trees.

Fortunately, the plant life seemed to have been well maintained. There were also several paths, some of them little more than narrow dirt trails, others wider and made of flat stones that had been set together. Mispacch led the way down one of the latter, which took them between two sets of hills and several clumps of trees.

With Nicole's full attention on the wilderness-like scenery

around her, it was almost a shock when they rounded the final hill and she saw the plain, gray arena wall looming up ahead. There was another large door like the one she'd come in through at the other end, closed and presumably locked.

But about twenty yards to the right of the main door was another, smaller door, more like the sliding doors in her part of the ship. This door, unlike the big one, was open.

Open, and guarded. A Micawnwi stood at one side, a halberd gripped in his hand as he watched the four of them approach. "You *are* going to tell him that I'm here to help, right?" Nicole murmured to Mispacch.

"Of course," Mispacch said hesitantly. "But I fear that the men may not welcome your assistance. You're an alien, after all, and it was clearly an alien power who brought us here."

Nicole felt her stomach tighten. "You could have said something about that before now."

"Would you have come if I had?"

Nicole glowered. No, she probably wouldn't have. At least, not until she had Jeff with her. "Just make it clear to him that I had nothing to do with your kidnapping. That I'm as much a prisoner as you are."

"Perhaps," Mispacch murmured. "Yet you work to fix the ship in which the Masters have imprisoned us."

Nicole stared at her. "You don't believe me, either, do you? You think I'm—?"

Abruptly, she stopped. The hell with this. "Nice meeting you," she ground out. "Good luck with that whole fighting and starving thing." She spun around and started stalking back toward the other end of the arena.

And jerked to a halt, barely in time, as Mispacch's two children moved onto the stone path in front of her. "Forget it," she snapped, and tried to sidestep them.

But the small Micawnwi again moved to block her, and again she had to stop short to keep from running over them. "Get out of my way," she ordered.

Neither child moved. They just stood there, their eyes lifted to hers, looking in their alien way exactly like the street children she'd had to walk past every day back home. Like she herself had been not too many years ago.

The hell with them. Nicole had managed to harden her heart to the street kids. She could damn well do it here, too.

Daughter One murmured something. "Please?" Nicole's translator whispered to her.

Nicole swore under her breath, not caring whether the children understood her or not. She didn't need this. Didn't need it, didn't want it, and the longer she delayed in getting back to Carp the deeper the pile of trouble she was going to be in. Sticking her neck out just because a couple of alien kids looked pathetic and said please would be an utterly stupid thing to do.

To hell with them. To hell with every single last one of them.

She spun back around to face Mispacch. "You want me to look at the dispenser, or not?" she demanded.

"Yes," Mispacch said simply.

Nicole cursed one final time, then gave it up. "You've got ten minutes," she said. "Move it."

The guard was still gripping his halberd as the group approached. But now that Nicole was closer she saw that he didn't seem all that comfortable with the weapon. He was fidgeting awkwardly with it, like a new gang member who'd just been handed his first gun. Whoever this Oracle was, it had probably been right to suggest they take a few days to learn how to use the things.

Still, it wouldn't take much skill for him to skewer her. She hoped Mispacch could make a compelling case as to why he shouldn't.

"Who is this?" the guard called as they approached. His voice was as nervous as his twitchy fingers. "Who is this you bring, Mispacch Woman-fifth?"

"This is the Sibyl, Varkos Boy-second," Mispacch called back. "She's offered her skills to repair the food dispenser."

Varkos's fur fluffed. "I am no longer Varkos Boy-second," he said stiffly. "I am Varkos *Man*-second."

"You're still a child, whether the men count you among them or not," Mispacch corrected, just as stiffly. "If I therefore choose to address you as—"

"Excuse me, but we're in kind of a hurry here," Nicole cut in. She *really* didn't have time for this. Especially not a stupid alpha-dog argument she'd heard a hundred times before. "You want to step aside and let us pass, Varkos Man-second?"

It seemed to her that the Micawnwi straightened up a little. "Wait here," he said in a formal sort of tone. "I'll inform Amrew Man-second that you wish entrance."

He turned and headed briskly through the door, the end of his halberd bumping against the jamb as he passed it. "He *is* still a child," Mispacch said sourly.

"I don't care if he's still in diapers," Nicole growled back. "In the real world you say what you have to to get what you want. *And* to not get poked by some kid with a stick."

"He wouldn't have hurt you," Mispacch said, still clearly annoyed at Varkos's attitude. "As a child, he would first have to be given an order by one of the dominants. Since none are present, he could only use force if you first used force against him."

Nicole grimaced. Only now he'd gone to fetch this Amrew character, who presumably was a dominant and *could* order the kid to skewer her. Terrific.

But it was too late to reconsider. Mispacch had barely finished her explanation when Varkos reappeared around the open door, a taller Micawnwi in tow. "This being is named the Sibyl," the younger one said, again in that formal-sounding voice. "Mispacch Woman-fifth declares she will repair the food dispenser."

"Hold on," Nicole said, holding up her hands. "I'm only here to *look* at the machine. I never promised I could fix it."

"Are you a woman?" the older Micawnwi asked.

"I'm a human female, yes," Nicole said.

The Micawnwi gave her a sort of backhanded wave. "Then you will not speak unless so requested."

It was all Nicole could do to keep from wrenching the halberd from Varkos's hands and giving the older Micawnwi a whack across the side of his head with it. "Are you Amrew Man-second?" she asked instead.

"I've already said that you will not speak unless—"

"Yes—right—got it," Nicole interrupted. "Varkos Man-second, be sure you let everyone else know that it was Amrew Man-second who didn't feel like being polite to a visitor who might have been able to help you." She looked at Mispacch. "I'll be back when the men start getting hungry, too," she added. "See you later."

She'd made it five steps down the path before Amrew caved. "Wait," he called. "*Can* you provide more food?"

Nicole stopped, permitting herself a tight smile. For all his pompous devotion to the rules, he was badly worried and ready to clutch at any hope. Even hope offered by an alien female.

The smile faded. Winning the mind game had been satisfying, but it wasn't the reason she was here. "I don't know, Amrew Man-second," she said, turning back to face him. "Let's find out."

For another moment he eyed her in silence. Maybe he'd just realized that he was no longer in control.

Maybe he also realized that his pride wasn't really important. Maybe. "Yes," he said, gesturing her forward. "Come."

Mispacch had said that the forty Micawnwi had been stuffed into ten rooms, which Nicole had assumed would be laid out in the same more or less rectangular pattern as the rooms in the humans' own hive area. Instead, this cluster was arranged into a circular pattern, with a large central area a little bigger than her hive's dining room and a group of smaller rooms angling outward from it like pieces of pie. Most of the doors of those rooms were open, and while she could see glimpses of sleeping mats and other bits of furniture, none of the rooms seemed occupied.

Which wasn't surprising, given that the central room was currently hosting a dozen of the group, all of them engaged in serious, violent, and very loud lunging and swinging practice with their halberds.

And unless these halberds were a lot lighter than the one Bungie had stolen, the way the Micawnwi were casually whipping the things around showed the creatures were a lot stronger than they looked. Maybe even as strong as Kahkitah.

Amrew gave a wordless shout, and the sparring and noise abruptly halted. At least they knew how to obey orders. "This alien is the Sibyl," Amrew announced into the silence. "She may be able to give us more food."

One of the Micawnwi took a step forward and made a sharp jab toward Nicole with the tip of his halberd. "That's her," he said darkly. "That's one of the beings who attacked us last night."

Uh-oh. "We didn't attack anyone," Nicole said. "We came in to look around, that's all."

"And to steal Borve's weapon!"

"That's not how it was," Nicole insisted, keeping her voice low and calm. She'd seen this same kind of twitchiness before, in men who were on the edge of losing it. "My companion saw your friend and thought he might be hurt. He went to see if there was any-thing he could do to help—"

"You stole his weapon!" the Micawnwi snarled, jabbing his halberd toward Nicole again.

"—and when you started shooting at him he grabbed the hal-berd purely by reflex as he tried to get to safety," Nicole finished.

The Micawnwi took a step closer. "We need that weapon," he said. "Where is it?"

"I don't have it," Nicole said. From the sounds of movement behind her, she had a bad feeling the other Micawnwi had closed the circle back there. "My companion disappeared with it."

"Then you'll find it *and* him," the Micawnwi insisted, taking another step toward her. "You *will* bring the weapon here." He jerked his halberd. "And your companion will pay for desecrating Borve's body with his foreign touch."

"There was no desecration intended," Nicole protested, start-ing to sweat. This whole thing was teetering on the edge of get-ting dangerously out of hand.

And then, to her surprise, Mispacch stepped forward. "Borve was already dead, Celenso," she said, planting herself not quite between Nicole and the halberd's spear point. "The Sibyl's pres-ence didn't help or harm that. Right now, we need food more than weapons."

Nicole shot a glance at Amrew. Shouldn't he be getting in-volved with this? But he was just standing there, watching the argument, making no move to intervene.

So much for Micawnwi dominant men.

Fortunately, Mispacch's intervention—or her logic—was enough. Celenso hesitated, then raised the tip of his halberd and stepped back. "Very well," he said. "But I'm going to watch her. Very closely."

Nicole eased out a sigh. "Help yourself." She turned to Amrew. "Can we get this over with? I'm on a schedule here."

"The dispenser is in there," Amrew said, pointing to the right at one of the open doors angling off the room they were all in.

Nicole looked through the doorway. The room was well lit, with no furniture that she could see. There was a vending-machine-sized thing nestled in one corner at the far end and a similar device fitted with something that looked like a water faucet in the other back corner.

There were also no other exits. Once she was inside, she was there until the Micawnwi decided to let her out.

If she had any brains, she would turn and make a run for it, hoping the element of surprise would be enough to get her past the halberds. Unfortunately, even as that thought occurred to her, she realized that it wouldn't work. If the numbers Mispacch had quoted were accurate, less than a third of the men were here in the practice chamber. The rest were probably out in the arena somewhere, and some of them had bows and arrows.

With enough lead time, Nicole might be able to outrun angry Micawnwi men. But no head start in the world would let her outrun an arrow.

Fighting back a grimace, she walked through the silent group and into the room. Celenso was right behind her. "There," he said, jabbing his halberd at the vending machine in the corner. "That's the dispenser. Fix it, or die."

nine

"Yeah, yeah, I got it," Nicole said, trying to filter her growing fear out of her voice. Kahkitah's words to her that first lunchtime flicked back to her: that he was confident she could learn how to fix things just like the repair team did.

He'd better have been right.

She walked slowly toward the machine, giving it a once-over as she went. It was little more than a big rectangular box, about six feet tall and three wide, with a display of colored lights near the top of the front panel and a six-inch-wide open chute coming out from the box's center with a wide hopper beneath it. On the wall beside the dispenser was a keylock similar to the ones she'd seen and used during their repair work.

"Well?" Celenso demanded.

"Keep your smock on," Nicole told him. There looked to be a couple of access panels on the dispenser's sides, and the whole top also looked like it might come off. The fasteners were the type used on equipment all across the ship, which meant she should be able to get the thing open and take a look inside. She reached into her vest pocket for her screwdriver.

Only then remembering she'd left the damn thing propping open the door at the other end of the arena.

She winced. This was going to be awkward. "You don't happen to have any tools, do you?" she asked, turning to face Celenso. "I seem to have misplaced my—"

And without warning, a voice suddenly bellowed from somewhere behind her.

She jerked, reflexively taking a couple of quick steps forward. The bellowing continued, and she had just enough time to realize it was coming from the dispenser itself—

"What are you doing?" the translation shouted into her ears. "Who are you? What are you doing here?"

Nicole looked at Mispacch, fighting hard to catch her breath. "Mispacch?" she hissed.

"It's the Oracle," Mispacch said, her body hair fluffing rapidly up and down. "The Oracle is speaking."

Nicole winced. And it didn't sound at all pleased.

"Who are you?" it demanded again.

Nicole braced herself. Playing big and tough had worked on Amrew. Maybe it would work here, too. "I'm Ni—I'm a Sibyl," she said firmly, switching words at the last second. The first law of survival in a dangerous situation was to never give your real name. "Who are *you*?"

The voice chattered again. "I am the Oracle," it said. "I speak for the Masters."

"Well, I speak for the *Fyrantha*," Nicole said. "I'm busy. What do you what?"

There was a brief pause. "Why are you here?"

"The Micawnwi dispenser hasn't been providing enough food," Nicole said, deciding to pretend she didn't know the reason that was happening. "I was asked to come and fix it."

The pause this time was noticeably longer. "By whom?" the Oracle asked. "The Micawnwi or the *Fyrantha*?"

Nicole opened her mouth—

And closed it again as the strangeness of the question suddenly struck her. How could the Oracle and his fellow Masters not know that? They probably didn't have the whole arena bugged—the thing was way too big for that—so it wasn't surprising that they hadn't overheard her conversation with Mispacch.

But surely they knew what the *Fyrantha* had said to her. Even if they weren't listening all the time, they must be able to go through the records and find out. Even simple Earth computers and phones could do that.

Unless they couldn't hear the *Fyrantha*.

But that was crazy. These Masters had to be the same people as Plato's Shipmasters. Surely they could hear their own ship.

But then why bother to bring Nicole and the other Sibyls aboard? Why bring Carp and Plato and the rest of them aboard, either? They couldn't hear the ship *and* they couldn't fix it?

What the *hell* was going on here?

"The *Fyrantha* told me to come here," she said, feeling the prickly sensation of walking out onto thin ice. The ship had indeed told her to come to the arena, but it hadn't said anything about the dispenser. If the Oracle and Masters *did* know what the ship told the Sibyls, this would blow straight up in her face.

But she had to take that chance. Every future lie she might tell depended on her knowing exactly what the Masters knew.

"The *Fyrantha* is mistaken," the Oracle said. "The machine isn't broken. The lack of food is necessary."

"Why, so they can starve to death?" Nicole scoffed. "What does that gain anyone?"

"There's more food available," the Oracle said. "Amrew Mansecond knows where it can be obtained."

"You mean by fighting someone else for it?" Nicole countered. "Why?"

"You will not touch the machine," the Oracle said, his tone

darkening. "Do you understand? The Masters demand you leave the machine alone."

Nicole grimaced. She hadn't known exactly what poking the Oracle like this would accomplish. Clearly, what it had accomplished was to make him mad.

Meanwhile, she'd picked up enough puzzling facts for one day. Time to cut and run. "I understand," she said. "In that case, I'll return to my other assigned work."

Too late. "You will not return," the Oracle said. "The Masters wish to speak with you. One will come soon and take you to them."

Nicole felt her throat tighten. "I have other assigned duties."

"You will wait there," the Oracle repeated harshly. "Amrew Man-second? Are you present? Speak, that I may know."

"I'm here," Amrew called from the doorway.

"The Sibyl is not to leave your hive," the Oracle said. "An emissary will be sent to bring her to me."

Amrew bowed toward the dispenser. "I obey, Oracle of the Masters." He straightened and gestured to Celenso. "Take her to Room Four."

Silently, her heart thudding, Nicole followed Celenso back into the central area, around the outer edge, and into the next of the pie-piece rooms. This one was somebody's living quarters, she noted as she walked through the doorway, with three sleeping mats, two rounded white chairs that looked like they'd been carved from giant plastic eggs, and a low oval-shaped table that matched the chairs.

Fastened to the wall in the back corner was another food dispenser.

"Wait a second," Nicole said, pointing at it. "There's *another* food machine?"

"It doesn't work," Amrew said as he backed out of the room. "Remain here until the Oracle's emissary arrives."

And just to make sure she did, he closed the door behind him.

Nicole took a deep breath. "Well, *damn*," she murmured. Whoever these Masters were, she was pretty sure that she didn't want to meet them. Not under these circumstances.

But they were all stuck in a giant can out in space. If the Masters wanted her, they would have her, and there wasn't much she could do except figure out how to deal with them.

Her best approach would probably be to back off the dominance act and try the good-little-girl-just-trying-to-do-her-job routine. She'd pulled that one a lot in the old days, usually when someone's half-baked scheme blew up in his face and she was the one the burned parties came after.

Unlike those situations, though, here she had the incredible advantage of being able to spin virtually any story she wanted about what the *Fyrantha* had told her to do without the Masters being able to call her on it. She still didn't understand how that worked, but it would undoubtedly come in handy somewhere along the line.

She looked at the food dispenser. Speaking of the *Fyrantha*, as long as she was stuck here anyway, she might as well see if the ship had some thoughts on how to deal with these things. Pulling out her inhaler, she gave herself a jolt.

Nothing. "Hello?" she murmured, frowning in concentration. "Anyone there?"

Still nothing. Not that the ship ever answered her, of course. Their communication had always been strictly one-way. But it had been worth a try.

She was debating whether or not to try a second jolt from the inhaler when she noticed the grips at the underside of the wall beside the food dispenser. Grips just like the ones Kahkitah used to open a section of wall when they needed to get behind it.

She looked back at the door, wondering if she should call Amrew in and point this out to him. If the wall in the other room worked the same way, it might let her get to the dispenser's inner workings, where she might be able to figure out how to boost its output.

On the other hand, having just been chewed out by the Oracle, Amrew was probably not in a cooperative mood. Better to wait until she had something solid to show him.

If she could get the wall open.

Most of the wall sections Carp's team worked with were huge things, fifteen or twenty feet long and eight feet high, and no one but Kahkitah could even budge them. This one also stretched all the way to the eight-foot ceiling, but it turned out to be only four feet wide. It wasn't light, but an experimental tug showed that it would be possible for Nicole to lift it high enough to at least take a look.

Dragging one of the egg-shaped chairs into position, she hauled the door up to chest height and nudged the chair beneath the edge with her foot. The chair gave out a discomfiting creak as she eased the wall's weight down on it, but it held. Crouching, she peered inside.

The space behind the wall was typical of those elsewhere in the ship: a set of equipment modules set back into a space just deep enough to hold them. In this case, that depth was about two feet, and the equipment consisted of twenty slender pipes coming down from somewhere above the ceiling and feeding into a cluster of boxes set into the wall from about six inches above Nicole's head to about her chest height. The boxes were connected together with more pipes, with one final large tube leading from the lowermost box to the rear of the food dispenser.

Interwoven among the pipes were several sets of wires that appeared to lead back to the keylock and to the darkened display panel on the front.

As with most of these equipment spaces, there was a lot of empty space around the boxes and pipes. No one was sure what that was for, but Carp had once suggested it was to accommodate new equipment in case some had to be added later.

She frowned, studying the layout. It reminded her of some of the filtering stations her team had worked on, where contaminated fluids were run through a series of filters and scrubbers and then sent back out the other side.

But those stations never had more than four inflow pipes, and both the inflow and outflow pipes ran horizontally. This system had four times as many inflow pipes and they were coming from above, with the outflow feeding into the dispenser. Apparently, the raw food material came in via the inflow pipes, got treated, mixed, flavored, and maybe textured inside the boxes, and the final goodies then rolled down the dispenser's chute into the hopper.

So were the Masters cutting back the supply of nutrients from somewhere in one of the floors above? Or had they simply cranked down the output from the dispenser?

Easing beneath the propped-open door, Nicole went over to the equipment cluster. During one of the crew's discussions, Jeff had mentioned that the simplest explanation was usually the best place to start figuring something out. The Masters *could* shut down all twenty of the input pipes. But if there was a valve or control box on the dispenser itself, that would be a whole lot easier.

And if there was a valve the Masters could turn off, Nicole should be able to turn it back on.

She was running her fingers along the sides of the boxes,

searching for a knob or slider or set screw, when there was a warning shriek of metal on plastic behind her.

And as she turned around, she saw the chair skid away across the floor and the suddenly released door swinging straight toward her.

Instantly, she dropped to the floor, landing hard on her knees beneath the processing equipment and twisting her torso around to face the door. The panel slammed shut in front of her face, delivering a sharp slap to her forehead and bouncing the back of her head off the rear wall.

For a few seconds she continued to kneel there, her knees and soles of her feet wedged awkwardly between the two walls, swearing feelingly as she clutched both of her head injuries and waited for the dizziness to go away.

Finally, the pain subsided and her head started to clear. Pressing her palms against the wall, wishing she'd never let Mispacch talk her into this, she pushed.

The wall didn't budge.

She stared at the flat metal bare inches from her eyes, a cold sensation prickling across her back. Squeezed in here like this, she didn't have the leverage to get the wall open. Her legs were stronger than her arms, but it would be impossible to maneuver them into position in the cramped space. There was nothing she could do but wait for the Masters' emissary to get here. She hoped like hell he wasn't dawdling.

And hoped even more that he paused long enough in this supposedly empty room to hear her banging on the wall. Otherwise, he might just leave, chew out Amrew for letting her escape, and take the search elsewhere.

Leaving her here to die.

Don't panic, she told herself firmly. Even if the emissary missed her, the Micawnwi lived in these rooms. Surely she wouldn't have to wait longer than evening for someone to settle down where they could hear her pounding on the wall.

She frowned as another odd thought suddenly struck her. There were no working lights in any of these between-wall equipment setups, at least none that she'd ever seen. Often there were indicator lights, but with this particular food dispenser shut down there was nothing like that, either.

So how was it she could even see the wall that was pressing in on her?

The faint light seemed to be coming from her right. Carefully, hoping she didn't whack her head on any of the equipment clustered around and above her, she turned to look.

There was light over there, all right: a sliver of soft glow coming from about twenty feet away along the between-wall space. Probably somewhere behind the room with the functional food dispenser, in fact. Maybe that was where and how the Masters were fiddling with the Micawnwi food supply.

And aside from a few small floor-level cables, there didn't seem to be any serious obstacles between her and the light. She should be able to work her way over there and see what was going on.

Not that the trip wouldn't be tricky. Many of these cables had rough-edged sheaths, and there was always the possibility of hidden bits of broken plastic that could slice into unwary hands in an instant.

But anything was better than kneeling here pounding on the wall and hoping someone found her. Maneuvering herself carefully around onto her hands and knees, she started crawling.

For once today, everything went smoothly. The cables were soft and yielding, there were no hidden dangers, and she even managed to keep from whacking her head again on the various low-hanging pieces of equipment.

The light turned out to be coming from a narrow gap beneath a wall section that hadn't quite closed properly. The segment itself was considerably narrower than the one she'd opened in the other room, no more than a couple of feet wide. Pressing her shoulders against the back wall, she settled her palms against the partially open wall, mentally crossed her fingers, and pushed.

It still wasn't easy. But unlike the larger wall section in the other room, it was at least possible. She managed to push it open far enough to get her legs up, and a moment later she was out. She let the section back down, being careful not to let it make any noise as it closed, and looked around.

She was in some kind of maintenance room, with workbenches on two of the walls and tool and parts cabinets at their ends. The wall section she'd come through had surprisingly rough edges, as if it hadn't originally been an access panel but had been cut out of something wider or even from a section of normal wall. Pulling the wall open again, she looked inside.

Just to the right of the opening was the Micawnwi's food dispenser, the one Amrew had shown her earlier. But unlike the nonfunctional one she'd examined in the second room, this one didn't have a nice simple pipe leading from the lower processing box to the machine's hopper. Instead, that pipe's center section had been cut out and replaced by a length of flexible tubing with a small box in the middle. The box itself had a display and a single knob, both of them marked with alien letters or numbers unlike anything else she'd seen aboard.

Nicole frowned. Most of the systems on the *Fyrantha* ran with digital electronic controls, though most also had manual backups or overrides. But this one just had a single control, and a not particularly accurate one at that. Something the Masters had cobbled together on their own, then, and not something that had originally been part of the ship?

Regardless, this was clearly how they were adjusting the food supply. Either they stopped by every day and turned the knob a bit to decrease the flow, or else the thing was programmed to handle the slow starvation automatically.

But not for long. A simple crank of the knob back to its original spot, and Mispacch and her children would eat again. She reached for the knob—

And stopped. Turning the knob would certainly change the setting. But which way would increase the flow, and which would just decrease it faster?

There was no way to know. She couldn't even go by the *Fyrantha*'s usual convention on such things—the strange markings could mean the device had come from somewhere else and didn't follow the usual turning convention.

But there was another way. Obviously, the tubing and its attached box were the mechanism the Masters were using to dry up the Micawnwi's food supply. All she had to do was cut out the box, weld or glue the ends of the tubing back together, and then seal this section of the wall so that the Masters couldn't get inside to mess with it again.

None of that should be impossible, given time and the proper equipment. Unfortunately, at the moment she had neither.

She hissed between her teeth. She could presumably get hold of a cutter and some of the workers' heavy-duty glue back in the main part of the ship. But that would take a while, and Mispacch and her children would continue to go hungry. There had to be something she could do right now to at least buy them some time.

Maybe there was. If the food supply was set to steadily decrease, and if the position of the knob was a direct reflection of that process . . .

Back when she'd been getting used to the translator on this side of her head, she'd sometimes accidentally run a finger along a sharp bit of metal and drawn blood. Now, reaching in under her hair, she did it on purpose. She squeezed a small drop of blood from her fingertip, then carefully touched it to the edge of the knob.

The blood wasn't very visible in the relatively dim light, and it should be even less so once it dried. If the Masters missed it, she should be able to come back tomorrow and tell which way the knob had been turned. Once she knew which way shut off the food, she would know which way turned it on again.

Of course, now that she'd done that, it was absolutely vital that whoever the Masters had sent to collect her didn't find her here. In fact, it would probably be best not to let them find her *anywhere* in this general part of the ship.

Crossing to the door, she pressed her ear against it. All seemed quiet. She touched the release, and the door whooshed quietly open.

The corridor outside was deserted. She listened for another couple of seconds, then slipped out and headed down the soft red flooring toward the arena door she'd seen as she and Mispacch approached the Micawnwi hive. Celenso or another guard would probably still be on duty, but if she was lucky he would be distracted by the Masters' emissary and she would be able to slip past him through the trees and bushes and make her way back across the arena and out the far door.

She hurried along a corridor that had the usual well-spaced doors on her right and flat wall on her left—the latter marking the cluster of Micawnwi rooms, she guessed—and finally came to another long corridor that headed off in the right direction. She stepped to the corner and looked carefully around it.

The door was there, all right, no more than fifteen yards away. Even from here she could read its oversized ID plate: *lefnizo*-four Door One.

She took a deep breath. Almost home. Now, if the access code for this door was the same as the one at the other end, and if she could get past the Micawnwi guard, and if she could avoid the Masters' emissary . . .

She was bracing her feet for a sprint to the door when she heard the sound of heavy footsteps coming her way.

She ducked out of the intersection, cursing silently. If she hadn't wasted time scoping out the Micawnwi food system . . . But it was too late to fix that mistake now. Nothing was visible down her cross-corridor, so the emissary must be approaching along the long hallway leading to the main arena door. She needed to find a place to hide, and fast.

Only there wasn't any such place, at least nothing she could get to fast enough and quietly enough. All the doors along her cross-corridor were currently closed, and all of them were the kind that whooshed when they opened. She didn't know how good the Masters' hearing was, but she didn't dare risk it. The nearest other corner was too far away for her to reach in time, not at the rate the footsteps were clunking toward her.

There was only one chance. Crossing to the other side of her corridor, the side toward the approaching emissary, she pressed herself against the wall, hoping desperately that he didn't have good peripheral vision.

The footsteps were nearly here. She froze . . .

And suddenly, there he was, striding purposefully past Nicole's position, his attention clearly on the door ahead, his even stride giving no indication that he'd spotted her. He continued on, disappearing past the cross-corridor as he made for the arena door.

Only then, when he was fully out of sight, did Nicole allow her lips to mouth a fresh curse.

Because the Masters' emissary wasn't Fievj or even another centaur, like she'd been expecting. The figure *had* been dressed in metal armor like Fievj, but this one was just a normal human-shaped person without the horse's body stretching out behind it.

And suddenly all her tentative assumptions as to what the hell was going on had gone straight down the flusher. If this new person-shaped thing was one of the Masters, then who was Fievj? Were there Masters *and* Shipmasters running around the *Fyrantha*? And if so, were they working together or were they enemies?

And which group was on her side? Or did she and the other workers and the Micawnwi not *have* a side?

From down the hallway came the sound of the arena door creaking open. So much for getting out of here ahead of the Masters' emissary. Now she would have to find someplace to go to ground until he left.

And hope that her disappearance didn't spark a frenzied search for her. Which, if the emissary had any brains at all inside all that armor, it probably would. On her side of the ship, where she was familiar with the layout of rooms and storage closets, she might have had a shot at eluding a search, or at least avoiding capture long enough to come up with a decent story to spin.

On this side of the arena, though, she didn't have a chance of finding something fast enough. She didn't know the rooms; she didn't even know the numbering system over here—

She frowned as something suddenly struck her. Provided the emissary in there spent enough time yelling at the Micawnwi for letting her escape, she might still have a chance.

Because the door the emissary had gone through was labeled Door One. The one at the other end of the arena, the one she'd come in through, was labeled Door Three.

Somewhere, there had to be a Door Two.

With the trees and hills obscuring the view, Nicole had never actually seen the far side of the arena beyond the stone building.

But she'd seen how the sky curved down in that direction, and she now had a pretty good estimate of how big the place was. Given the positions of Doors One and Three, the logical place for Door Two would be somewhere at that end.

Her estimate was right on the money. Half a dozen hallways and turns later, she came to a short corridor that led straight to another of the massive arena doors, this one's tag identifying it as *lefnizo*-four Door Two. Slipping around the last corner, she ran to the door, her hand shaking with exertion and nerves as she punched in the code the *Fyrantha* had given her earlier that morning. The lock snicked; gripping the edge of the door, she pulled it open.

Beyond it, just as she'd hoped, were the trees and grassy hills of the arena.

She stepped inside, a sense of relief rolling over her as she pulled the door closed. One of the stone paths like the kind she'd seen on the Micawnwi side was directly in front of her, winding around a clump of bushes and disappearing over a low hill ahead. She had no idea where it ultimately led, but it hardly mattered. This wasn't greater Philadelphia, where a wrong turn could take you into a bad neighborhood or get you hopelessly lost. All she had to do was walk straight ahead, leaving the path and slogging through the grass if necessary, until she reached the far wall. At that point, a simple right-hand turn would take her to Door Three and back to the hive.

She'd gone about twenty yards, and had just noticed that there was an open door back behind some trees to her right, when there was a sudden rustle in the bushes ahead. One of the weasel-like people she'd seen on her first visit stepped into view, planting himself in the middle of the path in front of her. His dark brown smock was covered with leaves and small branches, and he was gripping a halberd just like the ones the Micawnwi had. He spat something—

"Halt!" the stern translation came. "Who are you?"

Nicole sighed. She'd been wrong. There *was* a bad neighborhood in here.

And she'd just found it.

ten

The rooms the guard took her to were laid out the same way as the ones in the Micawnwi hive, with a large round area in the middle and a group of pie-piece-shaped rooms extending outward from it. Here, though, the whole area seemed deserted. No one was in the round room, and she could hear no conversation coming from any of the other rooms, either.

The weasel with the halberd behind her gave a short, soft whistle.

There was another moment of silence. Then, a voice came from one of the rooms to Nicole's right.

She turned to see a second weasel walk into the round room— "Well, well," the translation came. "If it isn't the Blue-clad."

Nicole frowned at him. *Blue-clad?*

And then it clicked. This was the same weasel who'd been shooting from the row of bushes during that first battle, when Bungie had sneaked off to try to grab one of the greenfire weapons.

The weasel who'd threatened to kill him.

"I am Sibyl, not Blue-clad," Nicole told him. She had no idea whether the bravado she had used on the Micawnwi would work at this end of the arena, but it was worth trying. "I speak for the *Fyrantha,* the ship we travel within."

The weasel bit out something. "Your ship must enjoy seeing blood, Sibyl," he said darkly. "I wonder what color yours is. Perhaps we'll find out. I am Hunter of the West Waterfall Narvae. I speak for this gathering of the Cluufes. What do you want from us?"

"Nothing," Nicole assured him. "I'm just passing through, heading across the arena to return to my people."

"The people who tried to steal our weapons?" Hunter countered pointedly. "The people who even now conspire against us with our enemies?"

Nicole blinked. "What are you talking about?"

"Don't feign innocence," Hunter said, his voice suddenly hard. "Do you think we don't keep close watch on our enemies? You were seen, Sibyl of the *Fyrantha,* first speaking with the Micawnwi and then traveling to their stronghold."

"Their strong—? You mean their *hive*?" Nicole snorted. "You must be joking. That place is no more a stronghold than this is."

"Do you think me a fool?" Hunter said contemptuously, waving a hand around them. "Despite the limited space available in a room of this size, they nevertheless cleverly practice their drilling and maneuvers inside, so that our observers cannot watch. That bespeaks both cunning and military skill, qualities this sorry collection of Cluufes sorely lacks."

He took a step closer, glaring up at Nicole. "And yet, despite that ranging of odds against us, you deliberately tilt those odds further by conspiring with them?"

"I'm not conspiring with anyone," Nicole protested. "Or against anyone, either. I came in looking for a missing person, Mispacch asked me to see if I could fix their food dispenser, and I went. That's all."

"Ah, yes—the food dispenser," Hunter said with the coldly triumphant air of someone who's just had his darkest suspicions confirmed. "Your weapon of choice. What kind of evil beings use the threat of hunger to force their victims to dance to their tune?"

Agree with him, a small voice in the back of Nicole's head urged. *Agree that it's unfair, promise you'll have a talk with the ship about it, and get the hell out of here.*

But even as she opened her mouth to make whatever soothing noises were necessary to get her out of this, that last image of Mispacch's children looking up at her from the path bounced unbidden into her mind's eye. "I agree," she said. "But even worse is when that threat is leveled against the helpless and powerless."

Hunter snorted. "We're all helpless, Sibyl of the *Fyrantha*. None of us came here of our own will or purpose. We're all slaves."

"But at least you have weapons and strength with which to fight," Nicole pointed out, nodding back over her shoulder at the guard still standing there with his halberd. "Others aren't nearly so—"

"You call *these* weapons?" Hunter spat. "These pathetic axe-spears? Phaw. The flash-flickers that we were given before—*those* were true weapons."

"Others aren't nearly so lucky," Nicole continued doggedly, wondering if Hunter's flash-flickers were the greenfire guns she and Bungie had seen. She wondered briefly what had happened to them, decided that for the moment she didn't give a damn about either question. "The Micawnwi women and children over there are being starved."

Hunter snorted again. "And you think their lack of food makes them unique? We, too, have just enough food for our own nourishment."

"I was told there's more in the stone building on your side of the arena," Nicole said.

"You were told correctly," Hunter agreed. "That supply is why we have enough for ourselves. Were we to lose it, the dispenser here in these rooms would have much of its supply cut off."

"Wait a second," Nicole said, trying to figure this out. "You have enough food in *here*? You don't even need the dispenser in the stone building?"

"Of course we do," Hunter said. "Weren't you listening? We must control the bastion or the room dispenser's flow will be cut off."

"So you don't actually need the other dispenser," Nicole persisted. Apparently the Masters had set things up so that the defenders never had to worry about food as long as they held on to the stone building.

But if they didn't need the food . . . "Would you consider just *giving* some of it to the Micawnwi, then?" she asked. "As long as you control the building, that should still be within the rules. Right?"

Hunter gave another snort. "And so again you seek to trick and destroy us," he said. "Or do you seriously think the Masters will be so easily fooled?"

"I'm not trying to trick—"

"Let me explain the realities of this place to you, Sibyl of the *Fyrantha*," he cut her off harshly. "We had to fight—to fight and to die—for what we have. The legged-snake creatures we were forced to battle defended the bastion with determination, and it was only through great energy and loss that we captured the bastion and drove them from the arena. You think we should then risk our lives again by meekly *giving* it to our enemies? What advantage would such a reckless act gain us?"

"Maybe stop the killing?" Nicole shot back. "They might not *be* your enemies if they had enough to eat."

"Or they might use the extra food and time to build their strength at the cost of our own," Hunter said. "No, Sibyl. If they're the strongest, they'll ultimately prevail. That's the way of the universe. We would be fools to voluntarily aid them in those efforts."

From one of the rooms came a voice. Nicole frowned, straining her ears—"This is the Oracle," the voice said. "Hunter of the Cluufes, I would speak with you."

Nicole felt her throat go dry. Time to get the hell out of here. "I understand and accept your position," she said. "I simply thought the subject worth bringing up."

"Hunter of the Cluufes?" the Oracle called again.

"And I thank you for your time," Nicole continued, raising her voice to try to cover up the Oracle's. "I'll be on my way."

Without waiting for his permission, she turned and strode back across the room. The guard, still standing in the doorway, looked questioningly over her shoulder at Hunter as she approached. Then, to her relief, he stepped aside. She passed him and headed out the door, wanting to look back and see what Hunter was doing but afraid that such a look might warn him that something was wrong.

She hit the stone path and lengthened her stride, trying to speed up without looking like she was hurrying. Her throat was tight with anticipation of an angry shout from behind her, her back tingling with the thought of the guard and his sharp-tipped halberd.

Just ahead, the path curved around a clump of trees. Nicole rounded the trees, putting herself temporarily out of sight of the Cluufe door—

And broke into a flat-out run, her feet pounding along the

stones, her sleeves brushing the edges of bushes and low-hanging tree branches as she raced along. She sprinted past a dirt trail heading off into the hills to her right, and she wondered briefly if that was one of the routes the Cluufes used to go up one of the craggy ridges to spy on the Micawnwi. If it was, and if there were any of them still up there, at least now they could only come out behind her instead of cutting her off from in front.

Twenty yards ahead, the stone path split in two, giving her a choice of angling to the left or to the right. She eyed the split, trying to figure out which would be more likely to take her where she wanted to go.

An instant later she nearly fell as a warbling scream erupted from somewhere far behind her, the sound sending a jolt through her muscles that briefly knocked her off balance. She was still trying to get her feet back under control when an answering call came from the distance ahead and a little to her left.

So they were on two sides of her. But at least now she knew which way she needed to go. The scream from ahead and left must have come from the stone building, which the Cluufes would have heavily guarded. The right-hand path must therefore lead away from the building, hopefully over the hills toward her usual arena door. She shot a quick look over her shoulder, wondering if Hunter or the guard had taken up pursuit—

And suddenly she toppled to the ground, her hands barely making it up in time to break her fall, her right ankle blazing with pain.

I've been shot! was her first, horrified thought as she sprawled among the tall grass and matting of dead leaves, the stabbing pain in her leg now joined by a throbbing in her chest and both wrists. Shoving herself back up onto hands and knees, wincing as more alien screams rippled back and forth on both sides of her, she frantically clawed her way to the nearest bush. She got behind it, realized belatedly that it gave her no cover whatsoever, and kept going. A couple of yards farther ahead was a line of bushes with tendril-like branches that shot up from the center and then flowed out and down like frozen bluish-purple spray from a fountain. She fought her way through the grass to the edge of the line, slipped between two of the bushes, and collapsed behind them onto her side. Curling up like a baby, she gripped her ankle, trying not to groan with the pain.

At least there was no arrow sticking out of her leg. That was something. There was no one charging in pursuit, either, at least no one that she could see as she peered back at the path through small gaps in the tendrils. The screaming had stopped—did that mean they'd given up?

She peered back at the path, realizing now what had happened. The flat stones of the walkway were slightly elevated above the ground on either side. Not much, no more than an inch or so. But it had been enough. With her balance already thrown off by her reaction to the Cluufe screams, her stupidity in looking behind her while she was running had landed her foot on the edge of the stones and twisted her ankle.

She clenched her teeth, gripping the throbbing ankle a little tighter. Was it broken? That was the big question. Jeff had told her how food was withheld when someone couldn't work, and even with crutches she might not be able to hobble to the team's work sites fast enough to qualify as doing her job. A sprain wouldn't be as bad as a break, but she might still find herself facing a day or two of not eating.

Assuming, of course, that she even made it back to the hive. If she got caught by the Cluufes, there was no telling what would happen to her.

She shifted her attention from the main path and her ankle

to the right-hand path she'd been aiming for before her accident. It was only a few yards ahead, and partially shielded from view by more bushes and tall grass. It had looked reasonably smooth—if she could get to it, she might be able to crawl along it and get the hell out of here.

In fact, crawling might be better than running. It would be slower, but staying low would make her harder for the Cluufes to spot.

Even more encouraging was the fact that the pain in her ankle was starting to fade. Maybe she hadn't done anything more serious than twist it. A nice, careful crawl out of the Cluufe area, then back up on her feet for better speed, and she might just make it. Unwrapping her hands from her ankle, she began slowly shifting around in preparation for getting up onto her hands and knees.

And then, just visible through the foliage, Hunter and the guard with the halberd emerged from around a clump of trees, hurrying along the stone path.

Nicole froze, silently cursing herself. Ankle or no ankle, pain or no pain, she should have hit that branching path the second she'd gone off the main one. Going to ground never worked for long—she'd seen way too many guys get nailed because they'd tried to hide and wait out a chase.

If it was the cops chasing them, they usually ended up in jail. If it was a rival gang, they usually ended up dead. Nicole still didn't know which of those categories the Cluufes fit into.

But there might still be a chance. If Hunter and the other Cluufe turned left at the fork and headed for the stone building, she might be able to get onto the other path before they realized she hadn't gone that way and turned back. The two Cluufes reached the fork.

And, of course, came to a stop.

Nicole mouthed another curse, watching as the two aliens looked around. Were they just going to stand there, trying to sort out which way to go?

Raising his head, Hunter called something. "Wishsinger?"

There was a pause. Nicole frowned—

And then, from along the right-hand path, the one she'd just been about to crawl onto, came a soft voice. "No one came this way," the translation came. "Shall I continue to watch?"

"No need," Hunter said. "If she didn't pass you, she didn't go that way. You'd have heard her running through the grass. Did you hear any noise at all?"

"I heard movement a few moments ago. Would that have been you?"

"It might have," Hunter said. "Or she could have passed on the other path. We'll continue to the bastion—with luck, we may trap her between our forces."

"Do I return to my watch duty, then?" the other Cluufe asked.

The guard beside Hunter touched his arm. "She may have left the path and doubled back," he warned. "If so, she may yet escape."

"She seeks food for the enemy," Hunter said firmly. "She'll have gone to the bastion to try to get it."

"Or the Masters may have taken her away by methods of their own."

"In which case all is futile anyway," Hunter snapped. "But until that's been proved, we'll act as if she may still be caught." He gestured toward the path. "Wishsinger, return to the stronghold and watch the large door, just in case Listmaker is right."

"Understood." There was a swishing of branches, and a Cluufe appeared, marching quickly down the right-hand path. He passed Hunter and the guard with a nod and hurried back toward the

Cluufes' hive. Hunter took another look around, then turned down the left-hand path, with the guard Listmaker following.

A moment later, Nicole was once again alone.

Without a single clue as to what the hell she was going to do.

She couldn't go back, even if she wanted to. Wishsinger would see to that. She couldn't go down the left-hand path, not with Hunter and Listmaker and whoever was at the stone building in that direction. That left only the right-hand path, the one she'd originally intended to take.

But did she dare risk it? One Cluufe had already come down from the hills and stone ridges. What if there were more? What if *that* was the route to their spy position above Micawnwi territory, not the path she'd passed earlier?

If so, there was a good chance that going that way would run her straight into their arms. She shifted position, wondering how far she could see up the path.

As she did so, her hand came down on something hard and cold.

She frowned, looking down. There was something just visible beneath the grass and matted leaves. Something dark gray, smooth, and metallic.

A lost weapon?

Carefully, she brushed away some of the leaves and grass. The metal didn't seem to have any kind of edge anywhere on it, like a knife or the axe part of the halberd. It was long and straight, but not round like the shaft of a spear. She tried to dig beneath it, but her probing fingers felt only cold flatness all the way down to the ground.

And then, abruptly, it clicked. It was crazy, but she'd seen way crazier things aboard the *Fyrantha* already.

She ran her fingers under the matted leaves, searching to both sides. There it was: a second line of metal, identical to the first one and running parallel to it about a foot away.

They weren't weapons. They were rails.

Sometime in the past, before the arena became an alien killing ground, there'd been some sort of *train* running through here.

She raised her eyes, tracking along the half-hidden rails. She hadn't noticed it before, but the bush whose flowing tendrils she was hiding beneath was just one of a whole line of the things. To her left they curved around the back side of the clump of trees she'd passed just outside the Cluufes' hive; to her right they rose upward, angling off toward a little dip between two of the larger hills. Midway to the hills, it also looked like there might be a place where the rails branched off to the left, possibly toward the stone building.

And with a surge of cautious hope, Nicole realized that the bushes provided a sort of covered tunnel for the rails. A tunnel that she could crawl through without being seen.

She had no idea how far the tracks ran, or whether they would even take her in the right direction. But for the moment, getting as far away from Cluufe territory as she could was enough of a plan. Easing up onto her hands and knees, wincing at the pain in her twisted ankle, she started crawling.

The trek was grueling. The tracks started out running more or less level, rising only slowly as they went through the low spot between the hills. But just beyond that they began to rise more steeply, not as steeply as the hills around them, but steeply enough to bring out fresh sweat on Nicole's forehead as she worked her way up the slope. Many of the dead leaves covering the ground were rough-edged and dug into the skin of her palms as she moved, leaving little indentations until she finally learned how to recognize and avoid them. Some of the grasses had edges that caught on the sleeves of her jumpsuit, and with her posture keeping her face aimed mostly toward the ground she continually worried that she would hit a low-hanging branch.

But at least the leaves and grass didn't crackle as she crawled through them, and there were no insects or spiderwebs she had to crawl through. It could have been a lot worse.

She didn't know how far she crawled, but it was only a few minutes before the tracks abruptly stopped, disappearing into a solid chunk of bare rock at the base of one of the jagged ridges. Nicole puzzled at it a moment, decided there must be a hidden door there, and spent a couple of minutes trying to find a catch or release that would open it. But there was nothing she could find. Dead end.

But at least she'd made it out of sight of the main Cluufe territory. Shifting into a sitting position against the cliff face, she massaged her sore ankle and looked around.

She was higher than she'd realized, though not as high as the tallest hills and certainly not as tall as the ridges and rock spires. She couldn't see anyone moving within her field of view, though with all the trees and other cover around her that didn't mean much.

More importantly, as she cautiously craned her neck above the branches she discovered the Door Three exit she was trying for was visible in the distance at the far end of the arena. Even better, she could see more bushes like the ones she'd just been following leading down in that general direction. If there was another set of tracks over there, she might be able to cover much of the remaining distance without being seen.

She was taking a closer look at the area, trying to figure out the best way to get to the line of bushes, when a figure came into sight around one of the hills, walking swiftly toward Door Three. A large, shiny figure.

The Masters' emissary.

Nicole clenched her teeth. So much for all her climbing and crawling and pain. She should have realized right from the start that he would head for that door as soon as he realized she'd escaped from both the Micawnwi and the Cluufes. She should also have realized that, without any need to hide or skulk around, he would reach the door long before she did.

And with that, the whole stupid game came crashing to a halt. Once he reached the door all he had to do was settle in and wait. That would leave Nicole with exactly two options: come out and surrender, or join Mispacch and her children in starving to death.

Still, there might be a way for her to wiggle out from under the worst of it. If she could come up with the right kind of story— probably something that made her look stupid, oblivious, or ditzy— the Masters might be persuaded that she wasn't up to anything sinister. If so, maybe they'd settle for some mild punishment, or even just a stern warning.

The armored figure reached the door and stopped. His first task, naturally, was to stoop over and remove the screwdriver Nicole had wedged into the opening, then pull the door all the way closed. For another moment he continued to face the door, doing something Nicole couldn't make out from her distance.

And then, to her surprise, he turned and strode briskly away along the arena's far wall, heading back toward the stone building and Cluufe territory.

Nicole frowned. The screwdriver alone should have showed him that she'd come in that way. Was he really going to be content with simply locking the door again? Especially when she'd already demonstrated she could open the thing?

Unless she *couldn't* open it anymore. Unless he'd just changed the keylock code.

She sighed. That had to be it. He'd changed the code, and

with her now securely trapped inside the arena he was off to find Hunter and the Cluufes and sic them on her.

But she might still have an ace up her sleeve. The *Fyrantha* had given her access once. Maybe it would do so again. Pulling out her inhaler, she took a whiff.

Nothing.

She chewed at her lip, watching as the emissary disappeared from view behind some trees. Earlier that morning, she hadn't gotten the keylock code until she was right beside the door. Maybe that was how it would work this time, too.

It would be risky, but she didn't see any other options. Giving her injured ankle one final squeeze, she got back up on her hands and knees and headed toward the other line of tunnel bushes.

There was indeed another set of train tracks hidden beneath them. They were buried a little deeper in leaves and grass than the first set, which made them a bit harder to follow but also lowered the risk of banging her knee on one or the other rail as she crawled along them. It was, she decided, a fair enough trade-off.

She passed two splits in the tracks along the way, one set heading back toward the Micawnwi hive, the other angling in the direction of the stone building. Each time, she made sure to pick the branch heading closest to the exit.

A few minutes later she reached the end of the rails and the bushes, and found herself no more than twenty yards from the door.

For a minute she crouched beneath the last bush, testing the tenderness of her ankle and wondering if the joint was up to a mad dash across the mostly open ground between her and safety. It was also entirely possible that the emissary had returned and was watching from cover, either alone or having brought a few Cluufes along to keep him company.

Whatever the situation, there was nothing to be gained by waiting. She pulled out her inhaler and tucked it into her palm where it would be ready. Then, taking a deep breath, she lurched to her feet. A burst of fresh pain shot up her leg as she put her weight on it, but the ankle held. Hobbling as quickly as she could, she made for the door.

There were no shouts of anger or triumph. Even better, there were no arrows or thrown halberds. She reached the door, throwing one hand up against the metal to brace herself and taking a good jolt from the inhaler with the other.

Exit the arena with the code three-four-nine-two-seven-six-one.

So he *had* changed it. Clenching her teeth, hoping the *Fyrantha* hadn't screwed this one up, she punched in the numbers.

And with the most gratifying sound she'd heard that day, the lock snicked open. Gasping out an unexpected sob of relief, she threw her full weight against the door.

Ten seconds later, she was back on her side of the ship, with the arena door once again closed behind her.

For a minute she leaned against the metal, shaking with reaction. Only now did it suddenly occur to her that if the Masters were smart they would have planted someone outside each of the arena's doors where they could capture her with ease.

But the hallway was deserted. Either her break for freedom had been faster than they'd expected, or else the Masters weren't very bright.

Either way, luck like this never hung around for long. She cleaned herself off as best she could—luckily, the dirt along the tracks had been dry, and it and the bits of leaves and grass were easy to brush off—and started limping down the hallway. Time to find Carp and the work crew.

And to come up with a good story as to where she'd been all morning and how she'd turned herself into a walking basket case.

There was a slim chance that they hadn't actually missed her, in which case all she would need to explain was her ankle. Or, if she was really lucky, hide the fact that anything at all had happened.

She reached the first cross-corridor and looked down it. No one. She continued to the next, trying to work out the best way back to their current work sites. The next corridor, she decided, and then the first right-hand turn off of that one.

She reached the corridor and turned into it, wincing with each step. No way she was going to hide this, she realized now. She'd better come up with a good story, and fast. She reached her next turn and started around the corner.

"Nicole!" a voice snapped from behind her.

She jerked and spun around toward the shout. Or rather, she tried to turn. Midway through it her bad ankle collapsed beneath her, sending her sprawling onto the floor. Through the sudden haze of fresh pain she saw Levi running up—"I found her!" he called, his booming voice hammering into her ears. "Carp?"

He dropped to his knees beside her, curving his arm around behind her shoulders to support her. "You all right?" he asked, his face taut as he looked her up and down. "My God, girl. What did you do to your head?"

"I was . . ." Nicole trailed off, letting her eyes drift away from him and putting some confusion on her face. With her attention focused on Hunter and the Cluufes, not to mention her twisted ankle, she'd completely forgotten about the double bump she'd taken to her head.

And that bump might be exactly what she needed to get out of this. Sometimes, if you could pull it off, the best story was no story at all. "I was heading to the hive, to the doctor," she said slowly, looking around the corridor as if seeing it for the first time. "Then . . ." She trailed off again.

There was the sound of running footsteps, and suddenly Carp and Jeff were towering over Levi, gazing down at her. Carp looked angry, his irritation visibly changing to concern as he spotted the knot on her forehead. Jeff just looked worried. "*There* you are," Carp growled. "Where the hell have you *been*? We've been looking all over the damn ship for you."

"I was . . ." Nicole started to point toward one of the doors lining the corridor, then paused and looked back and forth. "I don't know," she said. "It was . . . it was a room. I'm sure it was a room."

"Damn," Carp said under his breath. "It can't be this soon. It's *never* this soon."

"Everyone's different," Levi said, his face and voice grim. "But she might pull out of it. Kuri did—remember?"

"Yeah. Maybe." Carp's nose wrinkled. "We need to get her to the doctor. And make sure she *gets* there this time."

"I'll take her," Jeff volunteered, stepping to Nicole's side and crouching down. "Can you walk, Nicole? I can carry you if you can't."

"No, I can walk," Nicole assured him. "I—Ow!" She broke off, peering down her leg. "What happened to my ankle?"

"Feels swollen," Jeff said, touching her bad ankle carefully. "Maybe you twisted it and fell and hit your head. Maybe it's not—"

"That's for the doc to figure out," Carp cut him off. "You need any help?"

"I don't think so," Jeff said, helping Nicole to her feet and slipping his arm around her waist. "Lean on me. As much as you want."

Nicole tried it. He was stronger than she'd realized. She leaned a little more, grateful to get her weight off that ankle. "Is this too much?" she asked.

"No, it's fine," Jeff assured her. "We're okay, Carp. I've got it."

"Then get out of here," Carp ordered. "Hold it—wait a second."

Maneuvering around Jeff's arm, he slipped Nicole's vest off her shoulders. "It's past lunchtime," he said, checking that the food bars and water bottles were still secure in their pockets. "Okay, get going. And let me know what the doc says."

eleven

Nicole had hoped that Allyce would be on duty at the med center. Unfortunately, Sam turned out to be the doctor on call.

And the doctor wasn't happy with her at all.

"Tripped and hit your head, like hell," he bit out as he carefully wrapped Nicole's ankle. "You went back into the arena, didn't you?"

Nicole threw a quick look at the door. But Jeff was already on his way back to the work site, and there was no reason for anyone else to be in this part of the hive right now. "You said Bungie had disappeared," she reminded him in a low voice, squeezing the edge of the table as a jolt of pain shot through her ankle. She was *not* going to gasp or cry or make any other sign of distress. Not in front of him. "I thought he might have gone inside."

"Had he?"

"Not that I ever found," Nicole admitted. "But it's a big place. He might have gone into hiding somewhere. It's possible he fell asleep and didn't hear what was happening."

Sam grunted. "What was happening, I gather, was you getting yourself beaten to a pulp. I hope you learned your lesson."

"What lesson is that?" Nicole countered. "That the next time I go in I should be better prepared?"

"That there'd better not *be* a next time," Sam shot back. "Whatever's going on in there is none of your business. Or mine, or anyone else's. Got it?"

Nicole looked away from him, glowering into a corner. He was right, of course. Whatever the Masters or Shipmasters or whoever were doing with the Micawnwi and Cluufes, it wasn't her job to get involved.

Especially since, judging from today's performance, it wasn't a job she was very good at. She'd do well to take a deep breath and just forget the whole thing.

Only she couldn't.

Mispacch and her children were starving. Amrew and his fellow dominants didn't seem to have a clue about how to get more food for them. Hunter and the Cluufes, in contrast, seemed calm and professional. They also seemed perfectly happy to let every last Micawnwi starve as long as they had plenty for themselves.

And on top of that, the *Fyrantha* had sent her in there. Practically ordered her to go, in fact. Nicole still had no idea why, but it had.

"What about Bungie?" she asked.

"What about him?" Sam countered. "Come on, he's fine. His injuries weren't life-threatening, and I patched them up properly. Wherever he is, he'll come back when he gets hungry or bored."

Nicole didn't answer. Especially since he was probably right.

Sam finished his work in silence, sealing her ankle inside something he called a pressure-retention cast, cleaning and dressing her two head injuries, then treating the abrasions, bruises, and scratches on her palms and knees where she'd crawled over the rails and through the undergrowth.

She could tell he was particularly intrigued by that last set of injuries, especially the tiny cuts she'd picked up from the dead leaves. But he didn't ask how she'd gotten them, and she wasn't in the mood to volunteer explanations.

Because no matter how hard she tried, she couldn't get the images of Mispacch's children out of her brain.

It was maddening. She didn't want those faces in her mind, staring up at her with hope or desperation or whatever the hell emotions their alien minds had been generating. Sam was right: what was happening to them wasn't her problem.

Not only was it exasperating, it was also mystifying. She'd seen plenty of hopeless children on the streets of Philadelphia, and she hadn't lifted a finger to do anything for them. Why was she suddenly feeling pity for these kids who weren't even her same species? Because their mother had graciously not squashed Nicole like a bug when she'd had the chance? Because they'd said please so nicely?

Or was it because there might actually *be* something she could do to help them?

"Finished."

With a start, Nicole dragged her thoughts back from her broodings. Sam had finished with her hands and was collecting his equipment together. "You'll want to use those for the rest of the day," he went on, nodding toward a pair of crutches resting against the other side of the table. Nicole frowned—she hadn't even noticed him getting them out of storage. "But you shouldn't need them after tonight. It's only a strain, should be fully healed in a day or so."

"Thanks." Nicole got a grip on the crutches and hauled them over to her side. They were much lighter than she'd expected. Certainly lighter than the weapons the Micawnwi had been trying so hard to figure out. "You said that thing Bungie brought back was a halberd, right?" she asked. "What do you know about them?"

Sam gave her an odd look. "What do you mean, what do I know?"

"Function," Nicole said, silently cursing herself. Why was she even bringing this up? "How do you fight with them?"

Sam snorted. "How should *I* know? Do I look like a Renaissance Fair weirdo?"

There were a dozen possible ways to respond to a question like that. Nicole resisted all of them. "I just thought that since you knew what they were you might know how to use them," she said instead.

"I know what they are because my brother had a book on weapons and armor when we were growing up," Sam said. "He liked the thought of breaking things. I liked the thought of fixing things. End of story. Now, stop talking nonsense and hobble back to your room."

"I'd rather go see how the team is doing," Nicole said stiffly. He could at least *try* to be cooperative.

"Then hobble back to your team, I don't care," he said, turning his back on her as he returned the unused bandages to their drawers. "Go anywhere you want. Just go."

A dozen retorts flashed into Nicole's mind. Again, she choked them back. Setting the crutches under her arms, she swung her awkward way across the room and out into the hall.

And nearly ran straight into Jeff. "Whoa!" he warned, catching her shoulders in a steadying grip. "Easy, there."

"Sorry," Nicole apologized, taking a moment to get her balance back. "What are you doing here? I thought you were back with Carp."

"I was." He let go of her shoulders and pulled a food bar and bottle of water from his vest pockets. "I just realized you never got any lunch. Thought you might be hungry."

"Oh. Right. Thanks." Nicole shifted her grip and her crutches and reached out a hand.

"That's okay—I can carry them," Jeff said. "And no, you're not going back to the work site. We've got enough to do for today, and you need to get off that ankle. Your room. Now."

"Yes, Doctor," Nicole murmured, starting up her awkward walk again. "How long were you standing there listening to us?"

"Not long," Jeff assured her. "Sam can be touchy sometimes, and I didn't want to interrupt. So what's this about halberds?"

Nicole felt her breath catch. He'd heard that part too? "What?" she asked.

"I heard you and Sam talking about halberds," Jeff said. "That's a medieval weapon that combines a spear and an axe, right?"

"Right," Nicole said cautiously. "You know about them?"

"A little." He grinned suddenly. "I was one of those Ren Fair weirdos Sam mentioned. Or my girlfriend at the time was. She liked the pretty dress-up stuff. I was mostly interested in seeing how the combat lined up with my martial arts training. And the open-fire barbecues, too. Those were really good."

"You did martial arts?" Nicole asked, frowning. He'd never mentioned anything like that before. "You mean like karate and stuff?"

"Not karate per se," he said. "It was an Okinawan system that taught both unarmed combat and the use of weapons—bo staffs, sais, and a few others. The weapons part was what I was mostly interested in."

"And you used halberds?" Nicole asked, trying to sort through the unrecognizable words.

"Oh, no, our stuff was a lot different," he said. "But some of the staff forms could probably be adapted to halberds. A lot of the moves are more for sweeping and deflection, though there's also stabbing involved." He waved a hand. "Plato doesn't like us talking about this stuff, by the way, so don't tell him."

"Not a word," Nicole promised, chewing at her lip. She had no idea whether the Cluufes or the Micawnwi were better fighters. But throwing a few new moves into the Micawnwi side of the mix might be exactly what Amrew and his crew needed.

Of course, the best solution would be to get the food dispenser fixed. But there was no guarantee Nicole would be able to get back there without getting caught, or that the Masters wouldn't unfix anything she did.

In fact, she might not even be able to get to the door on that side of the arena anymore. Depending on how mad the Masters' emissary had been at her disappearance, she might find that door blocked by a bunch of very hostile Micawnwi.

Offering to teach them some new fighting moves might buy her way to the door. And even if she couldn't fix the dispenser, those new moves might let them push the Cluufes back long enough to get the extra food the children needed.

Neither of those options struck her as all that good. But if she could get one of them to work, the Micawnwi would at least have gained a little time. "Do you think you could show me some of the techniques?" she asked.

"You have a spare bo staff lying around?" Jeff asked dryly.

"No," Nicole admitted, wondering briefly what he would say if she told him that there *was* a spare halberd lying around the *Fyrantha*. "How about one of these crutches?"

"They're pretty short," Jeff said, eyeing the crutches dubiously. "But I guess I could at least show you the principles. Not out here, though—if Plato caught us there'd be hell to pay."

"Well, I've been sent to my room anyway," Nicole pointed out. "Not a lot of space in there, but we could try." She frowned. "Only you're supposed to go back to work, aren't you?"

"Eventually," he said. "But not until Levi misses me. I can certainly spare you a couple of minutes."

He was as good as his word, a rare quality among Nicole's usual circle of acquaintances. He got her settled on her bed, comfortably propped up against all of her pillows, then spent five minutes showing her a couple of routines he called katas before excusing himself and heading back to rejoin the crew.

But those five minutes were enough. The dizzying display of spins, jabs, and sweeps clearly showed that there was a lot more that could be done with sticks than just spearing and axing. If she could teach the Micawnwi some of those moves, they might be able to counter the Cluufes' extra speed and agility.

If she could teach the tricks. And *if* she could first learn them herself.

She spent a few minutes after Jeff's departure trying to do just that. But it was quickly clear that the maneuvers were harder to do than they were to watch.

But that was all right. Once the workday was over, she would get Jeff to teach her the most useful of the techniques. Then, in a day or so when her ankle was healed, she would go back into the arena and give the same lessons to Amrew and the other Micawnwi men.

If she could do that, or figure out how to fix the feeder—or both—she'd have done everything she could. Maybe then she'd finally be able to get Mispacch's kids' faces out of her mind.

Even if that was all she accomplished, it would be worth it.

Nicole had expected it to be easy to get Jeff to come to her room after dinner. Surprisingly, it wasn't. In fact, it was like he'd been expecting her to ask, because he had a whole set of excuses already prepared as to why he couldn't.

It was an impressive list. It started with what the others would say if the two of them went off somewhere together, then moved on to what *Bungie* would say if he found out they'd gone off somewhere together, and finally ended up at the tired argument of whether a nice girl like her should even be learning about nasty things like weapons in the first place.

The whole thing reeked of Plato, though how he'd found out about the afternoon weapons demonstration she couldn't guess. Apparently, Plato's no-fighting policy extended to even fake fighting like weapons practice.

Unfortunately for Jeff, Nicole had her mind made up. She countered each of his arguments with one of her own, making sure to tag each of them with Jeff's half-buried affection for her as a crewmate and as a woman, along with his overall dislike of Bungie. She eventually clinched the deal by pointing out that Bungie's temper and responses were unpredictable, and that until her ankle was fully back to normal she needed a way to protect herself in case he got violent when no one else was around.

Sam had said her ankle would be mostly healed within a day, and she guessed Bungie wouldn't surface again until long after that. But Jeff didn't know the latter, and probably wasn't thinking about the former.

By the time he left her room that evening, Nicole had the basics of stick fighting under her belt. She wasn't good enough to actually take on an opponent, and her footwork was still pretty shaky, but hopefully she would be able to teach the Micawnwi some of the techniques.

The only question left was when she could get back to the arena and do that.

By morning, that last question had answered itself. Her ankle seemed back to normal, and though she treated it with extra care as she moved around her room, it remained strong and pain-free. She would take the crutches along today just in case, but even without them she should be able to get across the arena to the Micawnwi hive. All she had to do was give Carp an excuse that would let her disappear for a couple of hours, and she would have done everything for Mispacch and her children that she could.

Getting away from the work crew turned out to be the easiest part of the whole thing. She got Carp and the others started on their tasks, and as they set to work she made a few twitchy movements with her leg, a couple of barely audible grunts, and an occasional grimace. Five minutes into her performance Levi noticed one of the grimaces, called Carp's attention to her obvious pain, and together they agreed she should go back to her room and rest.

Nicole gamely argued the order, just not very hard. Three minutes later she'd been relieved of her lunch-supply vest—minus the inhaler, which she'd already tucked into one of her jumpsuit pockets—and was lurching her crutch-assisted way back toward the hive. She made it out of their sight and, just to be on the safe side, continued on toward the hive for another half minute. At the next convenient cross-corridor, she turned toward the portside hull hallway and headed for the arena.

She had expected to find that the Masters had changed the keylock code on the door since her escape the previous afternoon. But the code was unchanged. A minute later, she was walking through the undergrowth toward the Micawnwi hive, her crutches tucked under one arm, watching her footing carefully to make sure she didn't reinjure her ankle with another bad step.

Fortunately, the ankle held, and after a short walk she reached the first section of stone-covered pathway. With safer ground beneath her she picked up her pace, making sure this time to stay clear of the path's edges.

She was nearly there when the whole crowd of Micawnwi strode into view from around the last hill. Three of them carried bows and quivers, the latter almost comically oversized given that each had only one or two arrows rattling around in it. The rest of the men carried halberds.

Nicole stopped short, her first panicky thought being that the Masters had alerted Amrew and sent them after her. A second later, she saw Amrew jerk as he caught his first glimpse of her. Clearly, he was as surprised by the meeting as she was.

Trake had always said that the way to take charge of a meeting was to get in the first word. Under the circumstances, it seemed worth trying. "Hello, Amrew," she called. "I've come to help you."

Amrew didn't answer. Probably waiting until they got closer, Nicole decided, and he didn't have to shout. She continued on toward them, eyeing their halberds and belatedly wondering if Jeff's techniques would work as well with that heavy axe head at one end.

She got to within ten feet of the crowd, and was starting to wonder if they were simply going to plow straight over her, when Amrew finally came to a halt. "Why are you here?" he demanded.

"I came to see if I could help," Nicole said. "I have some special techniques for fighting that you—"

"No," Amrew said flatly.

Nicole blinked. "What do you mean, no?" she asked. "Look, if this is because I bailed when the Oracle told you to—"

"We don't need your help," he said, again cutting her off in midsentence. "Nor do we want it. We'll rise and fall on our own strength and courage."

"If by *fall* you mean the Cluufes will cut you into roadkill, yes, you probably will," Nicole retorted. "Are you seriously saying you'd rather die than accept help from someone who's not a Micawnwi?"

Amrew made a sort of squawking sound. "We will rise and fall on our own," he repeated. "We don't need the help of a woman."

Before Nicole could even find a response for that one, Amrew hunched one shoulder and strode past her. The other men followed, passing around her on both sides. Nicole turned, watching in disbelief as they continued on down the path. Of all the stubborn, *stupid*—

"They won't listen."

Nicole turned back. Mispacch was standing just in view at the side of the hill, her two children clutched to her sides. Even since just yesterday the two smaller Micawnwi seemed to have gotten thinner. Probably her imagination. "They're fools," she told Mispacch.

"We do as we've always done," Mispacch said. "That's the way of all life. The path is found that seems best, then is faithfully followed."

"That's nice," Nicole said sarcastically as she walked up to the three Micawnwi. "Only this particular path is going to get them all killed."

"You don't know that," Mispacch said. "They're very strong. With hand weapons, strength can be the deciding factor."

"Maybe," Nicole said. Mispacch could be right, she supposed. Based on the size difference alone, the Micawnwi were almost certainly stronger than the Cluufes.

But the Cluufes were fast. Did fast trump strong in this kind of fighting?

She didn't know. But right now, that wasn't her problem. She'd gotten within reach of the arena door, and all the men who might have stopped her were gone. Time to see what she could do with the food dispenser. "I guess we'll find out," she said, handing her crutches to Mispacch. "Here—hold these for me, will you? I'll be back in a minute."

She headed down the path toward Door One, going as fast as she dared. "Where are you going?" Mispacch called after her.

"Got an errand to run," Nicole said. "Just stay put."

She reached the door and punched in her code. Fortunately, it worked at this end of the arena, too. She pushed the door open and peeked out into the gray metal hallways beyond.

Once again, the place seemed deserted. She slipped through the opening, closed the door behind her, and headed for the room where she'd found the choke valve on the Micawnwi's food supply.

She was in the final corridor, within sight of her target door, when she heard the sudden clink of metal in the distance.

She froze, crouching against the nearest wall, her ears straining. There was another clink.

And then, almost too soft to hear, she heard voices.

Human voices.

A chill ran through her. Plato was the overseer for eight different work crews, and though each group lived in a different hive area and seldom mixed with the others, she'd seen several of them in passing. Certainly she'd met all the other Sibyls. Along the way, she'd also wormed enough information out of Carp and Kahkitah to get a feel for which areas and clusters of decks each of the crews was assigned to.

The problem was that all of those work areas were on Nicole's side of the arena, the impressively huge area she'd always assumed was most if not all of the *Fyrantha*. If the voices she was now hearing were from a repair crew, it seemed likely they were an entirely different group from the ones under Plato's control.

But that would imply there was enough area on this side of the arena to warrant basing another crew here. Maybe even more than one.

How many more people had the Wisps snatched and brought aboard, people that Plato never mentioned? Where were all of them, and who was running their crews?

How big *was* this ship, anyway?

She didn't know. But in the meantime, she had more important things on her mind. The distant voices didn't seem to be getting closer, which hopefully meant they weren't going to be a problem for her. Straightening up again, she hurried the rest of the way to the room and popped the door. Time to see if yesterday's trick had paid off.

It had. The nearly invisible touch of blood she'd put on the knob had rotated a tiny bit to the right. Assuming the Masters were still working their policy of slow starvation, that must be the direction that slowed down the food supply.

Smiling grimly, she turned the knob all the way the other direction.

The new bounty wouldn't last long, she knew. The minute the Masters checked the knob they would realize it had been messed with and would undoubtedly put it back. The Micawnwi needed to get what they could while the getting was good.

And with the men all off playing soldier, there was only one person who could do that.

Mispacch and her kids were waiting where Nicole had left them, each of the children holding one of the crutches, all three staring off in the direction the Micawnwi men had gone. "Okay," Nicole said as she came up to them. "The dispenser should give you some extra food now. It won't last, though, so you'll need—"

"What?" Mispacch interrupted, her fur flaring. "Extra food?"

"Right," Nicole said. "But the extra won't last more than a day—maybe only a few hours—so you need to get in there and pull out everything you can right now. Stockpile it away someplace where it'll be hidden. And *don't* talk while you're doing it— I'm pretty sure the Oracle can hear everything that goes on in that room, though I don't think it can see. Got it?"

"Yes," Mispacch said, her fur rapidly flaring and flattening. "Yes, I'll get the other women onto the task at once." She snatched the crutches from her children's hands and handed them to Nicole. "Here—I have to go. Thank you, thank you." Grabbing her children's hands, she loped back toward the Micawnwi hive.

Nicole let out her breath in a tired but contented sigh. And that was that. She'd now done everything she could for these people. Time to back off, put the whole thing out of her mind, and get on with her life.

She retraced her steps back to her end of the arena. She saw no sign of Amrew or the other Micawnwi men along the way, but she also didn't hear any shouts or other sounds of battle. Had they given up? Or were they just being cautious with their approach?

She'd cleared the final set of low hills, and was thirty yards from the exit, when she finally spotted them. They were lined up on the mostly flat area where she'd seen that first battle, the one with Hunter and the Cluufes and the greenfire guns on both sides. It was the only really level area in the arena, which might explain why everyone picked it to do their fighting.

Or else it was because this was the end with the stone building. If this hunger squeeze was the Masters' standard game, it made sense that the hungry group would always come to this end to attack, while the side that already had the stone building and its extra food dispenser would be fighting just as hard to keep it.

She hadn't paid much attention back in grade school, especially the history lessons. But she did vaguely remember something about the British having to walk in straight lines during the American Revolution while the colonists got to hide behind trees and rocks.

Apparently, the Micawnwi were big fans of the British approach.

Sure enough, as she peered at the trees and bushes in the distance she could see the shadowy forms of the Cluufes moving around outside the building. The Cluufes' archers would be somewhere in the area, too, maybe inside, where they'd have some cover from the attackers.

She refocused on the Micawnwi. Now that she thought about it, she realized that Amrew's three archers were nowhere to be seen. Had he sent them into the hills where they could shoot down on the Cluufes? That would make sense. In fact, she could see a couple of locations from here where a bowman would have the height and the cover from trees and bushes to avoid being instantly seen.

But that wasn't her concern. Luckily, she didn't seem to be the fighters' concern, either. She kept a wary eye on the looming battle as she made for her door, but neither side seemed to be paying any attention to her.

More importantly, neither side was shooting at her. So far, that was the best part.

Though now that she thought about it, Amrew's bowmen probably didn't have enough arrows to waste on her anyway. Distantly, she wondered if the Micawnwi had already shot off most of them, or whether the Masters were just as stingy with arrows as they were with food.

She'd punched in the keylock code and pushed the door partway open when, with a hoarse shout that her translator apparently couldn't handle, the line of Micawnwi lowered their halberds and charged.

Nicole paused, her hand braced against the door, staring with morbid fascination as the aliens raced through the grass, dodging bushes and grass clumps and warbling more untranslatable words. It was like seeing a bad car wreck about to happen, impossible to look away from even knowing it was going to be ugly.

The attackers were about twenty yards from the nearest Cluufes when there was a flicker of movement through the tree branches and three of the Micawnwi jerked and toppled to the ground, arrows now sticking out of them. Two of them were still alive, Nicole saw: one writhing in pain, the other gamely trying to lurch his way back to his feet. The third just lay there, unmoving, probably dead.

A second later there was an answering volley from up in the hills, right in the area Nicole had thought of as being a good shooting position. But if the Micawnwi arrows had any effect, she couldn't see it. Maybe the Cluufes' more stationary positions meant that their wounded or dead collapsed without any visible fuss. Maybe the Micawnwi archers had missed their targets. If Nicole had to bet, she would bet on the latter.

But if the Micawnwi didn't have much skill, they had courage to burn. The remaining attackers didn't even break stride at the loss of three of their number. They kept going, their halberds pointed ahead of them, converging on the stone building and the Cluufes crouching half-hidden there.

They were maybe ten yards from the building when a half dozen Cluufes rose out of concealment on both sides of the Micawnwi line and charged. The Micawnwi at those ends, clearly startled, turned to face this unexpected threat. At the same time, the Cluufes beside the stone building rose from their own positions, leveled their halberds, and charged the center of the Micawnwi line.

And the nice, neat battle line dissolved into chaos.

Still, it wasn't as badly one-sided as Nicole had expected. The Cluufes were definitely faster than the Micawnwi, darting back and forth and jabbing their halberds at the bigger aliens' torsos or legs. They seemed more skilled with the weapons, too. But as Nicole had already noted, the halberds were pretty heavy, which put a limit on how fast the Cluufes could make the long sticks change direction. The Micawnwi, while not as expert, could nevertheless whip the things around like they were extra-long broom handles.

And while a couple of fighters from both sides were already staggering back out of the battle with blood leaking from them, so far only the one Micawnwi who'd been shot seemed to have actually died. It was, Nicole guessed, going to be a long-drawn-out day.

Nothing to do with her. She took one final look and started to turn back to the door—

And jerked around again as a fast-moving object caught her eye. It was Mispacch, for once without her children, rounding the hill behind Nicole and racing across the level ground toward the raging battle.

"Mispacch!" Nicole shouted, reflexively gesturing even though the other now had her back to her. "What are you *doing*? Come back!"

"I have to stop them," Mispacch called over her shoulder, her voice barely audible above the clash of metal and the snarls and shrieks of the fighters. "We have food now. I have to stop them."

"But—" Nicole broke off with a curse. The extra food wouldn't last—she'd already said that. Hadn't Mispacch understood? "Get back," she shouted again, taking a step toward the alien woman. "You're going to get hurt."

"I have to stop them," Mispacch said again. "I have to try to save Amrew."

"Why, because he's the leader?" Nicole snarled.

"Because he's my life-mate."

Nicole felt her mouth drop open. Amrew was her husband? The same man who'd decided that she and her children should go without food so that he and his buddies could be comfortable was her *husband*?

And now she was charging into battle to try to *save* him?

Nicole drew her lips back in a snarl. *Damn* it all.

Throwing down her crutches, she headed toward the battle, pounding along the ground without the slightest consideration for her ankle. She'd seen this same insane thing played out over and over: traumatized girl sticking with abusive man, taking whatever garbage he dropped on her, never complaining, always making excuses for him. And then, if and when the cops or some rival finally took him down, crying her eyes out over what she'd lost.

That wasn't going to happen again. Not here. Not now.

Even with a touchy ankle Nicole was faster than the more lumbering Mispacch. But Mispacch had a good lead, and Nicole was still fifteen yards back by the time the Micawnwi reached the swirling chaos.

And it was only then, as Mispacch braked to a halt and began looking around for Amrew, that Nicole suddenly realized that she was about to charge into a fight without a weapon.

But Nicole could fix that. A few steps in front of her was the Micawnwi who'd been killed by the Cluufe archer. Lying in the grass beside him was his abandoned halberd.

Nicole had lugged one of the things down the *Fyrantha*'s hallways, and even after Jeff's instructions she had no illusions as to her chances of wielding it with even modest skill. But then, she wasn't planning on launching any real attacks. All she had to do was get far enough into the chaos to grab Mispacch and haul her out of there, by one leg if necessary. If she could wave the halberd around enough to keep everyone else back, that was all she needed.

Ahead, someone shrieked—Micawnwi or Cluufe, she couldn't tell which. The halberd was right ahead now, and she slowed to a halt, reached down toward it—

An instant later she let out a startled gasp as a pair of hands closed solidly around her upper arms.

Her first instinct was to kick at her attacker, slashing her foot backward as hard as she could. A second later she lurched and nearly fell forward as her kick connected with absolutely nothing. She flailed, trying to regain her balance, the hands clutching her arms the only thing that kept her from falling flat on her face. She twisted her head around to the right, wild thoughts of biting her attacker flashing through her mind—

"You little fool," Plato snarled as he yanked back on her arm, pulling her fully upright again. "Come on."

Nicole looked to her left. Jeff was on that side, holding her left arm, his face grim. Not as angry as Plato's, but angry enough. "What the hell are you doing?" she demanded.

"What the hell are *you* doing?" Plato countered. "I said come *on*."

Nicole tried to resist. But they were bigger and stronger, and there were two of them and only one of her. They spun her around and hauled her back through the grass toward the door.

They were nearly there when Plato suddenly pulled her close to him. "You went that direction by mistake," he murmured into her ear. "You didn't leave the arena because the painkillers from your accident got you all confused and you headed the wrong direction. Got it?"

Nicole frowned. "What?"

He gave her arm a sudden, hard shake. *"Got it?"*

"Okay, okay, I got it," Nicole said hastily, frightened in spite of herself. Mispacch going nuts she could understand. But *Plato*?

A second later they reached the doorway, and the two men pulled her through.

Standing silently in the middle of the long hallway—hell, *filling* the middle of the long hallway—was Fievj.

twelve

Nicole stopped short, her heart suddenly thudding as the big armored centaur gazed silently at the three of them. Dimly, she felt Plato and Jeff let go of her arms, and a moment later she heard the arena door close behind her.

Fievj still didn't move or speak. Out of the corner of her eye Nicole saw her two companions come alongside her, and cold metal brushed her right hand as Jeff handed her back her crutches. She closed her fingers around them, wondering briefly if she should put them back in position under her arms.

Not much point, really. Fievj had already seen that she was walking fine without them.

The silent figure finally stirred. "Leave us," he said. "I will speak with her alone."

Plato made as if to say something, looked at Nicole, and apparently changed his mind. He gestured, and he and Jeff gingerly walked past the centaur and headed down the hallway. As they turned the corner into a cross-corridor, Plato gave Nicole one last, lingering look.

And then they were gone. "Is there a problem?" Nicole asked, perversely deciding to once again get in the first word.

"You went inside the testing arena," Fievj said. "Why?"

"The *Fyrantha* told me to," Nicole said, wondering if she was pushing it to try that same excuse twice in a row. Surely there was a logbook or something Fievj could check to see what the ship was telling the Sibyls to do.

Apparently, there wasn't. "Tell me what it said," Fievj ordered.

Nicole shrugged, automatically slipping into liar mode. Rule one: Never tell a big lie when a small one would do. Rule two: Never add detail that wasn't asked for. "It told me there was a problem with the Micawnwi food supply and that I should go look into it."

"Did the ship also tell you to flee when the Oracle told the Micawnwi to keep you there until an emissary could arrive to speak with you?"

"The *Fyrantha* told me there was other work to be done," Nicole said, keeping her voice steady. Like every other lie she'd ever told, this one was already showing signs of digging her into a hole. "I'd seen that I couldn't fix the food dispenser, so I left."

"Even though the Oracle had ordered you not to leave?" Fievj demanded.

"I'm a Sibyl," Nicole said with as much dignity as she could manage. "I speak for the *Fyrantha,* and I answer only to it."

For a long moment the centaur gazed at her in silence. Nicole forced herself to look him straight in his blank faceplate, trying to ignore her pounding heart. "Why you?" he asked at last.

"Why me what?"

"Why did the *Fyrantha* send you into the testing arena?"

Nicole frowned. Hadn't she just answered that one? "I'm a Sibyl," she repeated. "I speak for the—"

"Why *you*?" Fievj cut her off. "Why not any of the hundreds of other Sibyls who've been called aboard?"

Nicole felt her stomach tighten. *Hundreds* of other Sibyls? "I don't know," she managed through suddenly stiff lips. How long had the Wisps been snatching people, anyway? "You'd have to ask the ship."

There was another long silence. "Before Plato and the other human went in you were running toward a battle," Fievj said. "Yet we were told humans don't fight. Explain your actions."

Plato's last tense whisper echoed through Nicole's brain. *Play stupid,* was what it had boiled down to.

And if she was going to play stupid, she might as well go all the way. "That was a *battle*?" she asked, putting some bewilderment into her voice. "I thought—Wait a second." She frowned in feigned concentration. "I saw Mispacch running toward some— I don't know what it was, but it was noisy."

"Yet you ran toward it?"

"I was a little confused," Nicole admitted. "I was feeling disoriented, and I asked her to show me to the door so I could get out and get to one of our doctors."

"How is it you were confused?"

"Probably the pain meds I was given." She had a sudden inspiration—"Maybe there was a bad reaction between them and the stuff in my inhaler. You hear about bad drug interactions on the news all the time. They're a big problem with humans."

Fievj held out a hand. "Your inhaler."

Nicole winced. So that he could check its contents and maybe run some tests with the painkillers and healing goo Sam had used on her? Probably.

And that wouldn't be good. Unfortunately, there wasn't a thing she could do about it. She could tell Fievj that she'd lost it, but a quick search of her pockets would quickly prove that false. "Drug interactions are different with different people," she warned as she pulled out the inhaler and dropped it into his outstretched hand. Up close, she could see that the armor plates on his hand and wrist were small and fitted intricately together, like one of the fancy mosaics she'd seen at that art gallery her grandmother had dragged her to when she was eight. "And be careful with that. I need it for my work."

"There are more," Fievj said, turning the inhaler over in his hand as if studying it. "Plato will get you another."

"Whatever," Nicole said. "Can I go now? I have work to do."

Fievj finished his examination and lowered his hand and the inhaler to his side. "You will first go to the medical center," he said. "The doctor there is ordered to isolate the cause of your disorientation. You'll tell him that."

"Yeah, I'm sure he'll be thrilled," Nicole said, trying not to sound too sarcastic.

"Yes, he should find the challenge intriguing," Fievj said. Apparently, human sarcasm was lost on him. "Go. I'll speak with you later." Turning around, he headed down the cross-corridor outside the arena door.

Let him go, a small voice urged from the back of Nicole's mind. *Just let him go. You're done with this.* She clenched her teeth— "What about the food dispenser?" she called after him.

Fievj stopped but didn't turn back to face her. "Explain."

"What about the Micawnwi food dispenser?" Nicole said, cursing herself for bringing this up again. "It's broken. It needs to be fixed."

"It's not broken," the centaur said. The horse's rear end was just more of the smooth metal, Nicole saw as she gazed down the corridor, with no sign of a tail. Odd that she hadn't noticed that before. "The only way for the Micawnwi to obtain more food is to fight the Cluufes for it."

He swiveled halfway around, his blank faceplate turning back toward her. "Do you care enough for their welfare to aid them in that battle?"

Nicole swallowed. *Damn,* but when was she going to learn to keep her mouth shut? "Why do they have to fight? I've been told the *Fyrantha* has plenty of food."

"They fight because those are the rules," Fievj said. "Do you wish to aid them in their battle for survival?"

"I don't think I can," Nicole said. "Besides, I have other work to do."

"You must make a choice," Fievj said. "You have two days."

"Two days?" Nicole asked, frowning. "Two days for what?"

"To choose whether to fight with the Micawnwi," the centaur said calmly, "or whether to allow them to starve." Turning away again, he resumed his four-footed march down the corridor.

Nicole felt her eyes widen. "Wait a second," she protested. "What kind of choice is *that*?"

Apparently, Fievj had said all he planned to for one day. He didn't even break stride as he continued along the corridor.

"Well, damn," Nicole murmured as she watched him go. *Now* what was she supposed to do?

"Nicole," a soft voice called from down the portside hallway.

Nicole turned. Plato was standing at the corner where he and Jeff had disappeared earlier. He beckoned urgently toward her, his head turned slightly as if he were listening for heavy centaur footsteps. With a final look at Fievj's receding back, Nicole headed toward him.

She arrived to find him alone. His face looked sweaty, she noticed uneasily, and his hands seemed to be rubbing restlessly along the leg of his jumpsuit. Something must seriously be bothering him. "Well?" he asked quietly, as if afraid Fievj would hear him.

"Well, what?" Nicole countered, peering behind him down the empty corridor. "Where's Jeff?"

"I sent him back to work," Plato said. "We *do* still have work to do, you know. What did the Shipmasters want?"

"So Fievj's one of the Shipmasters?" Nicole asked. "I thought he was with the Masters."

"They're the same group," Plato said shortly. "What do they want?"

Nicole shrugged. "The same thing you do: to tell them why I was in the arena."

Plato's lip twitched. "And?"

"I spun him the tale. He either went for it or he didn't—I don't know which. Oh, and he took my inhaler."

Plato frowned. "What for?"

"He didn't say," Nicole said. "Probably wants to run some tests. I told him my confusion might have been a drug interaction between it and the pain meds."

She expected a lecture for having gone off script that way. But he just nodded heavily. "As good an excuse as any," he said. "Let's pray that he accepts it."

"I can act more confused if I need to," Nicole offered. "Right now, that wouldn't be very hard. What the *hell* is going on?"

Plato snorted. "You already know more than is good for you," he said grimly. "More than is good for all of us. I told you once, and I'll tell you again: Do *not* go into the arena again. Ever. The lives of every man and woman aboard the *Fyrantha* depends on it."

With an effort, Nicole managed not to roll her eyes. Overblown melodrama was always the last resort of someone who couldn't win an argument on facts or logic. "You want me to stay out?" she asked. "Give me a good reason."

"I just gave you one," Plato said. "If you go in there again, we may all die."

"Right," Nicole said. "And if I *don't,* some of the people in there are *definitely* going to die. Women and children are going to starve to death."

"I know." Plato took a deep breath. "Don't take this wrong . . . but in all seriousness, let them. A few more lives—" He broke off. "Look. Humanity has a long history of fighting. Of warfare. But the Shipmasters can't know about that. They can never know about that."

"Why not?"

"Doesn't matter," Plato said. "Just believe me when I say that if they find out about our history the consequences will be devastating for everyone aboard. So don't go back in the arena. And for God's sake, don't *ever* get involved with their fighting."

"Even if they're going to die?"

"They're going to die anyway," Plato said harshly. "You can't stop that."

Nicole glared at him. But down deep, she knew he was right. She'd seen how the battle had been going, and there really was no way she could have influenced the outcome. Not without Bungie's gun or one of Hunter's old greenfire weapons to even out the odds.

"Come on," Plato said, closing his hand around her arm. "I'll take you back to the medical center. Allyce has gone to *tevenri*-twelve-sixteen to help with a big accident, but Sam should still be here. Let's find out what kind of mess you've made of your ankle this time."

Sam wasn't nearly as vehement on the subject of the arena as Plato was, or at least he didn't launch into Plato's ridiculous claim that everyone aboard was going to be slaughtered in their sleep if she so much as looked into the arena.

But he was still pretty firm.

"Plato's right," he told her as he carefully removed her pressure cast. "Whatever's going on in there, you don't want to mess with it. Weapons and fighting—not a good idea."

"Right," Nicole said sarcastically. "I don't know if you noticed, Doc, but you and I met across a gun. Weapons and fighting aren't exactly new to me."

"That was in Philadelphia, not a battle arena inside an alien-controlled spaceship," he pointed out. "The rules are completely different."

Nicole snorted. "Maybe there were rules in your part of town," she said acidly. "There weren't any where I lived."

"Of course there were," he said. "Every society has rules. Who was top dog in the neighborhood, who moved off the sidewalk for whom, how much a fence paid, what you told the cops when they came looking for someone you knew. Those are all rules."

"More like the law of the jungle."

"It's still rules." He nodded toward the front part of the ship. "They have rules in here, too. Only you don't know what they are. And you probably won't even know you've broken one until it's too late."

Nicole sighed. But like Plato, Sam was probably right. Besides, as she'd told herself over and over, what happened in there was none of her business. "Maybe," she said.

"No *maybe* about it." He waved at her ankle. "Lucky for you, your little adventure doesn't seem to have damaged any of my handiwork. You should stay off it the rest of the day, though."

"I think I can manage that," Nicole said, watching dully as he rewrapped the pressure cast around her ankle. Suddenly, she felt very tired. The morning's hectic activity had taken more out of her than she'd realized. "Can I go now?"

"Sure," Sam said. For a moment he gazed into her face, a slight frown creasing his forehead. Then the frown cleared, and he turned away. "Oh, and Plato said you need a new inhaler," he added. "I'll have one ready for you in the morning."

"Thanks." Carefully, Nicole eased her feet back onto the floor. Her crutches were resting against the table; with a moment's hesitation she took them and positioned them under her arms. "Might as well baby it for the rest of the day."

"Good idea," Sam said. "Go get some rest. I'll see you at dinner."

Nicole had planned to rest for only an hour or two, then go back to Carp and the others and stay with them until they finished.

It was with disbelief and chagrin that she awoke to find that the afternoon and most of the evening had slipped past, and that it was already three hours past dinnertime. Giving her face a quick splash of cold water to help her wake up, she hurried off to the dining room.

Some nights one group or another stayed after dinner, taking advantage of the tables and access to snacks for games or conversation. But this wasn't one of those nights. She arrived to find the room empty.

Except for one lone person still sitting at his favorite table away from the door.

"*There* you are," Jeff said cheerfully, looking up from the puzzle board he'd been working on and waving to her. "I was about to give up and head to my room."

"Yeah, sorry," Nicole said, looking over at the serving counter. All the trays were gone, but the automated equipment back there was always ready to mix up another meal. "I can't believe I slept that long."

"Sam said you might," Jeff said, getting to his feet and heading for the serving counter. "No, here—sit down. I'll get you some food."

"Thanks," Nicole said, changing direction and dropping into one of the chairs at his table. "How come you're still here?"

His back wrinkled in a shrug as he punched the keys on the serving control. "You haven't missed a meal since you came aboard," he said. "I thought you still might show up. And that you might want some company."

"Company's always nice," she agreed, frowning at his back. There was something in his tone that warned he wasn't just talking about making chitchat. "Anything else you had in mind?"

He turned back to face her. "I thought you might want to talk about what happened in the arena," he said bluntly. "And not just today."

Nicole pursed her lips. All things considered, Jeff had proved to be a pretty loyal friend. And Plato hadn't said she couldn't talk about it. "You want the whole story?" she asked.

"All of it," he assured her.

"Okay," she said. "Get comfortable. This could take a while."

She told him everything, from Bungie's first sloppy sabotage of the arena door all the way to where Jeff and Plato had charged in and pulled her away from that morning's battle.

Midway through her description of the greenfire guns, her meal arrived. Jeff set it silently in front of her, resumed his seat, and continued to listen.

The meal was long gone by the time she finally finished the story. "So," she said. "What do you think?"

He was silent for another few seconds. "I think there's something wrong with it," he said.

"The story?"

"The situation," he said. "Even if we assume this is someone's version of dogfighting or gladiator combat, it doesn't make sense. Where are the crowds who should be watching the carnage? Where's the line of people betting on the winner?"

"Probably somewhere out of the way where they won't get hurt," Nicole said. "They're not going to sit out there where they might get stabbed or shot. I mean, between the Cluufes, the Micawnwi, and whoever the Cluufes chased out a couple of weeks ago, we've already got at least three different alien groups the Shipmasters have been playing against each other. They must have their system pretty well locked down by now."

"Okay, that's reasonable," Jeff said. "But then where was the reaction when you suddenly charged into the middle of it?"

"I think that was what the emissary was for," Nicole reminded him. "The armored guy."

"That's the centaur, right?"

"No, Fievj is the centaur," Nicole said. "I meant the other one, the two-legged armored guy who came to the Micawnwi after I tried to fix their food dispenser."

"Oh, right. Him." Jeff shook his head. "I don't know. Maybe you're right. Maybe it's just a show for them. But they still seem way too casual about the whole thing."

"Maybe they haven't done anything because they haven't figured out what to do," Nicole suggested. "Fievj said I was the first Sibyl who the *Fyrantha* ever sent into the arena. This may be as new to them as it is to us."

She lifted a finger. "Which reminds me. Have you ever heard any numbers on how long the Wisps have been snatching people from Earth?"

"Not really," Jeff said. "Plato's been here fifteen or sixteen years, and I think that's the longest of anyone. Why?"

"Because Fievj said there'd been hundreds of Sibyls here," Nicole said. "I figured if we also knew how long they'd been doing this, we could get an idea of how many work crews were aboard."

"There are eight," Jeff said, frowning. "I thought you knew that."

"There are eight on *this* side of the arena," Nicole countered. "But there's at least one team on the other side. Maybe more."

"Hold on," Jeff said, frowning harder. "There's more ship past the arena? Are you sure?"

"I already said I got out of the Micawnwi hive on that side," Nicole reminded him.

"Yeah, I know," Jeff said. "I assumed you were just talking about a service corridor or something."

"Trust me, their portside hull corridor looked just as long as the one on our side," Nicole said. "If it is, the *Fyrantha* could be twice as big as we all thought it was. Even if it is, hundreds of Sibyls could mean they've been doing this for a hundred years. Maybe longer."

"Right," Jeff said, staring off into space. "But you're not going to get that number by counting Sibyls. There's the whole—" Abruptly, his eyes came back into focus. "Never mind."

"Never mind what?"

"Never mind counting the Sibyls," he said. "We'll ask Plato in the morning. Maybe he's heard the Shipmasters mention how long they've had Wisps raiding Earth for workers."

"Yeah, good idea," Nicole said, studying his face. There was definitely something he wasn't saying.

And judging from the speed at which he'd gotten off the subject of Sibyls, it was something he *really* didn't want to talk about.

But none of that resolve was going to help him now. Not when he had Nicole's curiosity aroused. Five minutes, and whatever it was she would have it out of him. "Speaking of Sibyls," she said.

A muscle in his cheek twitched. "Yes?"

"I was just wondering—"

She broke off with a flicker of annoyance as the door behind her whooshed open. Great—someone had decided to crash the party, and just when she needed to have Jeff's full attention on her. She turned around in her chair to see who it was.

And felt her jaw drop.

It was Bungie. And he looked terrible.

Really terrible. His face was shiny with sweat, his hair was matted across his head, his defiant beard stubble looking even worse than usual. His jumpsuit was rumpled and had scattered smudges of dirt and oil on it. He was gripping a short pole that he was using for a cane, but even with its help he was limping pretty badly. The pole puzzled Nicole until she realized it looked like a shorter version of the shaft part of the halberd he'd stolen from the arena. Apparently, he'd found a way to break the weapon in half.

And on top of it all, he looked hungry. The whole package reminded Nicole of one of the stray, half-wild dogs roaming the Philadelphia streets.

Some of those dogs looked weak and pathetic. Others looked mean.

Bungie looked dangerously mean.

"Well, well," he said with that fake cheerfulness that always sent shivers up Nicole's back. "Not intruding, am I?"

"No, not at all," Jeff said, far more calmly than Nicole could have managed right then. "Nice to see you up and about. Especially so soon after having been used for archery practice."

"Oh, yeah, I'm just the picture of good health," Bungie shot back, flashing a look at Nicole. "Maybe I should pose for a poster or something."

"Good idea," Jeff agreed. "Something along the lines of *Train Wrecks I Have Known*?"

"Yeah, you're a real funny guy," Bungie growled. "What the hell are you doing here?"

"I could ask you the same question."

"You're the genius," Bungie said, still watching them as he started lurching his way toward the serving counter. "See if you can figure it out."

"That's okay—I think we've got it," Nicole said, breaking her paralysis and scrambling to her feet. "Go ahead and sit down. I'll get you some food."

"See?" Bungie said, gesturing at Nicole. "See that? There's a woman who knows how to take care of a man."

Nicole winced. Tired, hungry, and probably in pain, Bungie was nevertheless looking for a fight. "Only the best for my work crew," she said, keeping her voice light. Maybe joking about it would keep Jeff quiet and in his seat.

Unfortunately, it didn't. "That's okay, Nicole," Jeff said, catching her arm as he also stood up. "You need to rest that ankle. I'll get him something."

"I want her to do it," Bungie said, his voice cooling a few degrees.

"We don't always get what we want, do we?" Jeff countered in the same tone. "Like the lady said, sit down."

Bungie drew himself up and got a fresh grip on his makeshift cane. "Why don't you come over here and make me?"

"Stop it!" Nicole snapped, shaking off Jeff's hand. "Both of you. Now, sit down—*both* of you—and I'll get Bungie some dinner. He'll eat it, and then he'll leave. Okay?"

"What's the rush?" Bungie asked. "Maybe Pretty Boy and I need to have a talk."

"Why stop at just us?" Jeff countered. Circling around Nicole, he headed toward the door. "Let's make a party of it. I'll see if Plato, Carp, and Kahkitah want to join us."

"Get back here!" Bungie snapped, lunging for the door. His injured leg was slowing him down, but he was also much closer.

And with a sinking heart, Nicole saw that he would get to the door first. "Jeff, no," she called. "Please—it's not worth it."

Jeff didn't reply. Nor did he change speed or direction.

Nicole swore helplessly under her breath. Here it came . . . and there was nothing she could do to stop it.

Jeff was still five paces away when Bungie reached the door. He planted himself in front of it, shifting his weight onto his good leg and adjusting his grip on the halberd pole section. Jeff kept coming, either not seeing that the cane was about to become a weapon or else seeing it and not giving a damn. He took two more paces . . .

Abruptly, he swiveled to his right, grabbed one of the chairs from the table he was passing, and flung it in an underhand arc at Bungie.

Normally, Bungie would probably have been fast enough to dodge something that big and bulky. But his bad leg made all the difference in the world. Even as he tried to duck away the chair caught him squarely across his chest, and with a curse he went down, landing flat on his back. Jeff lunged forward—

An instant later he staggered back as Bungie kicked the chair with his good leg, sending it crashing into Jeff's shins. As Jeff fought to regain his balance, Bungie lurched up onto one elbow and swung his stick hard toward Jeff's knee.

But Jeff was quicker than Nicole had realized. He did a quick shuffle-jump backward that got him just far enough out of the way to send the swinging stick ricocheting harmlessly off the chair instead. With another curse Bungie rolled up into a crouch, whipping the improvised weapon back and forth to keep Jeff away. He got a grip on the chair, and started to lever himself back to his feet.

He was halfway up when Jeff did a sort of sweeping kick that sent the chair sliding sideways and out from under his hand.

With his support suddenly gone, Bungie toppled forward. He managed to get his hands in front of him in time to break his fall, but in the process the end of his stick caught its tip against the floor, and the impact knocked it out of his hand. As his outstretched hands hit the floor, Jeff stepped around the chair and kicked the weapon away. "Little boys shouldn't play with sticks," he chided. Reaching down, he got a two-handed grip on Bungie's jumpsuit and hauled him to his feet. "Now, let's sit down—"

The rest of the sentence disappeared into an agonized gasp as Bungie's left hand shot outward, jamming palm-first into the center of Jeff's chest. He staggered backward toward the wall, gasping for air and fighting to regain his balance. Bungie took a step to follow, his right hand darting inside his jumpsuit and emerging again clutching something shiny. He whipped the object across Jeff's face—

And with a muffled grunt Jeff twisted his head to the side and slammed backward into the wall, a smear of bright red blood suddenly blazing across his forehead. Bungie kept after him, and Nicole saw now that the shiny thing was some kind of knife, its tip red with Jeff's blood. "Jeff!" she snapped. "Bungie—no!"

But Jeff was still standing braced against the wall as if pinned there, his chest heaving, his hands swiping at the blood flowing into his eyes. Bungie kept coming, the knife held low and ready for a final killing stab.

There was no time for Nicole to weigh the consequences of what she was about to do. No time to think about Bungie's temper, or how long and hard he held on to grudges, or the rumors she'd heard about how far he would go to settle a score. All that mattered was that Jeff was going to die unless she did something. Grabbing the tray on the table in front of her, scattering the empty dishes as she flipped it over, she hurled it with all her strength across the room.

Bungie saw it coming. But again, his bad leg robbed him of the agility he needed to avoid it. The spinning tray caught him squarely across the side of his head, spinning him halfway around and nearly dropping him to the floor again. He managed to stay on his feet this time, and with a snarled curse he turned back to his attack.

But Nicole had bought Jeff the time he needed. He was still gasping for breath, but his left hand was now pressed against his forehead to stanch the blood flow, his eyes were open and aware, and he was able to take a couple of hasty steps sideways out of reach of Bungie's knife.

Bungie lunged toward him again, clearly still intent on finishing it. But with his bad leg, and without the element of surprise, he had no chance. And they all knew it.

All of them except maybe Bungie. He took yet another step forward; Jeff responded by taking another step to the side, putting the downed chair between them. As he did so, he got a grip on the back of another chair, ready to pick it up and throw it if necessary.

And with that, Bungie finally got the message. "Not bad," he said, rising slowly out of his fighting crouch but keeping the knife ready in his hand. "But not good, either. I could still take you, right here and now."

"Go ahead," Jeff panted. "I've got nothing else to do tonight."

"I don't think so." With his eyes still on Jeff, Bungie backed up to where his makeshift cane had landed. "Don't worry, we're not done yet. But *I'll* be the one picking the time and place for the next round." Stooping down, he picked up the cane and headed again for the door.

"Come on, Bungie, this is crazy," Nicole called to him in as cajoling a voice as she could manage. "What are you going to do out there? Besides, you never got anything to eat. Let me get you something, and you can eat it and go. We promise."

Bungie snorted. "You hear that? Now she's making promises for you. What kind of pansy lets a woman take over his life?"

"She's right, you know," Jeff said. "Where are you going to go? There's no place on the *Fyrantha* where you can hide."

"You don't think so?" Bungie asked, a hard-edged smile touching his lips. "Let me tell you something, Pretty Boy: this ship is a hell of a lot bigger than you realize. I've found stairways you've never seen—stairways, rooms, whole decks. I can hide out just fine until my leg heals. Or even until you've forgotten to watch your back. Hell, I could hide until you die of old age."

"Sounds great," Jeff said. "Provided you never have to eat again. I'll make sure you don't get anything else here."

"There's plenty of food if you know how to find it," Bungie assured him. "Plato and Carp think they've locked up all the meal bars. They're not even close. There's lots of other fun and nasty stuff out there, too. See you around. I hope you and the little bitch are happy together."

He hit the release and the door whooshed open. "'Cause you won't be happy for long. You should tell her all about it sometime. If you've got the guts."

With that, he lurched through the doorway and was gone.

Even as the door whooshed shut, Jeff was rounding the chair and heading toward it. "No!" Nicole snapped, breaking into a sprint that managed to get her to the door just as he was reaching for the release. "No," she repeated, catching his arm. "Let him go."

"I can't," Jeff protested, struggling to pull free. "He's here, he's hurt—"

"So are you," Nicole said firmly. "I've heard stories about him,

Jeff, and what he's like in this mood. He'd knife you just for the hell of it without caring what happened to him afterward. Give him some time to cool down."

Jeff glared at her, then looked at the door again. But between his heaving lungs and his bleeding forehead he wasn't in any shape to fight. Unlike Bungie, he was smart enough to realize that. "I suppose," he said, some of the stiffness going out of his shoulders. Pulling out one of the chairs at the nearby table, he sank into it. "*Damn,* but this stings."

"I'll bet it does," she said, wincing at the blood still oozing out from beneath his hand. "Sit tight. I'll go get Sam or Allyce."

"No—stay here," Jeff said, catching her hand as she started toward the door. "You're not leaving until I can leave with you."

"But—"

"He's just as mad at you as he is at me," Jeff said, holding her with the same determination she'd just been holding him. "Anyway, this looks worse than it is—head wounds always bleed like crazy. Grab me a few napkins and a big glass of water, will you?"

Nicole clenched her teeth. But she wasn't all that anxious to run into Bungie in a deserted hallway, either. Crossing to the serving counter, she keyed for a glass of water, pulling out a wad of napkins from the dispenser while it filled. She returned to the table and set the napkins and water in front of him. "What do you need me to do?" she asked, turning the fallen chair upright again and sitting down facing him.

"Mostly, just keep me company," he said, picking up two of the napkins and pressing them against the cut. "I can handle this. You suppose he really has found himself a hiding place?"

"What?" Nicole asked, frowning at the sudden change of subject.

"Bungie said he'd found places where he can hide," Jeff said. "But he shouldn't have. Not here. Going down below our work decks you just run into yellow crew's territory; go up and you get the green and purple crews. Does he really think he can dodge all of us forever?"

"He's probably just blowing smoke," Nicole said. "He does that a lot."

"Unless he's found a way past the arena, like you did," Jeff said darkly. "Don't forget how much time he spent looking around while he was supposed to be working. I don't know how tall the ship is, but it's possible he found a passage that goes over the arena. Or under it."

"Or through it," Nicole said, grimacing. "He could have been able to catch the code I put in on our second trip. No, wait, that doesn't work," she corrected herself. "The Masters changed that one. If he'd gotten in with it he couldn't have gotten out again."

"Unless he got out before the code was changed."

"In which case, he can't get back in now," Nicole said. "So if he *did* go through, any hiding places he found on the other side are now useless."

"Let's hope so," Jeff said. "Because wherever his hiding place is, it apparently comes stocked with weapons. The thought of him with an arsenal isn't a happy one."

"I think that stick was just a section of the halberd he stole," Nicole pointed out.

"I was talking about the knife."

"Which I think was just the halberd's tip," Nicole said. "Either he managed to break it, or else it's designed to come apart."

"Actually, that makes sense," Jeff said reluctantly. "Easier to put on a new tip or axe head when it breaks than to replace the whole weapon. But don't forget he said he'd found other good stuff. He may be just blowing smoke, like you said, but it's better to assume the worst."

"If he'd found other weapons, he probably would have brought one with him," Nicole pointed out.

"Unless it's heavy or bulky," Jeff said. "Remember, he wasn't expecting to find anyone here tonight."

Nicole winced. Or if the other weapons weren't as easily concealed as the halberd-tip knife. Men like Bungie liked being able to hide their trump card.

"Let's just hope that if he found something it doesn't work anymore." He peered at the napkin in his hand. "Okay, I think it's stopped bleeding. Time to start cleaning up."

"Yeah," Nicole said, standing up. "I'll get some more napkins."

Jeff's assessment of his injury turned out to be correct. Once all the blood had been cleared away, the actual wound was little more than a long, reasonably shallow cut. "See?" he said, touching it gingerly. "No problem."

"Right—no problem," Nicole said, wincing. "You're just lucky he missed your eyes."

"I was thinking that, too," Jeff said, his tone going a little brittle. "I imagine next time he'll try to aim better."

Nicole shivered. "We need to stop him, Jeff."

"If you recall, I was trying to do just that when you interfered."

"You'd have gotten yourself killed." She forced a smile. "Not to mention getting into trouble with Plato over his no-fighting rule. Speaking of which, what are we going to tell him about that?" She pointed to his forehead.

"No idea," Jeff said. "But we've got until morning to figure it out."

"Yeah." Nicole watched in silence as he collected the bloody napkins from the table and piled them on the tray she'd thrown at Bungie earlier. "What did Bungie mean about having the guts to tell me something?"

"Nothing," Jeff said. "Maybe I can sneak into the med center and get some of the docs' healing goo. I'd hate for this thing to scar."

"Jeff—"

"In the old days I could have passed it off as a dueling scar," he continued, getting to his feet. "Though why people thought it looked cool to show off a fight they'd obviously lost—"

"Jeff, stop," Nicole said, grabbing his sleeve. "Please. Just tell me."

For a long moment he gazed at her, a dozen emotions flickering across his face. Then, with a sigh, he sat down again. "It's the inhalers," he said quietly. "The stuff that lets Sibyls be Sibyls. They . . ." His lips compressed, his gaze dropping to his lap. "It's going to kill you."

Nicole stared at him, feeling the blood draining from her face. "What?" she asked carefully.

"Not right away," he added hastily, looking up at her again. "Not for months—maybe longer. I heard that the green crew had a Sibyl once who lived over a year."

"A year," Nicole said, the word coming out hard and cold and flat. "A whole freaking year."

Jeff winced, his gaze dropping again. "I know. I'm sorry."

Nicole swallowed hard. So that was what Carp had meant about it never happening this soon, back when she'd faked her dizzy spell. He'd thought it was the inhaler killing her faster than usual. It was also why Jeff had told her that knowing there'd been hundreds of Sibyls aboard wouldn't help her figure out how long the kidnappings had been going on. "So what's the average?" she asked.

Jeff shook his head. "I don't know. I could ask."

Nicole blinked away sudden moisture. "Why bother?"

"I suppose." He sighed. "I'm sorry, Nicole. I wish it was

different. I really do. Especially—" He gestured almost shyly. "With you."

Surreptitiously, Nicole touched the empty pocket where she'd had the inhaler earlier. Maybe Fievj had done her a favor by taking it.

Not that it mattered. Sam and Allyce had a whole cabinet full of the damn things. "Well, life in Philadelphia was risky, too," she said, striving to put a little lightness in her tone. Not for herself, but for Jeff. "Come on—Bungie should be long gone by now. Let's dump the evidence and get out of here."

"With a quick stop first at the med center," Jeff said, standing up. He, too, was clearly trying to put away the dark tone. Probably not for himself, but for her. "Then I'll walk you back to your room."

thirteen

It was just as well, Nicole reflected as she stared into the nothingness of her darkened room, that she'd gotten plenty of sleep that afternoon. Because it was abundantly clear that she wasn't going to get much tonight.

She was going to die. Sometime in the next few weeks or months, she was going to die.

In a way, it was almost funny. Back home in Philadelphia, she'd thought about death a lot. Maybe it was the sort of neighborhoods she lived in that had kept that dark reality continually at the edge of her mind. More likely it was the fact that she was hooked up with Trake's group, where everyone lived life on the most insanely ridiculous part of the edge.

The bitter irony was that she'd grown to actually feel safe here on the *Fyrantha*. In fact, it was the safest and the most secure that she'd ever felt in her entire life. On top of that, she was doing useful work, she was treated mostly with respect, and the people in her crew trusted her.

She'd become so comfortable, in fact, that she'd even been toying lately with the idea of opening up to a couple of them—Jeff, probably, maybe Kahkitah—and trying to see if she could make them into friends. Not assets she could exploit and manipulate, or protectors she could hide behind in a crisis, but real, genuine friends. The sort of friend she hadn't had since second grade.

No point in that now. No point wasting any time and energy when she was just going to die.

And for what? So she could hear the *Fyrantha* tell her where it hurt, so that Carp and the others could fix it? Why? None of the work they did ever seemed to make a scrap of difference to how the ship functioned. There was always plenty of food and water, the lights and heat never went off, and the clothing and dishware always got cleaned, or disintegrated and reassembled, or however the ship handled that particular chore. As far as she could tell, everything was running just fine without any of them being here.

So why *were* they here? Why was she here?

Why was she dying? For what reason? For what purpose?

There were no answers. She hated that.

But there were two things she *was* sure of. First, there was no way in hell she was just going to sit back and take this. She'd come too far, and had too much to lose, to just roll over and die on some make-work project for the Shipmasters' benefit. She would find a way to stop this, or at least postpone it as long as she could.

And second, if dying was inevitable, she was going to die doing something important.

The usual schedule for her crew was to get up around six thirty in the morning, gather together at seven for breakfast, then head out to the equipment closets about seven thirty and be at work by eight. Never in all her time aboard had Nicole seen anyone in the dining room before six thirty. Just to be on the safe side, though, she made sure she was there by six.

And so, naturally, this was the one single morning that someone got there ahead of her.

"Good morning, Nicole," Sam said, waving at her from his table near the serving counter. "You're up early."

"I couldn't sleep," Nicole said, fighting back a scowl. Of all the mornings, and of all the people. "Thought I'd get a jump on the day."

"You're probably starving, too," he said. "You missed dinner, didn't you?"

"No, I came in after everyone else was finished," she said. Jeff might have talked, or someone might have heard the commotion, and either way she didn't want to draw attention to herself with unnecessary lies. "But I didn't have very much."

"Well, there's always more for the taking," Sam said, gesturing toward the counter. "Help yourself." He lowered his voice. "And as it happens, I've even got the perfect way for you to start the day. Come over here."

"What is it?" Nicole asked, frowning as she walked to his table. Sam was usually barely even polite to her, and was prickly with everyone else even at the best of times. Seeing him cheerful, even friendly, was setting off quiet warning bells in the back of her brain. "You figure out how to reprogram the food system for cornflakes or something?"

"Better," Sam said. He reached down to the floor beside his chair and brought up a strange-looking bottle. "I got it to make whiskey."

Nicole felt her breath catch in her throat, old thoughts and feelings and reflexes pouring suddenly back from places in her brain she didn't even know were still there. Memories of the familiar scent, the rich dark flavor, the numbing of pain and anger, the welcome oblivion.

And in that single heartbeat, all the weeks of being clean and sober were gone. She wanted a drink. She wanted to drink, to get drunk, and to forget.

To forget that she was dying. And that nobody cared.

There was a glass already on the table in front of her. Odd that she hadn't noticed it there before. Sam tipped the bottle, and the clear amber liquid rolled smoothly out into the glass. One finger . . . two fingers . . .

"More?" Sam asked.

With an effort, Nicole found her voice. "No," she heard herself say. "That's fine."

"Okay." He straightened the bottle and pushed the glass another couple of inches toward her. "Enjoy."

Nicole stared at the glass, noting how the little ripples glistened in the room's indirect lighting. The aroma filled her nostrils and her mind, triggering a hundred more memories, good and bad and hazy. She hadn't realized until this moment how much she'd missed this glorious, glorious escape.

Only she couldn't escape. Not from the *Fyrantha*. Not from her ultimate doom. She was stuck here for the rest of her now shortened life.

So were all the others. Sam and Plato might live longer than she did, but their only way out would still come in the form of death. The only way out for any of them.

Including Mispacch and her children.

For another moment she continued to stare at the whiskey, struggling between the two sides of her as they pulled in opposite directions. But she'd made her decision. She was going into the arena, and she was going to try one last time to get Mispacch and the others a steady supply of food. If it worked, or even if it didn't, she would be done with it.

Either way, Sam and his bottle would still be waiting. And she would either celebrate her victory or obliterate the bitterness of her failure.

"Thanks," she said. "Maybe later."

For a moment there was nothing but the sight and aroma of the whiskey. Then, Sam's hand appeared into her focused view, pulling the glass back a few inches. She followed the movement with her eyes, noting that the drink was still within her reach. Maybe just a sip or two, just to get the taste . . .

"You sure?" Sam asked. "It can help you through rough times."

With an effort, Nicole raised her eyes from the glass and focused on Sam's face. He was gazing back at her, a strangely intense expression in his eyes. "I know," she said. "Like I said, maybe later."

His expression seemed to harden. "You're going in again, aren't you."

Nicole grimaced. "You've been talking to Jeff."

"Jeff?" Sam shook his head. "No. What does he have to do with this?"

"Nothing," Nicole said. "He had some thoughts on the subject."

"I'll bet he did," Sam said. "So did Plato. You *do* realize it's useless, don't you?"

Nicole snorted. So that was why Sam was suddenly all friendly and pushing booze on her. He and Plato figured that if they got her good and drunk, she wouldn't be in any shape to go into the arena. Not until it was too late. "What, feeding hungry people is useless now?"

"'Give a man a fish and he eats for a day,'" Sam quoted. "'Teach a man to fish—'"

"Yeah, yeah, I've heard it," Nicole cut him off. "What's your point?"

"My point is that there's no way to teach the people in the arena to fish," Sam said.

"Sure there is," Nicole said. "You changed the dispenser controls. Why can't they?"

"Because the Shipmasters control the whole situation," Sam said bluntly. "I got away with tweaking the dispensers because they let me, or because they haven't noticed yet. But they're not going to let that happen in the arena. No matter what you do in there, they can always undercut you or simply undo whatever small victory you achieve. You'll have wasted your time and risked your life for nothing."

"Nice speech," Nicole said sourly. "You come up with that all by yourself? Or did Plato write it for you?"

"That was mostly Plato," Sam said without embarrassment. "But he's right. No matter how you look at it, what's happening in the arena is a no-win situation. The best thing you can do is take a deep breath and forget everything you saw in there."

"You didn't see Mispacch's kids. I did."

For a moment he just gazed at her. "Okay, then," he said. "Your decision. Your consequences. You going to get something to eat before you go?"

Nicole looked over at the serving counter. That had indeed been her plan. But with Sam sitting here watching . . . "That's okay," she said. "I'll grab a couple of food bars and some water from one of the supply closets along the way."

"Okay," Sam said. He hesitated, then dug into one of his jump-suit pockets. "Oh, and you might need this."

Nicole felt her stomach tighten. Resting on his palm was a fresh Sibyl inhaler.

She looked hard into his face. Did he know what the inhaler was doing? That the drug inside it was slowly but surely killing her?

If he did, she couldn't see it in his face. Certainly not on top of all the frustration and disapproval already there.

Besides, even if he did, it didn't matter. Her lifestyle and

decisions back home had been driving her just as surely toward
an early death. Did it matter whether she died young on the
streets or in the *Fyrantha* arena?

Not really. Except that here she might be able to do something
meaningful first.

Unless Sam was right. Unless there was nothing meaningful
she *could* do.

He was still holding out the inhaler. Gingerly, she took it,
knowing it would look suspicious if she didn't. If Plato found out
Jeff had given away their little secret, there would probably be
hell to pay.

Besides, as long as she didn't use the damn thing, it couldn't
hurt her more than it already had. Probably.

"Thanks," she said, sticking the inhaler into her pocket. "See
you later."

"I hope so," Sam said gravely. "Good luck."

Nicole's plan had been to get her food bars from the supply closet
closest to the arena door, on the theory that there was no point
lugging a heavy vest any farther than she had to. But as she left
the dining room she was already having second thoughts. If Sam
was already up and moving, some of the others might be up as
well. If so, it would be better to avoid any other encounters by
taking a more roundabout route to the arena.

The last thing she wanted was to get to that distant closet and
find Carp and Kahkitah waiting for her. The better approach, she
realized, would be to instead hit the closet closest to the hive,
since no one was so eager to get to work that they got their tool
vests there.

No one, apparently, except Jeff.

"Morning," he said, straightening up from the closet door where he'd been leaning and giving her a tentative smile. "I figured you'd come here."

"Really," Nicole said, frowning as she looked him over. His forehead cut was still pretty visible, but it was already starting to heal. He probably used some of the special cream from the med center. To her mild annoyance, he also looked better rested than she was. "I thought everyone would figure just the opposite."

Jeff shook his head. "This is the closet farthest from where we've been working lately. Any food and tools you take from here won't be missed as soon."

"Oh," Nicole said a bit lamely. That part hadn't occurred to her. "Well, congratulations—you win a free breakfast."

"That's all?" he said with feigned disappointment. "I was hoping for an all-expense-paid trip to the famous *Fyrantha* arena."

Nicole felt her eyes narrow. "What's that supposed to mean?"

"It means you're going into the arena to help that woman and her children," Jeff said. "And I'm going with you."

"No," Nicole said firmly.

"Why not? You don't think you could use an extra hand?"

"I don't think you have any business going in there," Nicole said. "You've got a long life ahead of you. You've got nothing to gain by going in there and catching an arrow."

"That's your idea of something to gain?" he countered. "Is that what this is about? You going out in a blaze of glory?"

"No, this is about getting Mispacch and her kids some food," Nicole told him. "And I don't have time to argue about it. Get out of my way, will you?"

He didn't budge. "What if I could get them that food without anyone else getting shot or hurt?"

Nicole snorted. "If you're talking about food bars, I already told you the Micawnwi couldn't eat them."

"I was thinking about something a little more elegant," he said. "You said the food dispenser had a display on it, right? Forty colored lights?"

"That right," she confirmed, thinking back. "There were several different colors."

"Perfect," he said. "See, I think those lights are the readout that indicates the formula of the stuff the dispenser is putting out. That's what the dispenser in our dining room looks like, except you don't see the lights because they're back behind the counter. And of course we get a variety of different menus, which I'm guessing the Micawnwi don't."

"If you can't see the lights, how do you know what they look like?"

"The thing broke down a couple of years ago and Levi and I had to get back in there," he explained. "I saw the display, and also the keypad entry thing that looks like it controls the mixture. If we can figure out the Micawnwi code, we should be able to reprogram another dispenser to whip up some extra formula for them."

Nicole looked back over her shoulder, a flicker of cautious hope rushing through her. "You mean we could feed them from here?"

"Well, no, not from here exactly," he hedged. "I could see the control system on our machine, but the thing had been welded shut. Probably to keep someone like me from messing around with the controls and accidentally poisoning everyone."

"Sam was able to make whiskey."

Jeff's eyebrows went up. "Really? Huh. He must have found a dispenser somewhere he could get into."

"Or else Plato unwelded ours."

"Could be," Jeff said. "Maybe we should hunt up the doc and ask which it was."

"He won't tell us," Nicole said.

Jeff started to say something, took another look at Nicole's face, and thought better of it. "Fine—we shouldn't need his anyway. What I was starting to say was that if the arena dispensers have to be changed every few weeks, they should be more easily accessible. If we can get to the *Cluufes'* dispenser, we may be able to reprogram it."

Nicole chewed at her lip. Hunter had implied that between the dispensers in their hive and the stone building there was plenty of food available for his people. That meant taking food for the Micawnwi shouldn't hurt the Cluufes any.

And if Hunter had been lying about that . . . well, he was the one who'd refused to share any of their supplies, even knowing Micawnwi children were starving. Serve him right if he got a little hungry himself for a change. "Okay," she told Jeff. "How do we get to it?"

He seemed taken aback. "That was the part *you* were supposed to know," he said. "You were back there, weren't you? You said you saw the mechanism."

"I saw the Micawnwi mechanism," she corrected. "But the wall on that side had been cut to give the Shipmasters access. I don't know if they did that to the Cluufes' side."

"Why not?" Jeff asked. "They're both part of the same game, aren't they?"

"Yeah, but they're playing different parts," Nicole said. "So far the ones on the Micawnwi side seem to be the ones that are supposed to attack, with the ones in the Cluufe section defending. They're starving the Micawnwi to make them desperate enough to fight. The Cluufes are supposed to have plenty to eat unless they lose the stone building."

Jeff shook his head. "What kind of sick monsters make someone else fight to the death for food? It's like a bad horror movie or something."

"Hey, *I* didn't make the rules," Nicole said. "Besides, it doesn't matter if the Cluufes have the same shutoff valve or not. I couldn't see the controls on the Micawnwi version from the back, and I don't see why the Cluufe side would be any different."

"Your classic no-win situation." Jeff hissed out a sigh. "Maybe Plato was right. Maybe we should just forget it."

"You want to quit, go ahead," Nicole said. "While you're thinking about it, you want to get out of my way?"

"I'm not quitting," Jeff insisted, stepping away from the closet. "I'm just saying we're no farther ahead than you were yesterday."

"Sure we are," Nicole said, brushing past him and opening the closet. There were two fully loaded food vests at one end. She pulled out one and slipped it on, then tossed the second one to Jeff. "Now we have a plan. Here—you can carry this one."

"There's lunch here for six people, you know," he reminded her, eyeing the vest dubiously. "How long exactly are you planning for us to be in there?"

"Don't know," Nicole said. "How hungry are you willing to get?"

"Point," he conceded, putting it on.

"We'll need some tools, too," Nicole continued. "Which ones will you need to reprogram the dispenser?"

His mouth dropped open an inch. "I thought you said we couldn't get to it."

"I said I couldn't get to it from the *back*," she corrected. "We might be able to get in from the front. Come on, come on—which tools?"

"From the *front*?" Jeff echoed. "Well, that could be handy. You couldn't have mentioned that two minutes ago?"

Nicole shrugged. "I wanted to see if you were as crazy about doing this as I was. Besides, I said we *might*. So which tools?"

He stared at her another second, then looked back at the

closet. "We should probably have both an electronics and a general tool set," he said, stepping to the racks and picking out a pair of vests. "You want me to carry both of them, I suppose?"

"You're the one with two good ankles."

"Right." Shifting both vests into one hand, he dug into one of his jumpsuit pockets with the other. "Well, if I'm going to carry everything else, you can lug this."

Nicole stiffened. Resting in his palm was another inhaler.

"You told me Fievj had taken your inhaler," he explained. "I forgot to grab you a replacement last night, so I picked it up this morning. Thought you should have it in case we need to talk to the ship."

"Sure," she said, trying not to be too sarcastic. "You get any rattlesnakes? We could probably use some rattlesnakes."

He winced. "Yeah, I know," he said, sounding embarrassed. "But as long as you don't use it a lot, you should be all right. Right? I mean, the other Sibyls use the stuff two or three times a day and still live for months and months."

"So you figure as long as I just take an occasional shot of the stuff, I should be fine?"

"Yeah," he said, wincing again. "Sorry—it was just a thought. If you don't want it—"

"No, I'll take it," she cut him off, jamming the inhaler into a pocket. "It's just . . ."

"It's just what?"

She sighed. "What you said just now. As long as I don't use it a lot, I'll be fine." She hunched her shoulders. "It's the irony of it, that's all."

"Irony?"

She stepped over and closed the closet door. "That's the same thing I said to myself when I first started drinking. Hell, it might even be the same words." She waved a hand. "Never mind. Let's go before someone catches us."

So far Nicole had been zero for two on her assumptions of how the morning would go. But she was pretty sure her third assumption would pan out.

She was right. Amrew and the rest of the Micawnwi men weren't at all happy to see her.

"What are you doing here?" Amrew demanded as Nicole and Jeff stood by the entrance to the Micawnwi hive. "Never mind," he added before Nicole could answer. "I don't care why you're here. Leave, now. We don't need you."

"Really?" Nicole countered, trying hard to forget that this was the man who'd casually forced his own wife and children into slow starvation. "From what I saw of yesterday's battle it looked like you can use every bit of help you can get. How many did you lose, anyway?"

"We came very near to victory," Amrew said. "That's what's important."

Nicole locked her gaze on the nearby sentry. "How many did you lose?" she repeated.

The sentry glanced furtively at Amrew. "Three," he said. "One dead and two injured."

"But the enemy also lost one to death," Amrew added firmly. "And we nearly reached the objective."

"Yes, you said that." Nicole gestured to Jeff. "This is Jeff. He's here to teach you how to fight."

Out of the corner of her eye she saw Jeff lean a few inches closer to her. "Nicole, I don't know how to use weapons like this," he murmured urgently.

"They're special techniques the enemy doesn't know," Nicole continued, ignoring his protest. "Give him one of your weapons and he'll show you."

Amrew seemed to measure Jeff with his eyes. Then, he turned his halberd to point upward and tossed it to Jeff. "Very well," he said. "Let's see what you have to offer."

Jeff took a moment to examine the halberd, turning it over a few times as he ran his eyes and hands over it and got a feel for its weight and balance. Then, with a final glance at Nicole, he began flipping it over and around, slowly at first, then faster and faster, carving out a complex pattern of swings, spins, and jabs.

Back in the hive, Nicole had seen him do similar moves with her crutches. But she'd never realized how much more could be done with the longer and heavier halberd. The extra length gave him a whole new category of maneuvers that the crutch hadn't let him execute.

If Nicole was impressed, the two Micawnwi were even more so. Amrew seemed stunned as he watched the performance, and the sentry was so enthralled that he didn't even flinch when the tip of the halberd suddenly jabbed through the air a foot away from the side of his head.

The show lasted maybe a minute. When it was over, Amrew was convinced. "I'll call the fighters," he said. "We'll begin training at once."

"Don't call them too far," Nicole warned. "You'll want to do your training inside the main room, not out here."

"How big is this room?" Jeff asked, craning his neck to see past the two Micawnwi. "You saw how much space we're going to need."

"I'm less worried about a shortage of space than I am about an abundance of Cluufe spies," Nicole said.

Jeff looked up into the forested hills. "Damn," he muttered.

"Why didn't you say something? I could have taken the demo inside."

"Sorry," Nicole apologized, trying to sound sincere. In actual fact, Jeff and Amrew had done exactly what she'd wanted, and exactly where she'd wanted them to do it.

Not that she was about to tell either of them that. Not yet, anyway. "But better late than never," she added.

"I suppose," Jeff said dubiously. He gave the hills one last look, then gestured to the Micawnwi. "You heard her. Let's get inside."

There were thirteen Micawnwi who Amrew apparently decided were healthy enough to participate in the training. They were crammed pretty tightly into the central room, and for a long time the session was a loud and raucous thing indeed. The Micawnwi were understandably awkward with the new techniques, and there was a good deal of clinking and thudding as the halberds rammed into each other or bounced off the walls or other Micawnwi.

But the aliens were determined, and Amrew pushed them hard, and as the morning progressed the clinks and bumps and untranslatable sounds that Nicole began thinking of as Micawnwi curses gradually faded away. By lunchtime the only sounds emanating from the training room were Jeff's or Amrew's orders and the faint swishing of halberds being whipped through the air.

Fortunately, the earlier confusion had gone on long enough to give Nicole the time she'd needed to go into the food dispenser room and carefully record the colored display lights onto her notepad with her stylus. During the worst of the noise, which would hopefully mask everything else from the ears of the listening Oracle, she'd also borrowed Varkos Man-second, the young sentry she and Mispacch had run into on Nicole's first visit, and had utilized his strength and size for one other task.

And with that, the preliminary work was done. Now, if and when they got to the Cluufes' hive, Jeff should have everything he needed to reprogram their food dispenser. Assuming, of course, that the rest of the Micawnwi could buy them enough time to pull that off.

She hadn't told Amrew that part of her plan yet. She could hardly wait to hear what he thought about it.

But that confrontation was still a little ways off. With the first round of training complete, Jeff announced a half-hour break and informed them they'd be pairing off for actual combat drills after lunch.

Nicole and Jeff found an out-of-the-way spot against the wall where they could eat their food bars without getting walked on. The Micawnwi men, Nicole noted, each got a small handful of some stuff that looked like trail mix from the food dispenser. From the snatches of conversation Nicole was able to overhear, it was clear that the Shipmasters had discovered her interference and returned the dispenser to its proper starvation level.

Not surprisingly, none of the women or children joined the men for their midday meal.

Given that Jeff had run the Micawnwi through a full morning's worth of practice, Nicole had assumed that the afternoon drills would be just as extensive. To her mild surprise, Jeff called a halt after only two hours, citing the balance between preparedness and fatigue, and told Nicole the fighters were as ready as they were going to be.

And with that, it was time to let Amrew in on the whole story.

At Nicole's suggestion the three of them headed out into the arena, where the Oracle listening from the food dispenser room hopefully couldn't eavesdrop. They sat down cross-legged facing each other, and Nicole explained the rest of her plan.

Amrew listened in stony silence. When she'd finished he stared at her for nearly five seconds. Then, deliberately, he turned to Jeff. "And what's *your* plan?" he asked.

A blazing retort flashed to Nicole's lips. But Jeff got there first. "That *was* my plan," he said calmly. "I worked it out yesterday while observing your battle."

Nicole felt her mouth drop open. What the *hell*?

Amrew looked as stunned as she felt. "It's *your* plan?" he demanded. "Yet you allowed a woman to express it to me?"

And then Nicole got it. Of course Jeff had had to say that. And he'd had to say it in exactly that way.

Her own fault, really. She knew what Amrew was like. She should have briefed Jeff on the plan and let him present it to the Micawnwi in the first place.

"Of course," she said before Jeff could answer. "Jeff figured that if a woman could understand it even the slowest of your fighters could, too."

"And you thought *I* was one of those slowest?" Amrew countered. "No matter. I declare the plan unacceptable. It carries an abundance of risk, and only a small chance of success."

"I'm sorry you feel that way," Jeff said. "Let's hear *your* plan."

"We attack across the plain," Amrew said. "With these new fighting techniques to aid us, we can yet drive the enemy from the stone bastion."

"Ah," Jeff said. "And you've tried the frontal assault strategy how many times already?"

Amrew's fur fluffed briefly. "Three. But with these new fighting techniques—"

"You have any arrows left?" Jeff interrupted.

"No," Amrew admitted. "But we only had ten to begin with. And the enemy has used all of theirs, as well."

"So you have no long-range firepower," Jeff concluded. "That means your entire strategy is to rush at the Cluufes and try to whack or poke them before they can do that to you?"

Another fluffing of the fur. "It's more honorable than you make it sound."

"No doubt," Jeff said, nodding. "How many of your original twenty-six fighters have you lost in your various attacks?"

Amrew rumbled something untranslatable. "Seven," he said. "Though two of those may yet recover enough to fight."

"Good for them," Jeff said. "Which won't help you this afternoon, of course. So seven in three battles. You really think doing the same thing yet again will yield any better results?"

Amrew flicked a look at Nicole, then lifted his eyes to the hills behind them. "You guarantee your plan will work?" he asked at last.

"There aren't any guarantees in warfare," Jeff said. "But I think this is the best shot you're going to have."

"My fighters won't like it," Amrew warned. "They want revenge for the deaths of their compatriots."

"Then your fighters need to be reminded of their objective," Jeff said coldly. "The goal is to obtain food, not to kill or maim a few Cluufes." He gestured to Nicole. "If you don't agree, or want to do it some other way, that's fine. Good luck, and we'll be on our way."

Amrew fluffed his fur again. "You leave me small choice. Very well—we'll follow your plan. But this had better work. When do we begin?"

Jeff looked at Nicole and raised his eyebrows. Nicole started to speak, remembered Amrew's automatic resistance to anything with a female voice attached to it, and instead gave a microscopic nod. "No time like the present," Jeff said. "Get your fighters out here and we'll give them a briefing."

"I'll also need Mispacch Woman-fifth and her children," Nicole added.

"A woman?" Amrew said disdainfully. "Why?"

"We need her to come with us to the Cluufe side," Nicole said. "If you'd rather, we could take Varkos Man-second or one of the other fighters instead."

"All the men are needed for the attack," Amrew said a bit huffily. "As you well know. Very well. Mispacch Woman-fifth and her children are searching for edible berries at the hills near the plain. I'll send a messenger to summon her."

"No need," Nicole said. She'd glimpsed Mispacch moving through the foliage when she and Jeff had first come in. "Jeff and I can go get her after he briefs the other fighters."

"Very well." Amrew rose to his feet. "Wait here. I'll bring the fighters."

He strode across the ground and disappeared back into the Micawnwi hive. "What do you think?" Jeff murmured.

"He doesn't like it, but doesn't see any other alternative," Nicole said.

"He also hates you being here," Jeff pointed out. "Maybe you ought to head out right now and find Mispacch. I can catch up once we're finished."

"I don't know," Nicole said hesitantly. "The tracks aren't easy to find. It would kind of defeat the whole purpose if I had to stand up and wave to you."

"Don't worry, I saw the bushes you described on our way in," he assured her. "I'll find you."

"Okay," Nicole said, reluctantly standing up. She didn't like leaving him alone with Amrew and the others. But he was probably right about getting her out of sight. "We'll wait a little ways up the path."

"I'll find you," he promised again. "Go on, scoot."

A minute later, Nicole was hurrying along the stone path back toward the distant exit door and the hidden path she'd found on her last visit. A few minutes to find Mispacch, plus another few minutes to get her and her children under cover while they waited for Jeff to catch up, and the plan would be under way.

Amrew was right. It had damn well better work.

Fourteen

Locating the end of the hidden track system Nicole had followed during her escape from the Cluufes was easy. Finding Mispacch and her children proved considerably harder. Nicole hadn't expected them to be in the exact place where she'd seen them earlier that morning, but she'd assumed they would be at least in the same general area.

But they were nowhere to be found. Cursing under her breath, she pushed her way across the wilderness, wading through the tall grass, circling around bushes, and ducking under low tree branches, all the while sweating as the clock ticked down in the back of her mind. If she couldn't find them soon, she might have to talk Amrew into letting her borrow one of the Micawnwi men after all.

She'd almost given up when she finally found the three of them sitting beside a small creek, scooping water with their paw-like hands. Mispacch looked up at Nicole's approach, did a whole-body shuddering thing that Nicole guessed was their version of a double take, and scrambled hastily to her feet. "Sibyl!" she said, bowing in greeting. "I hadn't thought to see you again so soon."

"You mean so soon after running out on you?" Nicole waved a hand. "Never mind. I need your help. Yours and your children's. You game for a little adventure?"

"Of course," Mispacch said, her fur fluffing up and down. "Thanks to you, our hunger is eased and we have strength again."

"Good," Nicole said. "Because strength is exactly what I need from you." She peered up through the tree branches at the craggy rocks in the distance. "That, and silence. Come with me, and quietly. The Cluufes may be watching."

Jeff was waiting at the track crawlway entry point, crouched beside the trunk of a tree that was topped by a dome-shaped branch-and-leaf canopy that reminded Nicole of the top of a Russian-style church she'd seen once in a picture. "About time," he murmured as Nicole and the three Micawnwi came up. "You get lost?"

"*I* didn't, no," Nicole said. "Where's Amrew?"

Jeff nodded toward the Micawnwi area. "About twenty meters that way," he said. "Any idea how long this cross-country thing will take? He needs to know when to attack."

"Got it covered," Nicole assured him. "Mispacch, I need you to send Daughter One back to Amrew. Have her tell him that Son One will come and let him know when we're in position and he can launch his attack. Can you do that?"

"Of course." Pulling her children close to her, Mispacch put her mouth to their ears and began murmuring.

"You think you can trust them?" Jeff asked quietly. "Not to screw up, I mean. It's not like anyone in here has any kind of professional training."

"Neither have I," Nicole reminded him. "So far, I'm doing okay."

"Really?" Jeff countered. "The way I read it, so far you've mostly just been lucky."

Nicole gave a little snort. "Yeah, getting my butt hauled across space so I can kill myself telling people like you where to stick their screwdrivers sure qualifies as lucky."

"You know what I mean," Jeff said. "By all rights, you should be up to your eyeballs in trouble with the Shipmasters right now. *Or* lying dead with a Cluufe halberd through your stomach."

"Not a chance," she insisted.

But down deep, she knew he was right. If Jeff and Plato hadn't plucked her out of the middle of that battle . . . "Anyway, since when did you become Rambo?"

"Me? Rambo? Never," he said, giving her a slightly superior look. "Rambo was Army. I was a Marine."

Nicole felt her mouth drop open. Her question had been pure sarcasm. "A *Marine?*"

He shrugged. "Briefly."

"And?"

"And we'll save that story for another time," he said, nodding toward Mispacch.

Nicole turned. The three Micawnwi had finished their huddle and Daughter One was moving through the overgrowth toward Amrew's position. "Time to go?" Jeff asked.

"Time to go," Nicole confirmed. "Mispacch, you and Son One follow me. Jeff, you bring up the rear. Keep it quiet, and try not to hit any of the branches. It might give away our position."

The trip back over the hills seemed quicker this time. Part of that, Nicole knew, was because she'd already done it once. The other part was the fact that this time her ankle wasn't throbbing with pain.

The only really tricky part was the transition from the first set of tracks to the second. Nicole stayed especially alert as she slipped across the open gap, but again she heard and saw no sign of Cluufe sentries. Mispacch followed her across, and then Jeff.

And with the three of them safely onto the final leg of the journey, Mispacch gave a hand signal to Son One, still waiting back on the other side of the gap. The child nodded and turned around, crawling swiftly along the tracks as he headed back to give Amrew the word. Assuming all of them traveled at more or less the same speed, Nicole's group should be in position just about the time Amrew gathered his forces and marched off to the plain for their attack.

At which point, the success of Nicole's plan would rest on Amrew's ability to keep the Cluufes' full attention tied up at the other end of the arena. She hoped he was up to the task.

The tracks came to an end just around the curve in the stone path where Nicole had started her sprint the previous day, and within sight of the place where she'd twisted her ankle. She and the others were in position, and Nicole was staring at the stone path, when it started.

The first sign was a sudden flurry of activity from the hive. She could hear voices, the words unintelligible but the tones clipped and taut. The voices were followed by the sound of hurrying feet, and a moment later half a dozen armed Cluufes appeared around the curve and raced down the path in the direction of the stone building.

Something brushed past Nicole's left leg and arm, and she turned to see Jeff come up beside her. "Looks like they got the message," he whispered.

"I guess so," Nicole whispered back. "Did you see any messengers go past? I didn't."

"There hasn't been time for messengers," Jeff said. "Probably one of their spotters up there signaled down to them."

Nicole frowned. "You mean with a radio or something?"

"More likely a mirror or shiny piece of metal," Jeff said. "A quick flash code would be simple enough to set up. This Hunter character sounds like he might have had some military training." He shrugged. "Or else was just a very attentive Boy Scout."

Nicole thought back to her first time in the arena, when she'd seen Hunter shooting at the stone building's defenders and then quickly moving away before they could shoot back. "I'd vote for military," she said grimly. "He's organized and he can shoot."

"All the better that they're out of stuff to shoot with, then," Jeff said. "Let's hope he stays at that end and directs the battle."

Nicole sighed. "And helps them kill a few more Micawnwi."

"If Amrew runs his side like I told him to, there shouldn't be any more deaths," Jeff assured her. "Lots of noise and fury, but hopefully no one will engage hard enough to get seriously hurt." From somewhere in the distance a warbling cry drifted across the arena. "There's the signal," he said, hunching up onto his hands and knees. "We've got ten minutes. Let's find out if they all cleared out."

"Yeah. Let's do that." Nicole gestured over her shoulder to Mispacch. "Come on, Mispacch. No noise—the Oracle will be listening."

The Cluufe hive was indeed deserted. With Nicole in the lead, the three of them hurried across the central area and into the dispenser room.

Now that Nicole knew what to look for, it was obvious that the colored light display on the Cluufes' dispenser was very different from the one on the Micawnwi's. Pulling out her notepad and stylus, she pointed Jeff and Mispacch to the wall beside the dispenser and then started recording the pattern of the lights. As she worked, Jeff and Mispacch found the wall panel's handgrips and Mispacch pulled the wall open. Jeff stepped into the gap, flicked on a penlight from his tool vest, and peered into the dispenser's inner mechanism. He nodded in satisfaction and gave Nicole a thumbs-up.

Nicole nodded back, forcing herself not to rush. If she didn't get the Cluufe settings exactly correct, she and Jeff would never be able to get the machine back to the way it had been. That would tip off Hunter that his hive had been invaded, and he would make damn sure Amrew and the other Micawnwi were never able to pull off this stunt again.

Besides, depending on how much output the stone building's dispenser had, messing this one up might condemn the Cluufes to slow starvation. Nicole didn't especially like the weasels, but she had no intention of doing that to them if she could help it. Especially not when they were probably as much pawns of the Shipmasters as the Micawnwi were.

Jeff gave a soft but surprisingly impatient-sounding hiss. Nicole ignored him, carefully finished marking down the light order, and then just as carefully double-checked it. Only then did she key back to the page with the Micawnwi settings and turn the notepad around to where Jeff could see it. He peered at the display, looked back at the controls, and set to work.

One by one, the lights on the display began to change. Nicole watched, trying not to fidget, knowing there was nothing more she could do. There wasn't enough room for two of them back where Jeff was working, and she couldn't help Mispacch in holding up the wall. Instead, she concentrated on keeping the notepad steady and strained her ears for any signs that the Cluufes might be returning.

Probably because she was listening so hard, she heard the quiet thump.

She frowned. The thump had been soft, but it had also been deep, like someone had hit a huge drum somewhere in the distance. Even stranger, the sound had seemed to come from all around her. Turning her head back and forth, straining even harder, she listened for it to come again.

There it was: the same thump. Only this time it was a double:

thump . . . thump. She kept listening, and a few seconds later she heard another single thump.

What the *hell*?

There was a soft snap of fingers, and she looked over to see Jeff give her another thumbs-up as he stepped out of the alcove. Nicole nodded, slipping the notepad back into her pocket and pulling out the three flattened arrow quivers she'd swiped from the Micawnwi hive and tucked inside her jumpsuit. She put the open end of one of them beneath the dispenser chute and tapped the button, letting a few of the food morsels roll out. She stepped over to Mispacch, dug a couple of the morsels from the quiver, and offered them to her.

Carefully, Mispacch lowered the wall section back into position. She took the morsels and gave them a long and careful sniff. Then, with a brief fluffing of her fur, she nodded. Jeff snapped his fingers softly and pantomimed eating; Mispacch nodded and popped the bits into her mouth. She rolled them around her mouth a moment, then nodded again.

Nicole took a deep breath, feeling her muscles release some of their pent-up tension. It had worked. She and Jeff had found the right formula, and for the moment the Micawnwi food troubles were over.

There was another of the soft thumps. Frowning, Nicole pressed the quivers into Mispacch's hands and pointed toward Jeff and the food dispenser. *Fill them up,* she mouthed silently toward Jeff. *I'll be right back.* Without waiting for him to answer or object, she hurried out the door and into the central room beyond.

Her fear was that the sounds were somehow related to the Cluufes' return from battle. To her relief, the areas of the arena she could see were still deserted. She walked through the doorway onto the stone path, wondering if the whole thing might have been her imagination.

She was still looking around when she heard yet another thud.

She chewed at her lip. Could it be her imagination? Jeff certainly didn't seem to have heard anything.

But Jeff was focused on his work. Anyway, the thud seemed to be closer and louder out here.

She took a few more steps out into the arena, trying to figure out what might make a sound like that. There was another double thump, again sounding closer than it had indoors, and this time she had the impression that it had come from the curved wall to her left that arched up into the arena ceiling. She walked toward it, trying to pierce the trees and bushes that hid the lower part of the wall from sight.

She'd made it past the first line of short trees when, ten feet directly ahead, there was a rustling in the bushes.

Instantly, she dropped into a crouch, pressing close against the nearest tree, her pulse pounding in her ears. Her first impulse was to leap back to her feet and try to make it back to the Cluufe hive. But she'd seen Cluufes in action, and if that was one of them she would never get back to Jeff and Mispacch before he ran her down. The hidden track crawlway was no better; she might make it there ahead of her pursuer, but it offered no refuge and simply by going there she would betray its presence and destroy any future usefulness it might have.

But she had to do *something*. Too late, she wished she'd taken the time to grab a wrench or heavy screwdriver from Jeff's tool vest. At least then she'd have a weapon. But all she had in her own vest were food bars, a couple of small and useless tools, and water bottles.

Still, even a water bottle was better than nothing. Carefully, she slipped one out of its pocket and got a grip around its neck. The bushes rustled again . . .

And a Wisp stepped into view.

Nicole huffed out the breath she'd been holding. What *was* it with these damn things? "What the hell are you doing here?" she demanded as the thing glided toward her. "In case you missed it, there's a war going on a couple hundred yards that way—"

Right in the middle of her sentence, the Wisp stopped in front of her, wrapped its long arms around her torso—

And just like on the day when she and Bungie were snatched out of the early-morning Philadelphia sunlight, she found herself totally paralyzed.

She tried to shout. Nothing. She tried to kick, or to twist her arms against the Wisp's grip, or to slam her forehead against the silver-threaded white skin two inches from her eyes. She couldn't do any of those things. The Wisp turned around and headed back the way it had come, carrying Nicole pressed against its chest.

She couldn't even find her voice to ask where they were going. Not that the Wisp was likely to answer.

They passed beyond the last line of trees, and in her peripheral vision she saw the smooth curve of the wall rising up behind her. Was there some other door back here that she'd never noticed? Maybe a hidden path alongside the wall that would get them past the Micawnwi and Cluufes squaring off over there?

Or had the Shipmasters finally gotten so annoyed at Nicole's meddling that they'd sent a Wisp to haul her across the arena and hand her over to the Cluufes?

Even as that awful thought struck her, there was a soft whoosh, a longer and deeper sound than the ones that usually accompanied the *Fyrantha*'s opening doors. A sudden blast of hot air burst out behind her, shoving against her back like a steady August wind. The Wisp walked straight into the wind, and Nicole saw its butterfly wings unfurl behind it. The hot wind continued to press at her, and Nicole felt sweat breaking out across her skin.

And then the Wisp carried her through a wide opening in the wall and into a deep blackness.

There was a moment of turbulence as the wind suddenly seemed to be coming from every direction at once. Then it settled down, only now instead of blowing against her back it was an even hotter and more powerful upward blast that tore at the legs and back of her jumpsuit. In that same confused heartbeat she had the horrible sensation of falling. Then the Wisp's outstretched wings caught the airflow.

And as the door they'd come through slid shut, Nicole found herself and the Wisp rising rapidly on the wind.

Don't worry, Nicole. I won't let you go.

Nicole felt a grimace trying to form on her frozen lips. It was the same thing that first Wisp had said, the one who'd snatched her and Bungie and Sam. Whatever the damn things were, they seemed to have one-track minds. *I'm not worried about falling, you idiot,* she snarled silently at her captor. *I want to know where the hell we're going.*

We journey to the uppermost part of the ship.

Nicole caught her breath. Or at least she would have if she'd had any control over her chest muscles.

The Wisp had *answered*? That hadn't happened the last time. It had never happened.

And the answer didn't even make sense. Why would they be going to the uppermost part of the ship?

No answer. Maybe she needed to focus her thoughts into a more direct question. With an effort, she forced back the swirling emotion and confusion. *Why are we going there?*

Great danger approaches. Only a Protector can help us.

As if to underline the silent thought there was another thump, this one much louder and closer than the others had been. Some problem with this impossibly dark shaft they were floating in?

Again, there was no answer. Apparently, she couldn't just wonder about something, but had to put it into a clear sentence and mentally spit it at the Wisp. *What are those thumps?*

That is the great danger.

She grimaced. That was helpful. *What is this Protector you mentioned?*

A Protector isn't a what. It's a who.

Mentally, Nicole rolled her eyes. *Who is this Protector?*

You.

A faint light suddenly appeared above them. It approached rapidly as the Wisp continued to ride on the updraft. A few seconds later, with another moment of turbulence as the wind shifted back from blowing upward to a hard shove against her back, Nicole and the Wisp bounced out through another open panel into a narrow metal-walled space.

The Wisp unwrapped its arms from around her and took a step back. Nicole collected her balance, took a couple of quick breaths to confirm her lungs were working again, and then looked around her.

They were at the bottom of a narrow, dimly lit stairway that headed up to Nicole's right, curving around to the left as it rose, then disappeared around a wide pillar. Beyond the edge of the pillar, maybe up at the end of the stairway, was a somewhat brighter glow. To her left was a corridor like all the others she'd seen aboard the *Fyrantha*. "Which way?" she asked.

The Wisp didn't answer. *Which way?* she tried again, thinking the question this time.

Again, no answer. Maybe the Wisp had to be touching her in order to read her mind.

But the creature was standing in the middle of the corridor, effectively blocking it, and it was facing toward the stairway. The implication was obvious. Turning to her right, Nicole headed up.

The stairway was surprisingly short, no more than twenty steps. Focusing on her footing in the dim light, acutely aware that twisting her bad ankle here in the middle of *Fyrantha* nowhere would be bad, she reached the top and stepped out onto more of the familiar soft red flooring. Only then did she raise her eyes to look in front of her.

This time, she caught her breath for real.

The room was round, like the teleport room, and about thirty feet across. Most of the space was sunk three feet below the level where she was standing, with a narrow walkway around the rim at her level and three steps leading down from her stairway to the main floor. Filling the room were nine consoles of various sizes arranged in two concentric circles, all of the consoles facing inward toward the center, all of them with rows of muted indicator lights glowing across their surfaces. The entire rim of the room was composed of some kind of thick glass, six feet high, sandwiched between an expanse of hazy blue below and a wide overhang of gray metal that seemed to stretch outward from the room's roof.

And between the overhang above and the hazy blue below, visible all around her through the glass, were stars.

Nicole had seen stars once before, during one of the short trips her grandmother had taken her on. There hadn't been many of them up there, fighting their twinkling way through the hazy glow from the distant city, but they'd been pretty enough. Her grandmother had tried to tell her that on a really dark night you could see thousands of them, but Nicole hadn't really believed her.

One of her schoolbooks had said there were billions. She hadn't believed that, either.

Only there were. There were billions of them.

And every single one of them was out there, blazing with cold fire across the pure black sky.

They were stunning. They were beautiful. They were terrifying.

For the first time, in the deepest core of her being, Nicole finally, truly, believed. She was indeed aboard a spaceship, somewhere in the middle of a huge and terrible universe.

And her home was lost far away in the distance behind her. Forever.

Somewhere, someone gave a little whimper. A moment later, she realized the sound had come from her.

But somehow, that loss really didn't seem important anymore. Slowly, she turned, drinking in the overwhelming display. Stars and more stars; hazy patches that might be clusters of different stars or patches of space fog; a wide band of haze that she guessed was the Milky Way that her grandmother had tried to tell her about—

And then, right at the corner of her eye, something flashed, and there was a loud, metallic thud.

She twisted around, grabbing the handrail for balance, peering through the glass into the starlit blackness. Something was out there, a shadowy object visible only as it moved across the stars. From the shadow came another flicker, followed by a swift line of light tracing between the shadow and someplace below Nicole and to her right. The line intersected with the *Fyrantha* down there, and there was another flash and thud.

And only then did the explanation abruptly penetrate her awe-struck mind.

The shadow across the stars was another spaceship.

A ship that was attacking the *Fyrantha*.

She blinked once, and in that flick of an eyelid the wonder filling her brain vanished. Looking away from the stars and the attacking ship, she focused again on the room and the consoles below her.

She'd been wrong before about all the consoles having glowing indicator lights. One of them was completely dark.

She looked over her shoulder. While she'd been gawking, the Wisp had climbed the stairs and was standing silently behind her. "That?" Nicole asked, jabbing a finger at the dark console. "Is that why I'm here?"

No answer. Cursing, Nicole bounded down the three steps to the main floor and hurried toward the console. Obviously, the console wasn't working. Obviously, the Wisp had brought her here to fix it.

Only she wasn't one of the fix-it people. She was just a Sibyl. "You need to go get Jeff," she called back over her shoulder. "Wisp? Go get Jeff."

There was no answer. Nicole reached the console and glanced back at the stairs.

Predictably, the Wisp hadn't moved an inch.

Maybe it wasn't rushing off to fetch Jeff or Carp because it knew there wasn't enough time. Maybe, like she'd thought earlier, it couldn't hear her unless they were touching.

Maybe it was just stupid.

Cursing again, Nicole shoved the console's chair out of the way and dropped down into a crouch.

There was a wide access panel stretching across most of the rectangular pedestal, she saw, running almost the entire height from the deck to the underside of the control board. Hooking her fingers into some of the ventilation slits, she pulled, and the panel popped out. Behind it was the usual collection of junction modules, function pips, modulators, and neatly laid-out wiring. Racked along one side of the main circuit board was a collection of spare parts, while the other side sported an equally impressive assortment of small tools. Apparently, whoever was supposed to man this particular group of consoles was also supposed to do their own repairs.

If the repair was anything complicated, the Wisp was out of luck. But if it was just a matter of swapping out a damaged component or two, she'd seen that done enough times that she could probably do it.

Unfortunately, there was only one way for her to figure out which of the components needed replacing.

Her inhaler.

There was another flash from somewhere out of Nicole's view, and another hard thud. Her choices seemed to be either slow death by inhaler or fast death by whatever the hell the attacker was shooting at them. Clenching her teeth, she dug into her vest pockets.

Only to find that both inhalers were gone.

"*Damn* it," she muttered, patting furiously at her pockets. No mistake. Somewhere along the line, probably during that long crawl along the tracks, she'd managed to lose both of them.

There was another thud. Grabbing a small work light from the tool section of the pedestal, she flicked it on. Fine. If she couldn't figure out which component to replace, she'd just replace all of them.

The first step was to pull out all the replacement components from the spare parts rack and lay them on the floor beneath their counterparts. Fortunately, they were all types she'd seen dozens of times before and she was able to grab the right ones without even having to cross-check their component numbers. With that finished, she selected the proper tools, which she'd also seen dozens of times, and set to work.

To discover that the procedures were harder than they had looked.

The junction modules weren't as easy to pop off their connections as she'd expected. The pips tended to drag their attached wires or get hung up on their mounting screws. The modulators and rectifiers and various types of simplex ellies all had hidden connectors that she never seemed to find the first time. And the solder gun's little liquid drips could glue the dispenser tip right to the wiring if she didn't get it away before the drops hardened. A dozen times in those first five minutes she wished like hell she'd sent Jeff out of the Cluufe hive to investigate the noise instead of going herself.

But she hadn't, and he wasn't here, and the flashes and thuds were getting worse. Swearing pretty much constantly now, she kept at it.

She'd replaced about a third of the components, and was starting to get the hang of the soldering gun, when the console suddenly came to life.

"Whoa," she muttered, twitching her hands back from the suddenly glowing components and the flashing power-alert indicators. The damn thing had been left *on?*

Probably just as well that it had. Otherwise, she would have wasted time replacing components that weren't broken. Climbing out from under the control board, wincing as legs that had gone to sleep started tingling, she gripped the edge of the board and looked outside.

Earlier, the area below the windows had been glowing a faint blue. Now, instead of a glow, the whole thing seemed to be blazing with blue fire.

And while the shadowy attackers were still firing their flickering pencils of light at the *Fyrantha,* there were no longer any thuds accompanying them.

For a moment she continued to watch. Then, struck by an odd impulse, she crossed the room again, climbed up the steps to the narrow walkway, and walked around the edge of the room. Jeff had suggested that the area in front of the arena had just been a few corridors deep. Nicole had insisted it was bigger than that. Maybe from here she could figure out which of them was right. She reached what she figured was the proper vantage point and peered through the glass.

The blue glow stretched out in front of her, as far ahead as she could see. She turned and looked behind her, just for reference, then turned forward again.

And as she did so, she felt the blood slowly draining from her face.

She could see what appeared to be the end of the blue glow behind her. Just barely, but she *could* see it. That distance should represent their work area, plus the other teams' work areas, plus the arena she'd just left.

But in the other direction, the blue glow just seemed to keep going. She couldn't see any end to it at all.

Which meant that not only was there as much ship in front of the arena as there was behind it, but there was considerably *more* ship in front of it than behind it.

The *Fyrantha* wasn't just big. It was *huge.*

For a long minute she stared out at the blue glow, trying to wrap her mind around this sudden revelation. As she did so, an odd thought occurred to her. The portside hull hallway was supposedly the leftmost edge of the ship. Tearing her eyes away from the blue glow stretching out toward the billions of stars in front of her, she looked to her left.

The blue glow didn't stop at the line where the portside hallway should be. Instead, it kept going, once again stretching out toward the stars. It didn't go as far as the ship did toward the front—she could see the edge of the glow out there to the side. But there was most certainly a lot more ship in that direction than she'd thought. At least as much as there was on this side of the corridor. Maybe more.

The *Fyrantha* wasn't just a flying ship. It was a freaking flying *city*.

Only every city she'd ever heard of had people living in it. The bigger the city, the more people.

So where were the *Fyrantha*'s people?

From somewhere behind her came a soft thud. She tensed, her eyes flicking back to the area where she'd seen the shadows flying across the stars. But if the attackers were still there, they'd stopped moving and she couldn't spot them. The sound came again, and to her relief she realized it wasn't another attack, but merely someone coming up the stairs.

An instant later, her brain suddenly caught up with her. *Someone coming up the* stairs?

Her first impulse was the one that years with Trake's group had sharpened to a reflex: run, or hide.

But the room had only one entrance, and that was already blocked by whoever was approaching. And with the room as open as it was, there was only one possible way to hide. Vaulting over the railing, she dropped down behind the nearest console. She pressed her back against the pillar, pulled her knees and elbows as tightly to her as she could, and froze.

The footsteps grew louder, and there was a subtle change in the sound as the intruder reached the outer walkway and headed down the three steps into the room proper. The sound continued on another few steps, and Nicole realized there were actually two of them. The second set also topped the rise and stepped into the room, and for a long moment there was silence as the intruders walked across the soft flooring.

Nicole clenched her hands into fists, hardly daring to breathe, trying to make herself as small as possible. If the intruders decided to take a walk around the room, or if they even just walked straight ahead to this end of the walkway, she was done for.

There was a sudden chattering as someone spoke in an alien language. Nicole twitched.

And then frowned.

"There," Fievj's voice came to her through her translator. "See the components scattered on the floor? It was a failed cross-link, all right. And someone beat us to it."

There was another chattering, this one in a different voice. "You're sure they couldn't have just fallen out of the replacement rack? The impacts *were* sending vibrations through this part of the ship."

"Vibrations hard enough to knock off the access panel and set it neatly alongside the support pedestal?" Fievj scoffed. "For someone in your position, Ryit, you sometimes have terrible powers of observation. No, someone was here, all right. The only questions are who were they and where did they go."

"Whoever they were, they left in a hurry," Ryit said. "Otherwise they would have put everything back."

"Unless they don't care about neatness," Fievj said. "But no, you're probably right. And of course, the most likely reason for them to hurry away is that they knew we were coming. That means the Wisps."

"Or the *Fyrantha* itself, speaking to a Sibyl," Ryit pointed out. "That's the most likely explanation, in fact. It could have warned one of the Sibyls, who then brought a human work crew here to repair the console."

"I don't know," Fievj said uncertainly. "That would require that one or more of the Sibyls was listening at the crucial moment. *And* that the humans could get here this quickly from their work areas. Neither seems likely."

"Well, I doubt it was the Wisps," Ryit said. "I've never seen any of them do the slightest bit of mechanical work."

"Though we've never seen the *Fyrantha* under such a severe attack, either," Fievj pointed out. "Even if they won't fight—"

"*Can't* fight," Ryit corrected.

"Even if they won't or *can't* fight," Fievj growled, "it's possible that repairing something crucial, like a shield generator cross-link, is within their design parameters."

"No," Ryit said firmly. "I've run the matrix, and they're absolutely incapable of such work. I mean, come on, Fievj—if we could get them to refit the ship, would we be bothering with these damned humans?"

"The humans may yet prove more useful than you think," Fievj said, suddenly thoughtful. "So: not the Wisps, and not the humans. Could there be someone else aboard? Some tech-capable group we haven't run into before?"

Nicole felt a small shiver run through her. An hour ago, she would have dismissed such a suggestion as ludicrous. Now, having seen the *Fyrantha's* true size, the idea that a whole army might be lurking undetected didn't seem nearly so impossible.

"I suppose," Ryit said, sounding doubtful. "But we've been under other attacks and had to run. Why show themselves now?"

"They haven't exactly *shown* themselves."

"True," Ryit said. "I suppose it's time to give the Caretaker a call."

Fievj made a rude-sounding noise that Nicole's translator couldn't decipher. "Is that really necessary? Surely you realize he's not nearly as truthful as he acts."

"Of course not," Ryit said. "But you can often learn more from liars than they realize, simply by paying attention to how they dance around your questions."

"Maybe," Fievj said with a sniff. "I'll wager you a planet he won't be the least bit useful."

"I'll take that wager," Ryit said. "Let me find a call switch . . . there's one."

"I'd love to see you do a matrix work-up on him sometime," Fievj said darkly.

"I've tried," Ryit said. "I can never get a proper fix on—"

"Good morning, Master Fievj and Master Ryit," a voice suddenly boomed. "I see you've again successfully evaded destruction at the hands of your allies."

Nicole frowned. At the hands of their *allies*? Weren't allies the ones who were supposed to be on your side?

"Your sarcasm is wasted," Fievj said stiffly. "Those were suppliers, not allies. They also have a history of turning on customers they believe to be weak. We of course anticipated their attack and repulsed it."

"You *repulsed* it? You ran like frightened herbivores when the shooting started."

"Only because the starboard-aft shields failed to fully activate," Fievj said. "You wouldn't happen to know anything about that, would you?"

"Crews have been working on the skinshield grid for the past several months," the Caretaker said. "Perhaps one of the repairs was incomplete."

"No, I think it was that one of the shield cross-links failed," Fievj said. "This cross-link, as a matter of fact."

"We were on our way here to fix it," Ryit added. "Fortunately for your precious *Fyrantha*, someone got here first."

"I don't suppose you'd have any idea who that person or persons might be?" Fievj asked.

"Of course," the Caretaker said. "It was the Caretaker."

There was a moment of silence. "The Caretaker," Fievj repeated, his voice oddly flat.

"Not me, of course," the Caretaker said. "I mean another Caretaker."

"There aren't other Caretakers," Ryit insisted. "You said so yourself when we first came aboard."

"When you first came aboard, there weren't," the Caretaker confirmed. "But the *Fyrantha* has been long in consideration, and has chosen a new Caretaker."

Nicole felt her eyes narrow. The Wisp had called her a Protector. Now this whoever-he-was was talking about a Caretaker.

Were they talking about *her*?

But that was crazy. She didn't even know what a Caretaker was. She certainly didn't want the job.

"Bungie," Ryit murmured, his voice suddenly dark.

"What about him?" Fievj asked.

"He and his team's Sibyl went into Number Four a few days ago," Ryit said. "Twice, in fact. The Sibyl may have gone in a third time." He gave a derisive-sounding snort. "Unfortunately, Teqel has lost track of her. Very sloppy."

"Work crews have penetrated the arenas before," Fievj said. "There's nothing anyone can do in there that can affect the rest of the ship. Not even a Sibyl."

"I'm not worried about her," Ryit said. "My concern is with this Bungie. It seems he's gone missing, and not into the arena. I'm wondering if he might have done this."

Nicole felt her lip twist. Right. Bungie, being helpful. Especially being helpful with electronics repair, which he'd spent the past few weeks actively ignoring. Besides, she knew for a fact that *she* was the one who had fixed that console.

Or had she?

She frowned. She'd replaced a few components, yes. But to be perfectly honest, she had no idea what had restarted the console.

Could it have been someone else? Not Bungie, of course, but maybe these other people Fievj had suggested might be hiding aboard?

"Well, Caretaker?" Fievj challenged. "Is this human Bungie the *Fyrantha*'s new Caretaker?"

"I have no name to offer you," the Caretaker said. "Merely the truth I've already spoken."

"Location, then," Fievj persisted. "Where can we find him? *Or* the Caretaker?"

"I have no more truth to offer you," the Caretaker repeated.

"As helpful as always," Ryit said acidly.

"I warned you," Fievj reminded him. "Come—there's nothing more to be done here. Maybe our intruder left a trail we can follow."

There were more quiet footsteps on the soft flooring, and then louder ones as the two aliens climbed the three steps to the walkway. Struck by a sudden impulse to see whether Ryit was the armored emissary who'd been walking around the arena, Nicole moved to the edge of the console and eased an eye around the edge.

It was all she could do to keep from gasping. Ryit wasn't wearing any armor. Neither was Fievj.

Only Fievj wasn't the centaurlike creature that his armor had implied. He and Ryit were both just normal, human-shaped beings, with tall, thin bodies, almost skeletal arms and legs, pale skin, and wispy tendrils of hair flowing down their heads and shoulders. Instead of armor, they wore exquisitely textured and decorated knee-length kimono-style robes, with wide black belts and colorful patches on their shoulders and just below the neck. She couldn't see their faces, but from the clothing she could almost imagine that they were nice elderly men, like the mall Santa her grandmother had taken her to see once.

Or at least she could have imagined that if both of the wide black belts hadn't also included wide black holsters with large guns inside them.

She waited, holding very still, until both aliens had disappeared down the stairway. Then, as Trake had always warned her to do, she counted to three hundred to make sure they weren't lurking out of sight waiting for her to come out of hiding.

The seconds ticked off into minutes. She was still counting them, wondering how much longer she should wait and how she was going to find her way back to the arena or the hive, when she caught a flicker of shadow rising up the stairway.

Instantly, she ducked back around the pillar, again pulling her elbows in tightly. The steps were fainter than either Fievj's or Ryit's, but that didn't mean anything. Most people could move very quietly when they wanted to.

She was still sitting there, her throat tight, when a Wisp came around the side of the console.

Nicole huffed out a relieved sigh. "Time to go?" she asked.

The Wisp pointed to the stairs. Nicole got to her feet, and together they crossed the room and walked down the stairs. As they approached the landing where they'd first arrived, the wall opened, and once again a blast of hot air washed over them. The

Wisp wrapped its arms around her, unfurled its wings, and stepped into the opening.

The shaft was just as dark as it had been the first time, and the air rushing up at them just as hot. But this time, without the terrifying newness fogging her brain, Nicole found the trip not nearly as unpleasant. In fact, by the time the big sliding door opened to reveal the trees and hills of the arena, she discovered to her mild surprise that she was almost sorry it was over. She'd always dreamed of being able to fly, and this was probably as close to it as she would ever get.

The Wisp set her down a few feet from the door. Then, it backed again into the shaft, and as the wall closed Nicole caught a final glimpse of the creature as it floated downward.

She turned back, listening hard. There were no sounds of battle that she could hear. Not surprising, given that Amrew was only supposed to keep the Cluufes occupied for ten to fifteen minutes and she'd been gone nearly an hour. Hopefully, Jeff and Mispacch had also long since made it back to the Micawnwi side with their stolen food.

Which left only the question of whether the Cluufes had settled back into their spots in the hive and the stone building, or whether they were still moving back and forth between the two locations.

Only one way to find out. Moving as silently as she could, she eased through the undergrowth toward the stone path.

She was approaching the last line of trees when something sharp suddenly poked hard into her back. She jumped forward, twisting around.

It was Hunter, his halberd leveled toward her, his mouth half-open to reveal a set of clenched teeth. "Oh, hello," Nicole said, instinctively dropping into innocent mode. "You startled me."

"You'll come with me," Hunter said, his voice sounding as clenched as his teeth. "You'll return our food dispenser to our use.

"Or I will personally slaughter your companion before your eyes."

FiFteen

Nicole's first impulse was to turn and get the hell out of there as fast as she could.

But Hunter had a weapon, and he was faster than she was. More importantly, if he was on the alert so were the rest of the Cluufes.

So instead, she turned around and walked through the trees to the path and let him take her back to the Cluufes' hive.

Hunter's threat had implied that only one of her fellow intruders had been caught, and all the way down the path Nicole wondered whether the prisoner was Jeff or Mispacch. Probably the latter, she finally decided.

She was wrong. Sitting in a corner of the food dispenser room, surrounded by four leveled halberds, was Jeff.

They'd taken his tool and food vests away from him, and his jumpsuit looked rumpled. Had they roughed him up? "Hey," she said as casually as she could.

"Hey," Jeff replied. His voice was also casual, but Nicole could see the tension lines in his face. "What happened to you?"

And now, as she looked more closely, she could see that there were bruises starting to form on his cheeks and jaw. They were faint, but she'd been hit in the face enough times over the years to know what it looked like. The Cluufes had roughed him up, all right. "Sorry," she apologized. "I was suddenly needed elsewhere."

He gave her a faint smile. "You probably should have said no."

"Wasn't really an option."

"Yeah," Jeff said in a tone that probably meant he didn't believe her. "Listen, you wouldn't happen to still have the dispenser code for the Cluufe food profile, would you?"

"As a matter of fact, I would," Nicole said, looking over her shoulder at Hunter. "It was never our intention to leave your people without food."

"You will set it right," Hunter said. "Now."

"And Jeff?"

"Your companion stays where he is."

Nicole shook her head. "Sorry, but I need his help with the machine." She gestured to the wall. "We'll also need this wall section opened up—the handholds are down there and there. My guess is that it's going to take all four of your friends here."

Hunter seemed to measure her with his eyes. Then, stepping forward, he rested the sharp tip of his halberd against Nicole's stomach. "Open it," he ordered.

The Cluufes weren't nearly as strong as the Micawnwi, and it did indeed take all four guards to wrestle the wall section open. At Hunter's instruction three of them then held it up while the fourth set two of the halberds in bracing positions between the open section and the back wall.

Nicole winced, remembering her attempt to brace a similar wall section with a rounded chair. But the halberds were sturdy enough, and the Cluufes had placed them correctly, and the section stayed open. "Now," Hunter said, stepping back as his men collected the other two halberds and moved back to guard the doorway. "Fix it."

It had taken Jeff about four minutes to reprogram the dispenser for Micawnwi food. It took the same four minutes to put it back again. Nicole double-checked the final settings, confirmed he'd done it right, then waited while Hunter cautiously sampled the result.

Ten minutes later, with neither nausea nor death having ensued, he declared himself satisfied. At his direction, the guards lowered the wall section and retrieved their halberds.

"Excellent," Hunter said. He gestured to his men.

And suddenly the four halberds were once again pressed against Jeff's torso. "Your final task," Hunter told Nicole calmly. "You're going to get me a weapon."

Nicole felt her stomach tighten. "You already have weapons."

"Primitive toys of generations past," Hunter said contemptuously. "I want one of the flash-flickers that took us to victory before the Masters spirited them away."

"You mean the greenfire guns?"

"Is that what the Masters call them?"

"It's what *I* call them," Nicole said. "Where do you expect me to find something like that?"

"I don't know," Hunter said. "Nor do I care." He pointed at Jeff. "But *he* cares. He cares very much."

Nicole looked at Jeff. His throat was tight, but he was clearly trying not to show his tension. "That's not fair," she protested. "We did what you asked. We gave you back your food."

"Besides, you don't need any other weapons," Jeff added. "From what I saw—" He broke off as one of the Cluufes shifted his halberd from Jeff's torso to rest against his throat.

"I want a flash-flicker," Hunter said, his voice gone deathly cold. "This meager space is little more than a prison. But it is *ours,* and our enemies will be taught to respect it."

"They won't return," Nicole said quickly. Unfortunately, she knew, that was probably the truth. There was certainly no chance Amrew could use this same trick again. "I promise."

"I don't believe you," Hunter said flatly. "Even if I did, it wouldn't matter. They have to be taught a lesson."

"But why?" Nicole pleaded. The thought of the Micawnwi at the wrong end of a greenfire gun, with only halberds to protect themselves . . . "You've got all the food you need, and they won't be back."

Hunter made a contemptuous noise. "I pity you, Sibyl. Do you truly believe that food is all a being needs to live?"

"He's talking about honor," Jeff said quietly.

"No, he's talking about pigheaded pride," Nicole retorted. "I can't even count how many times I've seen someone get killed over that."

"And you'll soon see it again," Hunter said. "But it won't be *our* blood that will pour out across these worthless plants. Now go and bring me something worthy of combat."

"If I refuse?"

"Then your companion had best prepare himself for more pain," Hunter said calmly. "If you don't bring me the weapon by the time the light dims this evening, I'll begin taking his toes and fingers."

Nicole stared at him. "You can't be serious."

"Deadly serious," Hunter assured her. "Once the light dims I'll remove one digit per hour until you arrive."

"You mean you want it *tonight*?" Nicole shook her head, a twitchy, jerky movement. "That's only six or seven hours away. I can't possibly find that kind of weapon that fast."

"I believe you can," Hunter said. "Which of us will prove correct, I wonder?"

"This is ridiculous," Nicole insisted, trying one last time to talk him down. But without leverage she was just stalling. "Why do you need it that fast?"

"Because the enemy is now relaxing in the warmth of their victory," Hunter said. "If we move tonight, we can take them by surprise."

Nicole clenched her teeth. He was probably right, too. By tomorrow the Micawnwi would be on the alert again. Tonight, maybe not so much. "Fine," she said. "If I get you this weapon, do you swear on your honor and the pride of the Cluufes that you'll let us go? *Both* of us?"

"I do so swear," Hunter said without hesitation. "We were never tasked with your defeat. There's no honor to be had in your destruction."

Nicole frowned. *We were never tasked with your defeat?* What was *that* supposed to mean? "But cutting us up is all right?"

Hunter lifted his halberd point toward the ceiling and stepped out of her way. "Go. Time is passing."

Nicole hadn't dared ask Jeff what had happened to Mispacch, not with Hunter standing there listening. The only other way to find out would be to go to the Micawnwi end of the arena, and she couldn't waste time doing that. Not with the image of the Cluufes hacking away at Jeff's body frozen into her mind like the ghostly image on her grandmother's old TV screen. She had to either get Hunter his gun, or else find a way to get Jeff out of there. The whole thing was making her sick to her stomach.

Especially since it was all her fault.

She could rationalize all she wanted to about the Wisp not giving her a choice before it snatched her. But the fact was she *had* had a choice. In fact, she'd had lots of choices. She could have stayed with Jeff and Mispacch instead of going off alone to check out the thumping noise. Or, if she'd decided it absolutely *had* to be checked out, she could have left her notepad with Jeff so that he could reset the dispenser. Or she could have backed away from the Wisp instead of just standing there and letting it grab her.

But she hadn't done any of those things. At every point along the way she'd made the wrong decision.

And to make it worse, not only was Jeff in danger, but so were the Micawnwi. If she got Hunter his weapon, they would die quickly, fried by whatever the hell greenfire guns fired. If she didn't, they would still die, only slower from starvation.

Let them die, Plato had told her. In fact, he'd insisted on it. In hindsight, she knew now that he'd been right.

They were going to die anyway. What difference did it make how fast or how slow they did it?

But Plato hadn't looked into their eyes, or seen the children's faces light up at his approach. Nicole couldn't simply abandon them.

Only it looked like she was going to have to.

It was just as well, she decided bitterly as she passed beneath the cold stares of the Cluufes guarding the stone building, that she didn't have time to go see Mispacch. She couldn't have faced the woman anyway, knowing she was going to betray them.

So, naturally, given the way her luck was running today, Mispacch was waiting for her at the Micawnwi end of the plain.

"Sibyl!" she called, hurrying out from concealment behind a tree. "I was so worried about you. About you both." Abruptly, her lumbering jog slowed as she peered back the way Nicole had come. "Where's your companion?"

"Not here," Nicole bit out.

And was instantly ashamed of herself. None of this was

Mispacch's fault. "What happened back there?" she asked, forcing a softer tone.

"We couldn't find you," Mispacch said, waving vaguely back toward the Cluufe hive. "Jeff waited as long as he could, then ordered me to return with the food while he searched further."

Nicole nodded. That was Jeff, all right.

And he would have stayed there, dodging Cluufe searchers and hunting fruitlessly for her, until Hunter eventually ran him to ground. "Did you at least get the food back?" she asked.

"Yes," Mispacch said, the concern in her voice briefly overwhelmed by gratitude. "I did as you suggested: two of the quivers went to the men while I concealed the third to share among the women and children."

"Good," Nicole said, feeling a small flicker of satisfaction. At least that part of the plan had worked.

Unless Amrew found out about it, in which case he would probably be furious with Mispacch and Nicole both. Though right now odds were he wouldn't live long enough to do anything about it. So much for the brief lifting of her mood. "I need to go," she said to Mispacch, edging toward the exit. "I'll try to get back later."

"Wait," Mispacch said, reaching behind her smock and pulling out Nicole's two missing inhalers. "On my return through the bushes I found these."

"Oh—thanks," Nicole said, taking the inhalers and slipping them into her vest pockets. Back in the upstairs room, those would have been awfully handy. Now, when she didn't need them, was of course when she got them back. "They must have fallen out of my pockets along the way."

"Yes," Mispacch said, sounding puzzled. "May I ask a question?"

"I'm sorry, but I really have to go," Nicole said, taking a couple more steps toward the door. "Save it for later, okay?"

"I understand," Mispacch said. "I just wished to know why the two devices smelled so different."

Nicole shook her head. "I have no idea what you're talking about."

"They smell different," Mispacch repeated. "One of them . . . it would almost seem that it would do you harm."

Nicole stopped, an eerie feeling settling into her gut. Only *one* of them would do her harm? "Why do you say that? How could you know?"

"Remember when you offered me your food," Mispacch said. "From the smell, I was certain it would harm us. I can likewise conclude from the smell of your food and the smell of the device that they cannot both be acceptable to your body."

For a long moment Nicole stared at her. Jeff had said the inhaler stuff was a slow poison. Was that what Mispacch was smelling?

But shouldn't both inhalers still smell the same?

Slowly, she reached into her pockets and pulled out the inhalers. "Show me," she said, walking back to Mispacch and holding them out. "Which one smells like it would hurt me?"

Mispacch took them and gave each a sniff. "This one," she said, holding out her right hand.

"Thanks." Gingerly, Nicole took it back and gave it a long, careful look. As near as she could tell, it looked exactly like the other inhalers she'd used during her time aboard the ship. She turned it over, studying every square inch of its curved surface.

And then, finally, she spotted it. Just below the place where the cylinder tube joined the rest of the inhaler was a tiny, almost invisible notch. "Let me see the other one," she said.

Mispacch handed it over. Sure enough, that one had no such notch.

Experimentally, Nicole ran her finger across the plastic. The notch was nearly invisible to the eye, but her fingernail caught it just fine. If whoever had given that one to her had known about the notch, he could have spotted it with a casual flick of his finger. "What about this one?" she asked, holding up the notchless inhaler. "Does it smell like it would hurt me?"

"It smells odd," Mispacch conceded. "But it's the same scent you had about you the first time we met."

Which had been right after Nicole had used the inhaler to get the arena door's keylock code. Which meant the notchless one, however bad it might be for her, was the kind she'd been using since she came aboard. The other one was apparently something else. Something far worse.

Sam had given her one of the inhalers. Jeff had given her the other.

Which of them was trying to kill her?

"I have to go," she said, putting the inhalers away and once again backing toward the exit. "Right now."

"Be careful," Mispacch called after her. "And come back to us soon."

Two minutes later, Nicole was back in the cool, gray corridors of the *Fyrantha*. Bungie had claimed he'd found hidden decks and rooms and supplies. Jeff had wondered whether some of those supplies might include weapons.

For the first time in her life, Nicole hoped that Bungie hadn't just been blowing smoke.

She'd left the main work area before getting any instructions from the *Fyrantha*, which meant her crew could be anywhere. But she'd noticed a pattern in the sequence of work sites, and she had a pretty good idea where they would be.

Sure enough, she found them just three corridors away from where she'd expected.

Kahkitah, watching with interest as Levi took apart a rein oscillator, was the first to spot her. "Nicole!" he whistled an enthusiastic greeting as she hurried toward them. "Carp, look—Nicole's come back!"

"About time," Carp snarled, wiping sweat and grease from his forehead with his sleeve as he stepped back out of the wall alcove. "Where the *hell* have you been? Plato had to get Yuliya from red crew to get us our work—"

"I need your help," Nicole cut him off. "Jeff's in trouble. I have to find Bungie right away."

"Bungie?" Carp echoed, frowning. "What for?"

"Has Bungie hurt him?" Kahkitah asked, his bird trilling going suddenly dark.

"No one's hurt anyone," Nicole assured him, deciding to skip over the previous night's incident. Jeff and Bungie's brief fight was irrelevant to the current crisis, and it never paid to overload Kahkitah with unnecessary details. "But that'll change if I can't find Bungie. The people in the arena have Jeff, and they're threatening to cut off his fingers if I can't get something for them."

For a second, the air was filled with a variety of surprised gasps and angry or disbelieving comments. In the midst of the noise, Carp's voice cut through like a halberd axe. "What do you need from us?"

If she'd been paying attention, Nicole thought later, she would probably have noticed Kahkitah's back suddenly stiffen and his eyes lock on to something behind her. But she was so focused on the task at hand that such subtleties didn't even register. "Bungie said he'd found stairways and decks that the rest of us didn't know about," she told Carp. "Do you know if there really are hidden places like that?"

The whole group abruptly went stiff and silent. Even then, she didn't catch on. "Well?" she demanded. "Are there secret stairways, or aren't there?"

"Yes," Plato's voice came from behind her. "There are."

Nicole spun around. The big-shouldered man was striding toward them, the look of an approaching storm on his face. Two steps behind him, his own expression strangely blank, was Sam.

Nicole felt a sudden shiver across her skin. If Sam was the one who'd given her the poisoned inhaler . . . But surely he wouldn't try anything out here, not with everyone watching. "You're sure?" she asked Plato. "Secret places *here,* in this part of the *Fyrantha?*"

"Again, yes," Plato said. "Why do you need to know?"

"She says Jeff's in danger," Levi said. "That she has to find Bungie—"

"Yes, I heard what she said," Plato cut him off. "I want to know *why* she thinks that's going to help her find him."

"Because I know him," Nicole said. "At least enough to know how he thinks. Are any of the stairs near the *marsarvi*-seven-seven area?"

"One of them is," Plato said, his expression starting to edge from angry to curious. "But there's nothing interesting up there. It's mostly just abandoned crew quarters, like the ones we're living in back in the hive."

"Are there any food dispensers?"

"Nothing that's working," Plato said. "At least, nothing we've ever found."

"But we didn't really search out the place," Carp added. "Bungie might have found something."

"Bungie's limping around on a bad leg," Plato countered. "He isn't doing a hell of a lot of exploring."

"What makes you think he's up there?" Sam asked.

Nicole focused on him. She'd known a few casual killers back at home, people who could murder someone and then go out and relax with a drink or two. Sam didn't seem like the type who could do that.

But neither did Jeff. And yet, *one* of them had given her a poisoned inhaler.

Which one? More importantly, *why*?

She didn't have time to figure it out. All she could do was keep going and hope she got some answers before it was too late. "Like I said, I know how he thinks," she told Sam.

"So he's somewhere in one of the deserted decks?" Plato asked.

Nicole felt her forehead crease slightly. Plato's voice had been just a little too eager . . . "Yes, he's in that area," she said evasively. "Thanks. I'll let everyone get back to work now." She turned her back on Plato and Sam and started walking quickly away.

Not quickly enough. "Hold it," Plato ordered, catching up with her and closing a big hand around her arm. "First of all, *they're* not supposed to be working; *you*—all of you—are supposed to be working."

"I told you, Jeff's in trouble," Nicole said tartly, trying unsuccessfully to pull her arm free. "Bungie may be the only one who can help."

"How?" Plato persisted. "What can a walking waste of skin like him possibly do?"

Nicole clenched her teeth. They were listening closely, all of them. And after all of Plato's warnings about fighting, this wasn't going to go over very well.

But she had no choice. "The Cluufes in the testing arena want weapons," she said. "Better weapons than they've got now. Bungie said he'd found interesting stuff in the hidden decks. I'm hoping he found something I can trade for Jeff's life."

Plato's expression didn't change. "Really."

"Really," Nicole assured him. "I'm hoping—"

"What makes you think Bungie's gone up the *marsarvi*-seven-seven hidden stairway?" Plato interrupted. "There are at least three other hidden stairways I know about, and probably some I don't."

"Because he went on one of his extended walks while we were working there," Nicole said. "When he—"

"Extended walks?" Carp put in. *"That's* what you call goofing off?"

"When he came back," Nicole said doggedly, "he had the kind of look I've seen on him before when he's found something he thinks might pay off someday."

"That's why you think he's there?"

"Yes," Nicole said.

For a long minute Plato just gazed at her. Then, to her surprise, he gave a curt nod. "Okay," he said, letting go of her arm. "Let's go. Sam and I will help you."

"He won't like it if anyone except me shows up," Nicole warned.

"I don't care what he likes or doesn't like," Plato retorted. "Besides, Sam needs to take another look at those arrow wounds. Come on, I'll show you where the stairs are."

"You want us to help?" Levi asked. "There's a lot of space up there to search."

"You got work to do?" Plato countered. "Then stay here and do it."

Carp grimaced, but nodded. "Fine," he said. "Everyone, back to work."

Reluctantly, Nicole thought, the crew turned back to their jobs. Nicole looked at the hard expression on Plato's face, and the empty one on Sam's—"We can take Kahkitah," she said suddenly. "Carp won't need him again until it's time to close the wall section."

"We don't need him," Plato said. "Sam and I can handle any lifting we need to do."

"It couldn't hurt to have a little extra muscle along," Nicole persisted. "Kahkitah, do you want to help us find Bungie?"

"We don't *need* him," Plato repeated, his tone warning her to drop the subject.

"We don't need him, either," Levi spoke up. "Nicole's right— he might be useful."

Plato hissed out an exasperated-sounding breath. "Fine," he said. "But if he comes, he does what he's told. *Exactly* what he's told. You got that, Kahkitah?"

"Yes, of course," Kahkitah said, sounding puzzled as he walked over to them. "I always try to do what I'm told."

"Sure," Plato said. "Is that it, Nicole? You want to bring some tools, too? Maybe a cutter, in case Bungie's built himself a bunker?"

"No, this is fine," Nicole said through stiff lips. "Can we go now?"

"Your wish is my command," Plato said sarcastically. "This way. Try to keep up."

sixteen

The stairway was six corridors away from the spot where Nicole's crew had been working the day Bungie wandered back before lunch with that self-satisfied smirk on his face. The entrance was between two other doors, covered by a slightly wider section of wall than the one Nicole had gotten through during her escape from the Micawnwi hive.

"This is it," Plato said, peering in at the dimly lit staircase as Kahkitah held the wall section open. "So. We go up, or down?"

"Neither," Nicole said, waving both directions down the hallway. "He's here. Somewhere."

"He's *here*?" Plato stared at her. "Then why the hell did you ask about hidden stairways?"

"Because he told me he'd found hidden stairs," Nicole said. "I needed to see if they really existed and where they were."

"So he *is* in there?" Sam asked.

"No," Nicole said as patiently as she could. "Look. If you're trying to hide from someone, you don't give clues about where you're hiding. Like if you find a secret room and want to hide there, you don't let anyone know that *you* know there's a secret room. But if you *don't* plan to hide there, you might tell people about it so that they'll *think* that's where you're going to hide. Right?"

"Okay," Plato said slowly. "But you might also say that if there *wasn't* a secret room and you wanted people to waste their time looking for one."

"Right," Nicole said. "That's why I asked if there were hidden stairs. He told me he'd found some stairs, so that meant he didn't actually go up them."

"But if he didn't use the stairs he could be anywhere," Plato objected. "We're right back where we started."

"No, we're not," Nicole said, looking back and forth between their confused expressions. This wasn't *that* hard to understand. "He figures I'll tell you about the stairs. He'll also want to know when you start a *real* search for him."

"I know!" Kahkitah whistled, waving one hand excitedly as he continued holding up the wall section with the other. "He's hiding someplace where he can see us!"

"See us, or hear us, or know some other way that we're here," Nicole confirmed, impressed in spite of herself. She would never in a hundred years have figured Kahkitah, of all people, would have followed her reasoning on that one. Especially since Plato and Sam clearly hadn't.

But if they hadn't gotten it before, they were on top of it now. "So he'll know when we're getting close," Plato said thoughtfully, "and when he's going to need to either run or get ready to fight. Huh. I wouldn't have pegged him as that smart."

"Oh, he's smart enough," Nicole said, a shiver running up her back. "Smart enough to get himself in trouble. Not always smart enough to get out of it again."

"He'll need a supply of food and water," Sam said, looking down the hallway. "Someplace to sleep . . ."

"I know where he is," Plato said suddenly. "Come on. Kahkitah, put that wall section back down. *Quietly.*"

He headed off the way they'd come. "Where are we going?" Nicole asked, hurrying to catch up.

"There's a room in the next corridor that backs up against the stairs," Plato said over his shoulder. "We've never figured out exactly what it is—a ready room, a lounge, maybe even a holding cell. It's got a supply of water and a walled-off section with a couple of beds."

"And he'd be able to hear someone in the stairway?" Nicole asked.

"Don't know," Plato said. "Probably. We checked it once, right after he went missing, but it was empty."

"He would have dodged around a little at first," Nicole said. "Probably had his eye on the room all along and just had to wait until after you searched it before he could move in."

"What about food?" Sam asked.

"Nothing in the room," Plato said. "But if he was able to figure out the lock code on the storage closets he'd have had access to food bars. The other thing about the ready room is that there's plenty of space for him to walk around and get his leg back in shape without having to come out into the open."

Nicole frowned suddenly. Bungie's leg . . . and Plato had even mentioned that the wounds had come from arrows.

But how could Plato know that? She hadn't told him, Bungie certainly hadn't told him, and Sam had promised to keep it quiet.

Unless Sam *hadn't* kept it quiet.

"So," she said casually, watching Plato out of the corner of her eye. "How long have you known?"

He shrugged. "Pretty much since it happened," he said just as casually. "Sam told me the morning after he patched him up."

Nicole turned and looked at Sam. "What did you *think* I was going to do?" Sam demanded hotly. "That idiot is going to get us all killed if we don't do something about him."

"He's right," Plato said. "If I'd had the resources, we'd have done a full sweep for him earlier. Now that we know where he is, we can finally end this."

"I hope so," Nicole said, another stray fact dropping into place. "So you were the one who switched out the keylock on the arena door?"

"What, you thought it had fallen out by itself?" Plato scoffed. "Not that it did a damn bit of good. What did you tell Jeff to make him go in there with you?"

Nicole shook her head. "Nothing. Going with me was his idea."

"Yeah, I'll bet." Plato hissed out a breath. "Okay, this is what we're going to do. We're going to nail Bungie to the floor, and we're going to get Jeff out of the arena. Then we're going to weld the doors shut and you will never go in there again. Deal?"

The faces of Mispacch and her children flashed in front of Nicole's eyes. But she'd done all she could for them, and more than anyone could reasonably expect. Certainly more than she ever would have expected from herself.

Anyway, she had enough troubles of her own right now. "Deal," she said.

"Good," Plato said, coming to a halt. "Here's the plan," he continued, lowering his voice and pointing to the door just ahead. "We'll pop the door and you'll go in. If he's asleep, you signal us and we'll come in and take him. If he's awake, talk to him or something and get his attention away from the door. Got it?"

"Sure," Nicole said doubtfully. Bungie probably wouldn't be that easy to distract, especially if he was already wary or suspicious. Still, there were four of them and only one of him. They should make out all right.

Unless, of course, he'd found something nastier than the halberd on one of the hidden decks and brought it down here with him. If he had, they could be in serious trouble.

If he hadn't, Nicole had just wasted an hour of whatever life Jeff had left.

Only one way to find out. Taking a deep breath, she walked up to the door and tapped the release.

The door whooshed open to reveal a space about three times the size of her room back in the hive. In the front part was a small table and a couple of chairs, with a water dispenser by a short counter midway back along the left-hand side wall. In the rear were the two beds Plato had mentioned, behind a partially open floor-to-ceiling grate. "Bungie?" she called softly. "Bungie? It's me." She took a step into the room.

And nearly had her shoulder ripped out of its socket as a hand darted out of nowhere to grab her right arm and yank her sideways along the wall.

She stumbled, her free arm flailing madly as she tried to keep her feet under her. She was still fighting for balance as Plato burst into the room behind her, his hands bunched into fists, his eyes tracking the direction she'd gone. He was barely inside the room when the hand let go of Nicole's arm—

And the blunt end of a halberd shot across Nicole's view and rammed squarely into Plato's stomach.

The big man gave an agonized grunt and doubled over, half turning as he staggered away. Sam, charging in right behind him, tried frantically to get out of the way as the weapon tapped Plato a second time and then shifted direction toward him. He was partially successful, taking a glancing blow off his hip instead of catching the end of the shaft full force in his gut. But even that lower impact was enough to spin him a quarter turn around and drop him with a bone-jarring thud onto the floor.

"You stupid bitch," Bungie snarled into Nicole's ear. "What the *hell* did you think you were doing?"

"We were worried about your leg," Nicole protested, rubbing her throbbing arm. "That's why we brought Sam—"

"Like hell," Bungie cut her off, grabbing her arm again and giving her another yank that sent her stumbling past him toward the corner. "You'll get yours after I finish with them."

Taking a couple of limping steps forward, he gave Sam another quick jab, this one ramming him in his stomach where the first blow had been intended to land. Sam's moans turned into gasps as he suddenly had to fight just to breathe. Plato, still hunched over with his hands gripping his stomach, turned back to face Bungie, his eyes brimming with anger and pain. Bungie changed direction toward him and raised the end of the halberd shaft again, this time pointing squarely between the big Greek's eyes. He cocked the weapon back over his shoulder, ready to land a blow that would put Plato out for good.

A sharp whistle cut through the air, the sheer force of it ringing in Nicole's ears and sending a violent shiver through Bungie that sent his attack harmlessly past Plato's head and shoulder. Bungie twisted back around, swinging the halberd toward the door—"No!" Nicole's translator snapped—

As Kahkitah charged into the room.

Bungie must have known in that instant that he'd lost. But he wasn't the type to give up just because it was the smart thing to do. He took a couple of quick steps back from the big marble-skinned alien, trying to reverse the halberd and bring its pointed end around in front of him.

But Kahkitah was already at full lumbering speed, and the halberd was too heavy. The spear end was no more than three-quarters of the way around when Kahkitah caught the shaft between the point and the axe head and brought the weapon to

an abrupt halt. There was a brief tug-of-war, and then Kahkitah wrenched it from Bungie's grip, spun it halfway around,
and lobbed it across the room to land with a bounce on one of
the beds behind the partition.

Bungie didn't waste any time with snarls or curses. Spinning
on his heel, he headed for the halberd as fast as his injured leg
would allow, clearly intent on retrieving it.

He got three steps before Plato snatched up one of the chairs
and hurled it into the backs of his legs, knocking him flat on his
face. Before he could disentangle himself, Kahkitah was on him,
grabbing his upper arms and hauling him to his feet.

Bungie kicked backward, catching the alien in his marble-
encased lower leg. Kahkitah didn't even seem to notice.

"Son of a *bitch*," Plato half grunted, half groaned, as he
staggered his way over to where Sam still lay curled up around
himself. "You okay?"

"I think he broke my stomach," Sam managed between gasps.

Plato shot a look at Bungie. "Is that possible?"

"Of course not," Sam bit out, trying to push himself up. "Give
me a hand, will you?"

With Plato's help, Sam managed to get himself up and into
the remaining chair by the table. Through it all Bungie watched
in silence, his expression a mixture of defiance, amusement, and
quiet fear.

"Okay," Plato grunted. He was mostly vertical now, though he
still kept one hand pressed against his stomach. "You—Bungie—
Nicole has a question for you."

"Yeah, well, I've got a couple of questions for her, too," Bungie
said.

"Shut up." Plato gestured to Nicole. "Go on."

"Those hidden decks and rooms you talked about last night,"
Nicole said. "Did you find any weapons up there?"

Bungie snorted. "If I had, you think I'd still be fooling around with *that* piece of junk?" He jerked his head toward the halberd.

"I mean it," Nicole insisted. "Was there anything that might have been a weapon? Or something that looked like one but was too big for you to carry back here?"

Bungie's forehead creased. "Why do you care about weapons all of a sudden? We being invaded or something?"

"Jeff's in trouble," Sam told him. "If she doesn't get a weapon—"

"Shut *up!*" Plato snapped.

Nicole winced. But the damage had been done. Bungie's frown disappeared, replaced by a sly smile. "So you find something to charge to the rescue with, or Pretty Boy gets the chop? Poor Pretty Boy."

"Did you see anything, or didn't you?" Nicole asked, her heart sinking.

"Oh, yeah," Bungie said in that same self-satisfied voice. "Hundreds of weapons—whole rooms full of them. You want me to show you?"

"He's lying," Plato said, looking disgustedly at Sam.

"No kidding," Nicole said, looking around the room. She'd hoped that Bungie's explorations might have turned up *something* she could trade for Jeff, even if it wasn't the specific weapon Hunter had demanded. But there was nothing here.

"Any chance you can make some other trade with these Cluufes?" Plato asked.

"I doubt it," Nicole said. "But I can try."

"You'd better get started," Sam said, carefully levering himself back to his feet. For a moment he wavered, one hand gripping the table, then just as carefully sat down again. "Go on. We'll take care of Bungie."

Nicole frowned. There had been something odd in his voice just then. "What do you mean?"

"Like I said, we're going to nail him to the floor," Plato told her. "Don't worry about it. Go on—we've got him."

Nicole focused on Bungie's subtly altered expression. Clearly, he'd heard the same strangeness in Sam's voice that Nicole had. "I should probably stay," she said. "Maybe I can reason with him."

"Yeah, a lot of good reasoning has done up to now," Plato said pointedly. "Just go."

"And take the halberd with you," Sam added. "Maybe you can trade it for Jeff or something."

"They already have those," Nicole said, her vague suspicion starting to harden into something ugly. "I'll help you get Bungie back to his room first."

"We can handle it," Plato said.

"I don't mind."

"*I said we can handle it!*" Plato snarled.

Nicole flinched back, a flood of bitter-edged certainty washing over her. "You're going to kill him, aren't you."

The room went suddenly very quiet. "Go back to the arena, Nicole," Plato said evenly.

"Why?" Nicole demanded. "Because you don't like him? Because he's a screw-up?"

"Because he's dangerous," Plato said. "More dangerous than you realize."

"Nicole, I saw Jeff this morning," Sam said. "I saw what Bungie did to him. We can't let him just run amok that way."

"So lock him in his room."

"The doors don't have outside locks," Plato said, glaring at her. "Why do you even care about this piece of trash?"

Nicole looked at Bungie. That was a damn good question.

She didn't owe him anything. If anything, he owed *her* for all the messes he'd caused aboard the *Fyrantha* that she'd had to clean up. She didn't owe him anything for Trake's sake, either.

Even if Bungie had done anything for the group to deserve that kind of consideration—and she doubted he ever had—that life was far behind her.

She didn't care about Bungie. What she cared about was doing the right thing.

It was a surprising thought. In fact, it was a terrifying one. After all these years of doing whatever was necessary to survive, this was no time to be parroting lofty ideals. Or even growing a conscience.

But that was, in fact, what it seemed to boil down to. Bungie hadn't done anything aboard the *Fyrantha* to deserve death. Certainly not a cold-blooded execution without a trial or an opportunity to defend himself, or even a final warning and one last chance to clean up his act.

Still, a conscience wasn't supposed to replace her common sense. She couldn't let Plato and Sam flat-out kill Bungie, but she also couldn't let him roam free around the ship. But there *was* one absolutely secure place where they could keep him isolated while they hammered out some kind of permanent plan.

The arena.

On one level, it was crazy. There were people in there, innocent people he might attack or otherwise make trouble for. He'd certainly never shown himself to care about innocents, and he wasn't likely to start now.

On the other hand, both the Micawnwi and Cluufes knew him, didn't like him, and would probably take a poke at him on sight. Any thoughts he might entertain about having free run of the place were likely to get squashed pretty quickly. He would need to find a place to go to ground, and he'd need to find it fast. On top of that, all the doors were locked with a code he didn't have, and Nicole and Plato would have complete control of his food supply.

They wouldn't want to keep him in there more than a few days, of course. But it should at least serve as a holding area until they could come up with something permanent.

The trick would be getting Plato to agree to it. And since Nicole was pretty sure that wasn't going to happen, it was all going to be up to her.

"I don't care about him," she said flatly. "I care about justice." Her eyes flicked to Kahkitah. "I'm guessing Kahkitah does, too."

"Kahkitah will do as he's told," Plato said just as flatly. "So will you." He hissed out a sigh. "I know how this looks, Nicole. But believe me, I wouldn't even consider it unless it was absolutely necessary."

"Necessary for whom?" Nicole countered, looking casually around the room. Plato and Sam were still recovering from Bungie's attacks and wouldn't be racing down the *Fyrantha*'s hallways at top speed anytime soon.

But then, neither would Bungie, not with his leg still on the mend. She would have to buy him some time, probably with the halberd. If he had enough of a head start, they might be able to get to the arena before the others could catch up.

"Necessary for all of us," Plato said. "I can't explain—not yet. But if we don't stop him, right here and now, he'll ruin everything."

"Yeah, he does that," Nicole said sourly, starting toward the rear part of the room. "Fine—whatever. You're in charge. You said I could take the halberd?"

"Yes," Plato said, his eyes narrowing. She'd given in way too easily, and he knew it. "Be careful—it's heavier than it looks."

"I know." Nicole walked past Kahkitah and Bungie without giving either of them so much as a glance and slipped past the partition. Up close, the beds smelled a little musty. She picked up the halberd and, holding it with the blunt end forward, started back toward the exit door. "You realize, Kahkitah, that killing is wrong, don't you?"

"Not all killing," Kahkitah said. "Sometimes it's necessary for the safety of an entire group." He craned his neck to look down at Bungie's profile. "Or so I've been told."

"Told by whom?" Nicole countered, coming to a halt two paces in front of Plato, with Kahkitah and Bungie another two paces to her right. "By Plato? By Sam? Because sometimes killing isn't for the good of anyone except the person doing the killing."

"I'm guessing you've had a lot of experience with that one," Plato muttered.

"And don't forget, he admitted right up front that he was a murderer," Sam reminded her.

"It was self-defense," Bungie protested. Clearly, he'd figured out Nicole was planning something. "He'd have killed me if I hadn't gotten him first."

"He deserves a fair trial before any punishment gets handed out," Nicole said. Casually, she turned the halberd so that the blunt end was pointing straight at Plato's stomach.

"He deserves whatever I say he deserves," Plato said, his eyes on the halberd. "Go on, get out."

"Sure," Nicole said, easing the halberd back a few inches as if preparing to follow up Bungie's earlier shot to Plato's stomach with one of her own. Plato spotted the movement and took half a step backward, pivoting slightly to make himself a less open target. "You know, I don't think I'll need this thing," Nicole continued, cocking it back a couple of inches more. "You take it."

Pivoting on her foot, she shifted to a two-handed grip on the halberd and threw it.

But not forward, toward Plato. Instead, she lofted it to the side, sending it straight toward Kahkitah's head.

Kahkitah might not be human, but in this case he had the

same reaction most humans did. Letting go of Bungie, he snapped both hands up to catch the object suddenly coming at him.

And taking a long step toward him, Nicole grabbed Bungie's hand and yanked him into motion, half dragging, half pulling him toward the door.

Plato, balanced to dodge or deflect an attack, was caught completely off guard. He cursed and lunged, but Nicole and Bungie were already past him, Bungie pushing his bad leg for all it was worth. Sam, still sitting by the table, tried to leap to his feet, but a quick shove from Bungie as they passed sent him slamming back into the chair.

The room behind Nicole erupted with Plato's curses and Kahkitah's confused whistles, and for a second she found herself flashing back to all the other frantic getaways she'd been involved in over the years. But she knew better than to let either the confusion or the memories distract her. The open door was three steps ahead, with the empty corridor beyond it. Only Kahkitah could catch them now, and whatever Plato ordered him to do she could hopefully talk him into something else once they were out of the Greek's earshot. Two more steps—one—

And as she sprinted through the doorway she slammed full tilt into a mass of shiny metal that suddenly appeared in front of her.

The impact knocked the wind out of her, sending a jolt of pain through her chest and a dazzling array of stars across her eyes. She bounced backward from the unyielding mass, slamming a split second later into Bungie as he collided with her from behind. He gave a grunt of his own and bounced backward, his bad leg collapsing beneath him and dropping him to the floor.

And as Nicole staggered sideways, fighting for balance and breath, Fievj stepped into the opening, blocking any chance of escape. "What's going on here?" he demanded.

"A small discipline matter only, Shipmaster Fievj," Plato said, his voice suddenly taut and strained. More strained even, Nicole noted uneasily, than it had been as he'd pronounced Bungie's death sentence a minute ago. "Nothing you need trouble yourself with."

"Indeed?" the centaur asked, taking a few more steps into the room as if for a closer look.

Only now that Nicole knew what he looked like without his fancy armor, she could see that his own front legs and the suit's rear legs strode along in subtly different ways. Fievj was doing the front part of the walking, while the armor's rear legs were somehow keeping up with him.

The armor itself she could understand, especially if he sometimes went into the arena where people might shoot arrows at him. But why in the world pretend he was a centaur?

"This man appears to be wounded," Fievj continued, pausing and peering down at Bungie. "How did these injuries occur?"

Sam and Plato exchanged quick glances. "It happened while he was checking a problem with one of the doors," Plato said, and Nicole could hear the slight hesitations in his voice that told her he was being very careful how he chose his words. "But he's been treated and should make a full recovery."

"He needs rest and further treatment," Sam added just as cautiously. "We were about to take him back to the hive medical center and then return him to his quarters."

"No need," Fievj said calmly. "I'll take him."

Another quick exchange of looks. "We appreciate the offer, Shipmaster," Plato said. "But we can get him back to the hive ourselves."

"You misunderstand," Fievj said. "He isn't going to the hive. He's coming with me."

Nicole looked at Bungie, still half sitting, half lying, on the deck. He was looking up at Fievj, a measuring look on his face. "He's right—I'm in pretty bad shape," he told the centaur. "I never should have been brought here in the first place. Just send me back to Earth and I won't be any more trouble."

"You'll heal," Fievj said. Extending his hand, he made an odd gesture toward Bungie with his armored fingertips. "Come."

"I might die if I have to stay here," Bungie warned, getting slowly to his feet.

"You won't die," Fievj assured him. "Not yet."

Bungie's face stiffened. He shot a look at Nicole, then looked back at the others still standing together across the room.

And as his eyes fell on Plato, Nicole saw some of the tension leave his face. Fievj was offering a vague, future death. Plato had promised an execution right here and now.

Like most of Trake's group, Bungie loved playing the odds. He didn't play them well, but he loved playing them.

"Fine—you're on," he said, taking a step closer to Fievj. "Lead the way."

"In a moment." Fievj turned his armored faceplate to Nicole. "You—Sibyl. You came looking for a weapon."

Nicole swallowed hard. With her whole attention focused on getting Bungie out of here, and then scrambled by Fievj's unexpected appearance in the middle of her move, she'd almost forgotten about Jeff. "Yes," she said carefully. "But not for myself. The Cluufes in the arena—"

"I know," Fievj interrupted. He half turned, reaching back over his long horse back.

And to Nicole's amazement, the top of the horse opened up, the metal armor sliding around and disappearing behind the side armor like an old rolltop desk one of her grandmother's friends had owned.

In the opening, racked neatly side by side, were six four-foot-long black tubes.

Greenfire guns.

"This is for you," Fievj said, reaching into the compartment and detaching one of the weapons from its clamps. "Return with it to the arena." He turned back and offered it to her.

Gingerly, an eerie feeling shivering through her, Nicole took it. The weapon was lighter than she'd expected, much lighter than the halberd. "But it has only three shots," Fievj warned as the armor rolled back into place over the storage compartment. "Use them wisely."

He gestured to Bungie. "Come," he said again, and turned and walked out into the hallway.

Bungie threw an unreadable look at Nicole, and then an all-too-readable smirk at Plato and Sam. "Nice seeing you again, kiddies," he said.

"Enjoy your last taste of freedom," Plato said, his voice dark and bitter. "From this point on, you're their slave. And sooner or later, you *will* die."

For a second, Bungie's smirk faltered. But it came back quickly, and with a final sneer he turned and followed Fievj into the hallway.

And Nicole was alone. With three of her companions.

Holding a gun that held three shots.

Was Fievj expecting her to shoot them?

Carefully, she turned around. None of the three had moved, either to rush her or to run for cover. "I need to leave now," she said between stiff lips.

"Let them die, Nicole," Plato said quietly. "You have to."

"Jeff too?" Nicole shot back.

She saw Plato's throat work. "Jeff too," he said. "Even now—

even with Bungie in their hands—we still have a chance. If you go back in there, it'll all be over."

Nicole shivered. The man was serious, all right. Deadly serious.

Which meant nothing, of course. She'd seen people get just as serious over the proper way to cook chicken. "You want me to stay out?" she demanded. "Then give me a good reason. Tell me what the hell is going on."

"You have to tell her, Plato," Sam urged. "She can handle it."

Plato shot a sideways look at Kahkitah. Then, he took a deep breath. "All right," he said. "Look—"

"Sibyl?"

Nicole spun back around. Fievj had returned and was again standing in the doorway. "Yes?" she asked.

"You will leave now," the centaur said. "Those in the test arena await you."

Nicole looked back at Plato and Sam. Their faces had gone rigid.

But there was nothing she could do but obey. "All right," she said. "See you later, Plato."

She'd hoped that Fievj might watch her leave the room and then return to wherever he'd left Bungie. That would give her a chance to double back and find out what this big secret was that Plato was finally ready to tell her.

No such luck. With his four feet softly thunking against the flooring behind her the entire way, he escorted her in silence to the arena and watched as she keyed in the code. She pulled the door open and stepped inside, and Fievj himself closed and sealed the door behind her.

She swore under her breath. So much for Plato and his big secret. Clearly, Fievj wanted her to deliver the greenfire weapon to Hunter.

First rescuing Bungie, and now making sure Jeff got out of here in one piece. Maybe the lives of their human workers were more important to the Shipmasters than she'd realized.

Or maybe Fievj knew something Nicole didn't. Could Hunter be planning to change the deal again? Maybe ask for something else once he had the gun?

Or was Jeff already dead?

With an effort, she shook the thought away. Surely Hunter wasn't stupid enough to lose the only leverage he had against her. Especially not before he had the gun he'd demanded.

Even more especially when she had the gun ready to point at him.

Of course, the gun only had three shots. But Hunter wouldn't know that. Nicole could march up to him, press the muzzle against his stomach, and demand they turn Jeff loose. Once the two humans were clear of the guards and back in the main part of the arena, she decided, she would throw the weapon as far as she could into the bushes and make a mad break for it. Hopefully, she and Jeff would be clear before Hunter could get the gun back.

At which point, of course, the Micawnwi would still have to face the Cluufes and their new weapon. But it wasn't like the Cluufes could mow down the whole bunch of them or anything. Anyway, she'd already done way more for the Micawnwi than anyone could expect.

Whatever happened from now on wasn't her concern. All she cared about was getting Jeff free and escaping this damn hellhole. Squaring her shoulders, she started across the field toward the stone building—

"Nicole!" a voice called hoarsely from the trees.

—and jerked to a stop again as a figure emerged from cover and loped toward her.

It was Jeff.

"About time," he breathed as he reached her, his tool vests bouncing and jangling together as he came to a halt. "The damn door is locked from this side. I couldn't get out."

"It's locked from both sides," Nicole growled, her stunned disbelief at his unexpected appearance starting to turn into anger. She'd knocked herself out getting this gun to trade for him, and then he'd just walked away from Hunter on his own? "How the hell did you get away?"

"I didn't," he said grimly. "They let me go when the guy in metal armor came in and gave Hunter a couple of guns."

Nicole stared at him. "What are you talking about? What guy?"

"He didn't introduce himself," Jeff said. "Just a guy in metal armor. He brought two of those"—he pointed at the weapon in Nicole's hand—"said he was was sending you in with one for the Micawnwi, and told Hunter to let me go."

Nicole looked down at the weapon, her head spinning. What the hell was going on? Hunter had demanded a weapon, so Fievj and his buddies just *gave* him one? And then—?

She caught her breath. And then Fievj had given her one, too. Knowing that she'd been helping the Micawnwi. Clearly anticipating that once Jeff was free she'd give it to Amrew. "Did he say anything about how many shots the guns had?" she asked.

"Nothing that I heard," he said, frowning. "No, scratch that—make that nothing, period. I know, because we walked out together. Well, unless he went back and talked with Hunter after I'd gone."

"Probably not," Nicole said. "They're not much for talking."

"I noticed." Jeff frowned. "What's the matter? At least both sides have guns now."

"What's wrong is that it's a scam," Nicole bit out, hefting the gun. "This one only has three shots."

Jeff's face went tight. "Oh, hell," he said quietly. "They're expecting a massacre. No, not *expecting*. They're *planning* a massacre."

"I don't know what they're planning anymore," Nicole said, her stomach tightening into a hard knot. "Why are they doing this to these people, anyway?"

"Maybe they just like watching," Jeff said. "Well, they're going to get their money's worth tonight."

Nicole let her gaze drift past him to the arena's trees and hills. There had to be a way to stop this. Something she could do to stop the battle and prevent the slaughter. Or something to at least give the Micawnwi a fighting chance.

And then her eyes fell on the tree she'd noticed earlier, the bushy-topped one that reminded her of the dome of a Russian church.

It was a lunatic idea. But it was all she had.

"No, they're not," she told Jeff firmly as she swung the green-fire gun up onto her shoulder. "Or at least they're not going to get the one-sided slaughter Fievj's expecting. Come on, we need to get to the Micawnwi hive."

"You have a plan?" Jeff asked hopefully as they headed off down the stone pathway.

"I think so," Nicole said. "Let's find out."

seventeen

Jeff wasn't wild about the plan. Neither was Amrew.

But neither liked the look of the black tube in Nicole's hand. Nor did they like her description of its firepower.

They especially didn't like the fact that the Cluufes had two of them.

What probably made it worse, at least from Amrew's point of view, was that even while he dithered about the plan, Mispacch and the other women had already accepted their own roles in Nicole's proposed strategy. Women, apparently, shouldn't be willing to take risks that the men weren't.

But no one had a better plan to offer. In the end, reluctantly, they accepted Nicole's.

Nicole had been concerned that they would have to cut down the dome-canopied tree near the exit, the one that had first sparked this whole crazy idea. It was certainly the most convenient, but the very fact that it was the one closest to the stone building would likely tip Hunter off that the Micawnwi were up to something.

Fortunately, there were two similar trees near the Micawnwi hive that would serve equally well. Nicole chose the one with the narrowest, bushiest branch canopy and had the Micawnwi chop it down with their halberds. Hopefully, any Cluufe watchers would think they were simply planning to use the tree to build a barricade across the entrance to their hive.

In fact, Amrew suggested that exact strategy as his men worked to take the tree down. But Nicole pointed out the fatal flaw: settling into a defensive position would gain them nothing but slow starvation. Their only hope was to take the battle to the Cluufes and make one final attempt to capture the stone building and its food dispenser.

A minute later, the tree was down. The next step was to strip off a carefully selected section of its branches. That part went quickly, with the men again chopping off the branches where Nicole directed them, leaving the debris to be collected and removed by the women and children.

Midway through the operation, Amrew once again made a suggestion, this time that the women stack the branches at both sides of the hive entrance. Mildly surprised that he'd actually come up with something that subtle, Nicole agreed. With luck, it would lull any Cluufes watching the operation into concluding that the whole tree thing really *was* part of a defense setup.

Once all the cutting was done came the task of removing the axe heads from all the halberds. It turned out to be trickier than Nicole had expected, and cost them the destruction of one of Jeff's wrenches before they finally figured out the right technique. After that, though, the job went quickly.

And with that, the preparations were complete. Now, it was just a matter of putting all the pieces together and getting everyone in place.

And, for Nicole, hoping privately and fervently that she hadn't just sentenced all of them to death.

———

The light in the arena was starting to dim to its nighttime level by the time Son One crossed the gap between the concealed sections of the hidden crawlway, gave the thumbs-up signal that Nicole had taught him, and continued on down the hill.

Jeff, sitting with his back against the leftmost of their pair of adjoining trees, leaned a few inches closer to Nicole. "Five minutes," he whispered. "You ready?"

It was, Nicole thought fleetingly, a stupid question. Her part of the operation had mostly ended when she'd loaded the four Micawnwi men with detached halberd axe heads and sent them and Son One up the crawlway to their positions near the Cluufe hive. All she had to do now was help Jeff figure out where the other two greenfire guns were, and she was pretty sure Jeff could do most of that by himself.

But right behind that thought came understanding. Jeff knew she had little more to do. His question was an effort to gauge how nervous she was about the upcoming battle. Maybe he was also trying not to let his own nervousness show.

So Nicole merely nodded, gazed at the view stretched out in front of her, and tried not to think of all the things that could go wrong.

There were plenty of them. The four Micawnwi waiting silently at the Cluufe end of the rail crawlway had instructions to wait until all the Cluufes were heading for the stone building before making their move. But Nicole's food raid had surely taught Hunter not to leave the hive completely unguarded, and he would probably be expecting the same kind of diversionary attack the Micawnwi had launched that time. Still, no matter how many guards he left behind, axe heads thrown with Micawnwi strength would be devastating weapons, especially against halberds.

Unless Hunter had left one of his two greenfire guns at the

hive. If he had, all the Micawnwi strength in the world would be useless.

Then there was the main attack itself, and all the things that could go wrong there. And finally, if Hunter *did* have both guns protecting the stone building, Jeff was going to have to take both of them out with only three shots. That was the trickiest part of all, especially if the Cluufes had spotters concealed up here in these same hills who would be charging down on them the minute Jeff's first shot revealed their position.

Nicole shook the swirling what-ifs out of her mind. She'd been in worse situations with Trake's group, and she'd lived through them. She would live through this one, too.

Pulling one of the water bottles from her vest, she uncapped it and took a sip. Jeff had argued against wearing their vests up here, pointing out that they could catch on something or even entangle their arms at a crucial moment. Nicole had argued in return that the vests' darker color would help mask the blue of their jumpsuits, thus providing a little better camouflage. And while the extra layer of material probably wouldn't stop a green-fire blast, it might be of some help against a glancing blow from a halberd.

In the end, they'd split the difference. She'd worn her vest, and he'd left his back at the Micawnwi hive.

She capped the bottle again and put it away, gazing out across the panorama. At the very least, this was a more impressive view than the back alleys where most of Trake's deals and fights had gone down. Where she and Jeff were sitting, on top of one of the forested hills near the crawlway, they could see the entire end of the arena, including the grove of trees where the stone building sat and the mostly flat section where all the battles Nicole had seen thus far had taken place. The stone building itself wasn't really visible, though she thought she could see a bit of its roof through the overhanging tree canopies. She could also see a few Cluufes guarding the building, though she could usually only spot one of them when he changed position or otherwise moved.

Those movements had been increasing steadily over the past couple of minutes. Jeff had once speculated that Hunter had spotters with mirrors positioned up on the rocky ridges. Certainly any such spotters would have to be blind to miss what was going on down in the Micawnwi part of the arena.

A smile tugged at Nicole's lips. The spotters might be able to see what the Micawnwi were doing, but whatever flash code Hunter had set up couldn't possibly be capable of describing the situation.

It was almost a shame, Nicole thought briefly, that she wouldn't get to see Hunter's reaction when he saw what the Micawnwi had in store for him.

A shiver drove the smile from her face. Given that Hunter's expression would probably be situated directly above the muzzle of a greenfire gun, it was just as well that she wouldn't be getting a closer look.

"Here they come," Jeff murmured.

Nicole craned her neck. There, just emerging from around a stand of bushes at the edge of her view, were the Micawnwi.

The Micawnwi, and their tree.

It was, Nicole had to admit, even more bizarre than she'd expected it to look. The tree they'd cut down was waddling its way across the landscape like a giant bug or humped green worm, its trunk held horizontal, its domed end pointing forward toward the Cluufes, the flattened side of the dome where the Micawnwi had cut back the branches facing downward with the cut ends of the branches about a foot above the ground. The Micawnwi women who were carrying the tree were invisible, spread out along the trunk and concealed by the leaf-covered branches.

"It's like a tank," Jeff murmured, clearly as awed by the sight as Nicole was. "A tree hugger's version of a tank."

Nicole grimaced. Tree hugger, yes. Pretty much literally, in fact.

But tanks had armor plating. All the Micawnwi tree had going for it was concealment.

Concealment, plus a small surprise lurking inside.

The Cluufes had undoubtedly been warned of their enemies' advance by their spotters. Still, Nicole could sense a moment of stunned disbelief as the men guarding the stone building finally got a look at what that advance consisted of.

But the confusion didn't last long. There was a shout from somewhere in that area, too faint for her translator to pick up on, and four Cluufes broke from their positions and headed toward the lumbering tree, their halberds held ready in front of them.

The Micawnwi and their tree continued forward, apparently oblivious to the approaching threat. The Cluufes spread out as they reached the tree, and in a neatly coordinated attack thrust their halberds through the canopy.

Or rather, tried to thrust them. To their obvious consternation, the spear tips barely penetrated the surface before the axe heads caught on the tangle of branches behind the outer layer of leaves. The Cluufes pulled the halberds back and tried again, a couple of them turning the axe heads sideways in the apparent hope that they would be able to slide between the branches more easily that way.

But the branches were just as thick in that direction, and once again the Cluufes had to pull back, simultaneously taking some rapid steps backward as the advancing tree threatened to run them over. There was another shout from the stone building, an insistent-sounding one, and the attackers once again stepped forward and tried to drive their halberds through the branches.

They were pushing at the weapons when the Micawnwi men, walking unseen within the cover of the tree's branches, counterattacked.

Only with their halberds' axe heads having been removed, there wasn't anything to catch on the branches. The Micawnwi halberds—really just spears now—stabbed outward through the leaves with complete surprise and devastating force.

A second later all four Cluufes lay motionless on the ground, dead, their blood slowly staining the arena's greenery.

"That should persuade Hunter to take this seriously," Jeff murmured. Picking up the greenfire gun, he balanced it on top of his right shoulder like a bazooka. "Shouldn't be long now."

Nicole nodded, easing a little farther to her left where she would have a clearer look at the area around the stone building. Even if Hunter had left one of the weapons with the guards at the hive, the other one was surely out here somewhere. Now that he'd seen that halberds were useless against the advancing Micawnwi, he had no choice but to bring it into play.

She was peering down at the Cluufe area, looking for signs of the black tubes, when a brilliant flash of green slashed across her vision.

From *behind* her.

She flinched, reflexively pressing closer to her tree. Jeff had also frozen in place, his head turned and leaning just a little away from the edge of the tree as he searched behind them for the shooter's location. Clenching her teeth, Nicole did the same, turning her head and easing it carefully toward the edge of the tree.

She was peering up at the trees and bushes dotting the hills above them, wondering if the shooter could be all the way up and back on one of the stony ridges, when there was a rustle of leaves no more than thirty feet away. A black tube slid into view along a branch, and a second green flash lashed out.

An instant later there was an answering shot from Jeff's tree that blew apart a circle of branches and sent a brief flash of yellow flame across the leaves.

There was a squeal from the hidden Cluufe, quickly cut off. The black tube sagged, then dropped to the ground with another crunch of leaves.

"Think I got him," Jeff murmured. "Stay here—I'll go check."

"No," Nicole said, looking back at the battlefield. The Micawnwi tree's leaf canopy now had a pair of blackened spots, each with a small circle of flame burning fitfully around it. But there was no indication the shots had hit anyone inside, and the tree was still moving its plodding way toward the stone building. "Stay here and watch for the other gun," she said, gathering her feet beneath her. "I'll go see."

"Nicole—"

Ignoring him, Nicole dodged around the side of her tree and headed back. The greenfire gun was still lying on the ground, its former owner having made no attempt to retrieve it. That was probably a good sign. Keeping low, she made her way around the bushes, trying not to make too big of a wave as she plowed through the tall grass. Whoever Hunter had given the second gun to might have noticed that his friend up here wasn't firing anymore, and she had no interest in making herself an easy target.

Three steps from the gun now. So far no one had taken a shot at her. She could see the vague shape of an unmoving Cluufe through the branches, and the gentle arena breeze was picking up the acid tang of burned something. She felt her nose wrinkle at the odor, told herself firmly that it was probably coming from the smoldering leaves and branches. She reached the greenfire gun and bent over to pick it up.

An instant later a Cluufe appeared from the bushes to her left and launched himself hard into her ribs, sending her flying sideways. Her foot caught on a tangle of grass, and she felt herself teetering on the edge of the narrow crest above the steep slope below. Her flailing hands managed to grab the edge of her attacker's leather smock, and in a confused tangle of arms and legs they rolled and slid together down the slope.

She was halfway down the hill when her back slammed into a prickly-leaved bush, bringing her to a sudden halt. The impact jarred free her hold on the Cluufe's smock, and she heard the swishing of the grass stop as he too came to a halt. Scrambling to her feet, she looked around.

She was a few feet above a small hollow dotted with more bushes and a single tree. The Cluufe was also on his feet and was already trying to scramble his way back up the hill. "Oh, no, you don't," Nicole muttered, and hurled herself at him.

The Cluufe was fast, probably much faster than she was, and on flat ground she wouldn't have had a chance. But he was also shorter than she was, and fighting his way up a steep slope. Nicole's second lunge got her to his level, and her third landed her hand solidly around his ankle just as he grabbed hold of one of the viny tree roots snaking down the hill.

He twisted half over, snarled something, and kicked hard at her hand with his other foot. Nicole snatched her hand back just in time for him to rake his sandal with vicious force along his own leg. He howled with rage and pain as she grabbed him again. Before he could line up another kick, she rolled over onto her back and then up onto her other side, twisting his leg as she rolled in an attempt to turn him around with her and break his grip on the root. He howled again, and a second later they were both once again sliding down the slope.

Nicole looked up past the leg she was clinging to as they bounced along, wincing as various lumps and semisharp objects dug into her body, wondering if all the howling had attracted any unwanted attention. The Cluufe bent at the waist toward her, and Nicole caught a flicker of something as he raised his hand above his head—

She barely managed to let go of his leg in time as he slashed a knife through the air where her arms had been. He slashed again as he grabbed another root with his free hand, snarling something at her. "Stay back," the translation came. "If you fight with our enemies, expect to die like our enemies."

"There doesn't have to be any more dying," Nicole insisted, grabbing on to a tuft of grass and bringing her own slide to a halt. His knife, she saw now, was the pointed tip of a halberd, the same weapon Bungie had pulled on Jeff back in the dining room. "We can work something out, all of us together."

The Cluufe's answer was to again slash his knife through the space between them and start pulling himself back up the hill. Biting out a curse, Nicole followed.

Or rather, tried to follow. Her vest snagged on a tree root, and it cost her two critical seconds to get it free. By the time she was able to resume her climb, the Cluufe had opened up a solid four-foot gap between them.

He'd gotten a fresh grip on his chosen root and was widening his lead when a green flash from above blasted a fire-edged black spot through the back of his smock.

For another second his hands continued to grip the root and knife. Then, both hands opened, and the weapon settled into the grass as his body began its slow slide down the hill.

Nicole looked up. Jeff was leaning out from his tree, the gun still pointed at the Cluufe, his expression tight. Suppressing a grimace, Nicole gave him a thumbs-up. *Stupid.* He was supposed to be watching for the other Cluufe greenfire gun, not bailing her out of a situation she could have fixed on her own.

Worse, his little act of white knighthood had just cost them half of their remaining shots.

He'd meant well. Just the same, he'd damn well better hope that the abandoned Cluufe gun up there still had some shots left in it.

She was still holding up her thumb and smiling her insincere smile when a green flash from the plain slashed across Jeff's chest.

He was slumped against the tree when Nicole reached him, his breath coming in shallow huffs, his face tight, both hands pressed against his left side. "Damn," she muttered viciously as she dropped to her knees beside him. "Damn, damn, *damn*."

"There's no need to get nasty," Jeff murmured.

"Shut up," Nicole bit out, easing one of his hands away. There was a charred hole in his jumpsuit just below his rib cage, with an equally charred hole in the skin behind it. "What can I do?"

"Afraid I'm going to need Sam or Allyce for this one," he gritted out. "But as long as you're here, you *could* take out the Cluufe who got me."

Nicole looked down the hill just as another green flash cut across the landscape and sizzled a cloud of burning leaves through the Micawnwi's tree. "Looks like he's aiming down the trunk," Jeff continued. "Don't know if he's hit anyone yet. But if he hasn't, he will soon."

"Yeah," Nicole said, picking up the greenfire gun and turning around on her knees to face the distant Cluufe gunner. She'd never even fired a real gun, let alone a high-tech alien thing like this.

But someone had to do it.

"Remember, there's no kick," Jeff warned as she balanced the tube on her shoulder the way she'd seen him do it. "No recoil. No drop, either. Just line up the barrel on the target, hold your breath, and squeeze the trigger. *Squeeze,* don't pull."

"Got it," Nicole said. Unfortunately, with only one shot left, she was going to have to let the Cluufe down there fire again in order to see exactly where he was.

From behind a row of bushes came another flash of green. Swinging the gun a few degrees to line up on that spot, Nicole took a deep breath and squeezed the trigger. Her own shot flashed out, almost hurtingly bright as it erupted directly in front of her eyes, and she saw a brief puff of flame from the matted leaves where the shot hit. She lowered the weapon, wondering how she was going to know whether she'd hit him or not.

Her only warning was a sudden rustle of leaves behind her. Before she could even turn to look, a hand reached over her shoulder and snatched the tube out of her hands.

Reflexively, desperately, Nicole grabbed at the weapon, managing to clamp one hand around it. An instant later she was yanked up and backward as her attacker jerked back on the tube. Still off balance, she lunged with her other hand and got half a grip on the other end of the gun. Scrabbling to try to get her feet under her, she spun herself around toward the would-be thief.

And for the second time that day found herself unexpectedly face-to-face with Plato.

"Let go," he ordered, locking his other hand around the tube and giving it another jerk.

"No," Nicole snarled back, a small part of her brain wondering why she didn't just let him have it. It wasn't like he could turn it around and shoot her—the damn thing was empty.

On the other hand, he could still use it like a club and beat her to death. Clenching her teeth, she tightened her grip. "How the hell did you get in here?"

He didn't answer, but merely stepped back and gave the gun another tug, again yanking Nicole off her feet. At this rate, she realized tautly, he would break her grip and have the gun all to himself within seconds.

He took another step back and again tried to yank the gun free. Once again, even while being pulled off her feet, Nicole managed to hold on. He was backing right along the edge of the hill, she saw as she fought to regain her balance, the same edge that she and the Cluufe had tumbled down a few minutes earlier.

Halfway down that slope, hidden by the tall grass and the fading arena light, was the knife the alien had tried to slash her with.

She had a chance now. One chance. And it depended on her getting hold of that weapon.

Feigning a kick at Plato's knee to distract him, she jumped forward and to the side and dropped off the edge of the hill.

Plato was strong, but even he wasn't strong enough to suddenly handle that much extra dead weight without a chance to prepare for it. Nicole's unexpected move had left him only two options: release his grip on the tube or get pulled off the crest along with her.

He chose the second, leaping sideways off the hill before he could be pulled off his feet and landing in a surfer's stance on the steep slope. For maybe ten or twelve feet he managed to stay mostly upright as the two of them slid downward together. Then his foot caught on a low bush and went out from under him, and a second later they were both on their stomachs, both still gripping the gun as they careened down the hill.

In the midst of all the bouncing, and with the flurries of

displaced leaves and grass giving her cover, Nicole managed to snatch up the Cluufe knife.

She and Plato came to a halt in the little hollow at the bottom of the hill alongside more of the prickly-leaved bushes. Plato was on his feet in an instant, once again trying to wrench the gun out of Nicole's hands.

And an instant later he staggered backward, nearly falling again, as Nicole let go. "You want it?" she called as he flailed awkwardly in the tall grass before getting his balance back. Under cover of his distraction she curled the fingertips of her right hand around the handle of the Cluufe knife and pressed the pointed end against her forearm where it would be out of his view. "Fine— take it. Just tell me what you're doing here."

His only answer was to spin the weapon around to point it at her. *Only three shots,* she reminded herself firmly. Fievj had said the gun had only three shots. "I see you're going to kill me," Nicole continued quickly, taking a step toward him. "Just like you and Sam were going to kill Bungie. You could at least have the decency to tell me why."

"It's nothing personal," he said at last, his voice low. "But you wouldn't stop. No matter what I said, you wouldn't stop. And you *have* to be stopped."

"Wouldn't stop what?" she countered, taking another step toward him. The end of the gun was almost within reach now. "Helping the Micawnwi survive?"

He shook his head. "You wouldn't understand. Or believe it."

"Try me," Nicole invited. "Just be sure to use small words, because I can't—"

And right in the middle of her sentence she leaped forward.

But Plato had clearly been expecting the move. He leaped backward at the same time, pulling the gun back just out of her reach. Lining it up on her chest, he squeezed the trigger.

Nothing happened.

His eyes were widening in disbelief as Nicole took another long step forward, batted the gun aside with her left forearm, and swung the knife around into attack position in her right hand. With the tip pointed at Plato, she charged.

But just as Plato was stronger than she was, he was also faster. Dropping the useless gun, he whipped his right hand across his chest, his palm slapping across her right forearm and deflecting the knife away from him. As Nicole's momentum continued to carry her forward, he swung his left arm back and up, evading the knife and then clamping down on her right elbow, trapping her arm solidly in his left armpit.

For a moment they stood pressed close together. Nicole gazed into his eyes, now staring back into hers from only inches away. "You going to kill me now?" she asked quietly.

She felt his chest expand as he took a deep breath. "I can tell them you were a fluke," he said, as if talking to himself. "That there was something in your brain that made you snap and go berserk."

"Or maybe something in my inhaler," she suggested. "Like the one you gave Sam to kill me with."

His eyes widened, just a bit. "You *knew* about that?"

"Of course," she said, watching him closely. "My friend Mispacch told me all about it. It *was* poisoned, wasn't it?"

He sighed. "I'm sorry, Nicole."

"Yes, you said that already," Nicole said. "So *now*, I suppose, you're going to kill me?"

His lip twitched, and once again, he took a deep breath—

And right in the middle of that breath, Nicole brought up her left hand, the one that had slipped the poisoned inhaler out of her vest pocket. Before Plato could react, she sprayed it squarely across his nose and mouth.

He jerked violently backward, as if trying to get away from her. But with their arms still locked together all that happened was that he dragged her along with him. She gave him another jolt from the inhaler.

And then, suddenly, his muscles loosened, and he staggered back again. Nicole tugged at her arm, and with a supreme effort managed to pull it free.

He collapsed to his knees, and for a long moment he held that posture. "Damn you," he murmured, his voice coming as if from a great distance. "You've killed everyone."

"Everyone in the *Fyrantha?*" Nicole shook her head. "I don't think so."

A bitter-edged half smile touched his lips. "Everyone," he corrected softly, "in the world." Almost delicately, he fell over onto his side.

He never moved again.

The other Cluufe greenfire gun was still where Nicole had last seen it, resting in the bushes at the top of the hill. Nicole retrieved it and returned to Jeff's side.

His eyes were closed, and for a moment she was afraid he was gone. But he was still breathing, though the breaths were coming slowly. For now, that was all she could hope for. Settling herself beside him, she hoisted the black tube up onto her shoulder and looked down the hill.

The Micawnwi and their tree were still moving toward the Cluufes and the stone building. But it seemed to her that they were moving more slowly now, and that the tree was wavering a little, as if those carrying it were starting to tire.

From the same clump of bushes as before came a green flash,

and a section of the tree's leaves burst into momentary flame. Swearing under her breath, Nicole lined up her gun.

And paused.

That was probably Hunter down there. He'd struck her as the kind of arrogant, control-freak type who'd make sure *he* was one of the ones with the cool weapons.

And she'd seen how Hunter handled this sort of thing.

The gun down there flashed again . . . and sure enough, this shot came from a slightly different part of the bushes. There was a short pause, and another shot lanced out from yet another spot.

A distant scream wafted up from the battlefield, and it was all Nicole could do to hold her own fire. But she did. She had to. She had no idea how many shots were left in her gun, and she couldn't afford to waste any of them firing at the wrong place. One more shot, she decided, and she should have Hunter's pattern.

Another shot lit up the ground and the tree, and Nicole winced at the answering scream. Hunter had his targets' positions now.

But so did she. Shifting her aim to the spot where he should turn up next, she set her finger on the trigger and held her breath.

And as he fired one final time, from exactly the spot Nicole had predicted, she squeezed off her own shot.

She'd expected nothing particularly noticeable to happen. Maybe if she was very lucky there would be a scream or wailing to show that she'd hit her target.

She hadn't expected the group of bushes to explode into violent, green-edged fire.

Apparently, a direct hit on one greenfire gun by another wasn't very good for them.

"Nicole?" Jeff's voice came weakly.

She looked at him. His eyes were slightly open, still brimming with pain but at least conscious again. "It's okay," she said. "I got him."

"Good." His mouth worked, as if he were trying to find some moisture. On impulse, Nicole pulled out one of her bottles and dribbled some water down his lips. "Thanks," he said, licking at the flow. "The hive. The Cluufe hive. You should get down there. They might need you."

Nicole hesitated. He was right, she knew. Even with both of the Cluufe guns gone, the small Micawnwi force they'd sent to the enemy hive might need help, especially if the explosion sparked a massive Cluufe retreat.

But how could she leave Jeff in this condition?

"You hear me?" he croaked.

Nicole grimaced. How could she leave . . . but what good would it do for her to stay? "I was just going," she said. Reaching down, she slipped the water bottle into his hand. "I'll be back as soon as I can."

"Take your time. I'm not going anywhere." He gave her a weak smile. "Thanks for the water."

"Sure," Nicole said. "Next time bring your own."

But his eyes were closed again. Swearing under her breath, Nicole stood up. For a moment she gazed out over the hills and trees behind her, picking out what she hoped would be the fastest route to the Cluufe side of the arena. Then, holding her gun close so that it wouldn't bump into anything, she headed down the hill.

As it turned out, she needn't have hurried. The initial encounter was clearly over, and three of the four Micawnwi men were standing guard at the entrance to the Cluufe hive, each of them now armed with a captured pike. Lying inside the hive just beyond the doors were the unmoving bodies of the fourth Micawnwi and at least three similarly unconscious or dead Cluufes. "You all right?" she asked as she rounded the curve in the path and walked toward them.

"Yes," one of the Micawnwi said. His voice was polite enough, but Nicole could sense his quiet distaste at having to report to a woman.

"Is the battle still ongoing?" one of the others asked, his tone a little more civil.

"Yes," Nicole told him. "But it shouldn't be much longer—"

She paused, turning back toward the far end of the arena. Was that the sound of footsteps coming toward them?

It was. Lots of footsteps. Lots of hurrying, frantic footsteps.

The Cluufes were retreating.

And they were heading straight for her.

Frantically, she looked around. But the action was pure reflex. There was no way she could get to any serious cover, not before the front of the wave arrived.

Which left her only one option. Taking a couple of quick steps closer to the Micawnwi, she turned to face the approaching Cluufes, rested the butt end of her gun on the ground beside her with the business end pointed upward, and waited.

Twenty heartbeats later the first group of Cluufes charged into sight around the curve of the path. They got another five or six steps, and the wave behind them had also appeared, before anyone seemed to notice the human woman standing directly in their path.

In a sudden tangle of surprise and confusion the whole pack came to a disorderly halt. Some of the ones in front snapped their halberds up into attack positions—

"Who speaks for the Cluufes?" Nicole called.

There was a moment of quivering silence. Then, one of the Cluufes in the back pushed his way through the crowd and spoke.

"My name is Listmaker," he called back. "With the death of Hunter the rule of command has passed to me." He flicked a glance behind her. "Do you speak for our enemies?"

"Amrew Man-second speaks for the Micawnwi," Nicole told him. "He's one of the people who are either coming up behind you, or are about to be. I speak only for reason and peace."

One of the other Cluufes snarled something. "What reason and peace do you pretend to speak?"

"Let's start with reason," Nicole said. "From your sudden arrival here, I assume the Micawnwi now control the stone building and its food dispenser. As you can see behind me, the Micawnwi also control your hive and *its* food dispenser. If the situation stays as it is, you'll all die, either stabbed or starved."

"We wouldn't die without taking many Micawnwi with us," Listmaker warned.

"I know," Nicole said. "It seems to me that enough Micawnwi and Cluufes have died already. More than enough. That's why I'm offering you a deal."

A ripple of suspicious murmurs ran through the Cluufe ranks, a wariness Nicole could also hear from the three Micawnwi behind her. "I figure that between the dispensers in the hives and the one in the stone building there should be enough food for everyone," she said, hurrying to get the words out before either side could try to override her. "Let's put the weapons away and work out a distribution deal."

"Impossible," Listmaker insisted. "The Masters have ordered us to fight. Only by defeating the Micawnwi can we be assured of survival."

"Only by defeating the Cluufes can *we* be assured of survival," one of the Micawnwi countered.

"Fine," Nicole said. "You've fought, and one of you has defeated the other. Game over."

Listmaker looked uncertainly at the Cluufe standing beside him. "Game?"

"Game, competition, trial," Nicole said. "Whatever the Shipmasters want from you, I'd say they've had their money's worth."

"You're not listening," Listmaker said. "If we don't retake the bastion, our food supply will dwindle and we'll be killed."

"If you keep fighting, you'll also be killed," Nicole pointed out. "Seems to me you've got nothing to lose by trying it my way." Some of the Cluufes in the rear of the group turned their heads suddenly to look or listen behind them—"And if you don't make a decision fast, it'll be made by Amrew and his friends," she added. "What's it going to be?"

Listmaker exhaled in a soft whistle. "What do you wish us to do?"

"Put down your weapons and come over here," Nicole said, her heart pounding as she stepped back and beckoned them over. Listmaker might be cooperating right now, but the whole thing was still balanced on the edge. A change of heart on his part, some last-minute treachery from one of his fellow Cluufes, or a flat refusal by Amrew to play ball would throw the whole lot of them into a final desperate battle for survival. With Nicole squarely in the middle of it.

But if she could get this done quickly enough . . .

Maybe Listmaker was thinking the same thing. Maybe all the Cluufes were. For whatever reason, they obeyed her order with remarkable speed, setting down their halberds and hurrying past into the limited space between Nicole and the three Micawnwi guards.

Just in time. Listmaker and the final handful of Cluufes had just reached her when Amrew and the main Micawnwi force loped into sight around the curve. Amrew waved his halberd high and crowed something. "There! Now make an end of it!"

Nicole let them get three more steps, making sure the Micawnwi in the back were able to see her. Then, without moving, she squeezed the gun's trigger, sending a brilliant flash of green fire up toward the ceiling. "Stop!" she ordered.

The Micawnwi skidded to a staggered and confused halt, a taller and hairier version of the Cluufes' own bewildered reaction to her presence a few minutes earlier. "What are you doing?" Amrew demanded.

"You've won the war," Nicole told him. "Congratulations. The killing now stops."

"It does not," Amrew retorted, starting forward again. "Vengeance for our deaths—"

And again came to a sudden halt as Nicole sent a second blaze of green fire into the sky. "The vengeance stops now, too," she said firmly. "We'll find a place where the Cluufes can be kept out of the way, we sort out the food so that everyone gets what they need—"

"This is *outrageous*—" Amrew snarled.

"And you all live happily ever after," Nicole ground out.

Some of the Micawnwi exchanged glances, and Nicole saw the tension starting to drain from their postures. For some of them, at least, the idea that the war might be coming to an end seemed to be a relief.

Amrew clearly wasn't one of them. "Why should we obey your orders?" he demanded. "You, a woman and an alien?"

"Because without me, you'd probably be dead right now," she said flatly. "Whether you choose to remember or not, *I* was the one who came up with the marching tree idea." She turned to Listmaker. "And *you* owe me because I'm the one who stopped Amrew just now from slaughtering you where you stand," she added.

"I wasn't arguing," Listmaker reminded her mildly.

Nicole pursed her lips. Could that actually have been a hint of a sense of humor? "You're right," she agreed. "So it's just you," she continued, turning back to Amrew. "One other thing." She lifted the greenfire gun a few inches off the ground. "I'm the only one who still has one of these. So. You going to cooperate and live? Or not?"

Amrew looked over her shoulder at the Cluufes. Probably wondering how many Micawnwi would be killed if they simply charged the smaller aliens right here and now. Nicole got a tighter grip on her gun . . .

And then, from somewhere in the distance, came a faint voice. Nicole frowned, trying to locate its source—

"I am the Oracle," the translation murmured.

Nicole frowned. Did that mean the voice was coming all the way from the food dispenser room? The Oracle must have the volume really cranked up. "Are the leaders of the Micawnwi and Cluufe present?" it continued.

Nicole looked at Amrew. He was staring past her toward the open door. "I am Amrew Man-second," he called.

"I am Listmaker," Listmaker added.

"Return to your hives," the Oracle said. "The test is over. Return to your hives, and prepare to be returned to your homes."

Nicole caught her breath. They were going to be sent back home? Did that mean *all* of them were going home?

"There's still unfinished business to be done," Amrew called, hefting his halberd.

"No," the Oracle said flatly. "There is not. Return to your hive. Now."

One of the Micawnwi touched Amrew on the shoulder. "It's over, Amrew," he murmured. "Come."

For a moment Nicole thought Amrew still hadn't gotten the message. Then, abruptly, he spun around and stomped through the group gathered behind him, forcing them to move hastily out of his way. The others, some with long, penetrating looks at the Cluufes, followed.

And as Nicole watched them go, feeling cautious relief sagging the tension out of her muscles, she saw a Wisp standing half-hidden behind the bushes at the side of the arena.

It didn't speak or beckon. But its eyes were on her, and its message was clear.

Once again, she was being summoned.

For a moment she considered simply saying no. She was deathly tired, and she needed to see to Jeff.

But saying no would take strength, and a willingness to argue or resist or fight.

And she was tired of fighting.

The Cluufes were heading back to their own hive now, and Nicole tensed one final time as the three Micawnwi who'd been guarding the entrance moved toward them, their fallen comrade cradled in their arms. But there was no trouble. The Cluufes merely stepped aside and let the Micawnwi pass. They continued on, following their fellows, while the Cluufes closed ranks again and continued through the doors into their hive.

A moment later, Nicole was alone.

The Wisp was still waiting. With a sigh, Nicole settled the greenfire gun up onto her shoulder and walked over to the shimmery creature. "Where are we going this time?" she asked.

The Wisp didn't answer, but merely turned and led the way through the trees to the wall. A second Wisp was waiting there, and as Nicole came up it gently and wordlessly took hold of the greenfire gun.

For a moment Nicole resisted. The weapon had proved useful, and might do so again.

But the Wisp persisted, and Nicole still didn't have the strength to resist. Opening her hand, she let the Wisp take it. The thing was probably nearly out of ammo, anyway.

Behind the first Wisp, a wall section slid open, sending a familiar blast of hot air into Nicole's face. As she walked toward the gaping shaft she felt the first Wisp wrap its arms around her.

A moment later, she was once again in the heat and darkness, riding upward on butterfly wings.

Don't be afraid, the Wisp's voice whispered in her mind. *You seek answers. Now, you shall have them.*

eighteen

The room the Wisp took her to wasn't the same one she'd visited the last time they'd spirited her away from the arena. This room was rectangular and much larger, both in length and in width, its only lighting coming from widely spaced glowing circles in the ceiling. That ceiling was higher than in most of the places Nicole had been, though not as high as the arena's. There was also no glass like in the other room, and no view.

It wasn't until the wall had closed behind her and she was walking across the floor toward the nearest light that she noticed that both of the room's walls were lined with boxlike compartments. They were reasonably large, maybe twenty feet on a side, with high walls between them and some kind of open metal gridwork forming their fronts and tops.

All the ones she could see were empty.

Her first thought was that they must be some kind of storage compartments, like the ones in her grandmother's old apartment building basement. Those had also had open spaces covered by chicken wire for ventilation.

But as she passed one of them she took a closer look. The door, which was part of the gridwork, had a lock on it. Even more ominous, in the two back corners she spotted a food dispenser chute and a water spigot connection.

The compartments weren't storage facilities.

They were prison cells.

"Welcome, Protector."

Nicole jerked, twisting her head around toward the voice. Standing directly beneath one of the ceiling lights was the figure of a man.

She blinked, squinting in the dim light. Not just a man, like how she thought of Kahkitah or Amrew as men even though they were aliens. This was a *human* man.

"Welcome, Protector," he said again.

Nicole glanced over her shoulder. There was no one there, not even the Wisp who'd brought her here. "You talking to me?" she called back.

"You are the Protector, are you not?"

"No, I'm a Sibyl," Nicole said.

"In point of fact, you're both," he said. Lifting a hand, he gestured. "Please; come closer."

Nicole looked again at the rows of cells. Was that why she was here? The *Fyrantha* itself was already little more than a prison for the people who'd been brought here. Was her part of that prison about to get much smaller?

"Please; come closer."

She suppressed a curse. If she turned and ran . . . but she didn't even know where aboard the ship she was, let alone how to get back to her room.

Besides, she told herself firmly, if whoever this was had wanted her locked away, it would have been simpler to have the Wisp put her into one of the boxes while she was still helpless in its arms. Listening to her footsteps echoing from the metal floor—no nice soft bouncy mat in this part of the ship—she walked down the corridor between the rows of cells toward him.

He didn't move as she approached. Nor did he say anything

as she came to a stop three feet in front of him. Now that she was closer, she could see that he was dressed in a flowing brown outfit of a kind she'd never seen before. His face and hair were strange, too, some ethnic mix she couldn't identify. "You going to lock me up?" she asked.

His face creased with a sudden smile. "One does not lock up a Protector," he said, his tone mildly chiding but the smile erasing all of the sting. "Especially when we've been waiting for you for such a long time."

"Yeah, sorry about that," Nicole said mechanically. His eyes were unnerving: deep and piercing, and shimmering with a faintly greenish-purple color. But maybe that was just a trick of the odd lighting. "I was told I'd get some answers."

He made an odd gesture. "Ask your questions," he invited.

"Let's start with the easy one," she said. "What's your name?"

"You may call me Ushkai," he said.

So he wasn't ready to give her his real name? Fine. Nicole had used aliases herself on occasion. "You said *we'd* been waiting for a Protector. Who exactly are *we*?"

"You're humans, of course," he said, the smile still going strong. "I'm sorry—is my translation using an incorrect word?"

Nicole caught her breath. She'd become so used to hearing people through her translator that she hadn't even noticed until that moment that Ushkai was speaking perfect, non-accented English at her, with the proper match of lips to words and everything. "No, the words sound right," she said. "You speak English very well."

He waved a hand modestly. "The *Fyrantha* speaks English. Ushkai himself never did, of course."

"I thought *you* were Ushkai."

"You misunderstand," he said, a hint of wistfulness touching his voice. "I'm the voice of Ushkai, or perhaps the presence of Ushkai. But I'm not Ushkai. Ushkai is long gone."

A chill ran up Nicole's back. "I don't believe in ghosts," she said, fighting to keep the sudden quaver out of her voice.

"Nor should you," Ushkai said calmly. "I'm in no way a disembodied spirit. I'm . . ." He hesitated again. "I'm merely a part—an aspect—of the *Fyrantha*."

Nicole stared at him, a sudden suspicion hitting her. In movies and TV shows there'd been these things called holograms . . .

Bracing herself, she reached out a hand and touched him.

Or rather, tried to touch him. Instead, her fingers went right through his clothing and skin.

She pulled her hand back. "You're a hologram?"

"Yes," Ushkai confirmed. "We thought Ushkai's appearance would be a more comforting means of communication."

"Ah," Nicole murmured. There was that *we* again. "So if you're the *Fyrantha*, who is this *we* you keep talking about?"

"We are . . ." Again, he hesitated. "The *Fyrantha* is broken, Protector. It's no longer properly an *I*. It seems therefore reasonable to call it a *we*."

"Really," Nicole said, not at all happy with the tingling sensation this conversation was sending across her skin. "Usually words like *I* and *we* are used for people, not things."

"Perhaps the language is wrong," he said. "Or perhaps we stand astride that line. I don't know the answer. Perhaps when we've been made whole again I'll be able to explain it more effectively." He smiled suddenly. "But of course that's why you're here, Protector, you and your people. To fix me."

"Well, if that's the reason, you're taking a hell of a roundabout time of it," Nicole said sourly. "The only thing my crew's been told to do is fix stuff inside the walls." She frowned as a sudden thought struck her. "Unless whoever's giving us our orders doesn't *want* you fixed?"

"No," Ushkai said. His voice was firm, but Nicole thought she could hear a hint of uncertainty. "No, that can't be. All of us wish to be whole again."

"Sure," Nicole said. *Maybe,* she thought. "How many of you are there, anyway?"

"We are four," Ushkai said, his voice still sounding preoccupied. Apparently, the thought that one part of the ship might not want to get back together with the rest had never occurred to him. "There's the part the Shipmasters control—that's the part that guides the ship and its daily functions. There's the part that talks to the Sibyls, the part that controls the Wisps, and the part that controls"—he touched his insubstantial chest—"me."

"So why are we wasting our time fixing the plumbing or AC or whatever's inside the walls?" Nicole persisted. "Why aren't we working on the main computer or whatever it is you've got?"

"The main computer?" Ushkai frowned. "Of course you're working on the main computer. That's where it is: inside the walls and bulkheads."

Nicole stared at him. "Those are *computers* in there?"

"They're all parts of the whole," Ushkai confirmed. "The *Fyrantha*'s original designers created it that way, so that a single critical attack couldn't destroy everything."

Nicole thought back to the round room at the top of the ship, and the other ships that had been shooting at them. "That sort of thing happen a lot out here?"

"More than just a lot," Ushkai said. "But you didn't know, did you?"

"Know what?"

Ushkai waved a hand. "The *Fyrantha* was originally a vessel of war."

A creepy feeling ran up Nicole's back. She'd seen pictures of warships in books at school. *Big* warships, like battleships and aircraft carriers.

All of them completely dwarfed by the *Fyrantha*. And a warship this size . . . "You said that's what it *was*," she said. "What is it now?"

"Ah," Ushkai said, smiling again. "The *Fyrantha*'s history is one of great legend and diversity. It began as a warship—Galaxy class—one of the—"

"Look, I don't have a lot of time right now," Nicole interrupted. "Just give me the highlights. What made it stop being a warship?" She gestured at the cells on both sides of her. "Was it a prison ship or something?"

"A *prison* ship?" Ushkai seemed aghast. "No, not at all. The Lillilli who found it drifting derelict in space had a far more ambitious and peaceful vision. They nursed it back to function, repairing the main systems and refitting vast parts of it. The room you were brought here from, for example, was once one of the fighter-craft hangars. The Lillilli took out the racks, landscaped it and put in a hidden track system for moving supplies around, and transformed it into a vivarium where visitors could stroll and watch animals in their natural habitat. The other hangars were likewise converted—"

"Wait a minute," Nicole cut in again. "A vivarium? Animals?"

"Of course," Ushkai said. "The *Fyrantha* was a zoo."

Nicole looked again at the cells. "So these were *cages*?"

"Holding and treatment spots, yes," Ushkai said, sounding strangely wistful. "This particular deck was a medical center."

His face hardened. "But there were others who saw different value in the *Fyrantha*. The current Shipmasters seized it many years ago and are now attempting to return it to its former warship capabilities."

Nicole snorted. "Really. Looks to me like they've settled for pay-per-view gladiator shows."

"You misunderstand the purpose of the test arenas," Ushkai said grimly. "Rearming the *Fyrantha* takes a great deal of money. Once the Shipmasters locate a new species of intelligent life, they use the ship's transporters to bring a group of random citizens aboard. They then pit them against another species to see which, if either, has the spirit and skill to become good fighters."

"Wouldn't they do better to look for a few real soldiers instead?"

"Perhaps," Ushkai agreed. "But finding and capturing soldiers takes considerably more work. Besides, the behavior of ordinary citizens provides a baseline with which the Shipmasters' clients can judge which peoples have the potential to be useful as combat slaves."

"Whoa, whoa," Nicole said. "What the hell are combat slaves?"

"They're those who are sent ahead of the main army," Ushkai said. "They trigger the traps and take the first volleys of fire, thus allowing their owners to escape some of that risk."

"Why in the world would they ever agree to do something that insane?"

"Because charging onto a battlefield carries a small chance of survival, and sometimes even military advancement," Ushkai said. "Disobeying their owners' orders means instant death."

Nicole chewed at the inside of her cheek. Unfortunately, it made sense. In fact, gangs back home would typically give the hardest, most dangerous assignments to their newest members. If they lived, they advanced. If they didn't, the gang didn't lose anyone valuable.

Like Trake always said, no matter where you were, it paid to be the one calling the shots.

"So when they find someone they figure won't mind bleeding for their bosses, *then* they go get the soldiers?"

Ushkai shook his head. "At that point the Shipmasters' role has ended. They receive payment, either currency or a shipment of heavy weapons, and give the planet's location to the buyers. It's the buyers' job to travel to that world and recruit or enslave, as they choose."

And like a punch to the gut, Nicole finally got it.

Plato, insisting the work crews never fight among themselves. Plato, ordering her to stay out of the arena, where she would be seen.

Plato, willing to kill her rather than let the Shipmasters discover that humans were capable of combat.

Only she hadn't listened. And now she'd screwed up. She'd screwed up everything.

"What happens now?" she whispered.

"They'll do more tests," Ushkai said. "They'll certainly watch you closely, you and the others. Eventually, they'll bring in more humans to test, or possibly use some of the work crews already here."

Nicole felt like she was going to be sick. Carp, and Levi, maybe even Allyce . . . "Damn."

"But there's still time," Ushkai hastily assured her. "They won't try to sell Earth's location until they have proof of your value to their clients." He held out a hand. "They may not even sell you at all. Only humans can handle the refitting process necessary to bring the *Fyrantha* back to full strength. They may not want to risk losing their supply of workers and Sibyls."

"Why?" Nicole asked. "I mean, why are we the only ones who can fix you?"

"I don't know," Ushkai said. "All I know is that the ship's original creators arranged it that way. I don't know why."

Nicole nodded slowly. If there were observations to be done, and tests, and probably some straight-up fighting, then there was indeed time.

"The question," Ushkai added, watching her closely, "is what you will do?"

Nicole took a deep breath. It made her throat hurt. "I'm going to stop them," she said. "Don't ask how. I don't have the faintest idea."

"But you will," Ushkai assured her. "You've already had ideas. Good ideas. Useful ideas."

Ideas that had gotten Jeff shot. "Yeah," Nicole murmured.

"But more than that, you're a Protector, chosen by the *Fyrantha* itself," Ushkai continued. "If there's a way to stop them, you'll find it."

He waved a hand. "And truly, the Shipmasters control very little of the ship. The central control areas, the main weapons emplacements, a few others. But many decks are hidden or sealed from them, accessible only to Wisps using the ventilation and heat-transfer ducts. They'll show you whatever you wish to see."

Those strange eyes suddenly bored into hers. "We can't help you much, Protector. We were designed to be passive, to be incapable of taking control from our masters. But what help we *can* give will be yours. None of us wish to be a warship again."

"Sure," Nicole said. "Is there anything else? I have to get back to my friend."

"Yes; your injured companion," Ushkai said, nodding. "The Wisps will help. From this point onward, they're at your command."

Nicole grimaced. For whatever good they could do her.

Still, it was an army, at least of a sort. At this point she needed all the help she could get. "Thanks," she said. "And you—you travel around a lot, don't you?"

"As you've discovered, I'm little more than the visible voice of the ship," he said. "You can call me from many places aboard. The Wisps will show you how."

There were a hundred other questions swirling around Nicole's mind. But they could wait. "Then I guess I'll see you later," she said.

She started to turn away, then turned back. There *was* one more answer she needed right now. "So why *me*?" she asked. "What did I do that made you think I was this Protector you were looking for?"

"You don't know?" Ushkai asked, frowning. "It was during your second visit to the Number Four arena. You saw one of the plants had been disturbed in the previous day's battle, and you tried to fix it."

Nicole stared at him. "*That* was the reason?"

"Of course." Ushkai cocked his head thoughtfully. "It's interesting, you know. The original word, the one the *Fyrantha*'s translator speaks as *protector*, actually has two different shades of meaning. Depending on intonation, it can be protector against danger from within, or protector against danger from without."

A stray memory clicked in Nicole's brain. Fievj and the other Shipmaster arguing with Ushkai in that upper room . . . "Caretaker," she murmured.

"That's the protector from within," Ushkai said, nodding. "That's my title, as well. Or at least the title by which the Shipmasters know me."

"And protector from without?" Nicole asked. "What's that one called?"

Again, his eyes bored into her. "Warrior."

Nicole swallowed. "So which kind of Protector am I?"

"I don't know," Ushkai said quietly. "Only time will tell. Farewell, Protector. For now."

———————

Jeff's eyes were closed when Nicole returned to his resting spot, and again her stomach tightened with a moment of fear. But to her relief, he stirred as she knelt beside him, and his eyes opened. "Everything done?" he murmured.

"For now," she said. "You feel up to a little trip?"

"Sure," he said. "You feel like carrying me?"

"I think I can do a little better than that." Nicole gestured, and the four Wisps she'd commandeered stepped into view.

Jeff's eyes widened. "I was kidding," he protested weakly.

"Yeah, well, I wasn't." Standing up, Nicole gestured the Wisps forward. "Easy now—be gentle with him."

A minute later they were walking down the hill toward the exit door, Jeff lying across four sets of Wisp forearms. "By the way," he said, wincing with the small bumps and jolts. "Did we win?"

Nicole grimaced. Plato dead, his plan for keeping Earth below the Shipmasters' radar unraveling in front of her. The Shipmasters, with armor and guns and a grand scheme for turning the *Fyrantha* back into a monstrous weapon of destruction. Alien beings, fighting to the death for the privilege of having their whole worlds turned into slave camps.

And Nicole and a fragmented ship's brain all that stood between the Shipmasters and their nightmare dream.

"Yes," she murmured. "We won."

Three minutes later she closed the arena door behind them, said a quiet farewell to Jeff, and watched as the Wisps carried him down the hallway toward the hive. Allyce would take care of him, she knew. Even Sam had no reason to hurt him. Not anymore.

The damage had already been done.

It was up to Nicole to fix it.

Another Wisp was waiting for her in the dead-end corridor that ran alongside the arena. Looped around its arms, just as Nicole had ordered, were the extra food and tool vests she and Jeff had left behind at the Micawnwi hive. "Okay," Nicole called to it, gesturing as she approached. "Open up."

In answer, one of the wall sections slid open, letting out a flood of hot air. The first step, she'd decided, was to get a better feel for exactly what this monster ship really was. That meant taking a tour.

Given the *Fyrantha's* size, probably a really *long* tour.

But that was fine with her. There would be questions when the Wisps delivered Plato's body back to the hive as she'd instructed. She'd rather not be there when Carp or Sam started wondering about her role in his death.

She didn't want this Protector thing that had been dumped on her. And the thought that she'd gotten the job solely because she'd played with a few dead branches to kill some time was maddening.

But Ushkai was convinced, and the Wisps were convinced, and if the Shipmasters weren't they would be soon enough. Unless she could find a way to convince all of them otherwise, it looked like the damn job was hers.

She just hoped she could figure out quickly what kind of Protector she was supposed to be. Caretaker . . . or Warrior.

The Wisp was waiting, an expectant look on its face. Awaiting the orders of its Protector. "I want to see everything," Nicole said, turning around and backing into its enfolding arms. "We'll start at the top and work our way down."

about the author

TIMOTHY ZAHN is the Hugo Award–winning author of more than thirty science fiction novels, including *Night Train to Rigel, The Third Lynx, Odd Girl Out,* and the Dragonback sextet. He has also written the all-time bestselling Star Wars spin-off novel, *Heir to the Empire,* and other Star Wars novels, including the recent *Thrawn.* He lives in coastal Oregon.